THE STUART
JAMES READER

Also by Stuart James

Frisco Flat
Bucks County Report
Judge Not My Sins

THE STUART JAMES READER

Three Full Novels

Frisco Flat

Bucks County Report

Judge Not My Sins

STUART JAMES

CUTTING EDGE

ISBN-13: 978-1-952138-88-1

Published by
Cutting Edge Books
PO Box 8212
Calabasas, CA 91372
www.cuttingedgebooks.com

TABLE OF CONTENTS

Frisco Flat 1
Chapter One 3
Chapter Two 11
Chapter Three. 27
Chapter Four. 41
Chapter Five 48
Chapter Six 63
Chapter Seven. 80
Chapter Eight 102
Chapter Nine. 113
Chapter Ten. 142

Bucks County Report 165
Chapter One 171
Chapter Two 177
Chapter Three. 189
Chapter Four. 202
Chapter Five 211
Chapter Six 222
Chapter Seven. 234
Chapter Eight 248
Chapter Nine. 258
Chapter Ten. 273
Chapter Eleven 290
Chapter Twelve. 303
Chapter Thirteen 312

Chapter Fourteen 323
Chapter Fifteen 337
Chapter Sixteen 341

Judge Not My Sins **343**
Prologue 347

Chapter One 365
Chapter Two 378
Chapter Three 390
Chapter Four 398
Chapter Five 421
Chapter Six 440
Chapter Seven 447

Epilogue 455
Afterword 459

FRISCO FLAT

CHAPTER ONE

I t was early morning and the dew-topped fields glistened under the bright sun that had cleared the foothills and was gradually working its way into the pale-blue sky.

Frankie Cargo gazed at the endless rows of head lettuce waiting for the crews to move into the fields. They still used the old ice-pack method on some of the farms and wooden crates were stacked at the ends of the rows. Back along the highway they had passed fields where the Mexican workers were already busy at it, only their bent backs and straw hats visible.

When he saw the stop light ahead he said to the driver, "You can drop me off at the light there."

The driver turned his head and smiled. "Okay, fella," he said. His hands on the big wheel were strong and assured. He geared down to make the stop, and the powerful Diesel roared in protest as though it knew that this was not part of the routine.

"If you get the green light I'll hop for it," Frankie said. They approached the light, the heavy rig losing ground. The light went from red to green. Frankie opened his door and put one foot out on the step. The truck crawled through the intersection.

"Thanks a lot," Frankie called. He swung out and jumped, slamming the door after him. His feet touched the ground and he ran a short distance, scattering the loose gravel, then he stopped. The truck geared up with the wail of the double-clutch, and the driver honked his horn once to say good-bye.

Frankie watched the square semi dwindle. A black car roared by, the wind throwing dust at him, and Frankie cursed the hurrying driver, while reserving a special place for truckmen. There was still a chill in the air and he turned up the collar of his brown leather jacket, the relic of some Air Force hero, that he had bought for a dollar in a salvage store.

He walked back to the intersection where the two-lane concrete sliced through the local black macadam road that ran north and south from Watsonville to Salinas. He turned left, walked a short distance on the blacktop, then stopped. He rummaged in his jacket pocket for a cigarette, brought out a rumpled pack. He took out the last cigarette, fitted it into the corner of his mouth, taking his time, letting his eyes cover the small cluster of buildings that hugged the road a hundred yards ahead. He tossed the empty pack, found a match and lit the cigarette. Then he braced his shoulders and started ahead.

He was not the kind given to nostalgia and sentiment, but he felt a strange twisting inside him as he passed the school on the edge of town. It was on the right, a yellow-brick building of one story; a squat, square structure set back off the road and hemmed in, front and back, by lettuce fields. Etched in concrete relief above the main doorway were the words: *Frisco Flat Public School.* He twisted his wide lips into a wry smile. This had been his prison for eight years. This was where he had first learned that the kids from Morse Landing—sons and daughters of fishermen and clam diggers—were the natural enemies of the kids from the town and the surrounding farms. This was also where he had first learned that, with his fists and his Sicilian temper, he could command a silent respect.

As those first fights came to mind, he reached up and ran a finger over the shiny scar tissue that tugged against the corner of his right eye. Then he touched the nose that had been twice broken and looked it. It was a fighter's face, not barroom-battered, but clean-punched; the face of a kid who figured that because he could lick everybody in school and on the docks, he could do the same thing for money—and found out that it was different.

But, while the face showed that he had been a fighter, it was the eyes that windowed what was inside him, reflected what he had learned from the fighting. They were gray, but not the cold, hard gray of the hater. There was a softness about the eyes, a look of knowing, a resignation that men get when they go out to fight the world and finally learn that it's themselves they're fighting.

"I've come back," he said to himself, and then frowned against the slight fear that touched him. The eight years had been a long time. He had left for the nasty business in Korea and it had seemed natural enough. When it was over he had wanted more than the fishing, so he hadn't come home. He looked at his hands and they were strong like the rest of his hard-muscled body. He would do something else with them now, work with them, and he could almost feel the albacore lines sliding over his fingers, the jigs seeking the depths of the dark water. But despite these thoughts the feeling of doubt nagged him. He knew it wouldn't be the same as before. The Old Man was dead. He had missed the funeral because Polo Girolomo's letter announcing that fact had taken two months to catch up with him. He had been trying for weeks to think of the Old Man as dead, and had found it impossible to envision.

He came abreast of the boxlike Safeway store and stepped up on the cement sidewalk that began there. The store was still closed, but he could see through the large windows the orderly rows of canned goods, the silent cash registers. He wondered if the fishermen shopped here now, but he doubted it, knowing the stubborn quality of the Sicilian and his devotion to the small store on the island with its aged smells of hanging cheeses and spiced meats. The market was for the farmers and labor-camp families.

The service station edging the town on the right was open and Frankie recognized Carl Bigley, who was rolling a rack of oil cans into place beside the pumps. Crossing the road, Frankie stepped up to the pumps. "Hello, Carl," he said.

Carl Bigley looked up and Frankie was surprised that his face had not changed in eight years. Carl had always been a fat kid, and now he was only fatter, the face still round, the jowls hanging, his thin hair still slicked down on his round head like a black cap. He looked closely, then blinked the lids over his little black eyes. "Ah," he said finally, sticking out a pudgy hand, "Frankie Cargo. I didn't know ya."

Frankie grasped the soft hand, then let it go. "Nice to see you again, Carl."

"You been away quite a while," Carl said, the words coming out in the labored, wheezy way of fat men. "When ya get back?"

"Just got in," Frankie said. "I'm on my way to the Landing now."

As though remembering something, Carl's expression changed, seemed to darken. "Too bad about your Old Man," Carl said.

"Yeah, that's why I came back. I just heard about it."

Carl was suddenly nervous and Frankie noticed his reluctance to talk further. "I ... uh ... I gotta get to work," he said. "Got to get the place set up." He was looking somewhere over Frankie's shoulder. "Look, Frankie," he said, running his tongue over his thick lips. "Drop around will you, and we'll kick over old times." Carl was afraid. Frankie noticed it, but said nothing. He nodded, smiling.

"Sure, Carl," he said, "I'll see you."

Carl turned away and scuttled off toward the office. A frown creased Frankie's forehead. He turned. A black-and-white car with a gold star on the door was parked on the road beyond the station. The words: *Sheriff, Monterey County,* surrounded the star. A hard-faced man sat behind the wheel, his expressionless eyes on Frankie.

Moving away from the pumps, Frankie started for the channel of store buildings ahead. He glanced once at the man in the car who was following him with his eyes. He didn't mind the inquisitive stare. It was something you got used to when you were on the road. He knew he looked down at the heels, and that all over the country there were cops and sheriffs with an eager eye and a quick fist for anybody they might grind under their heels for the fun of it; picking on the itinerants because there was nobody to give a damn about what happened to them.

Frankie passed the car, crossed a side road and mounted the main sidewalk. He stopped and looked back. The sheriff's car was pulling up before the service-station office and Carl was standing there waiting. He watched while Carl spoke to the driver, saw Carl turn once and look in his direction, then jerk his head back. For some reason the scene made him uneasy. He couldn't put his finger on it, but something was wrong. Carl Bigley was afraid to talk to him, that much he knew, and the sheriff was interested in him. He shrugged and walked on.

He passed through the small town without stopping, noting that it hadn't changed much in eight years. Frisco Flat was what it had to be, nothing more or less. It straddled the road which had once been the main highway from San Francisco to Los Angeles. It was still a well-traveled thoroughfare, since Frisco Flat was a supply center for the farmers, and its stores were geared to their needs and wants without trying to compete with the Sears store in Salinas. The one small movie house showed Mexican movies on week ends only, and those businesses—like Harry's Bar— catered to the Mexican laborer. The farmers went to Salinas or Watsonville for their leisure and the fisherman stayed on the island.

At the north end of the town, where the road started up a long hill, was a diner, and Frankie turned in here. It was the old-fashioned type of diner, shaped like a railroad car and painted a dirty yellow with red lettering along the front. *Frisco Flat Diner.* A sign hanging over the road said: *Eats.* A sandwich sign below that announced: *Truckers Welcome.* There was a sliding door which Frankie pulled aside.

Two customers sat at the counter which ran the length of the place. They wore khakis and heavy work shoes. Frankie moved along the narrow aisle to his left and halfway to the end he mounted one of the round stools and propped his elbows on the marble counter. The waitress was facing the tall coffee urn, straining on her toes to reach over the top and pour in the container of hot water. She wore a white nylon uniform that pulled up on the backs of her knees, and stretched tight across her heavy buttocks. She finished the chore and came along the counter.

"What's yours?" she asked, pulling a strand of graying hair off her sweating face.

"Coffee, black," Frankie said. There was something familiar about the woman's face, but Frankie did not remember her. He watched her back when she went to draw the coffee. She looked about forty, but waitress work doesn't help a woman, and she might have been younger. She came back and put down the heavy mug and a spoon.

"I seem to know you," she said.

"I was thinking the same thing. I used to live at the Landing. Name's Cargo."

"Frankie Cargo," she said, smiling. "You used to come into the Greek's in Watsonville when I worked there. Geezus, that was forever ago. You sure were a tough little wiseacre." She laughed aloud, remembering. "My God, never thought I'd forget you."

"I remember you dumping a milk shake over my head."

She laughed and her body shook, her heavy breasts jiggling in their harness. "First and last time I ever did that."

He had been sitting at a table with the crowd from the high school. The waitress was younger and the body—now fat—was solid and rounded. She was the chief topic of erotic conjecture among the young men. When she passed close to the table Frankie had suddenly reached out and patted her on the buttock, saying. "Some ass." She whirled and struck like a viper, pouring the milk shake she was delivering over his black curly hair.

They were now both remembering. She slapped a red hand to her hip. "It got kinda spread out," she said. "Anybody said it was nice now I'd probably hug him half to death."

Frankie smiled, enjoying her talk. Then the smile left her face and she said, "Geez, that was too bad about your father. I read about it in the paper."

Wondering why his father's death was of sufficient interest to be mentioned in the newspaper, Frankie was about to ask for more details when the door slid open. He saw the waitress swallow hard, her lips compressed. There was a flicker of fear in her eyes. She was looking past him to the door. He followed her gaze, turning his head, and the sheriff was there, closing the door after him.

He was a big man, taller by three inches than Frankie who was just under six feet. He wore a tailored khaki shirt tight across his wide shoulders. He was big at the waist, but it wasn't fat. His arms were long, and big hands and wrists protruded from his sleeves. He wore a white Stetson and the brim shadowed his square, wide face; a face with a belligerent jaw and a cruel, wide mouth. The eyes were cold blue and wide set on either side of the large nose. There was a wary, suspicious animal quality about the man; not cunning or intelligent, but the primitive look of a man born to violence. He was a natural for the badge on his shirt. He moved to the right and Frankie noted that he was light on his feet. He took a stool and the waitress moved down to wait on him.

Frankie returned to his coffee, but he could not shake the feeling of uneasiness that pressed against him. He felt an urgency to get home. He tried to remember Polo's letter, seeking an answer for the fear that rode him. There was nothing. Just that his father was dead and that he should come home. Something about the house and his father's boat, the *Evalena*.

He didn't finish the coffee. He dropped a dime on the counter, then went to the cigarette machine at the end of the diner.

He deposited his money, got a pack of Marlboros and went to the doorway.

"I'll see ya," he said to the waitress.

She was watching him, but she didn't answer. He opened the door and left. He felt the sheriff's eyes on his back. Suddenly he was in a hurry. He had to see Polo. There was something wrong here, and he knew that it was tied up with his father. He had been in Frisco Flat only fifteen minutes, yet he knew the sheriff was stalking him. He didn't like the feeling, but Polo would have the answers.

CHAPTER TWO

Officially, Morse Landing does not exist. It is not mentioned on the maps of California, nor is it included in the directory of towns and cities. But it is there nevertheless, a tarnished fact of shacks weathered a silver gray, the pungent smell of fish, the mud flats lightly powdered by the cement plant which was the Landing's original reason for being.

When John Morse took over the limestone quarry and began the manufacture of cement, he elected to ship his product by water. His plant was on the top of a slope that dipped down a quarter of a mile to the beach and the waters of the northeast corner of Monterey Bay. It was rough water, so he dug a harbor in the natural marshes behind the beach, deepening it for tugs and barges. To protect the harbor he built a stone breakwater at the entrance. In time, the ocean's surge worried away at the sand and mud and a small island was formed; a narrow spit of sand just two hundred yards wide and a half-mile long, a barren sand-duned refuge for gulls and crab grass. The place was called John Morse's Landing and the barges came from San Francisco to carry away the cement which was produced in the dusty white plant on the inland side of the highway.

The Landing lies a mile north of Frisco Flat. The macadam road sweeps uphill from the small town and when you reach the crest of the hill, there—to the left—is the Pacific Ocean. It is always surprising to emerge suddenly from the low valley of farms and find yourself so close to the water. The fields, broken only by their varied design, run down right to the water. From this vantage point you can also see the complete half-moon of Monterey Bay, and at the southern end, Monterey itself, a city of white houses that seem to march straight up the pine-covered hills. To the north, but more obscure, is the outline of Santa Cruz and the roller coaster on the boardwalk.

Dipping then, the road curves down to the fork which marks the beginnings of Morse Landing. The main road veers to the right, climbs past the cement plant, and continues through the strawberry fields to Watsonville. The other road at the fork goes straight. It, too, is blacktop, but it is narrow and full of potholes, its shoulders unkempt and ragged with weeds. John Morse made this road and he was responsible for the row of shacks on the right; built for his workers in the early days—green lumber painted white—now dirty gray and weathered, dried out and warped, the walls defying any plumb line, the roofs twisted and canted. They are occupied by clam diggers and their pinch-faced women and wild, ragged children.

To the left, as you start along this road, is a derelict cemetery, the modest stones settled at odd angles. There are evidences that there was once a white picket fence. It is a desolate little square, choked with tough brown grass, the rectangles of the old graves clearly marked by depressions, like the mouths of a dozen old crones. There are some withered flowers drooping in tin cans.

Frankie slowed his steps as he passed the cemetery, and wondered if his father was buried there. He stopped and lit another cigarette. There were two fresh mounds, both of them marked with the white wooden crosses supplied by the county. He turned his head away and continued along the road, glancing at the shacks as he passed, hearing the shrieks of women, the laughter of children. The men would be out on the ocean side of the island, gouging the sand with their rakes.

At the end of the row, the road was joined by the cutoff from the north. He turned left, passed the line of shacks that were perched on stilts out on the mud flats, rickety catwalks joining them to solid ground like flimsy anchors.

A wooden, one-lane causeway joins the island to the mainland. A battered red pickup rattled across and Frankie stood aside until it passed, then he stepped onto the causeway and walked to the middle where he stopped and leaned on the wooden railing. He took a last drag on his cigarette, and flipped it into the water that moved beneath him, the surge rippling small waves against the wood pilings. It was shallow under the causeway and the seaweed was visible just below the surface, weaving rhythmically. Frankie was looking north where the boats were tied. There was something wrong with the scene and he noticed it immediately. The boats were all painted the same color; the hulls white, the decks gray, the cabins and hatches trimmed with green. As long as he could remember, the boats had always been painted to the taste of the individual owner, and clustered at the docks they had presented a carnival appearance. Now there was a uniformity about them, and for some reason he could not fathom, the fact bothered him.

He looked up at the cannery building which John Morse had constructed after the fishermen came to the island. It was as ugly as always, a huge box with small windows; the big doors facing the bay wide open, giving it the appearance of a monstrous glutton waiting to gorge itself on fish. The building was painted gray like the decks of the boats and a new sign above the door said: *Barlow Canning Co.* This was new to him and he wondered who Barlow was and when he had taken the place over from the Morse family.

Thinking of the Morses, he lifted his eyes to the bluff that rose above the breakwater, and looked at the house which sat on the top overlooking the sea, the island, the Landing. This was the Morse house, a rambling Spanish colonial structure. With the sun on it at this hour, the white walls were pink-tinged and the tiled roof was a deep red. To him, the house had always been the unapproachable castle, the symbol of wealth, home of the lord. He had always viewed it from below.

He brought his eyes down and surveyed the rest of the island. The houses there were sturdier than the places on the mainland. They were built low with easy-slanting peaked roofs and they nestled without pattern into the valleys of the dunes. They seemed to have burrowed there, seeking warmth and protection within the breastlike mounds of sand. His eyes passed over the pale-yellow three-story structure of Della's Hotel at the end of the causeway, then traveled further to the left and stopped on a small, weathered shack. He took a deep breath and swallowed, and he felt suddenly alone. The house would be empty.

Straightening, he pushed away from the rail and started walking. He heard the sound of a car behind him. It reached the causeway as he stepped off the end. He heard the clatter of loose boards and turned. Without slowing, the black-and-white sedan with the star on the side, roared over the causeway, made the sharp turn to the right and headed towards the cannery.

The road to the left, which serviced the dozen houses strung along it in a staggered line, was unpaved—a pair of tracks were worn into the hard-packed sand. The sand felt good under his feet and he quickened his pace.

He paused before the house, then mounted the small porch and tried the door. It was unlocked as it had always been. The knob turned in his hand and he pushed the door open. He stepped inside and closed the door after him. He had imagined the room larger and its limitations surprised him. There didn't seem to be enough room to move around in. One corner held the overstuffed chair he remembered and the heavy floor lamp, the shade patched with tape. There was a lumpy couch against one wall, a wooden rocker and several tables; one larger than the others supported a neat pile of magazines. He had expected the signs of a disordered man's life, since his mother had died while he was in Korea, but the room was clean and neat, as though someone had been caring for it. He was about to explore the other rooms when he heard sounds in the kitchen. He stopped and stared at the doorway.

A girl stepped into the doorway. Frankie stared at her with surprise and she stared back. At first her look was casual, as though she had been expecting someone, then abruptly it changed to surprise. She wore a sheer slip that clung to her. She had been combing her hair. She seemed to freeze, the comb poised in the midst of a downward sweep through the thick black hair that fell over her shoulders.

Frankie enjoyed the moment of appraisal. The girl was worth staring at: tall, long-legged and ripe-bodied, with a strong, narrow waist that accented the fullness of her breasts and the flair of her hips. The black hair framed her oval face, the slightly tilted nose, the wide, full-lipped mouth, the large blue-gray eyes. In that moment Frankie felt a twinge of jealousy towards whoever it was she had been expecting.

There was no sound except her quick intake of breath. She pulled the comb from her hair and dropped her hand to her side. Then she said, "Who are you?" in a husky voice, and, "What are you doing in here?"

"I might ask you the same thing," Frankie said. "My name's Cargo, and unless I'm mistaken, this is my house."

"Oh," she said softly, and the disappointment in her voice was matched by a look that passed over her face. Then her manner became defiant and she said, "Springer said you wouldn't be back."

"I'm back, and I don't know any Springer."

"He's the deputy sheriff," she said.

"You still haven't said what you're doing here."

"Springer said I could live here. He said ..." Her explanation was interrupted by the sound of a car sliding to a stop in front of the house. Frankie saw the girl's hand fly to her mouth, saw the look of fear in the wide eyes. He heard the car door slam, then heavy steps on the porch.

Jake Springer came through the door without knocking, as though he owned the place. He glanced once at the girl, then he said to Frankie, without preamble, "Barlow wants to see you." He snapped the words out so that it was a command.

"I don't think I know you," Frankie said, anger rising in him at the implied threat in the man's voice.

"You don't have to know me. You ain't gonna be around long enough to know me. Let's go!" He still stood just inside the doorway, and he seemed huge in the small room. His hands hung at his sides, but there was a tense readiness about him.

"Who's Barlow?" Frankie asked, realizing that Springer was a man used to being obeyed without question.

Springer's eyes narrowed and his hands came up to his belt, the fingers spread on his hips. Frankie noted the handle of the sap in Springer's rear pocket, the pearl-handled six-gun hanging western-style along his right thigh. "You better just shut your mouth and get your ass in gear, Cargo," Springer drawled.

"You can tell Barlow, whoever he is, that I'll be here when he wants to see me."

Frankie heard the girl catch her breath. He had almost forgotten her. His eyes went to her, then he knew it was a wrong move. In that split second Springer moved.

Lunging forward, Springer slipped the sap from his pocket and began a sweeping arc for Frankie's head. Caught off-balance, Frankie crouched and brought up his left arm. The sap landed on his upper arm. The pain shot down to his fingers, and the arm was numb and useless. But Springer was in close now, and Frankie bulled in before the sap came into play again, and drove a hard right into the deputy's midsection.

Springer grunted, a mixture of pain and surprise in his face. Frankie drove another right in below the heart, then quickly moved back a step and smashed the hard right hand to Springer's jaw. The big deputy reeled away, crashing into the table, spilling the magazines. Frankie crouched, waiting, working the fingers of his left hand, trying to bring life back to the left arm he knew he was going to need.

An angry snarl came from Springer's throat. He pushed away from the table and came in with a rush, swinging the sap as he moved. Frankie danced back instinctively, but the room was too small and his legs touched the couch. He tried to duck under the sap, but it caught him on the side of the neck, staggering him, pinwheels of light exploding in his head. Frankie threw himself forward, clutching at Springer's arms, hanging on until his head cleared. Springer whirled him, taking advantage of his size and weight, and threw him across the room.

Frankie landed on his knees by the door. He had gained the respite and his head was clear. He knew Springer's kind, sensed the natural next move. Springer came forward, as Frankie knew he would, and lashed out with a booted foot, aiming for Frankie's head. Moving his head a fraction of an inch, Frankie let the foot miss, then he reached up and caught the heel with both hands. He twisted it hard, and pushed up, coming to his feet in the movement. Springer crashed to the floor hard, but he was already coming up by the time Frankie was in position for him.

Springer squinted upwards, seeing Frankie poised in a fighter's stance, waiting, both hands ready. He came to his knees, then dived forward, the sap making a circle. It was unexpected and Frankie took the full shock of the sap on his left calf. His leg buckled and he went to his knees. Springer had rolled and was sitting. Frankie lashed out and caught Springer full in the face. Blood spurted from the big man's ruined nose, ran over his cheeks. Springer bellowed with rage and flung himself at Frankie.

Frankie brought his right leg back and as Springer came down, he kicked out, catching the man in the groin with his heel. Springer screamed and rolled away.

Breathing hard, his body a mass of shooting pain, Frankie pulled himself to his feet. He staggered, reaching out to the wall for support. Springer was already on his knees. Frankie stared blankly at the man, knowing the empty frustration of fighting a losing battle. It seemed that nothing was going to keep Springer on the floor. He still clutched the lethal sap. And even if he did stay down for a while, he was still fighting behind that badge, and Frankie had spent enough time in jerktown tanks to know that he had no chance of winning this fight. But he knew that there was no stopping either.

Springer regained his feet. He staggered back and hit the far wall. Frankie waited. The deputy was gasping for breath, and the pain in his guts drew his mouth tight. He shifted the sap to his left hand, and lifted the six gun from its holster.

"I oughta kill you, Cargo," he snarled.

The girl made a sound, a terrified cry that caught in her throat. She was still standing in the doorway. Frankie knew that he was staring at death. His mind tried to think of a way out, but he knew he could never cross the room before Springer fired. There was the girl, and he wondered if Springer would kill him like this with a witness. And he wondered if the girl would really be much of a witness.

"You're gonna go see Barlow," Springer said. "He said to bring you there in one piece, or I'd blast your guts out right here. Now you head for that door like you're walking on eggs, or I'll put a slug right in your spine."

Frankie turned slowly and started for the doorway. Springer stepped in behind him and he felt the hard muzzle of the revolver at the base of his spine.

Sam Barlow's office occupied the northwest corner of the cannery. It was two rooms; the first containing three desks and several file cabinets. A thin girl with mousy brown hair tied at the nape of her neck sat at one desk, her nervous fingers racing across the keys of a typewriter. A wasted, dour-faced man hovered over another desk, a pen in his bunched fingers adding figures to a crowded ledger. The third desk was unoccupied, but its top was cluttered with timetables and invoices; the desk of the cannery foreman who seldom sat at it. A frost-paned door lettered *Mr. Barlow* separated the outer office from the carpeted sanctum where Sam Barlow sat behind his wide, high-polished mahogany desk, drumming his fingers monotonously, a benign smile fixed on Frankie Cargo who stood before the desk, his hands folded behind his back.

Barlow turned his gaze to Springer, who stood by the doorway. "You may leave now, Jake," he said, his voice modulated to an easy conversational tone.

"I don't know, he might ..."

"Now, Jake," Barlow interrupted, a slight edge appearing in his voice.

"Well ..." Springer blustered, "okay. But I'll be right outside if he starts anything."

"You might do well to wash your face, Jake," Barlow said. "You look like you've been dragged through a steam winch."

Springer glowered, his eyes dropping to his shirt front which was spattered with his blood. He growled, saying nothing, and left the room.

"I must apologize for Jake," Barlow said. He stopped then, and gestured towards a straight-backed leather chair which faced his desk from the corner. "Please be seated," he said. Frankie took the seat. "I'm afraid that Jake is a bit impulsive," Barlow said, still smiling. "When I told him I wanted to see you, I meant it as a request. I'm not a violent man myself, Mister Cargo, and I'm sorry if Jake was rough."

Barlow's manner reminded Frankie of someone else, someone in the past, and he placed him immediately. It wasn't his appearance. Barlow was a handsome man, immaculately dressed. He sat behind his desk with calm assurance and his show of overt friendliness might have been a true impression, except for his eyes. While his face smiled, and his words held a ring of genuine concern, the blue eyes were hard and cold, unemotional and merciless. He reminded Frankie of a fight promoter in Denver, a rotund, red-faced man who had easy-talked him into a supposed set-up fight; and too late, Frankie had found himself overmatched with a killer. He had been led to the slaughter and the promoter had cleaned up on the betting. Frankie was listening carefully to Barlow, but he was also watching the eyes.

"I wanted to talk to you about your father's boat," Barlow said. "I imagine you returned to dispose of his small estate, and I would like to make you an offer for the boat."

"It's not for sale," Frankie said. His body ached and he wanted only to end this interview and find Polo.

Barlow's eyebrow lifted. "You have plans for the boat?" he asked.

"I figure to fish with it."

"Hmmm," Barlow said, leaning back into his chair. "That makes the picture a bit different then, doesn't it." He paused and eyed Frankie thoughtfully. "You realize, of course, that the boat isn't in the best of shape. Your father was a bit short on funds before the end, and he let things slide a bit. If you'll pardon my saying so, Mister Cargo, you don't appear to be...ah...exactly prosperous after your travels. The *Evalena* is going to take some money, quite a bit of money, I'm afraid. You might do well to think over my offer."

"I'm pretty handy with a boat."

"So I've heard. You have quite a reputation on the island. But there are things that even loving care won't cover. The insurance, for instance, has lapsed; and your father sold his radio a month or so before his death. I hate to bring up things like this, but I want you to see what you're getting into; and I can use another boat for my small fleet. I'll give you five thousand cash for her."

Frankie realized that Barlow was politely pushing him into a corner, but even on his knees he wouldn't have expected an offer of five thousand. When he had left, the *Evalena* was worth twelve thousand, and the price of good fishing boats had gone up. He would have laughed, but he knew that Barlow wasn't making a joke. Barlow was telling him to grab the five thousand and run, because the price could only come down, and a boat without insurance was worthless at the bottom of the bay. It was all moving too fast. His mind ran back to the truck driver who had picked him up at the intersection above San Jose. That was less than two hours before, but it seemed much longer. He felt like a man in a race, with no idea of the finish or the prize or even the reason for the contest. He had to slow things down. Too many races were lost in the fight for position at the first turn. He sensed that Barlow was an opponent, and the man behind the desk seemed to have been in the race for quite a while, and he was setting the pace.

"I guess I could use the money," Frankie said, hedging, buying time. "But I'd really like to see the boat first and see what's what."

"Take your time," Barlow said. "Like I said, I don't really need the boat, but I can use it." He laughed lightly. "But don't wait too long. The price might come down."

The laugh masked a knowing hardness that showed through the eyes. Frankie saw it and knew that the price was already coming down. He rose from the chair. "I'll let you know," Frankie said. He wanted to tell Barlow where to head in, but he had to see Polo first. He knew, instinctively, that Barlow was an enemy. Why, he didn't know, but an enemy, nevertheless, and a dangerous one. As he shook Barlow's proffered hand, he knew that he disliked the man more than he did Jake Springer. The deputy was a bastard, but his approach was plain, the kind that Frankie recognized and could meet with his fists. But Barlow was vicious behind the guise of friendliness. It was the difference between a rattler and a copperhead. They were equally poisonous, but the latter struck from behind without warning.

Barlow was still smiling when Frankie left. The girl at the typewriter looked up when Frankie came into the outer office. He smiled at her and she went back to her work, as though she didn't want to be touched by his look. The smile hardened to a grim line, and he wondered where Springer was. He opened the door and stepped out into the sun-warm morning. The sheriff's car was still there, but Springer wasn't around. Frankie stretched his sore arm and touched his fingers to the ache in his neck. He turned and looked down at the boats and the men busy on their decks. He recalled some of the faces, but mostly they were strangers. His eyes ran along the floating docks trying to pick out the outline of the *Evalena,* but he didn't see it. He wondered about that, then he started for Polo Girolomo's house.

As he approached the slanting front porch of the little house that was no better or worse than its neighbors, he suddenly felt a welling sensation of well-being begin to rise in him. He had to fight down an urge to run the remaining distance, shouting Polo's name. On the way home he had been thinking a great deal about the old days; that time of growth on land and sea. In retrospect it had been wild and exciting, and in every mental image, there was Polo with his wide, toothy smile, the black mop of tousled hair, the loud, brash, profane voice, the wide, stocky body and the hard fists always ready to swing. Identical in age, Frankie and Polo were contrasts in temperament; Frankie, somber, decisively quick, cool in his anger, quiet in his laughter; Polo, a follower, loudly loyal, powerful and explosive, quick to laugh, a rollicking satyr with the girls. They had played and fought together, fished side by side, working and playing in a steadfast friendship that seemed unbreakable. But the Korean war and the taste of life beyond the Landing had filled Frankie with the unrest that had kept him away for eight years. Now he was back, his feet were on Polo's front porch, and he knew that he wanted to forget those years, cast them off as though they hadn't happened, and pick up his previous life where it had left off. Barlow and Springer were far back in his mind. He hammered the door.

"Polo!" he shouted. "Open up!" He was happy and he wanted to hear Polo's loud voice. "Polo, damn it, open up!"

The door opened a crack and he saw a pair of wide, dark, frightened eyes. Then it opened still farther, just enough to show him the woman there, the door held in her hand. She stared at him, seeming ready at any moment to slam the door. A small child with curly hair, its mouth ringed with jam, clutched at the woman's faded cotton dress. Her face was still young, and with some attention she would be pretty, but her hair was pulled away from her face severely and she wore no make-up. The cheap, square-necked dress was shapeless and her loose breasts sagged beneath the fabric. She was bare-legged and her feet were slid into scuffed slippers.

"What do you want?" she whispered hoarsely.

"I'm looking for Polo Girolomo," Frankie said, attempting to smile away her obvious apprehension.

"He's not here," she said.

"Oh," Frankie said, losing the smile. "He still lives here, though."

"Yes."

"Where can I find him?"

"He's fishing," she said.

"When will he be back?"

"Tomorrow, maybe the next day."

Frankie was beginning to resent the half-closed door. He had spent half his youth in the Girolomo house, as though it were his own. "His parents here?"

"No, they've moved away."

"How about his brothers and sister?"

"They're gone. They're all gone." The woman's expression did not change. The fear was still in her eyes. Frankie gazed at her, the question forming in his eyes. He furrowed his brow. "I'm Polo's wife," the woman said.

Frankie regained his smile and he regarded the woman warmly, looked down at the child, Polo's child. "I'm Frankie Cargo," he said. "I'm an old friend of—"

"I know," she said, and there was a hint of despair in her voice. Frankie frowned again and she said quickly, her voice urgent and imploring, "Go away. If you're a friend of Polo's, go away. You will only bring him trouble. Nobody wants you here. Go away and leave us alone." She slammed the door.

Frankie stood there, his jaw slack with surprise. He knew the woman was still behind the door, waiting for him to leave. He burrowed his hands into his jacket pockets, turned and decended the few steps to the sand. He stood looking at the boats, but not thinking of them.

Polo's wife was terrified. *You will only bring him trouble.* What trouble could he bring Polo? Trouble with Springer or Barlow? That didn't figure. *Nobody wants you here.* Why not? What reason could the people here have for not wanting him around? It just didn't figure, none of it. He had no enemies on the island when he left, and he hadn't been near the place before this morning. His mother had died, and his father had died. His father. He recalled the waitress in the diner. *I read about it in the paper.* There had to be a connection with his father. Somehow the name, Cargo, had become a curse—and it had to tie in with the Old Man.

He rubbed the toe of his shoe in the sand thoughtfully, then he started to walk. He touched the blacktop and walked right, his stride long and determined. He turned in at the small Italian grocery store near the causeway. The faded sign over the door said: *Angelo Cardoni & Sons.* Bells jingled as he pushed through the doorway, and once inside he paused to breathe deeply of the heady odors. The low ceiling was hung with a variety of cheeses and spiced meats, long, slender salamis; there were pickles in barrels, and dried herring, piled boxes of torrone, bags of pistachio nuts, zeppolas impaled on a long stick.

Amidst the clutter of foods, leaning on his counter, his eyes squinting from within their wrinkled, leathery pockets, behind the small steel-rimmed spectacles which perched on his big, hooked nose, Angelo read his out-of-date copy of *Il Figaro*. He raised his head at the sound of the bells, and craned his neck forward, blinking his eyes.

"Ai paisano," Frankie said.

"Ah, ah," Angelo muttered, his mind clicking. "Ah, yes, yes, it's you, Frankie. Good, good. You're back. Good, good." He leaned on his hands, his shoulders stooped.

Frankie stepped to the counter, reached across and shook one of the gnarled hands. There were no customers and he was glad. "A long time, paisan."

"Too long, yes, but you're back. That is good. The young people leave here now, it is good to see one come back." He held his hands, palms together, in front of him, as though he were praying; then he clapped the hands once. "You're going to fish?"

"I don't know, Angelo. I just got back." He paused, then he asked, "Angelo, I want to find out about my father."

The old man shook his head slowly. "Bad," he said, "very bad."

"What's bad, paisan?"

"To die like that. A bad way for an old man to die." He looked down at his hands and continued to shake his head.

"Angelo," Frankie said, his voice soft as though he were almost afraid to ask the question, "how did my father die?"

The old man lifted his eyes. "He was killed," he said.

"Killed?"

Nodding his head slowly, Angelo looked past Frankie to his dusty windows. "They find him out there on the mud flats in the morning. He was beaten to death and thrown into the water when the tide was up. A bad thing."

"Who ... who did it?"

Angelo shrugged and lifted his hands, palms up. "Who knows? He was killed. That's that."

"But why? Why would they kill the Old Man?"

"They?" Angelo snapped, seizing on the word.

"I mean whoever did it. Why would anyone..."

"They!" Angelo interrupted, a fire glowing in his old face. "That is the good word. They!" He jabbed a finger at the counter. "They bought all the boats but your papa's. They owned everybody, but your papa. He laughed at them, sneered at them. He took his life from the sea. He was a man, and they feared him. There was no place here for a man. One man might make the others think about the time when they, too, were men. So they killed him."

"Who? Who killed him?"

"Who owns all the boats?"

The name was on his lips, but he didn't say it. Why would Barlow kill his father just because he owned his own boat and wouldn't sell?"

"A man wouldn't kill just to get a boat when he has plenty of boats," Frankie said.

"There was more," Angelo said. "He knew things."

"What?"

"Who knows? He knew something about Barlow. He was my friend, but he did not tell me. I saw him and he was very angry. He told me that the island would soon be good again."

"Then what did he do?"

The old man spread his fingers and stared down at them. His head was shaking. "He went and told the deputy sheriff," he said.

CHAPTER THREE

When Frankie left the store he wore a troubled expression. Angelo had brought him up to date on what had happened on the island, making marked insinuations between the facts, stoking the centuries-old fires of Sicilian vengeance. The old man had more than implied that Frankie's first duty, now that he was home, was to find his father's killer. And he made no bones about his assumption that Barlow was the guilty party.

"I don't want any trouble," Frankie said to himself, as he walked towards the boat yard where Angelo had told him the boat was docked. "I've had all the fighting I want in this life. I want to work. I want to be left alone. The Old Man is dead, he's under the ground. I loved him, but he's gone. He can't come back, no matter what I do. One way or another I've been fighting somebody or something for eight years; and I haven't won once. Now I just want to work in peace." He looked up at Polo's house as he passed, then glanced at the cannery. He passed the marine gas-station, and the boat yard was next.

The high fence surrounding the boat yard was new, but it didn't surprise him. A fence or a lock was never necessary in the old days, but things had changed, and he was already accepting the changes, expecting them. Inside the fence the boat yard was about the same as he remembered it. A square area crisscrossed with narrow-gauge railroad track, one section of the track sloping down and running into the water. Five small boats were in the yard, stiff and forlorn in the cradles that supported them. They were in various stages of being scraped and painted. There was no one working on them when Frankie entered the yard through the wire gates that were swung wide.

He stood and looked around. It was getting too warm for the jacket, so he shrugged out of it and draped it on one shoulder. A long low building on the right was the office and machine shop. He could see through the office windows that the room was empty. He shrugged and started across the yard. A long, floating dock ran out on the left of the tramway, and before he reached it, he made out the familiar lines of the *Evalena*.

He stopped short of the water and gazed at the boat, seeing if he still had the eye for a deep-water hull. He pursed his lips thoughtfully and scanned her slowly from bow to stern. He was pleased with what he saw; not because the *Evalena* looked too good, but because his eye took in her defects, the things a landsman would miss, and he knew that he was still of the sea.

To an unpracticed eye she would have looked a scaberous, paint-flaked hulk. There was nothing about her to evoke romantic images of life at sea. The bowsprit guy was hanging loose, canting the radio mast to the right, pulling both outrigger poles to an odd angle. Her deck was a clutter of rags and cans, thrown there by men working on other boats. The wheelhouse glass was caked with film and salt scum, and over-all she was dusted a dirty white with the refuse from the nearby cement plant. Rust from her toggles and braces ran in staggered lines down her sides, and she seemed to be hogged amidships.

But Frankie was looking at other things. The *Evalena* was a "Monterey" hull, the bow high and scimiter-shaped, cleaving a sweeping line to the wavering water. He knew there was double planking in that bow and solid ironwood beaming, the beams pegged clear through in the old way and put together to allow for the stress of a pounding sea. Her low, scuppered rail dipped down and swelled out, for she was broad-beamed amidships to allow for the roll in a deep trough. She rose in the stern and her fantail was rounded to reduce drag. She looked hogged because there was too much water in the bilge—he estimated a good twelve inches—and this wouldn't be doing the big Chrysler-Crown engine any good. The wheelhouse was low and rounded and set well forward, giving more space for fish holds and working deck. Like her sisters of that forgotten mold, she was a plodding, unspectacular craft; but there never has been a small boat to beat them when the Pacific gives the lie to its name.

There was no doubt about it, the *Evalena* needed work, but as far as he could see, it was mostly surface stuff; new braces, painting, scraping. The first thing to do was to get the engine going, to pump her out.

The dock swayed and rocked under his feet. He walked to the boat, stood a moment surveying her full thirty-foot length, then vaulted over the low rail to the deck. He went to the wheelhouse. There were sliding doors on both sides. The doors were unlocked and he slid the port-side door back and stepped inside. The wheelhouse deck was two steps down, about two feet, which gave a man good headroom at the wheel. The wheelhouse was small and compact. There was a ledge under the fore windows, the binnacle and compass over the wheel on the port side; the two-burner butane stove and metal sink on the starboard. An open doorway to the fore stepped down to the forecastle which contained two bunks and storage space. The wheelhouse was open, aft, and there was the engine and the sloshing, overfilled bilge. He rummaged for a flashlight, found nothing. He stooped into the engine chamber and struck a match. There was a lot of rust on the engine.

His stomach sickened as he held the match over the engine. "Bastards!" he snapped through his teeth. The distributor had been smashed, the wreckage hung by the wires. He struck another match and bent closer. One of the heads had a straight crack running across it. On close examination he could see where the rust had been broken away, and the edges of the cracks were clean metal. He let the match go out and hunkered down on his heels.

His fists were tightly clenched, and a low, burning anger spread through him, rising and choking in his throat.

The engine was out of commission. It had been a fast job of wrecking, not serious enough to ruin the engine, but enough to make things difficult for someone without the money for repairs. It had been a recent job, too, and he guessed it had been done within the past hour, after his talk with Barlow. New rust would have formed in the crack in a day or two.

Crawling out of the engine room, he straightened in the wheelhouse. He gripped the wheel and cursed silently, looking up towards the machine shop. He knew that this was just another taste of what Barlow had in store for him, then he found himself wondering why he automatically blamed the damage on Barlow. He didn't know the man, and all he had to go on was Angelo's statements. But it was plain that Jake Springer was Barlow's man, and he had the instinctive feeling that Barlow had been his father's enemy. Along with the boat and the house, he had inherited trouble.

He looked out towards the breakwater where the sea was battering the rocks with incessant fury and boiling away with frustration. "What do I do, Old Man?" he said aloud. "I don't want any of this. They're pushing me, Old Man, and I guess I'm like you when it comes to pushing—I won't take much of it." He waited, as though expecting an answer, but there was only the sea sounds, the screaming gulls, the steady slap of waves, the distant shouting of men on the boats, the barking of the sea lions off the breakwater, the laboring chug-chug-a-chug-chug-a-chug chug of a boat rounding the backwater and positioning for a sprint at the breakwater opening.

He knew the feeling of helplessness, but his mind was already racing ahead, tackling the problems he could see. As things now stood it might not be too bad. He had forty dollars and some change. A new head and distributor would come to about thirty. He could have the engine running in a day, then he could pump her out. He could patch up the rigging, then, if he could get gas and oil on credit, he could make a run for fish. The albacore season was at its peak, so he ought to be able to fish a ton or so before the week was out. He looked up at where the radio direction finder had been screwed to the wheelhouse roof, then to the ledge where the radio had left its marks. It was going to be rough working the coast without a radio; he knew the sea and the wind could be more vicious than Jake Springer on his worst day.

Sliding the door back, he stepped to the deck. He closed the door after him.

"Hey, you!"

Frankie turned towards the yard and saw a burly figure advancing from the direction of the machine shop.

"Whatta ya doin' on that boat?"

"What's it to you?"

The man was at the end of the dock and he stopped, his jaw set angrily, his eyes narrowed. The wasted stub of a cigar jutted from the corner of his thick-lipped mouth. He hefted the crescent wrench in his right fist. He advanced closer.

"Whatta ya, wise guy?" he growled. "Ya gotta be taught to stay off these boats?"

"This happens to be my boat," Frankie said, "and you'd better take it easy with that crescent or you'll be gagging on it." His voice was hard and there was a readiness about him.

The man stopped. He looked over the taut, hard-muscled body, the obvious signs of the ring fighter on the face. He lowered the wrench. "You the Cargo kid?"

"My name's Cargo, yes."

"Well, I'm just taking care of the boats."

"You taking good care of them with that wrench?"

The man's eyes narrowed again. "Whatta ya mean by that?" he said. "I work on the engines with this wrench."

Frankie knew he was looking at the man who had wrecked his engine. But he also knew that there could be no proof of it. He smiled thinly. "You do a pretty good job," he said, accentuating the sarcasm in his voice.

The man ignored the statement, but his face colored. He said, "You gonna take that scrap heap outta here?"

"Just as soon as the screw turns," Frankie said.

"You mean as soon as you pay me the hundred bucks for two-months storage."

"Ain't that kind of high for storage?"

"I don't set the prices, fella, I just work here. I didn't ask for that hulk to be tied up there."

Frankie knew the answer, but he asked the question anyway. "Who owns the boat yard now?"

"Sam Barlow," the burly man said. "But I run it, and I'll collect the money when you're ready to go."

Wherever he turned, Frankie ran into the name of Sam Barlow. He felt the man weaving a web around him, and with each turn he seemed to become more entangled in the choking strands. What was worse, Barlow didn't seem to be fighting him openly. He was making his moves legally and this was infuriating. Barlow was money and power, a rough combination. It would be natural for the *Evalena* to be stored in the nearest boat yard to await the claim of the deceased's next of kin. The law would have the boat impounded, and there was nothing illegal about it. Besides, Jake Springer was the law.

Frankie nodded and smiled. He walked off the dock, passing the man. When he touched the land he turned. "By the way," he said, "I can't prove anything about what happened to that engine, but if the guy who did it sets foot on that deck again, I'll ram his cigar down his throat." He whirled, swinging the jacket up on his shoulder, and stalked across the yard. He felt the man's eyes on his back.

He stopped again at Angelo's store and the old man was still leaning over the counter.

"Angelo," Frankie asked, "have you still got your old car?"

"Of course. It is not so good, but it gets me here and there."

"I'd like to borrow it to run down to Monterey. I got to get some parts for the engine."

A spark kindled in the old man's eyes. "You're going to stay."

"Yes," he answered.

"I was afraid," Angelo said. "Five thousand dollars can look like a lot of money."

"It is a lot of money."

"Yes, but there are other things."

"There are."

"And that's why you are staying."

"That's why. And how did you know it was five thousand?"

Angelo shrugged. "That's what he paid most of the others. He made it so they couldn't live, then he bought them cheap. They thought they were selling a boat, but they forget that a body is mostly sweat, and many times their lives had already soaked into the boats. Use the car. It is yours whenever you need it."

"Thanks, Angelo. I'll be going this afternoon."

He left the store and stepped into the road. He looked down at the water. More boats were leaving, the blue-white vapors coughing from their exhausts, the water boiling under their sterns. Groceries were being loaded aboard some of the boats which were still tied to the docks, and men were on the decks, making ready for sea. He saw their eyes turn up to him, and he realized that they already knew who he was. An old-timer waved and he waved back. He saw them talk together, and he knew that they were talking about him. He had friends aboard many of those gray-and-white boats, but he knew that they would also have wives with the frightened eyes of Polo's wife, and they would be silent, watchful friends. They would not raise their hands against him, but neither would they help him. He knew that he was alone. There was not a man on the island, with the exception of independent Angelo, who could afford to take his side. Barlow had them under his heel at sea, and Springer's badge hovered over them on land. But they looked up at him from their work and their eyes were hopeful. He had been a hellion before, a fiery lad with a brooding Sicilian temper; and at age fourteen he had fished with the best of them. He was his father's son. They were men still steeped in the history of their Mediterranean island, where blood was thick and the vendetta was a point of honor. They would already have heard of his fight with Springer and his refusal of Barlow's offer. They would not, could not help him now, but there might be a time.

Frankie felt warmed by their eyes. He turned away and began to walk. He had to get the *Evalena* to sea, and to do that he needed money.

Frankie hesitated on the front porch of his house, his hand resting on the door knob. He had almost forgotten the girl and now he wondered if she was still there, and if he should knock. He shrugged lightly, turned the knob and pushed the door open. He stepped into the empty room and closed the door behind him.

Sounds came from the bedroom. "Hello," he said, his voice more gruff than he wanted it to be.

She appeared in the doorway off the living room. She was dressed now, wearing a white blouse and a full skirt that covered her knees.

"You're still alive," she said.

"Yeah."

"I'm glad."

"So am I." He smiled, and suddenly he felt too big for the room. He swung the jacket from his shoulder and dropped it on a chair. He jammed his hands in his pockets. "I didn't get a chance to meet you," he said.

She leaned against the doorjamb and returned his smile. He liked the way her mouth curved; it wasn't a patent smile with a lot of teeth, but a slow inward smile. "You were pretty busy," she said.

"Yeah." There was a long pause, but he didn't want the conversation to die. "I ... uh ... I didn't get your name before."

"I didn't say it before, but it's Tosca."

"For real?"

"For real. My old man was an opera nut."

"It's nice," he said.

"A name's a name."

"You're Italian?"

"My father was. Sorrento is the rest of the name. My mother was Irish. That's where I got the eyes."

He wanted to say something about the eyes, but he didn't. He shifted on his feet. She noticed his discomfort and she pushed away from the doorjamb and came into the room. "How about some coffee?" she said. "It's on the stove."

"I could use it."

She passed him and went into the kitchen. She walked with an easy, undulating swing, moving through the house as though she belonged there. He liked it. He was glad she was there, partly because he did not relish the idea of being alone in the house with all its memories probing at him. He recalled how she had looked, framed in the kitchen doorway, her good body filling the slip, her hair falling over her bare shoulders. The thought warmed him, and he tried not to think that she was somehow connected with Jake Springer.

The kitchen was a small, narrow shed slanting off the main house. It brought back to him the years he had seen his mother in the small enclosure, the strange hours of breakfasts and suppers between boats. The stove was butane, and there was an old icebox, and a crude handmade cupboard painted white and draped with a faded curtain, and a porcelain-topped table and three chairs. The coffee was heating, and the girl faced the stove. He took one of the chairs at the table and watched her hungrily, knowing that he would want her soon.

She brought the coffee and poured it into a heavy mug, and pushed it in front of him. She put the pot back on the stove.

"None for you?" he asked.

"I have to finish my packing," she said. "I'll be getting out of your way."

"You're leaving?"

"You'll need the house."

"What makes you think I'll be staying?"

She stood looking down at him, her hands on her hips. "I don't know about a lot of things," she said, "but I do know about men. You're going to stay."

"You're sure of that?" He held the cup in both hands, his head tilted up to meet her steady gaze.

"A man doesn't get a face like yours by running away," she said.

He brought his eyes back to the cup. "I won't be using the house," he said. "I just came to see if my father's papers were around. I'll be staying on the boat." He took a sip of the hot coffee. "I'd like you to stay," he said.

She settled into a chair opposite him. "Maybe you won't," she said. "I work for Sam Barlow."

"So does everyone else," he said, meeting her eyes again. "That's your business."

"You don't know what my business is?"

"Like I said, that's your—"

"I'm a percentage girl at Della's."

"Geezuz, does Barlow own that, too?"

"Barlow owns everything on the island."

"Does he own you?"

"I work for him," she said. "I hustle drinks for him and I put up with a lot of pawing for him."

"For a living, or because he owns you?"

She laced and unlaced her fingers, staring at them. "It's a little more complicated than that," she said. "A girl like me isn't welcome everywhere. Here, at least, I don't have to worry about the do-gooders and the crooked vice cops. I get left alone here, so I guess Barlow owns me, in a way."

"So it's a job."

"Some job." There was a note of bitterness in her voice. "This was your mother's house," she said. "Do you know what your mother would think of me?"

"Every day of my mother's life she would rather have been back in Sicily," Frankie said. "But, instead, she was here in this house. She did what she had to do. And she knew what it was to be lonely. But she was a realist, or at least she took things as they came. Life for her was a matter of survival, like it is for most people. I think she would have liked you."

Tosca rose from the chair and went to the small window that looked out onto the wind-swept dunes. "When you came in here this morning, I thought you were Springer."

"I know. I figured that, anyway."

She turned and faced him. "And you still want me to use this house?"

A crooked smile brightened his face. "You're trying awfully hard to make me hate you," he said.

She took a deep breath, her breasts straining against the white blouse. "Yes, I am."

"Why?"

"Because I don't want you to. Because, really, I want you to like me; and I know it's too late for anything like that. When you went out of here on the end of Jake's gun I wanted you to come back. I knew you'd come back."

"And you knew I'd fight Barlow."

"Yes."

"And you want me to fight Barlow."

"Yes."

"Why?"

"I … I don't know." She turned back to the window, not wanting to meet his eyes. "I guess … well, I guess it's because I've always known the Barlows in this world, and I've never had the courage to fight them myself. Since I can remember I've always been a face and a body. Somebody has always wanted it, and I learned at an early age that most men can be conned out of anything by thinking they're going to get it. It's an animal kind of thinking, but it's easier than slinging hash. And, of course, the Barlows can always use a girl with that kind of thinking. You get to hate the Barlows, but you find out you need them, and then you become afraid of them because they can't be conned. Only the soft, lonely one can be conned. It makes you feel great to know that you can only hustle the ones who ache as much as you do." She was silent, staring through the window, and her shoulders were slightly hunched.

"You think I can be conned?"

She turned to him and her eyes were moist. "Yes," she said. "Yes, you can be conned, because you want to believe me. I know the signs. It's in your eyes when you look at me, it was there the minute I saw you. You've been taught not to believe in anything, so you want to believe in everything. You're ready to reach out and grab and take your chances. It's like you've got a great big empty hole inside of you and you want to fill it. I know—I've got it, too."

"That's bad?"

"Yes, that's bad. If I can see it, then Barlow will see it. And if he can't get to you any other way, he'll use me."

"Will it work?"

"I…" Her eyes dropped and her voice was small. "I don't know."

"You have to pick a winner."

"Yes, perhaps."

"And you figure I'm a loser."

"No." She looked directly into him. "I think you'll win. I don't know why, because everything is stacked against you, but I think you'll win."

"Then what are you worrying about?"

"If Barlow should break you, I might be able to pick up the pieces and then maybe you'd forget that I was on the other side. It might make up for some of the lonely ones, wipe out some of the years. If Barlow goes down, then I'm just a loser."

"Maybe it's not that cut and dried."

"I don't know. But I do know that it will be better if there isn't any reason for Barlow to put me against you. Better if we're not involved."

"You know what I think," Frankie said, "I think we're already involved. I think we were involved the minute I walked in here. We've already talked too much not to be involved."

"It's not good."

"Maybe not, but we were involved this morning."

She sighed, turning back to the window. She spoke as though from a great distance. "It was before that," she said. "I think it was when Polo first talked about you."

"You know Polo?"

"He comes into Della's. It started when he lost his boat. He had borrowed money from Barlow, like the others, and Barlow suddenly foreclosed and took the boat. He might as well have cut Polo's heart out. He had to go to work for Barlow on shares. Then he started talking about you. He used to sit in Della's and tell me about you. You became sort of a god to Polo and the more he talked, the more the other fishermen began to listen, and pretty soon they were all believing that when you came back they would get their island back. They had to have something to believe in, and it seems that you were quite a boy when you were here. I began waiting for you myself."

"And now I'm here."

"Yes, now you're here."

"I'm afraid I'm not much the hero type."

"Springer might disagree. And whether you like it or not, you're the hero type now. And now you know why Barlow can't have you around. He controls this island like a small kingdom, but he does it with fear and hunger. You're a symbol now, because Polo and the others needed hope, and Barlow will have to break you."

"And he'll use you."

"Yes."

"You know what I wanted to do when I first saw you?" She turned from the window and there was unhappiness in the blue-gray eyes. "Yes, I know."

"I still do."

"You're asking for trouble."

"Trouble I got by the ton." He rose from his chair, took two steps forward. She didn't move and he gripped her arms. Her chin lifted and his mouth came down upon hers. His hands went over her shoulders, his fingers seeking the hollow of her back. He drew her to him, his senses reeling as she clung to him, returning his pressure, losing herself in the intense fervor of the kiss.

He pulled away slowly, taking a deep breath. "I think we're involved," he said.

"You're crazy," she whispered. "You're crazy."

He held her at arm's length. "I guess so," he said, "but I like it. For the first time I feel like I'm home. If there has to be trouble, then that's the way it is. I want to belong to something, to somebody. I'll fight for it, if I have to."

"You'll have to."

He nodded soberly. Then he grinned. "In that case I had better get started," he said.

CHAPTER FOUR

ngelo's car was a vintage Chevrolet. Where the salt air had eaten away the paint, it had been daubed with red lead until it resembled army camouflage. The fender bolts were loose and they flapped after every bump. The engine was loud and at certain speeds there was the wail of a bearing gone astray.

Frankie fought the wheel shimmy until the speed was up to thirty, then the ancient jalopy settled down to relatively smooth handling. He dropped the speed going through Frisco Flat, paced himself to make the light at the intersection, then turned right onto the concrete highway. He leaned on the gas and got the speed up to forty.

Monterey was ten miles away, and Frankie was thinking ahead, his mind already there, ordering the engine parts, judging the installation time. In the back of his mind was the problem of money. He was going to need a few hundred to get the *Evalena* beyond the breakwater. He would have to borrow, and he wondered about the chances of getting a loan on the boat.

The siren startled him. He tensed automatically, his fingers gripping the wheel. He caught his breath and his eyes flicked to the rear-vision mirror. Jake Springer was riding his bumper, the blinker flashing on the top of his car.

Cursing silently, Frankie pulled off the concrete. He fought back a desire to hit the brakes suddenly, hard, and came to a smooth stop. He shut off the engine and pressed back into the seat, his hands light on the wheel in a gesture of resignation. He looked straight ahead. A car door slammed and he waited.

"Well, well, well."

Frankie turned to face Jake Springer who stood by his window, hands on hips, the mocking smile on his face.

"You again," Springer said.

Frankie sat, saying nothing. He hadn't expected Springer to be on his back so soon, but he had no intention of giving the deputy any trouble. There was enough stacked against him already.

"This your car?" Springer asked.

"No. It belongs to Angelo Cardoni." He said it, in spite of the fact that he knew Springer already knew it.

"Out," Springer commanded, still smiling.

Frankie opened the door and slid out from behind the wheel. He closed the door after him.

"Turn around," Springer said. "Lean against the car with your palms open."

Frankie turned and leaned against the car. Springer came up from behind and patted him down, the routine frisk for punks and hoodlums. Frankie could hear the passing traffic slow down as it passed. The anger was rising in him, but he didn't move. When Springer finished, he ordered, "Turn around." Frankie turned.

"Let's see your license."

Frankie took his wallet from his rear pocket. He took out his driver's license and handed it over.

"New York," Springer said. "Big city type, huh?" He waited, tapping the license against his palm. "How long you been in California, Mister?"

"Two days."

"Two days. Hmmmm. You don't waste any time breaking the laws in the little hick towns, do you?"

"What law did I break?"

"You mean you didn't see that light back there?" Springer was grinning broadly.

"I saw it."

"Do they go through red lights in the big city?" He made a clucking sound with his tongue. "Hate to do it," he said, "but I have to do my duty. We got laws here, and I just have to enforce them. Nothing personal, you understand, just the law." He handed the license back. "Just hold onto that a minute." He walked to the front of the car and looked at the plate. He came back, pursing his lips thoughtfully. "How do I know you didn't steal this car?"

Don't fall into it, Frankie cautioned himself, biting down hard on his teeth. He's pushing, just waiting for you to let go.

"Angelo will tell you he loaned it," Frankie said.

"He will? How do I know that?"

"We could go back to Morse Landing and ask him."

Springer smiled. "Yes, we could do that. But I'll tell you what; I think you have an honest face, and I'll just take your word for it." He reached into his back pocket and took out his summons book. He flipped the pages and rested it on the hood of the car. "Your license," he said. Frankie handed it over again, and stood aside while Springer filled in the spaces on the printed sheet. When he finished, Springer tore the sheet from the book and handed it to Frankie with the license. "The fine for running a light is twenty dollars," he said. "You have five days to pay or make an appearance in Salinas." He smiled again. "Be sure you drive more carefully in the future." He turned away and walked back to his car.

Frankie took a deep breath and let it out slowly. He folded the summons and stuffed it into his shirt pocket. The license he replaced in his wallet. He opened the car door and slid behind the wheel. He turned the key and kicked the starter. The engine coughed and caught, roared and settled into a drone. He grasped the gear shift and pulled it down into low.

Turning his head to check the highway, and finding it clear, Frankie eased off the clutch, pulled onto the concrete, and drove off. He didn't glance back at Springer, but he knew the deputy would be sitting there, probably laughing, knowing that he had shoved in another barb, had shown Frankie Cargo just a little more of what he was up against.

Frankie's anger sent the blood throbbing against his temples. He knew the frustration of a man used to fighting who finds himself in combat with his hands tied. He knew the incident was only the beginning of the harassment he could expect from Springer. And he knew he would have to take it all. There was only one way to fight back and that was with the *Evalena*. He had to forget everything else and get the boat to sea.

He reached that spot beyond Fort Ord where the highway divides and starts up a long grade. He kept to the right lane, the old car chugging and overheating, the steam oozing from under the hood and spraying the windshield. The sun was strong and hot, but he had to use the wipers. The car was barely moving as he reached the crest of the hill, but once over the top, it moved with greater speed, the wind cooling the radiator.

Below and beyond, the blue-green bay was a glittering basin. On the left was the sprawling army camp, yellow-ugly and uniformly barren. To the right against the dunes were the firing ranges and the wind carried the intermittent volleys of rifle fire, the hollow pop of automatics, the occasional hoarse sergeant's-bellow. It brought back the days of Korea.

He had thought he was finished with that kind of fighting, the back-against-the-wall fighting, the tense, watchful kind of living where rock or bush might have your death waiting behind it, when you were afraid to close your eyes to sleep. But it hadn't ended, not yet, anyway, and he cursed softly. Coming home was supposed to be the end of it, and now he wondered if there was ever an end to it. He thought of his father face down in the mud flats. Perhaps that was the way it ended.

He turned right on Del Monte Avenue, passed the clutter of junk yards and greasy-looking lunch rooms, finally reached the congestion of Monterey.

Parking the car in the Fisherman's Wharf parking lot, he crossed the street to the marine supply store that still called itself a "Ships Chandlers."

The parts he needed took all but five dollars of his money. He put the new head and distributor in the car and went back down the street to the bank. He managed to get in a few minutes before closing and the girl in the loan department showed her irritation.

"We're about to close," she said loftily.

"I'll only take a few minutes," Frankie said.

"Couldn't you come in the morning?" She wiped the perspiration from the down on her upper lip.

"I have to come from Morse Landing," he said. "If I could just see the man who handles the loans for a minute or two."

"Well...I don't know." She pushed back from the desk and stood. "I'll see." She tapped across the marble floor, her full skirt whipping against the backs of her knees. She disappeared into a wood and frosted-glass cubicle, then returned. "Mr. Holmes will see you," she said.

"Thank you," Frankie said, giving her a full smile that melted her icy stare and brought her shoulders back to press her full breasts tightly against the pink cotton shirtwaist. The movement was slight and fleeting, but it made Frankie think, *Some things, at least, don't change.*

He entered the cubicle and faced the middle-aged man who sat behind his neat desk, his hands clasped and his smile ready. Frankie took a chair.

"I'm looking for a loan," Frankie said, coming directly to the point.

"Ah," Mr. Holmes said, the smile fixed.

"I have a fishing boat that's clear, and I..."

The fixed smile went down ten degrees, but Mr. Holmes listened.

"...would like to get a five-hundred-dollar loan against it."

"I am afraid we haven't been making loans on fishing boats for some time," Mr. Holmes said sadly. "Since the sardine business collapsed we've had some rather bad experiences."

"But this is an albacore boat. It's worth at least ten thousand."

"The purse seiners are worth a lot more, but we're just not in the boat business. We have heavy loans against half the boats out there in the harbor."

"This boat could be sold tomorrow for five thousand."

The banker built a pyramid with his fingers and stared at them thoughtfully. "You're fishing the boat now?"

"I will be by the end of the week. I have repairs to make."

Mr. Holmes changed his expression slightly. "You have full insurance coverage?" he asked.

"Well, that's one of the things I need the money for. My father died and the insurance lapsed."

"I'm sorry," Mr. Holmes said with gravity, the studied banker's expression of refusal, "but we couldn't consider such a loan. It's not that we have anything against the fishermen. They're an integral part of our economy. But I'm sure that you can see our position. Boats are a bad risk, at best, and in your case—with a boat that is not in operation and not covered by insurance. Well, it's just impossible."

"But I was offered five thousand for it just this morning."

"If I were you," the banker said, still smiling as he would at an untutored child, "I'd accept the offer."

Frankie rose, his shoulders slumped with resignation, realizing the futility of argument. "Well," he said, forcing a smile, "I guess that's that."

"I'm sorry."

"Thank you, anyway."

He passed the girl at the reception desk, returned her small smile. The guard opened the door for him and he stepped into the street.

No loan. He walked along the street slowly, passing the string of bars that became more noisy as he neared the wharf. He chewed his lip thoughtfully. No dough for insurance. Okay, he could take his chances without it. No down payment for a radio. He could chance that, too. He had the parts for the engine. He fingered the five dollars in his pocket. That wasn't enough to eat on for a week, and he would need gas and oil for a week at sea. And there was the little matter of the storage charge at the boat yard, plus a fine to pay. The thought of the fine brought his blood up. There had to be someone to stake him. He had the feeling of being caught in a mirror-maze, and looking for an exit, and every door led to a blind alley, and the reflection in every mirror was not his own, but was Springer and Barlow, and they were both laughing at his helplessness.

He tasted blood and realized that he had bitten into his lip.

When he reached the parking lot, Angelo's car would not start. The final straw. A great day, a really great day. It was almost impossible to realize that he had been filled with hope only nine hours before, when he had hopped off the truck at Frisco Flat. He sat in the car laughing at the situation. "Home," he said aloud, "Oh, baby, am I home!"

He rummaged in the rear for a small wrench, then he started with the gas line to see where the trouble was.

CHAPTER FIVE

It was dark when he eased the car across the clattering causeway and parked in the rear of Angelo's store. Climbing out, Frankie slammed the car door. He stretched, enjoying the sensation in the muscles of his back. He stood rubbing the back of his neck, enjoying the smells of the night, the sounds of the surf and the background of the juke box from Della's Bar.

The creak of a screen door turned his head. "That you, Frankie?"

"Yes, paisan. I just got back."

"I heard the car," Angelo said.

Frankie walked to the small screened porch. He sighed deeply and sank down onto one of the steps, leaning back on his elbows and staring up at the night.

"How did you do?" Angelo asked.

"I got the parts for the boat."

"Good. How long will it take to repair the engine?"

"Should be done tomorrow."

"And then you fish." There was a note of triumph in Angelo's voice. Frankie could have dispelled it with a word, but he didn't want to talk about it. Tired from the drive and the frustration of things piling up against him, he could only think of lying down someplace and not thinking.

"I gotta get some sleep," he said. He grunted, pushing himself to his feet. "See you tomorrow," he said.

"Sleep well, bambino," Angelo said.

Frankie caught his breath, then swallowed hard. Those were the same words his father had always used, said in the same way. Frankie turned and walked away, laboring through the sand until he reached the roadway. There were lights on many of the boats and men were there working; some cleaning up for the night, others getting ready for the sea. The voices from the water were subdued, as though the night cautioned them to silence.

Stopping by the outline of a path that led through the dunes to the beach, Frankie thought of sleeping in the sand. But he turned his head towards Della's and he suddenly had a taste for beer. He swung the jacket up on his shoulder and set out at a brisk pace.

It was more than thirst that was carrying him towards the hotel. He wanted to see the girl. Her image came back to him in fresh detail and for a moment he could smell the soap-perfume woman's scent of her, and feel the outline of her body against his, the breasts soft-giving on his chest, the arms clinging, pulling. His stomach muscles contracted and he hurried up the steps with impatience and pulled open the glass-paned door.

It was a square room, drab and badly lighted. The once-yellow walls were almost brown. The floor was bare wood and worn by generations of feet. A bar commanded one side of the room, the wall back of it mirrored and old-fashioned, its shelves cluttered with bottles. Five wooden booths stretched along the opposite wall and at the far end of the room the juke box was a bubbling, moaning rainbow.

The bartender stopped wiping the bar and looked up as Frankie entered. He figured him for another fisherman and went back to his wiping. There were half a dozen men at the bar and four girls. Their conversations stopped and they turned to look at Frankie. They went back to talking, but the tones were different and Frankie knew that they were talking about him.

"Sonavabitch!" A deep voice bellowed from the shadows of one of the booths. "Frankie! Frankie!"

Polo Girolomo came crashing out of the booth, his grin broad and happy. A T-shirt and blue jeans were stretched over his wide, powerful body and he came across the floor like a bull. "Gahdamn," he shouted, throwing his arms around Frankie, crushing him. "Gahdamn!" He stepped back and looked closely. "Oh, sweet Jesus, you beautiful sonavabitch, am I glad to see you." He slammed Frankie on the shoulder, jarring him off-balance. "I heard you were back. I've been waiting for you."

"It's good to be back, Polo."

"Oh, great! Great!" Polo grasped Frankie's arm and dragged him across the room. He stopped and faced the bar. "Hey, everybody, this is Frankie Cargo."

The people at the bar, including three of the men that Frankie knew from before, smiled and nodded.

"Oh, brother," Polo shouted, "I can't get over it. You're back, you're finally back." He pulled Frankie to the booth. A Mexican girl was sitting there, dark-haired and young, her toothy smile turned up. "Sit," Polo said. "C'mon, we need a drink to celebrate. Move over, Dolores. Frankie, meet Dolores. Dolores, Frankie."

Frankie nodded at the girl, who moved in against the wall. The bench groaned under Polo's weight as he pressed in next to the girl. Frankie slid in the opposite side.

"Harry, bring a bottle," Polo shouted toward the bar. He turned to Frankie and slammed his palms down on the table. "Just let me look at you. Oh, baby, am I ever glad to see you. This place has been like a damn graveyard since you took off."

It was the same Polo, Frankie mused. A little older, a bit heavier, but just as loud. There were some lines around the eyes that didn't come from laughing, but you had to look close to notice them. The brash, lusty voice brought back a surge of memories, all pleasant, and Frankie had to smile.

"Ha, ha, that's what I like to see, the old Cargo smile. Frankie, boy, we got a lot to talk over."

The bartender brought the bottle of whiskey and fresh glasses with ice. Polo poured. Dolores was ignored as the two men lifted the glasses. Polo's face became solemn as the glasses touched. They made no toast, but their eyes held for a moment, saying a great deal, then they drank deeply.

"I have so much to say to you," Polo said soberly.

"That's two of us," Frankie answered.

"You've really been busy."

"You're right. I'm up to my ass in trouble."

Polo frowned and shook his head, as though trying to collect his thoughts before speaking.

"Mind if I have a drink?" the girl asked tartly. "You two laughing boys are great company."

"Oh, sure," Polo said, grinning and turning to the girl. He poured her glass. "Good old Dolores," he said, patting her arm. "A real card."

Frankie's eye strayed over the bar looking for the girl. He arrested his glance once to stare for a moment at the burly figure of the boat-yard manager. He turned back to Polo. "What's that guy's name?"

"Wha'? Where?"

"The guy with the cigar. The one who runs the boat yard."

Polo twisted and looked, then brought his head back. "That's Carazon," he said. "A mean sonavabitch."

"I'd like to kill him," Frankie said, gritting the words through his teeth. "Right now I'd like to carve out his guts." He was looking past Polo. The girl wasn't there, and the fact angered him. He was staring at the closed door at the end of the room next to the juke box. That door, he knew, led to a hallway and the stairs that went to the rooms upstairs. His mind was probing beyond the door and once again he saw her standing in the doorway to the kitchen, and her nonchalance under the eyes of a stranger prodded his growing anger. He talked against it. You have no claim on her, he said to himself. Twelve hours ago she did not exist for you. Her life is her own. Her body is … no, stop it. You're acting like a damn fool. What makes you so sure that she's up in one of the rooms?

Polo had been watching him intently. "Frankie," he said. "Frankie, stay loose."

"What?"

"I said, stay loose. That's what I want to talk to you about first of all. You're going too fast."

"Don't mind me," the girl said. "I just come with the place."

"What do you mean?" Frankie said, ignoring the girl.

"Things are changed here," Polo said with a pained expression, as though he hated to say it.

Frankie stared at his friend, trying to get behind the simple words, not wanting to believe that Polo was afraid.

"I mean you gotta go a little slow," Polo said. "For Jesus' sake, Frankie, believe me. Slow down. I wasn't even off the boat before I was hearing about it. You ain't up against a bunch of ginzos from Monterey that you can take care of with your fists. You've made some enemies that—"

Frankie felt a sickening in the pit of his stomach when Polo suddenly ended his sentence, quick fear in his eyes, and flicked his head around at the sound of the door opening at the end of the room. Frankie watched the door open and recognized the woman moving into the room.

It was Della. She was huge, a tall woman with a massive head. Her hair was gray and piled atop her head. Age and indulgence had loosened her flesh; it seemed to hang off her face and drape over her chin in folds. A cigar was imbedded in the face, held up by thick, loose lips. Dark eyes glinted from within their flesh pockets. She wore her soul for all to see. The greed was there, the cruelty, the wanton hunger. A faded cotton dress covered her huge shapeless body like a shroud. She moved with shuffling steps, unable to lift her feet, grunting as she came forward, breath wheezing through the clenched mouth. She stopped to survey the room and the only sound was the juke box wail, an insipid caricature of merriment. Her eyes fell on Frankie and stayed there. She moved across the floor like a great upright slug, until she stood over the booth.

"You the Cargo kid?" Her voice was harsh, grating.

"I'm Frankie Cargo, yes."

"Get out," she said, flatly. "I don't need your kind of business in my joint."

"Now, wait a minute, Della, I'm not—"

"Get out. Take your wiseacre ass out that door and don't come back."

Frankie did not move. He was breathing heavily. He glanced across at Polo, but Polo was looking down at the table. The girl was pressing against the wall, her eyes wide, waiting, praying. Frankie looked up at the woman. "Is this an order from Barlow or Springer?" he asked.

Her black eyes flashed. She shuffled back a step. She snapped, "Carazon! Chito! Harry! Throw this wise little bastard through that door!"

Carazon came first, the cigar twisting in his mouth, his body crouched, fists hanging low, a look of happy anticipation on his face. Chito was behind him, small and strong, his pocked face worried. Harry came around the bar, unhappy, but ready to do his job, a heavy bung-starter in his hand.

Frankie weighed his chances. They came to zero. Carazon would probably fight fairly. Chito would have a knife that he would use. Harry would just stand aside until he could beat his brains out. Frankie heard the girl muffle a cry. He and Polo could take the bunch, but he knew that Polo was not going to move. This in itself filled him with fury. He came out of the booth. He pressed his back to the table and waited. He heard Polo rise behind him and sudden hope surged through him. He faced Carazon and his head exploded.

Sharp, shooting pain. The blow was expert. One shot at the bunch of nerves at the base of the skull. This much he knew in those last seconds of awareness. The blow from behind. The blackness, the sickening fall from a great height.

He was groping, his fingers seeking, clawing. It was cold, like wet snow. He opened his mouth to call for help, choked on the sand, tasted the grit. He opened his eyes. His senses returned slowly. He was face down in the sand. He closed his eyes again and did not move. He was tired. He tried to sleep, but his body was awakening. The pain reached him.

Oh, my God! He stirred, lifting a hand to press against his head. He brought his knees up to his stomach. He held his head with both hands, opened his eyes. He was on his side and he could see that he was on the dunes. "Oh, sweet Jesus," he gasped. He tried to sit up, but the pain increased and he fell back. The sound of the juke box was close. He twisted his body. The outline of the hotel rose above him. He was back of it.

They dragged me out and dumped me, he thought. He forced himself up. His head ached, but that was all. He had expected broken bones, but he was intact. He sat there several minutes, breathing heavily. Slugged from behind. Polo. His shoulders slumped. Polo, what have the bastards done to you?

A full moon was up over the hills showering the scene like an arc light, dancing shadow lines over the water, ghosting the boats and the buildings, unmasking the dunes. He felt bathed in light. He wanted to burrow into the sand, crablike, to hide his shame. The others, yes, but not Polo. He felt the shame of a man found wallowing in garbage. Polo was the focal point of his misery. He saw again the frightened face of the woman in the doorway, Polo's wife, and the whimpering sound, Polo's child; and in the back of his mind he wanted then to fight for Polo and everything that had been before, and now this desire seemed wasted and dirty.

"To hell with you," he snarled aloud, lurching to his feet. He staggered, felt his knees shake under his weight. The sand slipped beneath his shoes. He caught himself with one outstretched hand, stood erect. He circled the dune, walking drunkenly, his legs widespread, his arms flailing for balance. He focused his mind on the sound of the surf, and moved toward it.

Topping a high dune, he stood swaying a little, his arms hanging at his sides, the pain throbbing behind his eyes. The moon-sprayed ocean stretched before him, the white ribbon of beach below. The damp, spray-breeze whispered over his face, caressing. The waves danced white, rolled, plopped on the sand with a weary gasp, as though trying in vain to reach the land; went back to the sea with a weary, suckling sigh. Weary. The weary sea. Trying again and again, worrying the sand, reaching and striving for something, but never reaching it, wearily.

Like me, Frankie thought, just like me. He wanted to lie face down in the water. He stepped off the crest of the dune, started down the steep incline. His feet tangled and he fell, rolling. Pleasantly soft. He rolled to the bottom. Mattress soft. He did not move. He stayed there, stretched out, propped up by the sand. He was tired and he closed his eyes, hugged his arms to him, savored the damp breeze that clustered his hair wet against his forehead. He felt his body relax and he wanted to sleep forever. He was through fighting. He could let it go, leave and pick up the loose ends somewhere else. He felt the relief of a man who quits a dull job, the elated feeling of freedom that comes before the pangs of fear of facing the world of the unemployed. He enjoyed the languid sensation, squirmed deeper into the loose sand.

He was like this when he heard the girl calling his name. The sound came from behind him.

"Frankie." A soft, searching voice tinged with the fear that she might find him. "Frankie."

Awakened gulls squalled angrily, circled and screeched. He listened, unmoving.

"Frankie, answer me." The voice on his left, still soft, but amplified by the night. The bell buoy answered her, heralded her, rejoiced in her. "Frankie." The distant foghorn at Point Pinos brayed sullenly. "Frankie, please." Plaintive and probing, the girl's voice.

He said nothing. He turned his head to the left. He saw her emerge from the channel of the dunes, step into the open of the beach; saw her stop, listened to her say his name over and over, as though she were repeating it to still her fears of the night and the noisy stillness, as though she were keeping him alive with the utterance of his name, his label, his identity.

The moon was full upon her, and he saw her clearly. The breeze whipped her full skirt about her knees. She was barefoot and she stood with her legs wide apart. He watched her look to right and left, say his name once again. Her voice caught and his name was gurgled and choked with a sob ending. Her shoulders sloped and she caught her face in her hands.

"Here," he said.

Her head snapped up. "Frankie?"

"Over here."

"Frankie." She ran, stumbling in the loose sand. A tiny cry of relief, of guttural joy, escaped her throat. She reached him, fell to her knees at his side, dropped her head on his chest, gripped his shoulders with her fingers. Her body shook. "They hurt you," she said.

He brought his arms around her. "I'm all right."

"I was so afraid." Her voice was on the verge of cracking.

"It's nothing. A headache."

"Oh, Frankie." She reached up and placed her hands on his head, squirming up closer to him until her face hovered over his. "Frankie, Frankie."

Tears had welled over, ruining her mascara. It was like dropping ink on a blotter. The blurred and erratic design was beginning to run over her cheeks. Frankie lifted one hand and wiped her eyes with a finger. He made two large smears.

"You're ruining your make-up," he said.

"I don't care." She was smiling down at him, her eyes glistening. Her panic was gone. He was here, unhurt.

"What *do* you care about?"

"I care that you're not hurt."

"That's all?" He enjoyed being able to talk this way, close, so that he didn't have to raise his voice above a whisper.

"More, I think. I don't know."

The night blanketed them, subdued them, cut them free from the reality that was yards away. The sea-air salt-kelp smells mingled with the damp, warm scent of her. Frankie pulled her face down to touch his, savored the pungency of the wind-wet black hair.

"Why do you care?" he asked.

"I don't know. It's crazy." She talked close to his ear, her lips moving against his cheek, her voice barely audible. "I came in to Della's to start work, and they were all talking about it. Something snapped. It was like a dam bursting loose and I was being flooded until I felt I was going to drown just standing there. I slipped out the back to find you, but you were gone. I saw your footsteps and you seemed hurt. I had to find you. I—I don't know. It's very strange."

They were silent, unmoving and then they became conscious of their bodies touching; something they had not noticed before, and this was strange to them, because they would have noticed this first of all, had either of them been with someone else. And realizing this, they drew themselves closer.

"Why is this?" she whispered.

"What? Why is what?"

"This. This thing we have. This feeling. No, it's not a feeling, it's more than that, it's ... I don't know. Why?"

"I don't know, either, but I guess it's like you're in a crowd and you're not looking for anyone in particular, and you see someone who sees you at the same time, and the crowd isn't people anymore, it's just a thing and you're two people. I don't know, but it's like that."

"But why us, why now?"

"I don't know, Tosca." He realized suddenly that he had never called her by name before. He said the name again, carefully, "Tosca."

"What?"

"Nothing. I was just saying your name. I never said it before."

"You said it this morning."

"That was different."

They were silent then, alone and together, each with separate-together thoughts.

"Tosca?"

"Umm?"

"I've been thinking." His voice was low and thoughtfully hesitant.

She did not move her face from his. "What?"

"Well, that maybe you're—"

"No." Her head came up quickly. "Don't say it."

"Tosca, I—"

She covered his mouth with hers, her fingers entwined in his hair, pulling him to her, silencing him. His need for her, his desire was like a hard fist in the groin that spread up through his body. He had wanted to tell her to leave him, that he was a lost cause, that she could only be hurt standing with him; but now his fingers sought the small of her back and he pressured her to him with all his wild need raging through him, telling her through his lips.

Pulling her head away she gasped for breath. He pulled her head down and burrowed his face in her hair. He was breathing heavily, his chest laboring against the hard press of her breasts, his mind sharp and alive, feeling every line of her body against his.

"I need you, Frankie," she whispered.

"I know."

"No matter what happens."

He sobered and the dark thoughts returned. His body relaxed under her. He ran his fingers lightly over her back.

"I'm losing, Tosca," he said.

"It doesn't matter."

"It does. It has only been one day and already they're beating me down."

"We can leave," she said. "Sell the boat and the house and we'll leave."

"It's too late."

"No." She pulled at him, forcing herself to him. He twisted his body and she slid to the sand. He turned over onto her back and hovered over her.

"I want to run," he said. "I want to just get the hell out of here. But I can't. I'm broke. You know that the word is out. I can only sell to Barlow, and now he can't buy. The whole island is watching this, it's him or me now. That boat will have to rot on the mud flats. That house will have to fall in, board by board. They'll be things for everyone to look at and know that Barlow cannot be beaten. If I leave, I have to leave the way I came, with nothing. And I can't leave like that."

"We can. Together we can. I'll work in Monterey. You can find something to do."

"No. It has to be here. I've always been fighting and I've always been losing. I never liked it, but it was clean. I always knew that I had been fighting. I don't trust myself to run away from this."

"What about us?"

He looked down at her for what seemed like a long time. "There can't be an us," he said. "They're going to hurt me. They could hurt you more."

"I don't care. Don't you see that? I don't care."

"But I do."

"Frankie, please, I—"

"Shhhh." He placed his fingers over her lips, touching her gently. "Let's not talk. It can't do any good, and I'm afraid we don't have a lot of time." He was kneeling and he pulled her up to face him. She trembled in his grasp. He leaned forward and kissed her lightly. "Go back now," he said.

"Frankie, please..."

"Go back. They'll be wondering where you are. And I have to think."

Subdued by the quiet force of his voice, she rose to her feet. She looked down, saying nothing, then she turned and walked away.

He watched her go, long-striding through the sand, the moonlight full upon her, giving her the appearance of a moving apparition.

She was about to turn beyond the dune when she suddenly cried out in surprise and terror as a running dark figure collided with her.

"Where is he?"

"My God, you scared me."

"Where is he?"

Frankie relaxed from his sudden tension, recognizing Polo's voice. "I'm here," he said, coming to his feet.

"Frankie," Polo gasped, "Oh, Jesus Christ, Frankie!" He ran forward, slipping in the loose sand.

The girl moved away from them and disappeared in the shadows of the dunes.

Polo reached Frankie and flung himself upon him, gripping his arms. Sliding down until he was on his knees, Polo cried, "Frankie, I had to do it. I'm sorry, but I had to stop you."

"Get up, Polo."

"They were ready to carve you up. It was the only way to stop it."

"Get up."

"Ya gotta forgive me, Frankie. Oh, please, dear God." He cried openly, his huge body shaking. "Frankie, you gotta realize I hadda do it."

Frankie pulled Polo's hands loose. He stepped back, then sat down on the sand. "Got a smoke?" he asked, his face breaking into a slow grin.

Polo lifted his head. A smile creased his face. "Frankie," he said, digging in his shirt pocket.

They lit cigarettes. Frankie leaned back against the dune. He still had Polo with him. He realized the foolishness of an open fight and he saw the wisdom in what Polo had done. "You still pack a wallop," he said.

"It hurt me more," Polo said.

"That's what you think."

They both laughed quietly. Polo leaned back and for several seconds they both stared at the sky.

"Polo," Frankie said. "I'm going to beat Barlow and Springer into the ground."

"When the time is right," Polo cautioned.

"Yes, when the time is right," Frankie repeated. They were both silent again, thinking, then Frankie asked, "Polo, why the hell does Barlow want this island?"

"What?"

"Why does he want the island? There's nothing here."

"He brings his girls in here," Polo said. "He's got a good traffic in Mexican whores. His boats pick them up in Mexico and he lands them here. He works a few in Della's, he supplies the labor camps with the real pigs and the rest he sells up the line."

Frankie wasn't surprised, but he wasn't satisfied either. "I don't know," he said. "He could handle that easy enough by just controlling Springer." He paused, then he asked. "Did my father know about the girls?"

"Sure, everybody knows about them."

"Then there's something else. He has to hang onto this island for a bigger reason."

"Like what?"

"I don't know. But when I find out I'll have that sonavabitch by the short hair."

CHAPTER SIX

I t felt good to be working. Crouched in the restricted space under the deck, Frankie sweated over the engine. The nuts on the head were frozen and he had to use a pipe extension on the wrench, bracing both feet against the bulkhead and levering with the full weight of his body. It was hard and the muscles of his body bulged and strained with every pull, but it was also soothing, working like this, doing something constructive.

When he and Polo had finally parted the night before, he had come back to the boat to sleep. He had been restless in the bunk, worry nagging him. He had slept finally and was awake at dawn. He then went to Angelo's store where he washed and had coffee. Borrowing tools from Angelo, he carried the new parts back to the boat, and had begun work immediately.

By mid-morning he was running his fingers over the oil-slick tops of the pistons, smiling, happy about the condition of the engine's guts. The new head was settled over the stud bolts before noon and he whistled to himself as he drew the nuts down, oozing the excess gasket cement over the block.

Finished, he leaned back against the bulkhead. The sweat was running off him, his shirt dark and wet. He ran a hand over his forehead and left a wide streak of grease. He was dirty and tired, but it was a good feeling. For the first time he felt hunger and realized that he had not eaten since the day before. He squeezed through the small opening forward and stood up to stretch in the wheelhouse.

Looking through the windows, he watched the working harbor. He felt a part of it, as if the intervening years of wandering had not happened. The motion of the boat under his feet, rising and dipping, shifting with the surge of the water, was natural to him. He could almost forget that the island had changed, could almost ignore the uniformity of the boats. But directly before him was the gray bulk of the cannery. He shook his head, shrugged, and climbed out onto the deck.

The sun was high and warm. The water sparkled. The sun-warmed kelp was strong-smelling. Sandpipers, beak down, scurried along the water's edge. Gulls lazed and pirouetted, screamed and swooped. Sea lions off the breakwater barked like dogs.

It was a good day. The night before seemed ludicrous and impossible in the light of day. It was too difficult to retain the violent aspects of it, and Frankie felt no anger. He leaped to the dock and started for the boat yard.

Carazon was hammering chocks under a boat. He looked up as Frankie passed. He glowered and tightened his grip on the heavy mallet, as though expecting a reprisal; but Frankie smiled and shouted, "A good day." Carazon frowned, unable to understand the friendliness. He watched Frankie pass through the gate and scratched his head, perplexed.

Barlow was standing on the steps outside his office. He smiled with his usual assurance as Frankie drew near.

"Hello, Cargo," he said.

"Hello, Barlow," Frankie answered, stopping to look up at the man, wondering about him, measuring him.

"You covered a lot of ground in one day."

"I like to keep busy."

Barlow laughed, but his eyes were coldly impersonal. "By the way," he said, "I might be able to help you out with that traffic ticket you got yesterday. Drop in my office when you have time. I have a little pull with the magistrate." He was still smiling, but it was a different smile. And Frankie realized that he had just been told that Barlow had the law sewed up from top to bottom. It was another warning.

"I might just do that," Frankie answered. "Thanks."

"Always glad to help out an enterprising young man," Barlow said.

Frankie nodded and moved off along the road. Barlow was the tough one. But somewhere there was bound to be a crack. A tree that is rotting inside can look solid, but the rot is bound to reach the roots and it topples. He figured the rot couldn't be far from Barlow's roots.

Sudden white movement caught his eye and he watched a dazzling Thunderbird approach the causeway. The car was going fast. It came onto the causeway without slackening speed and clattered across, slowing before the end, but sliding into the turn and touching the sandy shoulder before straightening and heading down the road towards him. Frankie stepped off the road. The car reached him and braked, the tires squealing.

The girl behind the wheel was blonde. Her hair was almost silver-blonde. Her skin was honey-blonde. She had a smile that radiated warmth and her eyes were a deep blue, the color the ocean is supposed to be and never is.

"Hi," she said. "You're Frankie Cargo."

"You're right," Frankie said, abashed.

"I heard you were back. I'm Arlene Morse."

The name rang a bell and Frankie registered surprise. The girl who lived in the castle. She had been there most of his life, but he had never spoken to her before. As a boy, peering through the castle gate, he had caught glimpses of her, but he had never been this close to her before. The only daughter of old John Morse. She had always attended private schools and in her teens she had gone East, according to the Frisco Flat *Times*, attending Miss Fine's School for Girls. Frankie recalled stories that had been spread around about her, stories bandied about by boasting fishermen who told of having encountered her in bars during her sporadic vacations at home. The stories were about the usual amatory adventures that working men like to tell about rich girls, and Frankie had never believed them. But now he was amazed that Arlene Morse should know who he was and that she would know he was back at the Landing. The girl seemed to read his thoughts.

"My cook was talking about you," she said. "That's where I get all my information."

Frankie felt awkward standing next to the car, now that he knew who she was. But he was rooted to the spot, fascinated, and he could not keep his gaze from wandering over her. She wore a shoulderless white linen dress that contrasted with the red leather of the car; a dress that clung to her, starting midway on her jutting, deep-valleyed breasts, tapering to her narrow waist, and flaring out to cling to her hips and legs.

"You're quite a celebrity," she said. There was a teasing quality to her voice. "*Muy hombre,* the cook says."

Frankie was uncomfortable under the intensity of her inquisitive stare. This type of girl had always confused him. He had encountered similar girls when he was boxing—thrill-seekers attracted to gladiators. He had always stayed away from them, not wanting to be an oddity, a part of a collection.

"I hear you clobbered that idiot, Springer."

"I'm afraid it was the other way around."

"Not according to my cook." She looked up towards the cannery. "When did you tangle with him?"

Frankie turned, saw Barlow still on the steps, looking down at him and the girl.

"You like fights?" he asked.

"Adore them," she purred. "Especially if the people I like win."

"Who do you like?"

"I like you." She said it in a matter-of-fact way.

"You don't even know me."

"That's what you think," she said. "You're the one who used to watch through the fence when I was playing. You didn't think I saw you, but I was watching as closely as you were." He laughed with her. "Then I used to watch you on the boats with binoculars." She pursed her lips thoughtfully. "You were too pretty then. Somebody gave you a nice face."

"A lot of people did that," he said.

"I'm glad. Now it's a good face. What are you doing today?"

The sudden question caught him off-balance. "Today?"

"Now. This afternoon. You busy?"

"I'm working on my boat." He indicated the condition of his clothes, the grease on his hands.

"You're really going to fish?"

"I hope."

"Barlow isn't going to like that."

"I'm afraid you're right."

"Tonight," she said. "You can't be working then."

"Well … I …"

"And you haven't been here long enough to have a girl friend, so tonight you're free. Eight o'clock, up at the house. I want to hear the story of your life." She put both hands on the wheel, then she reached down and moved the gear shift into low. "You have no idea how I rushed down here to see you before some local girl pinned you down." She smiled broadly, touched the gas pedal. The small car leaped ahead. She made a U-turn in Barlow's parking area, and waved as she roared past.

Frankie watched her go. He was still stunned by the suddenness of her attention, and baffled by her interest. He couldn't figure it. There were a few answers that came easily to mind. She was a bored rich girl eager to bask in the shadow of violence. She was a girl looking for a good lay. Both of these were logical, but there was still the fact that she *had* remembered him from childhood. Was it possible that she had really been interested in him. It was a flattering thought, and he warmed to it, giving rein to his ego. But it didn't make sense. What the hell did Arlene Morse have in common with Frankie Cargo? Answer: nothing. But he couldn't deny that she was a beautiful female, and in some instinctive way he knew he was going to make love to her, and soon. And despite his misgivings, he knew that he was looking forward to it.

Lunch with Angelo was a series of questions parried with stock answers. The old man seemed disturbed that Frankie was not seething with hate, and he was intent on fanning the flames of vengeance.

"They beat you last night."

"No, Polo knocked me on my ass."

"Polo is one of them? A traitor to the blood?"

"No, he was just stopping the fight."

"You're sure?"

"I know he stopped the fight."

"His wife is against you."

"She's got good sense."

When he left Angelo's he stopped in the street and looked down toward his house. He was thinking of Tosca. He wanted to see her. But he was also thinking of Arlene Morse. For the first time in his life he had feelings of guilt about a woman. He knew that Tosca was real, and there in the sand when she had clung to him, she had been a woman. There weren't many like her. He knew this, believed it, wanted it; but he still thought of Arlene with anticipation. He tried to rationalize it, say to himself that he had to stay away from Tosca for her good, that he was shielding her from the violence that was inevitable; but it didn't work. He knew that he was kidding himself. And in the back of his mind was the nagging presence of the idea that Arlene Morse could be the lever to upset Barlow. He didn't like the idea, it did not fit into the pattern of what he thought of himself, but he knew that he was going to be there at eight o'clock.

He turned away and went back to the boat yard. Carazon was not in sight. He went directly to the *Evalena,* back to the engine and engrossed himself with the distributor.

When he was finished, he brought two gallons of gas from the tank behind Angelo's store. He crossed his fingers and pressed the starter button. Nothing. The batteries were dead. He cursed silently, then he snapped his fingers, leaped to the dock and strode to the boat yard office.

"Carazon!" he called through the doorway.

"What?" The answer came from a back room. Frankie waited for the man to show himself and smiled when Carazon stepped into the room, noticed who it was and leaped back, instinctively knotting his fists. "What do you want?"

"I got a little job for you," Frankie said. "I want you to run your charger down there and give me a booster."

"You crazy? Why should I charge your batteries?" Carazon was genuinely baffled.

"Because I'm a customer here."

"Whatta ya talk? Whatta ya mean, customer? Get up some cash, you'll be customer."

"What are you worried about? You have the boat. You want to make it rough for me to get out, so run the bill up higher and make it tougher."

Carazon squinted and twisted his cigar. It made sense, except that he wasn't supposed to trust Cargo. But he had no specific order to go by, and he could overcharge on the bill for the services. That would make Barlow happy. "Okay," he said, "I'll get the stuff."

With the charger on the batteries, the engine turned over, coughed several times, then exploded into action, the cloud of blue-gray exhaust spreading out over the water. With the screw disengaged, he gave it full throttle, the powerful Chrysler-Crown pounding, the gauge showing a full charge. Frankie slammed his hands together with joy. Just feeling the shiver of the deck under his feet was elation enough. But he had to keep Carazon going before he had a chance to talk to Barlow. He went back on deck.

"I'll need a tankful of gas," he said.

"The price just went up," Carazon said, smiling, feeling that he was pulling a fast one. It was something he could brag about later to Barlow.

"Guess you got me," Frankie said. "I'll pull over to the tanks."

He ducked back inside, then put his head out and shouted to Carazon to toss the lines. Clear of the dock, he put the engine in reverse, easing the throttle off. The boat shuddered into action, backed out into the bay. He threw it into forward and turned the wheel over. The boat responded to the power and the rudder, wheeling smartly, stern down. He crossed to the gasoline dock, came in with a light bump, idled the engine and leaped to the lines.

Carazon filled the tanks. At the same time Frankie took the opportunity to fill the water tank with fresh water. When the gas gauge tipped over to full, and Carazon was wheeling in his hose, the *Evalena* was almost ready for sea. Frankie backed her out and came back to his dock, where he tied up. He left the engine running to give the batteries a full charge, then he went to work on the rigging.

The lockers under the forward bunks were filled with fishing gear, wire and turnbuckles.

Frankie started on the canted mast, laughing to himself as he thought of what Barlow would say to Carazon when he found the *Evalena* gone in the morning...

The big house was surrounded by a high iron fence. Frankie paused before the massive gate that crossed the drive. It was locked. He rattled it once, then he looked for a bell. It was imbedded in the stone pillar on the right, a brass button. He pushed it and waited.

He looked behind him at the winding road he had just climbed. He looked out over the island. It was still light, but there were lights on in the houses. Behind him the cement plant was dazzling white in the glare of spotlights.

There was a buzz, followed by a slow click, and the gates slid aside, controlled from the house. He stepped inside the grounds, continued up the drive, walking slowly. It was the first time he had ever been inside the gate and he thought about all the times he had stood outside with his face pressed to the fence and wondered about the life in the big house.

The house was Spanish colonial. White plaster walls of thick adobe, the windows thick-silled. Stone columns and heavy vigas supported the portale that ran the length of the building. It was low-roofed, sloping, with half-round red tiles. It was a sprawling house of many rooms. It sat on the bluff overlooking the sea as though it belonged there. The grounds were carefully landscaped with an assortment of shrubs and flowers.

Arlene was standing on the portico before the large hand-carved oak door. She was wearing white slacks and a white blouse that did good things for her. She wore thonged sandals. It occurred to Frankie that he hadn't seen her standing before, but he wasn't disappointed. Sitting or standing, she was beautiful.

"You're on time," she said.

"I didn't think you were the waiting kind."

He reached her and she turned and moved into the house. He followed, admiring the smooth motion of her hips.

She led him into a large room that was furnished with heavy, carved furniture, the kind you see in the haciendas of Mexico. There were many couches, piled with pillows, and the floor was covered with hand-woven rugs. It was a warm, comfortable room with enough clutter to make it livable. Arlene crossed to a large cabinet. There were several bottles on the top, along with glasses and a bucket of ice.

"What's your poison?" she asked.

"Sour mash," he said. He wasn't a drinker, but he knew that sour mash bourbon was a good drink.

"Mix?"

"Just ice."

She poured the liquor and handed him the glass. She lifted her own glass. "I'm ahead of you," she said.

"I'm a slow starter."

"Not the way I hear it," she said. She moved past him, walked into the bowels of the room, and settled gracefully into one of the couches, curling her legs under her. She looked at him soberly. "Come talk to me," she said.

He crossed to the couch and sat down. He lifted his drink and took a swallow, looking at her over the rim of the glass.

"Why did you come back here?" she said.

"Felt like coming home, got tired of beating around. A lot of reasons, I guess."

"Are you sorry?"

"Sorry?"

"Sorry you came. The way things are with Barlow, I mean."

"I don't enjoy getting pushed around, but I don't think I'm sorry. No, I guess I'm glad I came back."

"So am I," she said.

"You? Why are you glad?"

"Because I've been wanting to see a man. And you're a man."

He didn't try to answer that. It was too leading. "Why do you stay here?" he asked.

"I'm running the cement plant," she answered.

He smiled and she said, "Don't laugh. I mean it. I'm a businesswoman. Behind this blonde façade I'm as tough as Sam Barlow will ever be." There was a change in her when she said this, and Frankie noted it. He realized that she meant it and that she was probably right. But in the next instant she changed again, and the female softness came back. "But that's not why I asked you up here," she said.

"Just why did you ask me?"

"For dinner," she said, smiling. She uncurled her legs and stood up. She gulped her drink. "And it's all ready."

He followed her into the dining room where a large table was centrally placed. The table was set for two at one end and the dinner was under silver covers on a serving table. He sat down and she served the meal.

"You always do this? I expected to meet the cook."

"Everyone has the night off," she said with a teasing smile.

They ate for an hour. She talked about herself, about her schools, her travels. He listened to the monologue with fascination. It was a life he had not known. As she talked he detected a wistful quality to her speech, and she wasn't talking to him as much as she was just reviewing her life and not enjoying it. They finished the dinner with brandy and went back to the living room.

"You like Brahms?" she asked, standing by the console phonograph.

"I guess."

"I'll play the First Symphony."

The music filled the room. He had expected lullabys. It was the only thing he knew about the composer. But this was different. It opened with stirring brass and full strings, the complete orchestra in strident melody. Then it was mellow and moody, but building up to crescendos that seemed to catch his breath. She stood with her back to him and he stared at her. She swayed slightly to the strong, moving music. She turned to him with her arms crossed, her eyes closed, her firm chin tilted upwards. The strings were militant, then melodious, the woodwinds suddenly coming in with a pastoral feeling and then the brass and the full orchestra. It was haunting music and he was caught up in the mood.

Arlene opened her eyes and smiled slightly. She came across the room and curled up on the couch next to him.

"I love this," she said dreamily. She looked at him, the deep blue of her eyes dulled. Her lips were wet from the drink, and they were parted, inviting. Although she sat quietly, unmoving, there was an urgency in her that reached him, that unknown knowing that can travel between man and woman. His hand trembled and he placed his drink on the table before him.

The music rose, crashed through the room. A deep-throated cello sang as he leaned towards her and placed his hands on her shoulders. There was silence between them. He could feel the blood pounding through her veins, sense the beat of her pulse quickening under his touch. Her breathing became heavy, her breasts rose and fell beneath her blouse. He drew her to him slowly. He lowered his face to hers. He heard her glass clatter to the floor. Her fingers searched his back. He touched his mouth to hers, lightly, brushing her lips, feeling the muscles of his body tense. She opened her mouth and pulled him to her, arching her body, darting her tongue against his.

His mind reeled. He crushed her to him. He pulled his mouth away and gasped for breath. She clung to him, forced her mouth back to his. He kissed her again, not daring to breathe. Her body was aflame under his touch. She pulled his arm from her shoulder and gripped his hand. She pressed the hand to her breast and squirmed against him with a lithe, animal movement. He moved his hand, caressing, and felt her breast harden under his touch. She moved her head back, her eyes closed, and writhed against the pressure of his hand.

Twisting suddenly, she was out of his grasp and standing. She took his hands and pulled him to his feet. She was against him, pressing against his rising passion, rubbing her face against his chest.

The brass rose and screamed as the tympani ended the movement, the strings joining in and carrying the music to heights that matched the wild howling in his brain.

He grasped her to pull her down upon the couch. She struggled free. "Not here," she gasped. She turned and ran across the room. He walked after her.

Entering the large bedroom a few steps behind her, he stopped. Not bothering to unbutton the blouse, she tore it from her, slipped it off her shoulders. There was nothing under it and her breasts were high and firm, golden as the rest of her, and dark-tipped. He gazed upon her, unbuttoning his shirt.

She slipped out of the slacks and her eager fingers tore at the sandal thongs. She fell upon the wide bed, her arms outstretched to him.

He kicked his clothing aside on the floor and went to her. She pulled him down and they sprawled, entwined, his mouth seeking hers. He held her tightly, feeling the press of her thighs against him. He kissed the hollows of her throat. He bowed his head and sought the erect tips of her breasts. She moaned with ecstatic joy and pressed hard against his lips.

"Now," she whispered, her voice frantic.

The music came from a distance and he felt the wild, urging rhythm, as he linked his body with hers. Then, suddenly, they were as one, uniting in passion, their senses mounting to incredible heights, the mind released, shut off, and only the nerve-wracking wanting striving for fulfillment and ending with a tympanic crash!

The house was stilled. The music had ended. There was only the sound of breathing returning to normal. Frankie rolled to his side. He bent to kiss her, but Arlene moved away. She was smiling.

"You're better than I thought you'd be," she said.

The words, the nonchalance with which she said them, broke the spell for him. He was confused and he wanted to quiet her. But she was suddenly changed, as though nothing had happened between them. She swung her legs off the bed and sat up. She smiled down at him. "Now you know about Brahms," she said. "He never fails."

Frankie felt used, as though he were nothing more than a stud she had picked out for her pleasure. He was hurt and angry. What had gone before was dirtied. He watched her pull the slacks over her long legs. For her it was over and he was no longer needed. It could have been anyone. She went to a closet and brought out a blouse.

"How about a drink?" she asked, buttoning the blouse.

He didn't answer and she walked back to the bed. She looked down. "What's wrong?"

"Nothing," he said. "Just a boy growing up."

"Not enough tenderness?"

"Forget it."

"Look," she said, "I mean it. You're wonderful."

"I said, forget it!"

"I couldn't forget it if I tried. I like you. But some people are different than others."

"Okay. Let's have that drink."

She rose. "Don't be angry," she said. She left the room and he retrieved his clothes and put them on.

The drinks were mixed when he entered the living room. His feelings had already been altered and he expected nothing from her now. He took the drink, raised his glass to her, and drank. Then he went to the couch and sat down. She sat opposite him.

"You need money," she said.

"I'm not for sale," he answered bitterly.

"And I don't have to buy you," she said. "You went to the bank in Monterey for a loan."

"Your cook tell you that?"

She smiled. "Some things I find out in other ways. So, you need money."

"I don't need your money."

"I don't intend giving any money. I told you I was a hard businesswoman. I want a percentage of your boat."

Frankie laughed. "For what?"

"To stop Barlow."

He paused. "What have you got against Barlow?" he asked, finally.

"Let's just say I don't like what he's done to the island, my father's island."

"What makes you think I can change that?"

"I think you could do damn near anything."

He eyed her curiously. There was something sincere in the way she had said that. He was swayed by her tone. "What kind of a percentage?"

"Barlow offered you five thousand. I'll take ten percent of that for five hundred."

"The boat is worth ten thousand."

"I told you I was a businesswoman. Your hands are tied. You need the money and I want that boat at sea."

"Does this give you ten percent of me, too?"

"I've already got more than that, and you know it."

He was silent. She was right. The thought annoyed him, but he had already put aside her cold attitude and at that moment wanted to take her in his arms. "It's a deal," he said.

She went to a table at the end of the room and picked up a check. "I made it out earlier," she said, handing it to him.

He glanced at it and frowned. "You were pretty sure of yourself."

"Yes."

"And of me, too."

"No, not exactly. If you thought you were in love with me you would have refused the offer. I'm glad you're not."

"You're sure."

"Yes. We're a physical thing."

"You, yes, but how about me?"

"Shall I put on some music?"

He smiled. "No thanks. I don't think I'm man enough." He rose and pocketed the check. She followed him to the door.

Standing on the portale, he asked, "When will I see you again?"

"I'll let you know."

He shrugged, nodding his head, sorry he had bothered to ask the question. Everything was sounding as if this woman had just bought him, and he was already begging for her favors. He walked away without looking back.

The gate opened as he approached it and he passed through. It closed behind him. He started down the winding drive, and when he had walked only a hundred yards he saw the lights of an approaching car. He stepped off the road and behind a cluster of bushes.

The car shot past him, giving him just a glimpse of black and white. He scowled and stepped back into the road, keeping in the shadows, but watching the car. It pulled up to the gate and stopped. The driver's door opened. He saw Jake Springer pass in front of the headlights and go to the bell on the gatepost. Springer passed through the light again. The car door slammed. Then the red light on top of the car blinked several times so that it could be seen from the house. The gate swung aside. The car drove ahead, and the gate closed.

Frankie stood there for several minutes staring after the car. It was obvious that Arlene Morse had opened the gate at the signal from Springer. Why was he going there? He had an answer for that. For the same reason that she had summoned him. But it could be something else.

He wanted to get up to the house and eavesdrop, but he would have to go over the fence and he knew that Arlene would have some sort of warning device for intruders. People didn't have locked gates unless they had an insurmountable fence. And Springer would love to have a good excuse to blast him.

Turning, he started along the road. He fingered the check in his pocket. None of it figured. Arlene wanted to get laid. Okay, he had obliged. But she wasn't paying five hundred for that. For what then? To knock Barlow off, as she said? Was Springer playing both ends against the middle? He would, the bastard.

CHAPTER SEVEN

Except for Della's, the island was dark and silent. He stood at the end of the causeway. It was warm and Della had her front door standing open. The rowdy sounds of the juke box came out to disturb the night. Laughter followed in discordant harmony. He could see into the smoky haze of the bar.

Tosca was standing by one of the booths talking to the occupants. She wore a tight black dress and black heels. Her jet hair spilled over her shoulders. She was smiling, one hand on her hip, a typical bar-girl pose. She was a different person from the girl of last night. Seeing her framed in the doorway from a distance, looking at her objectively, the tight dress selling her sex, she was just another hustler. The girl last night had been frightened and earthy. He saw her barefoot, her full skirt whipping about her bare legs, felt her trembling against his chest, and he could not believe that it was the same person who was now standing in the bar.

Which girl was she? He damned himself for thinking that, for asking the question. Who was he to question anyone after tonight? No matter what the reasons, he had sold something of himself tonight and he felt the loss. But it was done and he could not buy it back.

And why was Tosca there? Yesterday she was there because she had to be there, because life dumped her in that spot the way it dumps everyone in their own particular spot, banker or pimp, it's all the same. But she was there tonight because he had sent her back there, because he was not big enough to take her away from Barlow's grasp, because he was afraid to accept another area where Barlow could strike at him.

He was piling up a lot of things that he didn't like about himself.

But he was going to be striking back. And sooner than Barlow would realize.

He walked to Angelo's and rattled the door until the old man awakened and appeared to let him inside. He produced the check and endorsed it.

"I want you to cash this and have the money when I get back," he said.

"You're leaving?"

He had to control the elation in his voice. "I'm putting to sea tonight. I'll need some food for a few days."

"Tonight? Now?" He glanced at the clock on the wall.

"Tonight," Frankie said. "And don't tell me I can't go through the breakwater. I've done it before."

Angelo smiled and danced happily. "You can do it," he said. "You have the blood." He crossed the room and threw on the lights of the store. He danced along the shelves, pulling down canned goods. He pulled salami from a hook, added some cheese. He put the food in a bag. "You have gas, water?"

"Got it from Barlow," Frankie said, winking.

"Wonderful," Angelo said, laughing, clapping his hands. "Wonderful."

Frankie took the bag in his arms. "Wish me luck, paisan," he said.

"My heart sails with you, son of my friend," Angelo said in Sicilian.

Frankie passed through the door. He went to the rear of Polo's house. He whistled softly. A head appeared from a window. "Frankie?"

"Yes."

"Be right out."

He waited and then Polo came through the screened door. He carried a pail in one hand. "I took the chum off the boat," he said. "Courtesy of Sam Barlow."

Frankie took the pail of chum, herring that was well salted, bait that would bring the albacore to the surface.

"I'll come down and help you get off."

"No," Frankie said. "I'm going to need you later and I don't want you to get hung up if something goes wrong."

Polo hung his head. "I guess you're right." He glanced back at the house and saw his wife's face in the window. "I wish to hell I was going with you, Frankie," he said. "But, well, you know how it is."

Frankie, too, glanced at the frightened face in the window. "I know," he said. "I better get rolling."

"Good luck," Polo said.

"I'll need it."

Frankie walked quickly towards the boat yard. As he went he wondered where Carazon lived. It was just possible that he slept in the shed at the boat yard.

Reaching the wire fence and the open gate, Frankie paused and listened. His eyes probed the shadows. Seeing nothing, he moved into the yard, walking carefully, his senses alert. He came to the water's edge and stepped onto the dock. It swayed lightly under his feet. When he reached the *Evalena* he stopped and looked back. Satisfied that he was unobserved, he climbed over the gunwales and went to the wheelhouse. He put down the groceries and the pail and went back on deck.

His eye checked the details of the boat. The mast was now straight. The outriggers rose up on either side of the mast and were lashed fast. The lines ran off the outriggers and he stepped to the stern to make sure that they were still gigged and coiled in the stern well. Everything looked right.

Headlights crossing the causeway brought his eyes up. He felt his heartbeat quicken. The car roared over the narrow bridge and squealed onto the island. Somebody was in an awful hurry.

Frankie leaped to the dock. He slipped the stern line and ran to the bow. The half hitch came away easily. He pushed the *Evalena* away from the dock and leaped to the deck. He scrambled to the wheelhouse, praying that the engine would turn over on the first kick. The headlights were probing the dunes up above him. He could hear the roar of the car's engine. Damn! Leave it to Springer to second-guess him.

He had wanted to drift out into the channel before starting the engine, but now he was filled with a sense of urgency that made his hands shake. True, he could wait until tomorrow and pay off the bills and then leave quietly, but he felt that it was important to throw this into Barlow's face. He had to steal the boat from under his nose and make his first trip with Barlow picking up the tab.

He pressed the starter. The flywheel whirred. The spark coughed. It seemed like long minutes before the spark exploded the gas in the cylinders and the engine roared into motion. He threw the screw into reverse, begging the engine not to stall under the pull. The boat swept away from the dock.

The car squealed to a stop. He was not looking there, but he heard the door slam, heard the shouting.

"Carazon! Gahdamn you, stop that bastard! Carazon, you dago sonavabitch, get your ass in gear!"

Frankie could hear the running feet. But he was in the channel. He threw the screw into forward and eased the throttle forward. He couldn't chance stalling now. Springer's feet pounded on the dock. The deck trembled under the power of the engine. He eased the wheel about. The stern dipped as he threw the throttle all the way in. The wash boiled in his wake. The bow rose and sliced the black water. He pointed straight for the rocks and the sand, peering into the darkness.

"Cargo, you bastard, I'll see you in hell!"

The crack of the service revolver pealed out over the silent water like the crack of a whip. Frankie jumped at the sound of it, his hands tightening on the wheel. The slug tore into the wheelhouse and Frankie ducked his head instinctively. Splinters flew against his face. Frankie grinned. In his wild anger, Springer was shooting for the wheelhouse where only a lucky shot would have a chance of hitting him.

But even a shot at the water line would not do any real damage. It could be easily plugged.

Making the turn in the darkness was tricky, and Frankie strained his eyes forward. Springer was still shooting, too excited to realize that he ought to be on the rocks at the channel entrance where the *Evalena* would be a sitting duck. Frankie felt the strong run of the sea. He pulled the wheel over to starboard. The boat swung into the turn and labored against the running tide.

Work horse that she was, the *Evalena* put her head into the sea with the tenacity of a bulldog. The tide was running in at this hour and the waves battered against the rocks and concrete of the breakwater, boiled and raged against this unmoving adversary, and turned the narrow opening to the sea into a maelstrom of leaping fury.

Frankie gripped the spokes of the wheel. The jagged rocks loomed, dark and foreboding on either side of him. He drove into the leaping, whitecapped turmoil and his laughing voice rose in happy song. The water battered his bow, the spindrift was flung against the wheelhouse like shot. He fought the sudden yaw of the stern that could send him broadside against the waves and toss him like a cork. The engine pounded amidship, the screw growling against the tide. His happy laughter was lost, mingled with the angry howl of the rushing water. He forgot Springer. Barlow did not exist. The sea was his element. He took her on her terms and bullied her.

The rocks were gone. Beach curved out on both sides behind him. He was through the opening. The bay stretched out before him. The bluffs of Santa Cruz were a distant shadow on his right. The lights of Monterey were a dim pyramid on the left. The bobbing red light of the bell buoy was directly off the starboard quarter. The *Evalena* rose on a final wave and dipped her bow into the trough, a graceful curtsy, her stern lifted to the men on the beach like the flagrant flip of the can-can dancer's skirt.

At the buoy, well beyond pistol range, he flipped on the running lights. He knew that the sight of the white light on the mast and the red and green on the sides would bring a growl of rage from Springer, who was sure to be watching. He smiled with glee, conjuring up a picture of Carazon's unhappiness when he had to tell about the battery charge, the gas and the water. It was too bad that Barlow couldn't know about the bucket of bait.

Hovering over the binnacle, now lighted, Frankie checked his course at due west. A few yards past the buoy he gave starboard rudder until he was two points below west-west-southwest. He held that course for five minutes, his bow drawing a direct bead on the Point Pinos light, then he made another change, heeling over until the light was due starboard. He checked the compass. West-northwest. He made several more changes, checking against the light and known landmarks until he was sure of the accuracy of the compass. Running without a radio was tough enough without having the compass off. Satisfied, he set a course, west-west-northwest, held it there, and rummaged for a cigarette.

He eased the throttle down a little. The race was over, and he didn't need the sixteen knots. He wanted at least twelve, but it wasn't important enough to run a log, and he settled on a guess. There was a light chop to the bay, just enough to slap the bow as he boiled along.

Fifteen minutes and he was clear of the bay. The sea changed to a gentle swell and he enjoyed the motion that he had not experienced for a long time. He had to try the iron mike, the automatic pilot that co-ordinated the rudder with the compass setting. He pushed the small lever forward, checked his reading, and leaned back against the far wall of the wheelhouse to smoke.

He waited five minutes, then checked the compass. He was still on course. He changed the setting several degrees, put it on iron mike and waited again. When he was satisfied that the mechanism was working properly, he went back to a course of due west, put it on automatic, and went on deck.

There was nothing to do now. He went to the stern and looked back. A mist obscured the distant lights and there was only the vastness of the sea and the sky surrounding him.

He sat on a hatch and lit a cigarette. He was feeling what every fisherman feels with the realization of the sudden, sharp division of land and sea. It is an overpowering loneliness that settles in the chest and seems to eat away at the innards until you feel small and helpless. There is always the longing for the solid security of the earth. Your world has shrunk to thirty feet of wood planking and you are a prisoner of your own making.

Frankie looked up at the sky and there is no sky so vast as the sky at sea. It is more like an enclosure. The stars rise out of one horizon and descend into another. It is a great, sparkling tent; a sequinned shroud.

The romantics would have the fisherman stand, spread-legged upon the bow, the spray in his face, elated freedom expanding his chest. Not so. He sits or stands in humble silence, more so at night. He is cowed by the immensity of the water world. And there is always the fear. The fear of being alone. The fear of the sea. The fear of whatever nature may unleash, fear wrought by hard experience. The fear of dying without friends, of dying cold and wet. Frankie felt all these things.

He stood and stretched. He listened to the engine. He picked his way forward and sat down on the air hatch over the sleeping area. He watched the water purl away from the slicing scimiter bow with satisfaction.

The next couple of hours were always watchful ones. He was running through the shipping lanes and he kept an eye out for the lights of freighters. A thirty-tonner could slice through a fishing boat without noticing the bump. It had happened too many times, and Frankie did not relax his vigil.

By morning he would be in the Japanese current where the water was warm enough for the albacore to run.

And now there was time to think. He folded his hands and stared down at the knuckles that were like knots from punching too many faces. He didn't want to think about fighting, but everything about him seemed to bear the marks of combat. He lifted his hand and touched the smooth scar tissue over his eyes, the width of his spread nose, the lips that were thinner once.

The land was severed from him now, the land with its demands upon him, and he was now of the sea. It was like a great mother enveloping him and he felt a kind of peace. But in the back of his mind were the nagging thoughts of the things unfinished on the land; unresolved fates of friends and enemies. The faces paraded before him until they became a mass of confusion. He shook himself and decided that he would be better off doing something.

Running without a radio, he had to depend on the compass and memory. It would be better to use charts. He went to the wheelhouse and came back with the water log, a cylinder on a long cord. He tossed it off the stern. Its revolutions in the wake would record his speed. He waited several minutes and pulled it in. He checked the instrument and smiled. Twelve knots as he had figured. He went back to the wheelhouse.

The chart table was hinged to the wall. He pulled it down, brought out the rolled map and spread it over the table top. He brought a rule and calipers and a pencil. He checked his watch, jotted down some figures. He placed a protractor on the chart, ran his rule and marked his position. With the calipers he plotted a day's course, noted the times and compass changes on a pad.

When that was done he rolled the map and folded the table back against the wall. Afterward, he went back on deck and sat on the forward hatch. He looked again at the sky. It was clear. He picked out Venus, then Orion. He turned his head to see the Big Dipper, followed it to the North Star. He glanced back at Orion, mentally tracing the image of the hunter. Hunter or hunted, he mused, which am I? Both, he imagined. He squinted his eyes, searching for Sirius, the Dog Star. Too early, he decided, giving it up.

The moon was high behind him and an endless path of light spread over the water before him. Phosphorescent algae rose along the port side and he marveled at the pale green light it gave off, remembering the first time he had seen it and how it had frightened him.

And now there was nothing more to see or do, just wait, and he could no longer keep the troubling thoughts below the surface.

There was not an inch of the boat that did not remind him of his father. This, in itself, was enough to make him melancholy.

His father, his blood, his flesh, his past, his tie to ancestry—murdered. And what was he doing about it? He hadn't even visited the man's grave. All he had done was wonder *why* they had killed him. Nothing more. Was Springer the killer? Yes, he told himself, emphatically. Then why is Springer still alive? Because... because... well, damn it, I don't have any proof that it was Springer. Then how can you be sure? It has to be him. Why not Carazon? I don't know, maybe it was him. But it's the same thing, Carazon, Springer—it all comes back to Sam Barlow.

Frankie's mind kept posing the questions and he flung back the answers to himself, trying to straighten the thing out. The engine throbbed. The wind came up and the wire rigging sighed overhead.

Why the hell does Sam Barlow have to control the island? Why would he kill for this? Whatever it is, the Old Man had found out something. But what? Frankie had gone through his father's few belongings and papers carefully. There had been nothing there with any connection to Barlow. It was a blank wall and it was maddening to face it and know that somewhere there was a doorway, elusive and hidden.

The minute he had arrived in Frisco Flat he had been thrown into combat with Springer and Barlow. He had been pushed off-balance because he hadn't expected trouble. But Barlow and Springer had been waiting for him. And since he knew neither man before yesterday morning, it had to be that he was simply picking up the fight where his father had left off, as though some referee had called time with the Old Man's last breath and things had stood still until he entered the picture. This was the only way he could figure it, because the situation was too advanced to be his fight alone. The events of the past two days had been in the making and waiting for him for months.

And he wasn't ready. He had just been rolling with the punches, trying to catch his breath.

And then there was Tosca. He had seen her and wanted her as he might any full-bodied sultry woman. You can pass a girl on the street and feel a longing to possess her. But then he had seen her again and something had grown between them in min-utes. He had been surprised and skeptical of her emotions on the beach, but now he realized that she, too, was a part of his life long before he saw her; that she had been waiting for him.

And what of Arlene Morse? He had met her and slept with her in one day. He had left her just hours ago. His mind and body had raged with longing for her in that short time, desiring, pos-sessing and rejecting in one long gasp. But she, too, had been expecting him, figuring him into some plan of hers. There was nothing accidental about any of it.

Was he in love with Tosca? If he was, why did he go to Arlene Morse knowing that he would take her to bed? Were love and sex separate things? It had to be. He couldn't remember all the women he had slept with, but he had loved none of them. What would it be like when both emotions came together and centered on the same woman. He came back to the original question. Did he love Tosca? He could not drive her image from his mind; she overshadowed Arlene. He knew that he wanted to be near her. Was this love? He shook his head and went back to the wheelhouse to check the compass.

And there, standing by the wheel, enclosed in the small dim-light world of the cabin, his thoughts returned to his father.

Help me, Old Man, he said softly. I'm fighting them and I don't even know what I'm fighting. You found out something that made them kill you. Let me find it. Let me find it, Old Man, and then let them come after me.

Before the sun, the sky and the water blended into the pasty gray light of false dawn, he shut down the engine. He went on deck and ran the sea anchor. He waited for fifteen minutes to check the rate of drift, then went below and slept.

He awoke with a start and sat up. The bunks were little more than mattressed platforms following the lines of the bow. Two men could sleep there, one on either side, their heads at the wheelhouse bulkhead, their feet at the bow point. He was dressed except for his shoes. He dropped his legs over the side and squirmed his feet into the waiting shoes.

Stooping through the narrow opening, he straightened in the wheelhouse and gazed through the windows at the sun-glittering water.

Rubbing his eyes with one hand, he reached out and pressed the starter. The engine turned over and he let it idle while he went on deck. The boat rocked gently on the marching swells. Blue exhaust rose from the stern. He grasped the sea anchor line and began to haul, pulling hand over hand, coiling with his left. He reached down, finally, gripped the metal rim of the canvas bucketlike anchor and hauled it over the side. He put it aside to dry in the sun, and went back to the wheelhouse.

He checked the clock. It was a little after eight. He pulled down the chart table and spread the map. Making quick computations of time and drift he readjusted his position. It was not exact, but it would be close. Then he meshed the screw with the drive shaft and throttled to twelve knots. When his course was west-west-by-west-southwest, he engaged the iron mike and went back on deck.

Leaping to the wheelhouse, he climbed the short mast. He loosened the storm binding on the outriggers, and slid down, jumping to the deck. Then he went forward of the wheelhouse where the mast rose from the bowels of the boat. He slipped the half hitch of the outrigger lines, gripping them with his hands. He flipped them, loosening the pulleys, then began to play the lines out. The stout, forty-foot outrigger poles leaned away from the mast and descended slowly, resembling booms coming off both sides. They came down until they tightened against their guy supports at mast and bowsprit. The *Evalena* now seemed to be winged and she dipped and rolled, quartering the swells.

Frankie moved aft and began playing out the lines. Eight lines of different lengths ran off each outrigger, attached to the poles with a length of spring to cushion the shock of a heavy strike. Each line was attached to the stern by another length of string, and on each line was a small bell to sound the strike.

The lines out, the jigs running deep to keep them taut, Frankie stood and surveyed his work. Everything was right. It was good that there were some things one remembered.

He went back to the wheelhouse and had a breakfast of salami and bread, brewing coffee on the butane stove.

The morning passed without a strike, and he saw no other boats. The sun was high overhead and hot. And then began the long, grueling period of watching and waiting. Fishing is never a matter of sitting and sailing. You stand, you pace the deck, you climb to the top of the wheelhouse. And you watch. The water stretches forever in every direction and somewhere in that glittering, undulating mass are the schools of fish. At any moment you may be passing within fifty yards of a full catch. But there are signs and you watch for them, constantly scanning. Where tides converge there are tide slicks and in these glassy avenues the plankton is collected. The fish feed here and you watch for the slicks. You look for birds playing over the surface of the water, for where fish are up there is something to eat and the birds follow for scraps. You look for the sudden white break in the water's surface, a momentary thing, but it might be the member of a school feeling frisky.

The sun's glare from the water tortures the eyes until you blink and squeeze the lids together to stop the burning that doesn't stop. For one man alone there is no break. Not while his decks are bare. And the strain and the glare and the waiting play tricks on the mind until you see tide slicks everywhere and every skittering spindrift is a ten-ton school.

By late afternoon Frankie ached. His eyes were red-rimmed and his pulse was a tom-tom against his temples. He went to the stern and sat on the hatch cover, rubbing his fingers against his head, cursing the sea. With a radio he would be getting reports from the various small fleets, telling where they were hitting fish, and he could run a course to cut their migrant path, and perhaps coax them up with chum.

The sun dropped, inflaming the water and sky until it seemed to Frankie that he was sailing into hell. As quickly as it touched the edge of the water, the sun sank away, leaving in its wake a glow of changing colors that ran from pink to purple.

Before dark, Frankie brought in three fish. He was standing by the wheelhouse, smoking. A jangling bell snapped him upright. He tossed the butt and ran to the stern well. He looked up to see which spring was taut. He pulled the line in to him, grasped it with thumb and forefinger of the left hand, and began to haul, coiling and holding, laying the line into the left with precise loops. The royal blue albacore skipped on the surface a few yards from the stern, white side turning up in the roiling wake. He brought it in, held, and reached for the gaff. He leaned over, thudded the sharp hook into the gills and swung the fish over his head, slipping the gaff and the jig with one movement. The fish flapped on the deck. Frankie tossed the jig and let the loops ride off his fingers. Another bell and he repeated the maneuver. Again. Three fish and it was over. Not much, but they were forty-pounders, and the ice was broken. He covered the catch with wet burlap.

By eight o'clock it was dark and he shut down, checking position and trimming the sea anchor. Now was when you usually tuned in the marine operator, the matter-of-fact female voice coming from San Francisco with news and the weather report.

Spattered with blood from the gaffing, spray-wet and smelling of sweat, Frankie settled on the bunk with a cup of coffee. The water lapped against the sides of the boat, cooing and gurgling. He was too tired to think and of this he was glad. He was mildly concerned about the weather and his position, but there was nothing he could do about either, so he kicked off his shoes, finished the coffee, set the alarm for four, lay back and fell asleep as soon as his head touched the bunk.

The morning was a wild, ringing, spring-stretched, joyous massacre. It was gray-light and calm—before his coffee—when the hungry school came for the silver-spinning jigs, suicidally impaling their tuna flesh upon the barbs.

Leaping up, Frankie put the *Evalena* into a wide turn that would cross and recross the school of fish, set the iron mike, and made a dash for the stern well.

He was there for two hours, hauling, gaffing, swinging the heavy fish over his head, running the lines, taking another. As a line went out another fish took it and the sixteen bells pealed with abandon.

The school sounded as quickly as they had come and one by one the lines were cleared, the bells silenced. It was a good haul and Frankie was elated. Blood was running through the scuppers. Frankie flushed the deck with buckets of water. Then he went for coffee and another long day of watching.

Now the waiting and the careful scanning was not the same. Now, when the eyes ached he could look back at the burlap-covered mound of fish. He could make a mental count. So many pounds, so much a pound. How many hours? How much an hour? So much for the loneliness, so much for the wet and the foul stench that was now his smell. And now there was also that weary good feeling when the muscles of the body respond to hard labor.

Frankie also had his hands to think about during the long afternoon. The hard, wet lines running off his hands had gradually taken away the unworked skin. It was always like this when you had been away from the boats for a time. His palms were a crisscross of pink flesh inflamed by the salt water. While he worked he had bit into his lip and stood the searing pain. During the afternoon the hands stiffened. In time they would be like leather.

He made another strike before dark, and when he shut down that night he moved like a sleepwalker. He fell into the bunk exhausted. He lay staring at the beams overhead. There were so many things that he had forgotten about fishing. Under the thin blanket his clothes were wet and caked with blood. The night would be damp and cold. His face was covered with a stubble of beard. He felt dirty. This was all part of the job. The glamorous life. Dirty, cold, wet and lonely.

In the morning he made another strike, and now he moved and worked mechanically. By mid-morning he sighted the Farralon Islands. He made a 180 degree turn and started back.

Late in the afternoon the weather changed. The sky turned gray. The water calmed, flattened out. He was more than two hundred miles out and he knew he was in for a blow. A ton of fish pressed the stern down. He pushed the throttle until he had sixteen knots.

Suddenly there was no breeze. The air was still. And then the wind began. It started gently, and gradually built up. It rippled the still water. It fingered the wire rigging until the guys hummed. It turned the water to chop. It whipped the tops of the waves, flinging the spindrift in dancing spirals.

The *Evalena* began to roll and pitch. Frankie took the rudder off automatic pilot. He took the wheel in his hands. Now it was between him and the sea. He could feel the pull against the rudder. Every motion, every shift came to his hands.

Frankie watched the sky darken until it was charcoal gray. The sea was building fast. The *Evalena* was sliding into the trough of the waves, then climbing effortlessly, cresting, dipping and sliding away.

It began to rain, a light patter against the windows that was somehow different from the flung spray. Frankie switched on the running lights. The binnacle light shadowed the small cabin, giving it life and furtive movement.

Frankie felt a gnawing fear, as all men do when they sense the rising power of the sea. For days you can sail on it and it is gentle as a lake; and you become confident and stop wondering about the dark water, stop thinking of it as a grave, stop thinking of the water closing over you, wondering how long it takes to drown and does it hurt. And then it rises up and you have the feeling that it is awakening, scornful of your confidence. It is all the monsters of childhood nightmares. It seems indignant. You feel like a trespasser pursued by an angry landlord. And you feel so small.

And now is the time of men. You can tremble and break under the strain of the unleashed anger, and some men do, and the flotsam of their boats is tossed upon the sands of the Monterey beach as though the sea must announce each conquest. There are those who suddenly turn upon the sea, bow up, fury blinding them, anger choking their senses. They fight the sea. And they may win for a time, but the sea is relentless, a Goliath that rises to fight again. And in the end the sea will win.

Frankie's fear gave way to careful determination. The Sicilians have been one with the sea since the waters first lapped over the rocks of the Mediterranean Isles. They respect the sea as they do their God. They supplicate before its wrath. They humble themselves before its power.

Filled with a mixed feeling of awe and elation, Frankie ran before the wind, quartering the waves. It was not much different from boxing a heavier, more lethal, opponent. He was feinting and covering, rolling with the punches; letting the adversary carry the fight to him, already going away from the blows as they landed. He was intent only on staying afloat. It was the way he had been taught.

The rain came in driving sheets. The waves were surging dark towers. The *Evalena* soared on the side of a wave, perched, quavering on the wind-whipped crest and dived down the far side, settling into the trough as though taking a breath, then rose again with the buoyancy of a chip.

Frankie let the sea carry him. He worked in the troughs where crosscurrents tried to force him broadside. He gripped the wheel, fighting to keep the bow against the running sea, then relaxed on the ascent. It was tiring, nerve-wracking work, and there would be no sleep.

Heavily loaded, the *Evalena* was taking water and the bilge pump was a monotonous thump that formed a harmony with the steady chug of the engine—sounds that echoed in the wheelhouse, sounds that were both reassuring and frightening. If either one of them should suddenly cease, the sea could gleefully claim another victim.

Hour joined hour and were welded into one long time of intense agony. Time became a matter of marching waves, and as Frankie fought exhaustion and his body screamed for respite, he became grim and began counting the waves aloud. And still later he began to sing, lifting his voice above the howling wind, the waves that hammered the small boat.

The dawn was gray with the unrelenting rain. The wind died. The waves receded as though seeking slumber. It was over. The sea rolled easily, though the rain continued. A light mist formed over the water.

Frankie checked his compass and put the wheel over until he was running northwest. There was no way to tell his position. He could only run on an oblique angle for the coastline and then go north until he reached the Point Pinos light.

He tried making coffee, but the butane stove sputtered and went out, the fuel exhausted. He ate a cold breakfast, this adding to the misery of exhaustion. But he was still afloat and he had his load of fish. It would bring in over three hundred dollars at the prevailing prices in Monterey. He wouldn't need Arlene's money. For the first time he felt that he could beat Barlow at his game.

By mid-afternoon he sighted the distant mountains of the California coast, the cliffs fringed with lacy fog. He changed course, heading north, keeping his distance from the treacherous rocks, straining his tired eyes ahead.

It was dark, the sifting fog lying close to the water, a damp, warm diaphanous cloud. He heard the bassoonlike bay of the Point Pinos foghorn before he saw the dim distant sweep of the mist-shrouded light. The next leg of the trip was to swing around the point at the bell buoy and follow the coastline to the Monterey breakwater; several miles of touch-and-go with the rocks and surf. At best, it was a tough job in the fog, and because of his exhausted condition, Frankie decided not to try it. He skirted the buoy at the entrance to the bay and ran northwest, well out of the usual fishing lanes, to shut down until morning.

He was in the stern running out the sea anchor when he started at the sound of a guttural, braying ship's horn. It was too close and he had a moment of anxiety, thinking he had misjudged his position and was stopped in the shipping lane. He tensed, holding his breath. He peered through the whirling fog. The horn sounded again, a mournful wail. The fog parted and he saw the ship's lights, above and beyond him, moving parallel to his position. He stumbled to his feet and ran to the cabin. He came back with his own manual horn. He held it to his lips, took a deep breath and blew. The sound rumbled over the water, magnified and echoed by the fog. The ship—close now—answered. He sounded again.

A searchlight probed the whirling mist, swept over him. A deep voice shouted an unintelligible sound. He was clear of the ship and he watched it pass with relief. It was obviously off course, even for a coastal freighter.

While he stood there watching, he saw something flung from the side of the ship pass through the shaft of the searchlight, heard it land in the water. The ship's horn sounded once more and the lights subsided, closed off by the fog. The final horn was a kind of greeting as though they had expected to find him there and he pondered this.

Stepping into the wheelhouse he started the engine. He put the bow over into the direction where the freighter had passed, and went on deck with his strong flash. The *Evalena* toiled slowly, dragging the sea anchor, and he played the strong light over the water, half expecting to find a bag of garbage.

He saw something glowing in the water ahead. He shut the engine down and drifted. He went to the side with a gaff hook. It was a round float with two loop handles. He hooked it with the gaff and brought it in. There was a chain on the float and at the end of this a watertight box. It was heavy and he grunted as he brought it aboard. He held the box with both hands and pursed his lips thoughtfully.

His mind was racing. During prohibition the rumrunners had used this same method of dropping booze for the speedboats that put out from Morse Landing. One of the highlights of the island's history was a gun battle between the bootleggers and the revenue agents. He hefted the box, tying it in with Sam Barlow. Was this it? Was this the key?

The sound of an engine droned over the water. He dropped the box and ran for the stern. He slipped the sea anchor line and tossed it. That was not the chug-a-chug of a fishing boat. It was the deep-throated roar of a Packard Diesel. Someone was coming to pick up their package. There was a chance of getting away in the fog.

Inside the wheelhouse he switched off the running lights, and threw the throttle full ahead. He made a fast compass check. The speedboat was coming from Morse Landing on his port side. He ran north.

He leaned from the wheelhouse, listening. The speedboat was idling and he heard voices.

"You hear that engine?"

"What do ya think, I'm deaf?"

"What do ya make of it?"

"I don't know, but I can guess."

"Cargo?"

"Who else would be nosing around off the fishing lanes?"

"Get the Thompson."

"With pleasure."

Frankie felt panic roar through him, tightening his nerves, and he slammed his palm against the throttle. The *Evalena* was doing everything she could. But it wasn't going to be enough. He had the night and he had the fog. But the engine was like a beacon for them. And if he shut down they would know it immediately and it would just be a matter of time before they found him. Frustration assailed him and he cursed silently.

The twin Packards roared into action.

He was less than a mile from the beach. He left the wheelhouse, pulling a life preserver with him. He slipped the bulky garment over his shoulders, tied it in front. The boat was on iron mike. He picked up the box and float from the deck, slipped the chain through one of the shoulder straps. He went to the stern and jumped.

The cold water was a shock. He bobbed to the surface, obscured by the boiling wake. He gasped for breath. He heard the speedboat roar past in pursuit of the steady chugging of the *Evalena*. He rose and fell like a cork on the boat's waves. He was angered and despondent. He heard the voices again, shouting now.

"I see him. There on the left. See?"

"Yes! Steady, I'll make a circle."

"No," the familiar voice shouted. "Come in on the side. It's a gas engine. The Old Man never changed over to Diesel. The tanks are on both sides."

Yes, Frankie thought, he would know that.

"Okay, boy, here we go! Let 'er rip!"

The chatter of the Thompson submachine gun was like the cough of death.

Piercing the wood hull, the slugs found their mark, tearing through the thin metal of the gas tanks. The explosion that followed was a mushrooming blast that rumbled and then erupted in a rising sheet of flame. The fire burned for a minute and then it was swallowed by the water.

Idled, the speedboat hovered nearby.

"Wow! That sonavabitch went down fast."

"Yeah," the familiar voice answered. "Kind of a shame. It was a nice boat."

"Do you think he got the drop?"

"Doesn't matter now."

"We better go back and scout a little to make sure."

"Okay."

The boat droned into motion and came back, passing a distance from Frankie, who bobbed in the water. They stayed in the area for several minutes, then they left, the roar of the engines dwindling.

Alone then, Frankie felt the cold seeping into him. He moved his arms and feet, began swimming slowly for the shore.

It was difficult to realize that it had actually happened. In a matter of minutes everything had been wiped out. The *Evalena* was now on the bottom.

He pushed through a cluster of dead, floating fish. Part of his catch. Those weary days of work when he actually thought he was fighting Barlow. Wiped out like that. But they had assumed that he had gone with the boat. They were wrong about that. And now it would be different.

His anger and hatred were slow-burning. His exhaustion was gone. He pulled for the shore with strong strokes. They thought he was dead.

The man with the Thompson. Frankie could recognize Polo's voice anywhere.

CHAPTER EIGHT

His feet touched the sandy bottom, a wave lifted him and he rose, twisting. He was dropped and his knees touched the bottom. The undertow tugged at him and he was too exhausted to resist. He swallowed salt water and gagged. Another wave took him and flung him forward. He landed hard. The surf ebbed away from his outstretched form. Another wave broke over him, moved him ahead, left him.

Lifting his head, Frankie gasped for breath. He dug his fingers into the sand and pulled, dragging himself up on the wet sand. He reached out and pulled again, moving like a slug. The surf lifted his legs, ebbed. He dragged his knees under him, lifted his body on stiff arms. He tried to crawl, but the effort was too great. He pitched over sideways. He closed his eyes and slept.

Chill-stiff, the salt spray sticky against his face, Frankie opened his eyes. He was cold and his body shook. He dragged himself to his feet and staggered up on the dry sand of the beach.

His mouth felt thick and swollen and a wave of nausea swept over him. He dropped to his knees and retched, his innards heaving with pain, his chest wracked with agony.

He sat. He took his head in his hands, closed his eyes tightly, and tried to bring his numbed mind into focus. The surf was a drum-beat, the wind a cold, but gentle probe. The sea lions barked in the distance and the gulls screamed. He opened his eyes to the sun-filtering dawn.

Daylight is the great deceiver. Passions, wild under the mask of night, are stilled. Evil, which stalks freely under the mantle of shadow, is obscured by sun glare. Violence, run rampant in darkness, is gentled, and death out of its element. The mind is prey to the deviousness of daylight. To sit on a beach with the dawn spread over the sky and to attempt to bring the mind back to darkness is a task. And a refreshed body will not be reminded of exhaustion. Terror, in such a setting, is inconceivable.

But there was the box and the float. Frankie untied the life jacket and slipped it from his shoulders. He lifted the metal box and examined it carefully.

He stood and walked to the rocks. He searched until he found the right rock, then he sat down and battered away at the box until he broke the seal and could pry the lid with the knife that was sheathed at his waist. He knew what he was going to find, but he unfolded the rubber inner lining, then carefully unfolded the heavy foil.

It was in several square packets. He lifted one of the squares and undid the wrapping. He brought the opened packet up to his nose and smelled it. He had been around the fight game and its fringe rackets long enough to recognize the white powder—heroin.

Barlow wouldn't kill a man over a shipment of whores, just as he wouldn't kill a man because he was fishing competition, or threatened his hold on the people of the island. But for this, a lot more people than Barlow would kill.

Frankie hefted the package in his hand, guessing at the weight. It was the pure stuff, the full-strength derivative of a good supply of morphine. Frankie had no idea of the marketable price of even a single deck, but he knew that he held a fortune in his hand. Just by figuring on what he had read of narcotic raids and the estimated coup by the agents, Frankie knew that the drop had been a big one, in the neighborhood of a quarter-million. And when the stuff was cut and passed along, it would bring in well over a million.

The men sent out to make the pickup, of course, would not know that. Barlow would never tempt the hired hands with that kind of knowledge. They hadn't searched the area close enough last night. To them it must have been just a routine pickup that got loused up.

But someone knew the real value of the loss. And when Frankie turned up alive, that someone was going to know the drop hadn't been lost. And that someone was going to want it back.

Hidden in the curve of a dune, Frankie worked his way up to the rear of his house, keeping to the shadow sides of the night-hidden mounds.

He stopped every few steps and listened. Then he moved ahead.

The night sounds: saw-toothed crab grass grating against his legs, cough of a dying engine, a cormorant's insistent caw, the juke box from Della's, muted car-hum from the highway, rasping screech of woman calling a child, insect symphony, lonesome pealing gong of the buoy, barking cur dog.

Frankie stopped in view of the small house. The windows were dark. He crouched and ran for the back door.

He had been walking, watchful, half hidden all day; sleeping for a time when he was in sight of the island. Avoiding the causeway, he had slogged through the mud flats and crossed to the island at the barren south end, wading through the waist-high water.

He pulled the hinge-groaning screen door and stepped into the rear shed, then into the kitchen. The house was silent. He picked his way through the darkened rooms to the bedroom. He lit a match over a small trunk, opened it, and pulled out camphor-smelling khaki shirt and pants. He removed his wet, muddy clothes and redressed in the dark, replacing his ruined shoes with a pair from the closet.

Voices stopped his movements. He was sitting on the edge of the bed, tying the shoes. His fingers left the laces and he rose, moved to the doorway.

"You didn't have to walk me." Tosca's voice.

"It's okay."

"Well, thanks."

"Just like that, thanks?"

Frankie eased the bedroom door closed until there was just enough of an opening for him to hear.

A board on the front porch creaked under weight.

"That's all, just thanks." Her voice weary.

"Maybe we could talk."

"I don't feel too well."

"What's the matter with me?"

"Nothing's the matter with you, Polo, I just don't feel like talking."

"We could be friends, you and me."

"We are friends."

"I mean, good friends. What's the matter, you think I ain't man enough for you."

"Go home to your wife, Polo."

"You maybe could use a friend."

"I won't ask you what you mean by that tone, but thanks for walking me, and I have to go in."

"It's because of Frankie, huh?"

"Let's not talk about it, Polo."

"He moved in pretty fast, old Frankie did. I wondered about you two down there on the beach the other night. I guess I shouldn't have been surprised."

"Good night, Polo."

"Hell, I'd be satisfied with seconds."

Her voice snapped angrily. "You couldn't get thirds or fourths, Polo. Go home to your wife. Isn't it enough that Frankie's dead?

He was your friend. You had him come back here. What kind of a person are you? Just get away from me."

"That's no way for a Barlow whore to talk. You might be insulting a special customer."

The door slammed. A silence followed. Then Frankie heard Polo curse, "Gahdamn high-class sheriff's whore!" Heavy footsteps crossed the porch. Then silence again. Frankie moved softly, pressing into the corner behind the door. He heard soft sobbing. He wanted to go to her, but he waited.

Tosca switched on a lamp in the living room. She crossed the room, pushed the door, and entered the bedroom. The door swung back, covering Frankie's corner.

Tosca's grief was audible in the tight, shaking sobs of true anguish. There was no whimpering. It was a mourning sound. Frankie heard a scraping sound and then the click of a suitcase latch. The closet door opened. Hangers rattled.

Frankie gave the bedroom door a push, and it swung away from him. Startled by the sudden movement, Tosca turned, her movement arrested, several dresses hung over her arms. She stifled a scream, gasping. The dresses fell to her feet. Her eyes widened.

"Tosca."

"Frankie," she whispered, her eyes round and wide with surprise.

"Don't be frightened."

"Polo said—"

"He said wrong. I'm not dead."

"Oh, my God."

Frankie crossed the room and stood before her. Her face was a mixture of fright, confusion and joy. A moment passed between them and they looked deeply into each other. With a small cry, Tosca sagged against him and he enveloped her with his arms, holding her, his face buried in her hair. She cried openly, breaking with relief, while her body shook.

"It's all right," Frankie said, soothing her.

"I wanted to die," she said.

"Don't talk about it."

"I was going to leave. I couldn't bear to stay here. They told me and I died inside."

"It's over and I'm here."

"Oh, Frankie, I love you. I love you, Frankie. I never loved anyone before, but I love you." She spoke breathlessly, wildly. "I'm not any good, and I shouldn't love you, but I do and I don't want to stop."

He lifted her chin with his finger. Tears stained her cheeks, swam in the depths of her glittering dark eyes, spilled over and ran in rivulets. Her mouth trembled. She started to speak. Her voice choked with emotion.

Frankie bent his head and met her lips. He kissed her tenderly, lightly. She clung to him, her hands clawing at his back, as though fearful that he was not real, that her mind was playing tricks. Her lips parted under his, and she sought him passionately. Their emotion was soul-deep, charged with the years of longing. It broke upon them, flooding them. Pent-up desires were unleashed, armors dropped like veils, and they found themselves in each other, giving, seeking, clinging, their embrace welding their bodies until the blood raged through arteries and veins like a boiling river.

Lifting his head, his breathing labored, Frankie looked into Tosca's eyes. His image was mirrored there, as though the kiss, the embrace, had stamped them upon one another for all time. She returned his gaze. Lost love suddenly regained, added to the excitement of the moment, and their exchanged looks were charged with an electric impulse that quickened their pulses.

"I love you," Frankie said hoarsely, the words strange on his lips.

"Frankie," Tosca whispered.

Moving away from her, Frankie reached out with both hands. His eyes never left hers, as his fingers sought the first button of her blouse. Her body trembled as he touched her, but she stood unmoving, her arms at her sides, her eyes loving and caressing him.

His fingers fumbled. She stood patiently. Her full breasts rose and fell, pressed eagerly against the blouse as it slowly separated to reveal the tawny, velvet-textured skin. The only sound was their breathing, hushed and expectant.

They denied their urgency. There was a purity in their precise motions. It humanized, while heightening their desire.

Frankie slipped the blouse over her shoulders and arms, let it fall to the floor. Her body arched towards him as he removed her bra and let it drop. Then she stood proudly before him, her chin high, unashamed under his eyes. He looked away from her steady gaze for the first time, his eyes lowering, gradually moving over her shoulders, following the urgent, voluptuous swell of her breasts. They were smooth-round, hard-bursting with emotion, the dark nipples rigid.

His eyes returned to hers, said the things of which his tongue was incapable. His hands traced the contours of her body to her narrow waist. He touched the fabric of her skirt. His fingers sought the zipper at the side.

When she stood before him, resplendent in her long-limbed nudity, he stooped and lifted her in his arms. Their eyes still held as he carried her to the bed and placed her down. Gazing down at her, he removed his own clothing.

He settled down next to her, facing her, and she came into his arms. Their bodies met, breast to breast, stomach to stomach, thigh to thigh, feet entwined, arms encircling, groping. His face brushed the black, silken spread of her hair on the pillow. He nuzzled the hollows of her throat. She twisted away and lifted a bared breast to his kiss, her body trembling under his response.

Lying in his embrace, the life-force surging through her, Tosca was virginal. Her past meant nothing. The hands that had touched her body were nothing more to her soul than the gloved fists that had distorted his face. She had given her body for survival and in the giving had warped her mind-image of herself and blighted her spirit. But she had secreted her love into a distant inward place where strange hands could not touch. And now she released this love, yielded herself to Frankie until no fiber of her remained untouched. He was her first man, and her body ached to be fulfilled.

His mouth upon her lips, his tongue sending sensation through her, Frankie moved his hands over her supple waist and wide-flaring hips.

Tosca groaned, unable to silence the rising turbulence of her feelings. Her body opened to him, eagerly and willingly and, receiving him, strained hard against him.

For Frankie it was not like being with a woman. He was suspended, breathless, his nerves high-pitched to wire tautness. It was not give or take. Together they were one undulating, pleasure-probing organism that was without individuality or identity.

Their passion rose on an even plane, mounting, mounting, and then it was a reeling, spinning, light-flashing panorama of ecstatic darkness that increased until Tosca's eyes rolled back into her head and the world crashed in, the fever-pitch climbing to climactic end.

Their bodies spent, their senses dulled with numbing satisfaction, they clung together in silence. There was nothing to say. There were no words. They had gone beyond the point of intellect. And returning, they sought solace in each other's new knowing.

Frankie finally shifted to his side, facing her. He brushed his palm gently against her lips. His fingers touched her face, crawled through her hair. Her love-damp eyes glistened and she smiled.

"I love you," she murmured.

"And I love you," he answered, and this time the words belonged. They were silent again, looking at each other, savoring their new experience.

"Could I have a cigarette?" Tosca asked.

Frankie leaned from the bed and brought back the package of cigarettes. "They're not much good," he said. "They were wet and I dried them in the sun. They taste strange, but I didn't want to chance buying any."

"I want to smoke one," she said.

Frankie lit both cigarettes and handed one over to her. They inhaled and expelled smoke together, lying side by side, their naked bodies gently touching.

The time of the cigarette is the time of knowing. This is the time when the soul is bared. Tensions are released and walls come down. There is the mask of darkness, hovering protectively. There is the closeness of responsive flesh. And a seemingly strong man will exhibit his flaws and weaknesses, unburden his mind to the silent listener. And a brave man will become more brave in the knowing.

"It tastes of salt water," Tosca said.

Frankie realized that she wanted him to talk, but he resisted, remaining silent.

"They sank your boat?"

"Yes," he said.

"They said you were dead, that your boat blew up."

"It did. They still think I'm dead."

"It wasn't an accident."

"No. They sank it."

"How?"

"Machine-gunned me." He told her what had happened.

"Did you see who it was?"

"I heard. It was Polo."

She was silent, stunned. She sensed his hurt, his disillusionment. "I'm sorry," she said.

"It's still hard to believe it. A week ago I would have believed that he was the only friend I had who was incorruptible. I still don't know why."

"There must be a reason."

"For killing me, yes. I understand that. I found a load of heroin that was dropped by a freighter. They came out for it, and they had to kill me. But I can't understand Polo doing it."

"He works for Barlow," she said.

"As a fisherman. I can see that. He has to eat, his family has to eat. But Polo was never a killer. He was wild and rough, but never cruel. But—but last night, he was eager to kill. You could tell it in his voice. He was hating and he wanted me killed."

"Men change," she said. "Believe me, I know."

"But why would he write for me to come back? Why did he make a hero out of me if he wanted to kill me?"

"There's a reason," she said.

"Yes."

They were silent again, each in his and her thoughts. Then Tosca asked, "Do you have the heroin?"

"Yes."

"What will you do with it?"

"I don't know. I've been thinking about it all day. I can turn it in, but it won't connect with Barlow. It would end the traffic here on the island, but there is no proof against Barlow or Springer. Somehow I have to use it to get Barlow."

"You can't stay on the island!" There was a note of terror in her voice.

"I can't leave," he said.

"They'll try to kill you again." Tosca's fingers pressed into his arm. "They'll know you have the heroin. Barlow won't stop at anything for a million dollars in dope."

"I know that, but somehow I have to let him act and be ready for him."

"I don't want you to do this," she said tensely. "I know it's selfish, but I want you alive. Once tonight you died for me, and now I have you alive. Next time it might not be the same. But I know you'll do what you have to do, and I want to help you."

A day before he would have turned her down, been protective of her. But now he knew that they were one, together, and that if either of them died, it was right for the other also to die. And he needed her.

"I need some background before I make a move," he said. "Somehow I believe it goes back to my father's death. There might be something there. They think I'm dead, so I have time. It might be a wild-goose chase, but I have to start someplace. I must learn about my father and play it from there."

"You'll let me help?"

"I want you to help." He leaned over her and kissed her again. She twisted into his arms.

"Frankie," she said, "I want to tell you more about me."

"No, don't say anything."

"But I want you to know. About Springer, I—"

"No." He put his fingers to her lips. "He couldn't possibly make any difference to us."

"But, Frankie, I—"

"I love you," he said, interrupting. He kissed her hard, and she brought her body close to him, twisting her sleek hips and warm pelvis against him. He felt his longing for her return.

CHAPTER NINE

The office of the Frisco Flat *Times* was in a garage behind a small white frame house, one of several identical houses in the dwindling outskirts on the north side of the town.

It was office and print shop combined. The *Times* was a small weekly newspaper with a circulation that depended on township legal advertising.

An old flat-bed press commanded the major portion of the garage. On the far side was a rebuilt letterpress and a hand-fed card press. The room was a clutter of cardboard boxes filled with unremembered samples of print orders, cast-off newspapers and just trash. The walls exuded the mixed odors of crankcase oil—from the original occupants—and printers' ink and stale newsprint. The wall studs served as shelves for all manner of junk, and the siding was a clutter of thumbtacked pictures, notices and old clippings, put there for a purpose and forgotten. The office was an old, scarred wooden desk in one corner.

"Well, now, I don't know," the thin, white-haired man at the desk said in his high-whine voice. "I remember that story and I probably got a copy of the newspaper. I don't keep much of a file. Sort of gave up that sort of thing when I came down here to be my own boss. That was, let's see now, that was twenty three—no, let me see, that would be twenty-four years ago. Long time, yes, well now, let me see. Yes, well." He cleared his throat and closed one eye, as though pressing his brain to think. "You wouldn't remember the date?"

"No, I'm afraid not," Frankie said. "Not the exact date."

The old man tilted back in his chair and scratched his head with a veined hand. "This is really important."

"Yes, I'd like very much to see that story."

"A murder," the old editor said, squinting. "You don't look like the law."

"I'm not," Frankie said. "It was my father."

The old man took a deep breath. His eyes blinked. "Ahhh," he said. "Cargo. Cargo, now let me see. Cargo. What's your first name?"

"Frank."

"Yes, Frankie Cargo. I used to see you around a few years ago." He paused, reflecting. "Say," he said, "Wasn't your boat the *Evalena*?"

"Yes."

"Then you're supposed to be dead. I got a report that your boat blew up."

"It did, but I got ashore."

"Damn," the editor said. "That's the trouble putting out a weekly. You get part of a story and nobody bothers to tell you the rest." He shook his shaggy, white head. "Tell you what," he said. "The pile of papers over there is my file. Now, if you want to rummage through them to find that issue with the murder story in it, you go right ahead. It was a banner headline. Don't remember what it said, but you ought to find it okay. Not many stories around here big enough for a banner."

"Thank you," Frankie said. "I'll try not to bother you."

"No bother. Matter of fact, I'm glad to have the company. You just go through them. It's kind of messy and there isn't any order to them, but you ought to find it."

Frankie went to the pile of newspapers that ranged along the wall. He pulled up a stool and sat down. He began shuffling through the newspapers. The editor hadn't been kidding. There were papers three years old next to issues a month old. Frankie filtered through them, stopping to glance over an occasional story. Some of the papers he opened, and flipped through the inside pages. An hour passed and he failed to find the issue concerning the murder. Then a familiar name caught his eye and he stopped. He lifted the newspaper. The name was Arlene Morse, and the story was a few short paragraphs on the bottom of the front page. He recalled all the notices he had seen about Arlene in the past. She was of the island's first family and her activities were always worthy of a mention.

Frankie read, pursing his lips and scowling thoughtfully. He whistled softly to himself. It was a short announcement of Arlene's marriage, stating that she had been wed in Baltimore. Frankie glanced up at the date line. *March 25, 1957.* The paper was two years old, the story forgotten. Frankie looked again at the body of the story. *Miss Arlene Morse was wed last week to Mr. Samuel Barlow of Baltimore…*

Frankie put the newspaper down, his original quest forgotten. He stared at the type, read the names again.

I'll be damned, he thought, I will be damned. Arlene and Barlow married. He folded the newspaper and picked it up. He rose from the stool and started for the door, engrossed in his perplexing thoughts.

"Get what you want, son?"

Frankie turned back quickly. "Oh." He had forgotten the old man. "Yes, yes, I did. Thank you."

"No trouble, son, glad to help out."

Frankie left the garage-office and walked slowly along the gravel drive to the road, tapping his palm with the newspaper. It was a twist he hadn't figured on. He wondered how many persons knew about Arlene and Barlow. Were they still married? Divorced? And why did Arlene want Barlow broken? Why would Arlene want to finance his boat unless…. unless…. Damn! Unless Barlow wanted him where his men could put him away with ease and have it look like an accident. If this were true, then he had walked into the thing with his eyes wide open. He had to see Arlene.

Reaching the end of the drive, he waited. As he expected, Angelo's old car turned in from the highway and came towards him. Tosca was driving. She pulled into the drive and he got into the rear seat.

Leaning over the seat, he kissed her. "Any trouble?" he asked.

"None. I told Angelo you wanted me to take the car and he didn't ask any questions."

"Good." He flipped the newspaper open and pointed to the story.

When she finished reading, she said, "What does this mean?"

"It means I have to see Arlene Morse."

"Again?"

He might have feigned surprise, but he knew that it wouldn't come off. Tosca knew that he had been with Arlene. "Yes," he said. "She might be the weak spot I'm looking for. There must be a way to get to Barlow."

"Strictly business," she said, a slight edge to her voice.

He smiled at her, flattered and annoyed by her insinuation, but careful to ignore it.

She put the car in reverse and backed out of the drive. She drove down the road and made a left turn onto the highway.

"You better get down," she said. "Everyone on the island thinks you're dead."

"That's good," he said. "They'll be relaxed."

"Not for long."

He curled up on the floor of the car. He looked up and he could see her shoulders and hair.

"Where does Barlow live?" he asked.

"He has a house in the valley."

"Have you ever seen him with Arlene?"

"No. I've seen him try to talk to her, but she cuts him in public."

"That could be an act. Somehow I can't get those two together in my mind."

"Hold your breath," Tosca said. "Springer is about to pass us."

Huddled in the rear, his body tensed, he waited. A car passed, the slip-stream rocking the old Chevy.

"That him?"

"Yes."

"What did he do?"

"Nothing. He just looked."

"Is he still going?"

Tosca was watching in the rear-view mirror. "Yes. He didn't even slow down."

"Whew. That's all we'd need now." Frankie struggled up, crouched on the rear seat and peered through the window after the retreating car. "He's making a turn," Frankie said, excitedly. "Maybe he's coming back. No, he's going down that road. He's— oh, oh, he's heading for the newspaper."

"Did the old man know who you were?"

"I told him."

"And he must have called Springer the minute you left."

Frankie slammed a fist into the seat. "Christ! Does he own everybody in this damn place?!"

"You better get down," Tosca said.

Frankie glanced ahead. They were approaching the cut-off to the island. "He'll be after us in a few minutes," he said. "When you get well past the cut-off, up there on the other side of the cement plant, you slow down. I'll hop for it. You keep going towards Waterville. When Springer stops you, tell him you're going there to shop for something."

"He saw us coming from Frisco Flat."

"Tell him you couldn't get what you wanted in Frisco Flat."

"He won't believe it."

"He can't be sure," Frankie said. "I won't be in the car, so there won't be anything he can do. I have to see Arlene before he gets to me."

They passed the cement plant. "I'm going to slow down," Tosca said. "There's a stand of bushes just ahead."

Frankie lifted his head and looked back anxiously. There were no cars on the road. The old jalopy slowed. He gripped the door handle, pushed it down.

"Be careful," Tosca said.

"Don't worry. I'll see you tonight. I can't get across to the island until dark." He opened the car door and jumped, hitting the ground and running. Tosca shifted into second and picked up speed. He hit the bushes at a run and dived, rolling. He regained his feet quickly, shook himself. He huddled into the bushes and waited. And not for long. He saw the sheriff's car come hurtling along the highway. He dropped prone to the ground. The car rocketed past in pursuit of the Chevy. He waited until it was out of sight over a hill, then he leaped to his feet and ran across the highway. He took the cover of the shrubbery on the far side and worked his way up the side of the hill, staying away from the drive.

When he reached the high iron gate, he looked carefully behind him, then he glanced up towards the house. He was remembering the previous visit. He pushed the bell button and then stood before the grating where Arlene could see him from the house. He waited and rang the bell again.

The gate swung back and he walked through. It closed after him. Wondering if he had trapped himself, he hurried towards the house.

Arlene was standing before the front door, the portale shading her. She was wearing short white shorts which accentuated her long, honey-blonde legs; and a jersey pullover in wide stripes that did the same for the rest of her. Despite his misgivings about her, Frankie had to marvel at her flawless beauty. She was staring at him strangely.

"Surprised to see me," he said.

"I thought you were dead." Her voice was husky and low. Her pale eyes were wide.

"Do I look dead?"

She did not smile, but relief passed over her face. "You look very much alive," she said. "Wonderfully alive." She came towards him and raised both arms, placed her palms against his chest. "I'm so glad," she said.

She's really playing it cool, Frankie thought, and then he wasn't sure of himself. If it was an act, it was a good act. But she was his only hope, and he had to believe that she was deceiving him.

"I came straight here," he said, lying. "Barlow's men sank the boat and I swam ashore."

"Come into the house." She curled her hand around his arm and led him through the door. They entered the large living room. She disengaged her hand and sat on the edge of a long divan. He sat opposite her, and looking at her, knew that she had changed. Her previous self-confidence was lacking; whereas she had been glib and talkative before, she was docile now, almost somber.

"I'll return your money," Frankie said. "The partnership never had a chance to get started."

"I don't care about the money," she said. "I'm just glad that you're alive."

"I didn't do very well against Barlow."

She twisted her hands. Tears suddenly welled up in her eyes, and she seemed frightened. She flicked her tongue over her lips. Frankie's eyes narrowed. He watched her closely.

"Did you sell the cannery to Barlow?" he asked.

Her eyes dropped. "I'd rather not talk about it."

"You don't really operate the cement plant, do you?"

"What do you mean?" Her eyes snapped. "Of course I do."

"Occasionally you do. You're there just enough so that it's natural for you to be seen coming and going."

Her hands were shaking. "What on earth do you mean?"

"There wouldn't by any chance be a lab in the plant, would there?"

Tiny beads of sweat appeared on the down of her face. Her hands fluttered to her forehead. Frankie watched her carefully, noting and recalling the telltale signs. Her lower lip trembled.

"You didn't know it was me at the gate, did you?" he asked.

"Of course I did."

"You were expecting someone else."

"No, I wasn't." There was a note of panic in her voice. Frankie realized that he couldn't have appeared at a better time. He hated the idea of taking advantage of her now that he knew about her, but at any other time she would have been the other Arlene and that would be much more difficult.

Moving suddenly, Frankie came out of his chair and lunged across the room. He gripped her right arm. She recoiled, startled. He turned the arm over. She pulled against him.

"You're hurting me!"

"Hold still."

"No, let me go!" She twisted, crying.

He looked down at the tiny, red needle marks on the inside of her elbow. He let go of her arm and she pulled away, shrinking back.

"Barlow do this to you?"

She snapped, as Frankie knew she would. The nervousness, the fluttering hands, a slight dilation of the pupils of her eyes, the marks on her arm. She was an addict badly in need of a fix. She buried her face in her hands and her shoulders shook. Frankie scowled with distaste. Not for Arlene, but for the man who had popped the first needle in her arm. For Arlene he felt pity. She was beautiful, she was wealthy. And no doubt she had her first fix on a sexual binge, looking for bigger kicks. Ugly, rich, beautiful, poor, it made no difference to the needle. One bulging vein looks the same as another. But somehow, there is something about seeing a beautiful girl on the habit, that makes the whole business more rotten than usual.

"Is it beginning to hurt?" he asked.

"A little. It's not bad yet, but I get afraid." Her lower lip trembled.

"You know I got the stuff the other night."

Her eyes lighted with hope. Frankie knew that he was going to hate himself for what he was doing, but he had to take advantage of the opportunity.

"Where is it?" she whispered, perspiration filming her forehead.

"I have it."

"Please."

"Who supplies you?" Frankie queried.

"Sam. He's supposed to send it today. I've been waiting."

"Maybe they won't come."

"Oh, God, please." She came at him, clawing at his shirt. She forced her body against his. "Frankie, please. I'll give you anything you want, anything. But don't let me be afraid. I can't stand the pain, Frankie, please." Tears spilled over her face. "Sam made me have the pain sometimes. If Springer told him I gave you money he'll make me suffer again. He'll make me crawl."

"You still married to him?"

Arlene stiffened, then her body relaxed. "You know," she said. "Yes, I am."

"And the other day when you stopped to talk to me. He put you up to it."

"No! I'm sorry. Frankie, I'm really sorry. I hate Sam. He made me like this, and I hate myself like this. I wanted to hit back at him."

"And I was easily available."

"Yes, I mean, no! Frankie, I'll admit I wanted you to hurt Sam for me. But also, I wanted to see you, to talk to you. I always wondered about you and I knew you looked at me."

"So you gave Barlow the cannery to keep the supply coming," Frankie said, keeping her talking.

"Yes."

"And you set up the lab in the cement plant to cut the stuff down."

"Yes. Oh, please, Frankie, if you have the stuff, help me."

"You told Springer about the money." He kept throwing the questions while she was frightened and confused.

"He thought you were here. He twisted my arm. I had to tell. Frankie, I can't stand pain."

"I don't have the stuff with me," he said.

Her face changed, clouded. "Can you get it?" she whispered. "Can you? It's not far away?"

"Too far," he said.

She took a deep breath. "Help me, Frankie." Her voice was small and helpless and filled with terror. "Do something, Frankie, it's going to hurt. I don't want to hurt, Frankie." She dug her fingers into him, thrust herself against him.

Frankie felt sick. This was the little girl from the castle, the unapproachable, the unattainable. The illusion shattered, he hated the man who had accomplished it. His compassion went out to the girl who trembled against him. He brought his arms around her. "There's nothing I can do," he said.

"Make me forget it, Frankie," she whimpered. "Do something to me. Take my mind off the hurting. You can make the nerves stop screaming. Do it to me, Frankie."

"Arlene, I can't."

"Please, Frankie. I'm begging you. You wanted me the last time. I need you now, Frankie." She twisted her hips against him, enclosed him with her thighs. She took her arms from around his back, gripped him lower and pulled him to her. "You do want me," she gasped. "I can feel that you do."

Frankie's mind railed against it, but his body was responding to her. He tried to fight himself free, but she clung to him savagely, her burgeoning breasts and flat belly grinding against him. "Stop the pain, Frankie. Do something." She tore at his belt buckle. She slipped the hooks on her shorts and tore them away.

Feverishly she writhed out of her shirt, baring her full breasts. Then, she sank to the floor, dragging him with her.

Reason left him and he took her in a mad, convulsive sprawling on the rug, their desire-riven bodies cleaving to each other. It was a wild, animalistic coupling without tenderness or meaning.

It was over in minutes and Arlene was not released from her ordeal, as Frankie knew she would not be. Her anxiety was only heightened, and now she was shaking with the fear, and the pain was just beginning, the pain that starts like a hard fist in the groin and spreads up in the guts like fingers of flame.

"I can't stand it!" she screamed, her long legs twisting under her.

Frankie was burning with hate and disgust, the latter emotion for himself.

"I'll help you get through this," he said.

"I don't want to go through it!"

A bell rang.

"It's him!" Arlene cried. "Oh, thank God, it's him. Sam sent it!" She scrambled to her feet, slipped on her shirt and ran to the wall. She threw herself against the button that opened the gate. She slumped against the wall, whimpering with relief. Her blonde hair hung over her face, disheveled. She wore only the jersey shirt.

Tense with a sudden panic, realizing that Arlene no longer knew he was in the room, and knowing what would happen if Springer found him there, Frankie got to his feet and looked quickly around the room. There was a doorway at the far end and he went for it. Opening the door, he stepped into a hallway. He closed the door, leaving just a crack, and waited.

There was a knock, the door opened.

"Well, Gahdamn, look at you."

"You have it."

"Sure I got it."

"Let me have it!"

"Easy now, easy. Don't get excited." Frankie strained to recognize the voice. He couldn't. It was a guttural voice. "Ain't ya gonna ask me in?"

"Come in, dammit, but give me the stuff!" Arlene's voice was on the verge of hysteria.

"Well now, ain't you a nifty looking piece. I see you been waiting for old Carazon." He laughed tauntingly.

"Give it to me, you fat, filthy bastard!"

"Maybe I will. Maybe I won't."

"What are you trying to do?"

"I need a little coaxing. Thought maybe you'd be a little nervous by the time I got here."

"Jesus Christ, shut up and let me have it."

"What do I get for it?"

"Oh, you bastards," Arlene wailed. "Well, get it over with. Come on, you stinking goat, get it over with!"

"You think I want you against the wall. No sir, duchess, I want it on clean sheets."

"Well, hurry up, you scum."

Footsteps crossed the room and then there was silence. Frankie opened the door. He stood inside the room, his face contorted with revulsion. He shook his head and his shoulders slumped. Arlene would get her fix. He hated Carazon, but he felt no better. He went across the room quietly and out the front door.

The afternoon sun was beginning its decline. White clouds wisped across the pale blue sky. The water below dazzled under the brilliance.

Passing through the front gate he went to the right and worked his way to the red clay cliffs that rose above the island. He found a rock that secreted him from view and settled down. There was so much to think about now, so much to do and he wanted to do it right.

He knew only one thing. He was going to carry the fight to Barlow and Springer. He was tired of hiding and trying to roll with the punches. He was going to force them to show their hand openly, and in the showing, hope that they came up with deuces and treys. He was holding an ace, he knew, and the rest would have to be bluff.

Barlow had to be stopped. Looking over his shoulder, he could see the red tile of the house, knew what was going on there, and was filled with loathing. He tried not to think of Tosca and Arlene at the same time. He loved Tosca and he pitied Arlene, but he had left Tosca, and less than an hour later was groveling on the floor with Arlene. It didn't make sense and he didn't want to think about it.

He stayed there, sitting, until late afternoon when he stretched out and slept.

It was dark when he awoke. The island had gone indoors and lights shone in windows. The cannery was a dark bulk. The water shimmered black. The moon was lifting over the hills.

Frankie retraced his steps to the drive leading down to the highway from the Morse house. He walked easily, without haste. He reached the highway and walked along the shoulder until he turned at the Morse Landing cut-off. He passed the stilt-houses, the weed-high mud flats. He stepped onto the causeway and strode across. He was rested and he felt good.

There was no fear in him. He had accepted his own death as a possible climax, and so be it, that was better than being half alive.

Coming off the end of the causeway, he angled for Della's Hotel and the persistent honey-hum of the juke box. He climbed to the small porch and opened the door without hesitation. Inside, he slammed the door behind him. His eyes roamed the circumference of the drab room. He picked out Carazon at the end of the bar, smiled back at the man's unbelieving stare. Della was spread over a chair at a round table at the end of the room, a solitaire hand before her. Her fat face attempted a scowl of displeasure. He gave the others a fast glance. Tosca was not in the room. He settled his gaze on Polo who sat in a booth with the Mexican girl named Dolores.

Polo was openmouthed. Frankie walked to the booth and slid into the opposite side.

"Paisan," he said, smiling.

"Frankie," Polo said, his voice shaken, "You're supposed to be—"

"Nothing to it," Frankie interrupted. "Some characters sank the *Evalena,* but I bailed out and made it to shore."

"You're like a cat," Polo said.

Frankie grinned. "Polo," he said seriously, "I got to talk a minute. Get rid of her."

"What do ya mean?" the girl said.

"Beat it," Polo said, shoving her out of the booth with his hip.

"Well, how do ya like that?" she said, tossing her head and moving to the bar.

Frankie leaned close over the table. "Listen, Polo," he whispered. "I got the jack pot. The *Evalena* doesn't mean anything compared to what I got for her. I can't tell you what it is, but it's hot and I need some help. Come in with me on this and you can tell Barlow to take a flying jump in the bay."

"What is it?" Polo forced himself to ask.

"I can't say," Frankie whispered. He looked up and around before bringing his head closer to say, "But it's worth a million bucks."

Polo whistled softly. He was too busy congratulating himself to ask himself any questions.

"What do I do?" Polo asked.

"Get your boat ready for a fast flying trip tomorrow night."

"I've got to go out tomorrow morning."

"Get out of it. Make sure that your boat doesn't go."

"It's Barlow's boat."

"You run it. That's what matters now. You'll be able to buy ten like it in a week."

Polo could see that Frankie was playing right into his hands, and Frankie sensed that Polo thought this, and he knew that he was playing the part right.

"Now I've got some relaxation to catch up on." He started out of the booth. "You have the boat ready," he said. "This is for old times' sake, buddy boy." He gave Polo a wide wink and left the booth.

Crossing the silent room, he went straight to Della's table. He was playing the thing exactly the way an arrogant, overconfident idiot would do it. He hooked a chair with his foot and brought it up to the table. He slumped into the chair and leaned his elbows on the table. "Della," he said, "you look like you wish I really was dead."

"What do you want?" Della said, hoarsely. "I thought I told you to stay out of here."

"I'm back, Della," he said. "And this time I got aces and spades. It's a pat hand, and I know how to play it. You know what I got." He emphasized each word, "It's a bomb, Della."

"Take your riddles some place else," she sneered.

"Don't play it tough, Della. I'm trying to do you a favor. I know you got orders from Barlow to rough me up the other night, and I'm not holding it against you. But play it cool now. Barlow and Springer are through. In two days I'll throw Springer's little badge in his face. You're okay with me, Della. Just make sure you're on the right side."

"You're outta your head." Her eyes narrowed in their fat pockets.

"Don't you believe it." The next thing he said was in a confidential tone. "Now, I like the way you run things here, Della, and there won't be any changes. But there won't be any Barlow in a week. This island is going to be Frankie Cargo's. And you're in." He paused, then he leaned back, smiling, and said, "And now I could use one of your broads. I'd like to sample a little of what I'm going to take over."

Della regarded him suspiciously. He was counting on her to humor him until she had complete control of the situation. She knew that since he was alive he might have salvaged the narcotics drop. She was bound to be in on the deal. And he was alive. So, Della was going to be thinking of her own skin. At the moment she couldn't be sure that he was merely bragging. But there was a way to keep him occupied until she could get to Jake Springer. It was just as Frankie had planned and hoped, and she rose to the bait.

"Take your pick," she grunted.

Frankie swiveled in the chair, carefully scrutinized every girl in the room. They all had their eyes on him. He returned his gaze to the girl, Dolores. If Polo was going to get the business, he might as well start now. "That one there," he said, nodding his head at Dolores.

Della waggled a sausage finger and the girl swayed to the table. Della jerked her head towards the door. The girl stopped to look at Frankie, then at Della. She shrugged and went through the door.

"We're gonna get along fine together," Frankie said, rising from the chair. He went through the door, feeling Della's eyes hard on his back, and closed the door after him. He waited behind the door until he heard the hard scuffle of footsteps, then he smiled and followed the girl to the second floor.

The hallway was dimly lit to hide the obvious scars of time. There were closed doorways on either side. Light shafted from an open door near the end of the hall and the girl stood there waiting.

Frankie walked down the hallway. It wasn't the room he had hoped for, but this was a minor thing. He cautioned himself against feeling that it was going to be too easy. It was only the beginning and the stars hadn't made their entrances. He entered the room ahead of the girl and went to the single window. He pulled the shade. He turned back and smiled at the girl.

She closed the door, coming into the room. "You got a bottle?" she asked.

"I didn't come up here to drink."

She shrugged, used to all kinds of answers, not caring. It was a job. She went to the wall switch to turn off the single light that shone from the ceiling.

"Leave it on," Frankie said.

The girl's hand stopped. She shrugged again. Some like it dark, some like to watch. It was all the same to her. Frankie had to feel sorry for Polo. A tired, nervous, sloppy wife and a bored, mechanical whore.

"You wanta get started?" the girl asked. "We ain't supposed to horse around up here for nothing."

"After you," Frankie said, gesturing to the bed.

In several fast movements the girl was undressed. She put her skirt and blouse over the back of the only chair in the room. Padding across the room, her pendulous breasts swaying, her buttocks grinding, she crawled onto the bed and rolled over on her back. She lifted her knees, smiled mechanically, then scratched her shoulder.

"What are ya waiting for?" she asked. "I ain't got all night."

Frankie was standing, facing the shaded window. He had hoped for window cord and there wasn't any. He went to the bed, and took up one of the pillows. He jerked the pillow case off.

"Hey," the girl said. "What are ya doing?"

"Just take it easy, Dolores. I'll be right with you." He tore the pillow case into three strips.

"Are you crazy? Jesus Christ, Della will blow her stack!" The girl was on her side, staring at him, certain that she had drawn a nut.

"Okay, now, Dolores. Over on your stomach."

"What? Hey, what is this? I don't go for any of this queer stuff."

"Over, Dolores."

"Like hell. I do it straight or not at all. You want the odd-ball stuff they got a girl down there that—"

He lashed her across the buttocks with the strips. It wasn't enough to hurt, but like most prostitutes, the girl reacted to punishment with obedience. She flipped onto her stomach. Frankie climbed onto the bed and straddled her. "Get your hands back," he said. She brought her hands around and he crossed them on her back. He took one of the strips and tied them securely.

"What kind of crap is this?"

Frankie did not answer. It amused him that the girl still did not know that she was being tied up. Her mind did not go beyond the reason she came to the room, and she was only questioning this strange innovation. Frankie reached out, gripping the sheet. He tore off a sizable piece and rolled it into a ball. With one hand he gripped the girl's hair and pulled her head back. She opened her mouth to cry out and he jammed the gag in, tying it securely in place with the second strip.

Dolores at last realized that something was wrong. She mumbled and began to thrash around on the bed. Frankie caught her flailing ankles and bound them together. He patted her on the buttocks. "Good-bye, Dolores," he said. "Thanks, but no thanks." He went to the door and opened it carefully. The girl followed him with frightened eyes. The hall was empty. He stepped out of the room and closed the door. He went down two doors and entered a room on the left.

"Who's that!?" A sharp, frightened male voice called.

"What?" A sleepy female voice.

"Go to sleep," Frankie said.

"Who the hell are you?"

They were both sitting up in the bed. Frankie went to the window and lifted it.

"What do you think it is, Grand Central Station?"

"Go to sleep." Frankie lifted one leg over the window sill and leaned out. As he had judged, he could just reach out and grasp the drainpipe. He swung out of the window and slid to the ground, leaving angry voices behind him.

The second his feet touched the sand he dodged into the complete shadows and ran, crouched, for the beach. The first thing Springer would do would be to close off the causeway. At the same time he would send a couple of men along the southwest bank, the only place where it was easy to wade off the island. He would then go to the hotel room. When he found the girl he would scour the island, feeling that escape was cut off. And when he didn't find his quarry anywhere on the island, his simple mind would form the logical conclusion that the people were hiding Frankie Cargo.

When he left the dunes and came out on the open beach, Frankie stopped. He pulled off his shoes and socks. He removed his shirt and pants. Tying everything into a neat ball that could be held around his neck by the knotted shirt sleeves, he ran along the beach until he was near the breakwater.

This would be the last thing Springer would expect. He veered to the left and plunged into the surf. He bobbed to the surface and swam out with strong, even strokes.

The water was cold, but he found it exhilarating. He swam straight out until he was well past the pull of the surf. He stopped, treading water, and looked back at the island.

He could see only a commotion of lights, but he knew that Springer or Barlow had the causeway shut off. He smiled to himself, imagining the comments when they found the girl and knew he had slipped out of the trap. All hell would soon be breaking loose.

And now there was another card face up. Polo knew how much the dope was worth.

He began to swim again, his strokes even and slow. Now that they knew he was alive—not just Springer, but everyone—there would be a scramble to get the heroin. And in that scramble someone might trip.

The ocean pulled at him as he crossed over the breakwater opening, but he angled away from it and pulled hard. The tide was already beginning to come in and he hated to think of trying to swim in the raging torrent that blasted between the rocks.

Once past the point of danger, he slackened his pace, resting. Then he changed his course and swam for the narrow strip of beach below the red clay cliffs.

When his knees touched sand he struggled to his feet and staggered ashore. He dropped down, breathing heavily. He sat there until he was rested, then he stood and his eyes covered the wall before him, remembering.

He had climbed these cliffs many times as a boy, day and night, and now he concentrated on the difficult trails that led to the top.

The night air chilled him. He untied his clothing. It was wet and uncomfortable, but it would keep the wind off him. The laces of his shoes knotted together, he slung them over his shoulder and started off along the beach, walking slowly, examining the terrain.

When he found the slight cleft in the rocks he began to climb. It was an inclined chimney, but there were good footholds and he moved up slowly. It was something the others would not know about.

Midway, he paused to rest. He was gasping for breath and the blood pounded behind his eyes.

He had to get to Arlene. Things would be popping now, and he had to get her to the police. He felt certain that he could frighten her into a confession. Everything depended on that. The needle marks on her arm would help. They were almost imperceptible, nothing like the ragged jobs done by cheap junkies, and they would never hold water the narcotics agents, but it might be enough to frighten Arlene.

And there was the fact that she hated Sam Barlow. If she had been telling the truth, she wanted Barlow put away. There were plenty of addicts who wanted off the stuff when they were feeling good and intentionally turned in their suppliers.

He felt for handholds, pulled himself up. When he reached the top he crawled over the edge and lay still, his eyes closed. He came to his feet and staggered forward. Twenty yards and he reached the high iron fence.

Alarms did not concern him now. He climbed the fence and dropped to the other side. Then he ran for the rear of the house.

It was brightly lighted. He came to one of the large, low windows and crouched, listening. There was only a monotonous, whirring sound from within. He strained his ears. A whirr, a click, a whirr. The record player left running. He was thinking of Brahms as he raced around the corner of the house and slammed through the front entrance.

He burst into the living room. The console was running. The room was a shambles. Cabinets were torn apart, drawers and contents strewn over the room. Cushions were slashed.

In the middle of the floor, a shapeless bundle in the midst of the wreckage, Arlene lay face down, her arms askew, her legs sprawled.

Frankie went to her slowly. "Arlene," he whispered to himself, "what more could they do to you?"

He dropped to one knee and gripped her shoulders. He turned her over. Her head lolled on her neck. Her nose was battered out of shape. One eye was swollen and blue-black. Her mouth was broken and teeth were missing. Her dress was shredded from her shoulders and her flesh was bruised. There were cigarette burns on her breasts. Her jaw hung slack and one eye was open, staring in death as if she were surprised.

"Poor, poor, wild, loony dame," Frankie murmured. He eased her to the floor. Her body was still supple and the flesh retained heat. So she hadn't been killed too long ago. He had at once thought of Carazon. Now he paused in his thinking. It could have been Carazon, but it didn't have to be. Someone had been here recently, but why had they killed her.

He kneeled, looking at her, shaking his head. "You hated pain," he said. He could imagine her when the cigarette touched her breast. Torture! No one tortured for kicks. Well, that was wrong, but why? They beat the hell out of her, burned her and finally killed her. Why?

When he came to his feet he was weaving. He felt drunk and sick. His eyes covered the disheveled room. He crossed to the bedroom and entered. It, too, was torn apart. He ran from room to room. The entire house had been ransacked.

If they thought she had the heroin. Yes! If they thought that the heroin was hidden in the house.

He returned to the living room and dropped to the torn divan where he sat holding his head and staring at the body of Arlene.

"Did I do this to you?" he whispered. "Did I have you killed?"

Springer knew that she had lent him the money to get his boat out. He might have figured that they were a partnership, that Arlene had put him up to getting the heroin. She wouldn't need Barlow or Springer if she had that supply for herself.

And there was something else pulling at the back of his mind. He tried to thrust it away, but it nagged at him.

Lying next to him, her voice apprehensive, Tosca had said: "Barlow won't stop at anything for a million dollars in dope." He pressed his knuckles into his eyes. No! His mind screamed. But how did she know? He hadn't told her the value of the drop. But she knew. He had thought of it at the time, but forced it from his mind, wanting nothing to blemish his love, wanting to believe completely.

He remembered back to that first morning. Tosca in that sheer lace slip, stroking her hair, waiting for Springer. And Polo's words: "Gahdamn high-class sheriff's whore!" And her words: "I want you to know. About Springer ...."

His brain was reeling dizzily. He wanted to curse. Was everybody rotten?

Trust her! another part of him shouted. Trust her! You love her so trust her!

She knew that he had been to Arlene's that first night. And he thought that only Springer had known. She knew the heroin was hidden. She knew he had come back to Arlene's that afternoon.

The rage burst from his constricted chest with a snarl. He thought of Sam Barlow. The man behind the scenes. Careful, handsome Sam Barlow. No, he wouldn't have been the one who beat her to death. Making her guts scream for morphine was more in his line. But Barlow had dealt this death blow just as surely as if he had been standing in the room.

Reaching out to the phone on the small end table, Frankie lifted the receiver. He dialed the operator.

"Number, please."

"Information."

"One moment, please." The clicking, the hum, the buzz.

"Information."

"The number for Samuel Barlow." His voice a low and flat monotone.

He got the number and dialed it. He waited, listening to the ring. A click. "Hello?"

"Barlow?"

"Yes, who is this?"

"She's dead, Barlow."

"What? Who is this? What are you talking about?"

"She's dead. Arlene is dead."

"You're crazy. Who is this?"

"Very, very dead. You ought to see her, Barlow. You wouldn't recognize her. You did it, Barlow. You killed her."

"What the hell are you talking about?"

"Your wife, you filthy bastard," Frankie shouted. "You went too far. This time you've got your ass in the sling. I'm going to kill you, Barlow." He slammed the phone down.

The hell with it! There was nothing he could do now; no way to prove Barlow or Springer guilty. But he still had the heroin. Let Springer come after it—oh, just let that bastard try. And he would. When he did someone was going to die.

Frankie lurched to his feet. He took one last look at Arlene, the anger burning in him, then he ran for the door. Before anything else he had to see Tosca. He might be dead before this night was ended, but he was going to know about her before he went. If she had lied to him, then she was going to go just the way Arlene did.

He ran down the drive, his feet slap-slapping on the macadam. He was still barefoot. Suddenly running into some gravel, he realized this. He had left his shoes at the house.

Skidding to a stop, he turned back toward the house. If the police found his shoes he'd be in real trouble. He tried to remember just where he had dropped them, but he couldn't. He could go back for them. But what difference would it make? He wasn't going anywhere tonight, except to Springer and Barlow. After that it wouldn't be a matter for the police. Springer was the law here and one way or another, the thing was going to be resolved.

He turned and ran on. He reached the highway and kept running. His mouth was open and he sucked air, his arms pumping. He had a stitch in his side and he gripped the place with his hand. When the pain was too great he slowed to a walk. His breathing restored, he began to trot.

Cars passed him, fingering the road with their lights, blinding him. He was oblivious to them, his mind concentrated on getting to Tosca.

At the turn-off to the Landing, he leaped off the highway and bulled his way through the tough weeds of the mud flats. The moon was up, but its light was not enough to make his going easy.

He slogged through the slime, beating the waist-high weeds from his path. He stepped into a pothole, twisting his ankle, and fell. He turned, gripping the ankle with both hands, his face tight in a grimace of pain. He struggled to his feet and pushed on, trying to shift his weight to his good foot. The pain gradually left him.

He saw lights probing aimlessly, and heard voices. They were directly ahead. He stopped running and ducked to a crouch, listening. His breathing seemed like a shout to him and he fought to stop the sound.

"He ain't gonna be out here."

"So who cares. I don't wanta see him anyway."

"Well, I don't like slogging in this mud."

"Better than running into him, I say."

"What's Springer want him for?"

"Who knows? We're supposed to look for him, that's all."

"I like to know what he done. Yesterday he's dead, now we're looking for him to arrest him."

"Why don't you ask Springer?"

"Yeah. Then you'd be looking for me."

The voices passed within yards of him, and Frankie held his breath until the lights moved away.

He edged forward, placing his feet, parting the weeds carefully. When he reached the water, he dropped to his hands and knees and crawled into it. He stopped when he reached his neck. Looking to the right, he could see the lights on the causeway, see the dark figures of the men milling about. Their voices were muted.

Turning his head, Frankie started across the open water separating the mainland from the island. It wasn't far and it wasn't deep. He pushed with his feet on the muddy bottom and worked his hands in a slow breast stroke. The bottom changed from mud to sand, and he had to crouch to keep himself covered by the water. He crawled out onto the island and spread himself flat, listening.

When he heard no sound except the lapping of the water, the whispering wind, the sea-lion bark, the distant noises, he lurched to his feet and ran for the protection of the dunes.

Then he worked his way up the island, keeping to the shadows. He skirted two houses that were nestled in the dunes, pausing behind each one.

It was like Korea. He was moving under the shadow of sudden death, and he was suspicious of every movement, every sound. A dog began to bark, a mournful wail.

There was a light in the window of his house. It was the living room. The kitchen was dark. He circled the house. The bedroom was dark. He came closer to the house, crawled to the side and raised himself slowly to the lighted window.

Tosca was sitting in the overstuffed chair. A magazine was in her lap, but she wasn't looking at it. Her usually vivid face was expressionless, as though she were in a trance. Her hands were folded atop the magazine pages and she stared at them.

Frankie lowered his head from the edge of the window. He moved quietly, stooped, to the corner of the house. It was too close to the causeway to open the front door without being seen. He retraced his steps and went to the rear.

The few steps to the screened shed creaked under his weight and he waited after each step. Every minute sound was like an explosion to him, magnified by his imagination. He opened the screen door, closed it carefully after him. His hand touched the knob of the rear door. He turned it carefully, soundlessly. It opened. He eased into the kitchen and left the door open. He crossed to the lighted doorway. He stepped into the living room.

Tosca's eyes flicked to him and her breath caught in a tiny gasp. Her hand flew to her mouth and her eyes widened. She said nothing.

"Why did you do it?" Frankie said, his voice low and quavering.

Her lips moved, but they offered no sound. Her head shook from side to side, her eyes wide and sick with fear.

"Why? Just tell me why you did it?"

"Because I told her to."

The voice was rasping and deep. Frankie spun and faced the bedroom and Springer stood there, grinning, the service .38 large in his hand.

Tosca broke. Her shoulders slumped and she held her face in her hands, muffling her crying.

Springer stepped into the room. Polo and Carazon appeared in the doorway behind him.

"You took a long time getting here, Cargo," Springer said.

"I've been busy," Frankie answered. He looked over Springer's shoulder at Polo. "Hello, old buddy," he said.

Polo smiled, and it wasn't the same Polo of the other years. What was the reason for the change, Frankie wondered.

"We gotta have a little talk," Springer said. "You're in bad trouble."

"You keep telling me that," Frankie said.

"You just wouldn't take a man's friendly advice," Springer said, hefting the gun in his hand.

"We always learn too late." Frankie forced a smile.

"You ain't got nothing to be happy about, boy."

"It's the American way," Frankie said.

"Polo," Springer said over his shoulder.

"Yeah."

"Wipe the smile off our friend's face."

Polo stepped forward, his wide, powerful body rolling on his short legs. He faced Frankie who was smiling at him.

"You haven't tried this for a long time," Frankie said.

"Not for a long time," Polo answered, grinning.

"Since we were twelve," Frankie said.

"Eleven," Polo said. "Your memory's no good."

"And yours is too good. You invite me back here just to settle that kid stuff?"

"Nah. We had to have somebody. You was just easy to get to."

"And the kid stuff helped."

"Some." Polo's eyes glinted. His huge fist drove into Frankie's midsection with the force of a sledge. Frankie doubled, grunting. Polo looped his right. It landed, bone against bone, snapping Frankie's head, sending him sprawling to his knees. Frankie held his stomach and shook his head.

"You ain't so good since you grew up," Polo said.

Tosca lunged from her chair. She dived across the room and dropped on her knees before Frankie. "Forgive me," she gasped, throwing her arms around his neck.

"Get that bitch off him!" Springer snapped.

Polo grabbed her arm and jerked her away. He pulled her roughly and spun her, crashing, into the chair.

Frankie snarled, moving. His fist came from the floor, driving up with the leverage from his rising legs. He caught Polo flush on the jaw with a jarring thud. For an instant they were two immovable bodies. Then the fist dropped. Polo's knees sagged and he pitched forward. He groaned and rolled over. He dragged himself to his knees.

"Come and get it," Frankie said. "Old buddy."

"Cut it, Cargo," Springer said. "I don't want to use this until I'm ready."

Frankie looked across at Tosca. Her eyes were imploring. "Do what he says," she said. "He'll kill you."

"You know him real well," Frankie said.

Her eyes dropped. Springer's voice broke the silence between them. "She's telling you right, boy."

"Maybe not," Frankie said, turning back to Springer. "You might want me dead, but you want what I got a lot more."

"And I'm gonna get it, too," Springer grinned.

"Says you."

"Sez me, is right. Carazon, get Polo up."

Carazon stepped forward and helped Polo to his feet. Polo shook his head clear. He glared at Frankie and his eyes were clouded. "You're gonna get yours, big man," he growled. "This island is gonna hear you whimper your guts out. I wish my old man was here to listen. All my life I heard, 'Frankie does this, Frankie does that. Why don't you do it like Frankie does? Frankie's the best fisherman on the island. Frankie's a war hero. Frankie, Frankie.' Well, that's over. I walked in your shadow all my life. Big, stupid Polo. Now this island is gonna see you cry, Frankie Cargo."

"You're sick, Polo."

"Not nearly as sick as you're gonna be."

"Can it," Springer said. Polo was silenced and Springer added, "I want this character tied up for our little trip. Turn around, Cargo, and get your hands behind you."

Frankie turned, facing the wall, and put his hands behind his back. He heard someone move up behind him, sensed sudden movement, then his brain exploded and the world spun in star-sputtering darkness.

CHAPTER TEN

Frankie smelled where he was before he opened his eyes. Fish. The pungent, stale, overwhelming odor of fish. Over the years it was enough to permeate any building. You could tear the walls of a cannery down and the smell would still be in the concrete foundation.

He felt cold concrete at his back. His head ached and then he remembered back to the instant of being hit from behind. He opened his eyes.

It was a basement, and he knew it was Barlow's cannery. The long room was stacked with packing cases. The ceiling was a grill of pipes used for steam canning. There were larger pipes along the walls. A single bulb with a blue glass shade hung by a cord from the ceiling. It cast its direct light over a table in the middle of the room. There were four chairs at the table. Springer and Polo occupied two of the chairs. They were both watching him.

Beyond the immediate circle of light the room was grimly shadowed.

Frankie was on the floor, his back propped against some packing cases. Tosca was next to him. They both had their hands bound behind their backs. He turned his head and his eyes met Tosca's. Why was she here with him? Was it because they had no more use for her? Or was it...?

"I love you," her lips said, without sound, forming the words carefully.

He closed his eyes and swallowed hard. He tried not to remember Arlene. He opened his eyes. "Did you tell them I was at Arlene's?"

She bit her lower lip. Her head bowed and she squeezed her eyes closed. A tear rolled over her cheek. "I'm sorry," she whispered.

"You're sorry!" He shouted vehemently, his voice reverberating through the cavernlike basement, startling both Springer and Polo.

"Shut up, you!" Polo shouted.

"You're sorry!" he snarled again. "Well, Arlene's sorry, too. She's dead! These animals beat her to death!"

"Shut up!"

Polo kicked back from his chair, knocking it to the floor. He ran across the short space between them. He lashed out with his foot, as he would at a placed football, kicking Frankie in the ribs. The blow sent pain through Frankie's chest and he rolled sideways, landing on Tosca's lap. He struggled up and away from her, as if she were poison. Polo slammed him across the mouth with the back of his hand.

"Now, maybe you'll shut up," Polo said.

"You better kill me, Polo. I swear, you better kill me. Because if you don't I'm going to break every bone in your rotten, treacherous body."

"Bravo." Springer was clapping his hands and laughing. "Bravo. A speech from the big bad Cargo."

Polo stepped back, breathing heavily and grinning at Springer's humor. Frankie's eyes were narrowed with hate. Polo went to the table and righted his chair. He sat down, tapping his fingers on the table impatient to vent his fury.

"Where's that damned Carazon?" Polo asked.

"He'll be along."

"Why don't you let me do it?"

"It's gotta be done right." Springer rose from his chair and came to stand over Frankie. He showed his teeth and his thumbs were hooked in his belt.

"You didn't play your part right, Cargo," he said. "You caused me a lot of trouble."

"I've just begun."

"No, Cargo, you're through. But it could have been nicer. For me, that is. It's six of one, half a dozen of another for you. You came back here to die. That's all, just die. But you made a mess of things. We asked you back here to be a fall guy. You were gonna be convicted of a murder." Springer was smiling, enjoying himself. "You were just right for the job. You had a motive and everything. And we needed an airtight case because this murder would get publicity. Nasty thing, publicity. That's when you need someone to sit in the gas chamber, someone ready-made. You were perfect, but you had to louse things up. You and Arlene. If you hadn't taken that boat out we wouldn't have this little problem. Just a little time was all we needed, but you had to louse it up."

Frankie's mind was rushing over Springer's gloating words, adding between the lines.

"Why don't we get it over with?" Polo asked.

"Shut your mouth!" Springer snapped.

Motive, Frankie was thinking. Motive. Who could he have reason to kill except the people in this room? Barlow! He had already told Barlow he was going to kill him. But for another reason.

"How much did my father know about you?" Frankie asked.

Springer laughed. "He didn't know anything. He came to tell me that Barlow was shipping whores in from Mexico. Wanted me to arrest Barlow." Springer laughed. "He was a funny old man."

"You killed him for that?"

"Me? You're jumping to conclusions, boy."

"You've got a lot of blood on your hands, Springer."

"The chain of events," Springer said. "And besides, he was an old man. He was going to die anyway. Whoever killed him did us a favor. You wouldn't have come back here unless the old man was dead, and we wanted you here."

A door slammed and Carazon walked into the light. He was carrying a tall stepladder.

"You took long enough," Polo said.

"Couldn't find the damn thing," Carazon growled.

Springer turned away from Frankie and crossed to the table. "Set it up over here," he said.

Carazon spread the legs of the ladder. Springer took two lengths of cord from the table and handed them to Carazon. "You know how I want it," he said.

Carazon nodded and began to climb the ladder. It wobbled and he said, "Hold the damn thing."

Polo held the legs, his head tilted back to watch. Carazon reached the top. He could then touch the ceiling. He took the cord and tied one end to one of the pipes. When both pieces of cord dangled from the ceiling, he climbed down and moved the ladder away.

"You'll remember this from Korea," Springer said. "I know you weren't a prisoner, but you must have heard. Get him up here."

Polo and Carazon came and lifted Frankie to his feet. They dragged him to the center of the room. Springer pressed the .38 into his stomach while Polo untied his hands. They took both of his arms and stretched them over his head. They put the tiny slip-knots over his thumbs and drew them tight. When they released him, he was standing on his toes, his arms over his head.

"Get that shirt off him," Springer said, his voice cold and mechanical.

Carazon stepped behind Frankie and gripped the collar of his shirt. The cord bit into Frankie's thumbs as Carazon jerked downward. Frankie bit his lips, but a strangled, "Agh!", escaped his throat. Carazon tried again, and this time the shirt tore away. The sweat was standing on Frankie's forehead.

"Now get the towels, and I want them good and wet."

Polo brought the wet towels. "Okay," Springer said. "Carazon, you go first."

The big man removed the cigar from his mouth and placed it carefully on the edge of the table. He took one of the towels, gripped it, wrapping it once over the back of his hand. He stood, straddle-legged, before Frankie. He brought his arm back, then grunting, he swung the towel.

It was like being hit by a length of chain. The force of the blow brought Frankie's weight down on his thumbs and the muscles of his arms screamed with the pain.

"That's just the beginning," Springer said. "Now, Cargo, you got something I want. You stole it and you hid it. I want it. Just tell me where it is and I'll give you a fast slug in the gut, absolutely painless."

Frankie closed his eyes, pressed his lips tightly together.

The towel cut the air and landed across his neck and shoulders. Frankie gasped and came up on his toes to ease the pain of his thumbs. The towel landed again.

"Stop it!" Tosca screamed. "Stop it!"

The towel came down again with stinging force, raising an angry welt across Frankie's chest. Carazon paused for breath. Wrapping his fingers around the cord, Frankie jerked his body up. His legs shot out like pistons, his heels slamming Carazon full in the face. The towel flew out of Carazon's hands and he crashed into the table, blood running from his nose and mouth.

"Next," Springer said, calmly, the amused smile still on his face.

Polo took the next towel, stepping up. He brought it overhead. Frankie looked him in the eyes. The towel landed with a loud crack, but Frankie's eyes stayed on Polo. And he kept them there throughout the ordeal, until Polo stopped, exhausted.

Tosca was sobbing, cursing them, begging them to stop the punishment, begging Frankie to tell them where the heroin was hidden.

Frankie was numb to the pain. A part of his brain seemed to be closed off, and it was as though his body did not belong to him. It was just a dull ache. He heard the voices from a distance, knew that Tosca was shouting and crying, but could not reason why.

"Okay," Springer said, "I'll have to take care of this one myself."

He took one of the towels and knotted the end. Frankie watched him through dulled eyes, not caring.

"Drop his pants," Springer said.

Carazon unbuckled his belt, unzipped the fly. The trousers dropped to Frankie's ankles. Frankie blinked his eyes, seeing Springer approach. He saw the white blur of the towel.

The shock cleared his head. He cried out for the first time. Springer swung the towel again.

Frankie writhed in pain. He was sick in the pit of his stomach. His body convulsed and he heaved. Springer hit him again. Frankie groaned. The pain spread through his guts like sharp, hot needles. He was wide awake now, every nerve in his body aroused to the sudden pain.

"Tell me, Cargo. Tell me where you hid the junk."

Frankie shook his head. The towel swished in the air. The hard, wet knot slammed into his genitals. He gagged on the scream that rose from his chest. He vomited again.

"I can keep this up, Cargo. When I'm done you'll never be any good again."

Frankie shook his head, the involuntary tears running from his eyes. Again the towel. Sharp pain. And again. The body rose to Frankie's aid, and blackness spread over him. His chin dropped to his chest.

When he opened his eyes again he was doubled up on the floor. His insides seemed to be torn apart. Springer was standing over him.

"You're a tough man, Cargo, a tough man. But I'm going to get that heroin, and you're going to tell me how."

Frankie did not answer. He had no will to speak. He clutched at his stomach. His trousers had been pulled up and the belt cinched.

"Get the girl over here," Springer said. "I should have used her in the first place."

Frankie caught his breath and his eyes opened. He flicked his eyes to Tosca. There was only the look of resignation in her face, as if she didn't care what they did to her now.

"Listen!" Polo said.

The basement was suddenly silent. Footsteps sounded on the floor overhead.

"The watchman?"

"I sent him home."

They waited, listening. A door opened and closed. The footsteps were on the stairs, coming down. Springer lifted his .38 and all eyes were on the doorway. It opened and Sam Barlow stepped into the room. He crossed into the light. His stern jaw was set and his brows were knitted over his eyes. His fists were clenched at his sides. He faced Springer.

"You didn't have to kill her, Jake," he said. He was fighting for control of his voice, but even so, there was a slight tremble to it.

"She gave me trouble," Springer said, the gun still leveled at Barlow.

"There was no reason to kill her."

"It was an accident."

The tension in the room was electric. There was no sound except heavy breathing and the voices of the two big men who faced one another.

"That beating was no accident. You killed her."

"Okay, okay, I killed her!" Springer's voice rose. "So what? She was a stupid little junkie with hot pants. I killed her. So what?"

"She was my wife." Barlow's voice was almost a whisper. "She was no good, but she was my wife."

"Balls!"

"She was a beautiful thing."

"She was a tramp!"

"I told you no killing," Barlow said. "You're through, Jake. Smuggling dope and women is one thing. But killing…" He shook his head. "I called the State Police, Jake. You're through. You forgot who was boss."

"Boss? I'll tell you who's boss. *I'm* the boss!" He slammed his chest and waved the revolver. "You're just the gahdamned front here, Barlow. You think you can sit on your ass while I handle the dirty work?"

"That's all you're good for!"

"Sez you! You've had it, Sam. I'm running things. You haven't got the guts for this operation anymore. It's gonna get bigger, and I'm running it—me, Jake Springer. You think you're God. Well, listen to me, Barlow. I brought this Cargo character back here just to go the route for your murder. I had your number a month ago. How do you think his old man got it? That was going to be his motive for killing you, you jerk."

"You shouldn't have killed her, Jake."

"It was a pleasure!"

Barlow threw himself forward, his face twisted with rage. The .38 exploded, the report magnified and echoed by the enclosure. Barlow's hands gripped Springer's shoulders, then the fingers relaxed and slid down Springer's chest. Barlow seemed to be resting. He didn't move.

Springer stood over him a moment, then he spun around. "Get that gahdamn broad over here," he snarled. "Polo, get that tarp and throw it on the floor."

Carazon was holding Tosca. Her black hair was disheveled and it fell in unruly waves over her shoulders. Her eyes were red and swollen from crying, but they still flashed with defiance. She lifted her chin and pulled her shoulders back. Her breasts rose and fell with her heavy breathing.

Springer gestured with the revolver. He spoke through clenched teeth. "You get this, you stupid broad. I told you what was going to happen to you if you crossed me up. You thought he was going to buy you out of this. You went for that love crap. Well, look where it got you. And don't think I'm going to knock you off. I got something better than that. When I'm done with you, you're gonna be working the labor camps. You wouldn't work at Della's and I let you off, but now you're gonna be a fifty-cent lay in a barracks.

"Maybe you ain't never seen that assembly line over there on payday. Well, you're going to. You take all comers. You just lay on that cot and spread it, and they come one after the other. In two months your own mother won't know you. Afterward, even the Mexicans won't want you, and then I'll throw you into the gutter." His face was flushed when he finished.

Whirling to Polo, he snapped. "Get that tarp down. Okay, now put her on it."

Tosca struggled, but both men threw her to the floor and held her pinned by the arms.

"You're gonna enjoy this," Springer growled at Frankie. "You ever heard of a gang-bang? Did they play that game when you were a kid? Well you're about to see one." He turned to Polo, his lips pulled back off his teeth. "Polo, you've been trying for a crack at this broad. Now you're gonna get it free. You're first." He reached down. His fingers caught the edge of Tosca's blouse and he tore it away, exposing her round, amber breasts.

Frankie pulled himself to his knees. Tosca's eyes were wide. Frankie stared at her.

"Oh, my God," he whispered. Both of her breasts were dotted with dark red burns, now blistered. "Oh, no." How many times had the cigarette touched her? And she had begged him for forgiveness. His eyes met hers. She shook her head and smiled.

"I'll tell you!" Frankie gasped.

"Where?"

"Let her go."

"Where?"

"Let her go and I'll tell you."

Springer laughed. "Who're you trying to kid, Cargo? This broad goes loose when I got the junk in my hand."

"C'mon, Jake," Polo said. "Let me take a crack at her while he's making up his mind."

"Polo," Frankie said, his voice rasping, "I'm going to castrate you."

Polo grinned and looked up at Jake Springer. "C'mon, Jake."

"Okay," Springer said.

"Get both her arms," Polo said to Carazon. The burly man shifted his position until his weight pinned Tosca's shoulders to the floor.

"You bastard, Polo!"

Polo grasped the hem of Tosca's skirt and pulled it up over her thighs. Tosca lashed out with her feet. She caught Polo in the chest and sent him over backwards. He got up, laughing.

"That's the way I like 'em," he laughed. "Plenty of fire." Polo crawled forward. He gripped Tosca's ankles and held them down. She twisted her body.

"Wow! Look at her go. Like a damn snake. Oh, baby, is she gonna be something." Polo's hamlike hands gripped her thighs, pressed her down.

"I'll tell you where it is!" Frankie shouted.

"Well, tell me!" Springer said.

"Get him off her."

"When I hear it."

"Get him off first."

"Not until I hear you singing."

Polo was hovering over Tosca. He leaned close to her face and she spit.

"Bitch!"

Polo's hand shot out and he slapped her hard across the mouth. Tosca cried out.

Frankie forgot the intense pain in his groin. He threw himself forward. He caught Carazon from behind, cupped his chin and threw him over backwards. He lunged across Tosca and smashed into Polo. They rolled on the floor together, but Frankie did not have the strength left to match Polo and the powerful fisherman drove a hard right fist into his face. Frankie dropped to his knees, then slid to his side, unable to move. He lifted his head. Polo was smiling.

"You better tell us where that stuff is, boy. Because one more minute and I'm gonna have this broad."

"All right," Frankie muttered, his mouth twisted with agony. "You can have it."

"Don't tell them!" Tosca screamed. "They'll only kill you when they know." She scrambled to her knees.

Polo turned and swung a backhand. It cracked against the side of her face and knocked her over.

"Let's hear it."

"Don't tell them," Tosca cried.

"Carazon, keep her quiet," Springer said. "Okay, Cargo. Tell us, and tell us right."

"You'll let the girl go?"

"Okay, we let the girl go."

"I buried it on the beach. Out by the point where you sank my boat. I swam ashore. Then I buried it."

"How do we find it?"

"You know where Three Peaks is?"

"I know it," Polo said. "Just this side of the point there's three big rocks that look like peaks from the water."

"There's a red clay bluff just below them," Frankie said, struggling for each word. "I planted it right at the bottom and covered the spot with a pile of rocks. You can't miss it."

Springer smiled broadly. "Now then, you see how easy it was?" He came around the edge of the table. "Okay, boys, we gotta get out of here."

"How about that?" Carazon said, nodding towards the body of Sam Barlow where a pool of blood was fingering out over the cement.

"That's easy," Springer said. "The original plan. Cargo killed him and he knifed Cargo. Two bodies. Open-and-shut case."

"How about three bodies," Polo said. He was standing in the shadows, a snub-nosed revolver in his hand.

"What?" Springer said, one eyebrow arched.

"Three bodies," Polo repeated.

"Don't be an idiot, Polo," Springer said.

"Just keep that gun hand down at your side, Jake. I got you dead center."

"You don't really think you can gun me down before I cut you to ribbons, do you?" Springer was grinning.

"For a million bucks I'll try."

"You're a dead man, Polo."

Carazon edged away from Springer, his mouth agape. In his eyes was wonderment and confusion. He realized that he had to take sides to stay alive, but he couldn't be sure which side was to be the winner, and which winner would include him in the winnings. Befuddled, he stumbled into the table. It tipped and crashed to the floor.

Polo's eyes flicked away from Springer for just an instant, but in that second, Springer brought the .38 up and squeezed the trigger. The explosion was hollow, the sound ricocheting in the basement. Polo staggered back, stunned. His hands dropped to his sides. He bowed his head and stared dumbly at the spread of blood on his shirt. He looked up and his eyes were wide with disbelief.

Springer stood loose, smiling. Polo started forward, his legs moving stiffly. Springer shot again. Polo winced under the impact of the slug, but he did not go down. It was as though his wide, powerful body was absorbing the bullets. He stopped and his fingers touched his stomach. Blood oozed through the fingers.

"Come on, Polo," Springer said. "Take another step."

Polo lifted the gun in his hand. It was slow motion, the muzzle rising steadily. Springer shot again. Polo went back a step. He bit into his lower lip until blood dribbled over his chin. He gripped his wrist and held the gun-hand up. Springer pressed off another shot. Polo's fingers loosened. The gun dangled a moment, then clattered to the floor.

Springer's laughter was wild. "Just saved me the trouble of doing it afterwards, Polo."

Polo's knees buckled. He went down gradually until he was kneeling. He crawled forward, his teeth bared.

Carazon gripped the edge of the tumbled table, his eyes wide, dodging between Polo and Springer. He saw the enjoyment in Springer's face, the grimace of death in Polo's. And he knew that Polo had been marked for the death before this evening. Springer was not going to leave any of them alive.

Taking a deep breath, Carazon leaped. He landed on Springer's back, his hairy arms around the deputy's neck. Springer staggered under the weight. Carazon hung on in terror.

Polo crawled after the fallen revolver.

In the distance there was the muted sound of a siren. Frankie caught his breath and listened. Barlow had called the State Police. Were they on their way to Arlene's? Had they been there? Were they coming to the island? The people must have heard the shots.

Were they doing anything. This was it. It was breaking apart at the seams.

"I'll kill you, Carazon!"

Springer whirled, flailing his arms. Carazon stayed behind him, his powerful arms pressuring Springer's throat. The deputy tried to beat his legs with the revolver. Carazon dodged the blows.

"You sneaky, yellow bastard!" Springer bellowed. He twisted his arm until he had the gun behind his back. He pulled the trigger. Carazon grunted. He loosened his hold and stumbled back a step.

"You shot me," Carazon mumbled with disbelief.

Springer turned. "Yes, and here's another little present." The hammer clicked on the empty chamber. Springer threw the gun. It hit Carazon in the face. Springer whirled again. Polo was still trying to reach the snub-nosed .32.

Frankie gathered his legs under him. He lifted himself and dived. His fingers curled over the butt of the gun. He was still rolling and he brought it up. Springer was coming for the gun in the same instant. Frankie fired point-blank. Springer howled in pain. He grabbed his left shoulder. He was still moving and he lashed out with his foot. Frankie felt the numbing blow on the side of his neck, but he rolled with the impact. He was on his back with Springer above him. The gun came up.

Springer dodged away, lifting one of the chairs as he moved. Swinging, he smashed the light. The room was plunged into darkness.

It was silent. Heavy breathing. Frankie probed the darkness. Springer was not moving. Polo was gagging. Carazon was weeping quietly. The siren was approaching. There was the hum of voices from outside. Frankie felt his sweat moisten the gun butt. He waited for movement from Springer. It had to be soon. The siren was clear now, like the wail of a banshee. Frankie moved his arm. With the elbow resting on the floor, he aimed towards the doorway. Then he waited.

Springer bolted. His heavy shoes slapped the concrete floor. He slammed into the wall and scrabbled for the door. Frankie fired. The bullet ricocheted with a high whine.

"Tosca, keep your head down!"

Springer found the door. The knob rattled under his grasp. Frankie fired at the sound. The bullet wailed off the wall. The door opened. Frankie saw the movement in the blackness. He fired again.

"Tough luck, Cargo!"

Springer's feet hammered on the steps.

Biting his teeth together, hard, Frankie dragged himself to his feet. He grunted with the pain in his stomach. He ran doubled over.

"Let him go!" Tosca screamed.

"No! This is it. I have to stop him now." Frankie's feet touched something soft and giving, and then he was falling. He threw his arms out to take the shock. He had forgotten that Barlow's body was between him and the doorway. He rolled when he hit. He forced himself up again. He groped forward.

"Frankie," Polo gasped, his voice a whisper. "Frankie, I didn't mean it. Help me, Frankie."

His hands touched the wall, and Frankie felt for the doorway, cursing the darkness. He heard the commotion above, heard Springer's bellowing voice.

"Out of my way, you miserable crumbs!" And the wild laughter.

And the siren.

"Please help me, Frankie."

And Carazon's terrified whimpering.

Springer was getting away. He felt panic. His hands rushed over the rough wall. His fingers touched a hinge. Elation leaped within him. His hands outlined the door. He gripped the knob. It seemed like a long time. Was he too late?

Fingers touched his back. He started and swung around. "It's me." Tosca's voice.

"Come on." Frankie jerked the door open. "Take your time," he said to Tosca. "I'm going to stop him." He tripped on the first step, but his hands supported him. He ran up the steps. The door at the top was open. He was in the main room of the cannery. Moonlight fingered through the outside door and he ran for the beam. He was on the short loading platform and a crowd of shadowed men surrounded him, the soft light on their faces.

"Where'd he go?"

"Springer?" A voice asked.

"Yes. Which way?"

The rasping cough of an engine answered him. The engine roared, then settled into the chug-chug-chug of a Diesel. Frankie leaped off the end of the platform. He stumbled into the group of men. He shouldered them aside.

The pain tearing at his insides, he forced himself to run, each step jarring him. He stopped before the wooden walk running to the floating dock.

Chug-a-chug-a-chug. The white hull, gray and shadowed by the night, was swinging out into the channel. The engine roared at full speed, a billow of exhaust rose off the water.

A red light blinked across the causeway with the clatter and rumble of a speeding car. Tires squealed.

Chug-chug-chug-chug.

Frankie glanced down at the gun in his hand. It was useless at this range, and he remembered when Springer had tried to stop him a few nights before. He turned and ran back up the slope.

The State Police car slid to a stop, the headlights on the milling crowd of astonished men before the cannery. Two uniformed men got out of the car. Doors slammed.

Frankie ignored them. He crossed the path of the headlights, running.

"You there, hold up!"

Frankie stopped at the commanding voice. He turned. "He's getting away," Frankie wailed.

"What are you talking about? What's going on here?"

"Jake Springer. He's in that boat."

"So what?"

"He killed Arlene Morse and Sam Barlow." Frankie was frantic.

Chug-a-chug-a-chug-chug. The boat was making the sweeping turn into the breakwater current.

"Who are you?"

"Gahdammit, man, stop him and talk later!"

"Just a minute. What are you doing with that gun?"

"I'm trying to stop him!"

"Just you hold on. I might have a few questions for you, buddy."

Christ, Frankie shouted to himself, were all cops the same? He turned and ran, bending low.

"Stop!"

Frankie kept running. He dodged away from the beam of the headlights. He was still barefoot and it helped his footing in the sand.

"Stop or I'll shoot!"

He lowered his head and kept running. The crack of the service revolver was carried over his head by the wind. He heard the whine of the slug. There were shouts from behind. He saw only the shadowed rocks of the breakwater. If he got there in time, he could still put a bullet in Jake Springer.

The dark water was churning white away from the bow of the fishing boat like a foamy ribbon. The soft sea breeze rustled over the island. The red-lighted buoy bobbed and twisted on the in-rushing tide, its bell a dreary, tolling bong-pause-bong-pause-bong. And above this sound, intermingling, was the coughlike, water-deep chug of the boat. And punctuating these sounds, the hollow pop of the revolver from behind and the angry shouts of the fishermen.

Frankie could not be sure what was happening behind him. He was running between the dunes. The State cops were reacting naturally. A running man was a fugitive and must be stopped. He thought he heard the loud voices of the gathered, curious fishermen telling the police to stop shooting. But he couldn't be sure. The men were certainly confused about what was happening. Perhaps Tosca told them. Then they would call off the police— maybe. But Springer had to be stopped. He was in flight now, racing without plan or reason for the cache of heroin. The million dollars had tipped the balance. Springer had killed Arlene because of it, an act he wouldn't have committed so boldly under other conditions. It was like tossing a special fly over the head of a cautious, clever trout; making the fish break its careful pattern and lunge for the prize. Even Polo had tossed caution aside to go after the lure. And just as a fish goes berserk when it takes the hook, Jake Springer had reverted to the basic animal trait to run and survive. His thinking warped by greed, his sadistic impulses had erupted in the orgy of violence that left Barlow dead and Polo dying and Carazon weeping in the terrifying darkness, the blood running out of his body.

As is always the case when ballooning violence suddenly bursts, cause and effect are alien to the mind. The human being rushes over the brink of reason and the primordial instincts— ever lying in wait—surge to the surface. Attack and kill!

Springer had played his hand for high stakes and he had already lost. His flight was a meaningless gesture. He had killed openly and left witnesses. He had done this without plan or deception—an affront to organized society; and thus society was equipped to punish him for this sin. A beast may roam and devour its prey in secrecy, but when it foams at the mouth and runs amok in the crowd, society clubs it down with a terrible vengeance. When Springer reached the open waters of the bay or ocean, the Coast Guard cutter from Monterey would already be on its way, radar-eyed and bristling with sharp 20 mm. teeth.

But Frankie was still swept up in the reason-numbing chain of events. He heard only the sound of the engine and that sound pistoned his legs, drove him on. His island blood rushed through him, and he knew only that he must kill the man who had killed his father, had degraded and beaten the woman he loved. He threw himself across the top of a dune and lay prone, the gun hand stretched out before him. He watched the progress of the boat.

Springer had put too much sweep into his turn and now his bow was quartered into the running sea. He was fighting the surge, and Frankie knew from experience, the muscle-tearing strain of the rudder cables against the wheel. And he wondered how badly Springer had been wounded. Was he strong enough to handle the wheel with one arm?

The powerful Diesel labored and the stern swung in until the bow was righted and was cleaving into the full force of the racing tide. Springer was headed straight for the breakwater opening. The bow dipped and water exploded over the scuppers, the flung spray a white curtain of flying lace enveloping the wheelhouse.

Frankie leaped to his feet. He ran along the top of the dune, leaped down the far side. He reached the projecting rocks of the breakwater opening. He braced himself in a rock crevice. He steadied the gun with both hands. The water below him smashed into the rocks, leaped up like a thing alive, and covered him. He shuddered under the icy blast. He watched the bow of the boat rising and falling as the sturdy hull breasted the battering onslaught and fought for its head. He was trying to draw a bead on the glass of the wheelhouse, trying to judge where Springer would be standing. But the target was leaping and staggering and salt water smarted his eyes, ran off his face. He cursed the darkness. He shouted an order to the sea to calm itself at once and give him his target. He raged against the elements, his fury dementing him, his frustration bringing him close to tears of anguish.

But the sea had a will of its own. It was a woman; fiendishly, diabolically leaping with playful strides at the toylike boat; dancing in the cool moonlight, lifting gauzelike spindrift from her cold dark belly-depths. Twisting and dipping like a frenzied, passionate nymph, the sea raged against the rocks and boiled away in lunging crosscurrents, embracing the jolting white hull in the crush of her black, liquid thighs.

Few fishermen would dare venture into the boiling maelstrom of the inrushing tide. And Springer was not a man of the sea. He saw only water—an element to be plowed through, as though he were driving through a thundershower. His man-ego dulled his senses to the living power of the sea-woman. But even had he known, he would not have caressed and cajoled the vindictive wench, seeking out her weaknesses. It would be his way to assault her as he was doing.

Frankie saw what was happening and his finger relaxed on the trigger.

While he should have been twisting and turning the wheel to ease the rudder against the sea, Springer was hanging on and plowing straight ahead. The crosscurrents swung the stern.

Frankie watched the bow turn slightly, slowly at first, then swing. A wave leaped against the broadside of the boat, staggering it. The sea danced back. The boat took its head, the engine driving it forward. The bow leaped clear of the water, poised a moment, and came down on the first jagged rock.

The crash was the gut-shattering scream of splintering wood.

Springer's hoarse cry rose above the gleeful, windswept, sea laughter. It was not a cry of terror. It was a bellowing, profane curse.

The stern was lifted and brought down with an agonizing crash.

Frankie stood up to watch. He was conscious of lights and voices behind him, but he didn't turn. He watched the dark figure struggle out of the wheelhouse and stand, clinging to the disintegrating wreckage.

"I'll kill you for this, Cargo! You hear me? I'll kill you for this! I'm the boss here! Me, Jake Springer! And I'll have your ass for this! You won't—"

The wave rose like a shroud. The cold tentacles of dark water grasped Springer and plucked him away.

Frankie's fingers loosened and the gun clattered on the rocks. He felt empty. The release of tension left him exhausted. He was wet and cold and his body shook. He turned from the sea and faced the group of stunned faces. They were fishermen and they watched the boat being torn apart, each harboring his own fear of the sea. Along with his angry God, the fisherman has the sea, the Great Mother who nourishes him and yet punishes with severity. The faces were somber with awe and each man saw his own boat on the rocks. Their lips moved silently. "Hail Mary, Mother of …"

Frankie climbed from the rocks. He walked into the group and they parted to let him pass. They were silent. Tomorrow they would talk, but now they were still in the grip of the violence which had burst around them. Death was too close to them now. The air seemed full of it. The daylight would clear things, and there would be much to say. And then they would only wonder in what way the violence of the night would affect their lives. Frankie walked away from them. He kept to the narrow road that ran along the island.

His shoulders slumped and his head was bowed. The hollowness within him was like a drum-beat. His feet dragged. He was tired, so tired. And he felt unreal. It didn't seem possible that all this had happened. He heard Polo's frightened, pleading voice. He closed his eyes and swallowed hard.

"Frankie."

He stopped and looked up. Tosca was standing in the road before him. She was barefoot. Her face was shadowed, but he could make out the outline of her hair falling over her shoulders. One hand clutched her torn blouse together. He walked and stopped before her. She looked up into his eyes and when she saw the dull pain there she lowered her head and leaned against him.

"It had to happen," she said.

"I know." He closed his arms around her and drew her warmth close to him. He buried his face in the sea-smell of her hair. He remembered the burns of her body and tears welled in his eyes. "Forgive me," he whispered.

"Don't."

"I'll never—"

"No."

"I want to tell you."

"I know what you want to say."

He held her quietly, tightly, wanting her, rejoicing in her. His mind went back to the cannery.

"Did Polo … ?"

"He's dead."

"Poor Polo," he murmured. "All those years. I never knew. He was always the big clown. And like all clowns he hated it. Always on my shirt-tail. When I went into the army he was turned down. I remember his Old Man used to give him that, 'why-can't-you-do-it-like-Frankie-does stuff.' All that hate storing up. And then the chance to be big, really big. Poor Polo."

"It wasn't your fault."

"I don't know. Maybe … maybe I should have seen it when we were kids. It could have been different."

"You thought you were friends."

"No. I just took it for granted that we were friends. I never thought about Polo feeling anything."

"You can't blame yourself."

"It wouldn't do any good anyway."

He pulled her to his side, holding her shoulder with his arm, and started walking.

"I'll have to talk to those State Police."

"They have Springer's gun. And Carazon is alive. He told them what happened."

"Then it's all over," he said.

She twisted in her stride and brought her body up to his, lacing her fingers behind his neck. She pulled his head down until their lips were close. "It's just beginning," she said.

He kissed her with the slow dizzying fervor of a first kiss.

THE END

BUCKS COUNTY
REPORT

For Richard Wormser and Judy with
gratitude and affection

Whenever a book is written about Bucks County, and there are many, the residents take it apart with glee, attempting to recognize their neighbors. I hate to spoil the fun, but all the characters in this book are fictitious, created from whole cloth from my own febrile mind. I write about a certain area of Bucks County only because I lived there and I like to describe physical locations I know. This story could have been placed in any small town. Essentially, it is a long lecture on morality and love and the various aberrations distorting human emotion. That, at least, is what I like to think it is.

S. J.

CHAPTER ONE

A truck passed on Bradley Road, the sound fading away as it crested the hill and dropped down into the valley. Then there was only the sputter and laboring chug of the power mower to break the morning silence.

Sylvia Thompson was standing at the window, idly smoking a cigarette and watching the young man who guided the power mower, when the phone rang. She ignored the ringing, keeping her eyes and her mind on the muscular back of the young man. When the mower reached the end of one of the long terraces which dropped down the width of the lawn to the pool beyond, the young man jerked the handle about and sent it on its return trip.

The phone persisted, and Sylvia grimaced. The young man wore a T-shirt stretched over his wide chest, and faded jeans hugged his narrow waist and thick thighs. He had a square, simian face with a tilted, insolent mouth, and a cropped brush of blonde hair.

When the annoyance of the phone became too great and it was apparent that it was going to keep ringing, Sylvia turned from the window, crossed the room with long-legged strides, and lifted the receiver.

"Hello," she said.

"Sylvia? This is Agatha Kelsey."

Damn, Sylvia thought, what does the dried-up old bitch want? "How are you?" she said.

"Fine," the voice said. "How are *you?*"

"Not so good," Sylvia said. "I'm working up a passion for the kid cutting the grass." It amused her to shock Agatha, and it further amused her to have people refuse to believe the truth merely because it was spoken in a matter-of-fact manner.

"Really, Sylvia!" Agatha Kelsey said, forcing a laugh. "The way you talk sometimes."

Sylvia had sat through her share of card games, coffee klatches and cocktail sessions with the women of Walkers Ferry, and she knew that behind the public facade there lurked the minds and morals of a gang of stevedores. "Oh, crap," she said, eager to give something for Agatha to talk about, "what's on your mind?"

"Sylvia," Agatha chanted, getting a breathless note in her voice which meant that she needed help for some Village Association project, "I have the most exciting news."

"Why don't you call the *Register*," Sylvia said. "They could use some news."

Agatha giggled as Sylvia had known she would. "No, I mean, really. Walkers Ferry is going to go down in history."

"The Russians going to blow it up?"

"Be serious," Agatha said. "You heard about Dr. Ira Wilson."

"The sex nut?"

"Sylvia, please, I'm trying to tell you something. Dr. Wilson is including Walkers Ferry in his study."

"Why?"

"Why?" The clipped question had thrown Agatha.

"Yes, why? What can he learn from this dried up bunch of biddies?"

"Sylvia, please, you're making it difficult. The study is called: *Sex in Suburbia—An American Phenomena*. He has picked Walkers Ferry because it is different, an unusual community."

It suddenly dawned on Sylvia that the phone call was not for mere gossip. As President of the Village Association, Agatha had probably been contacted and asked to line up volunteers for the Wilson interviewers.

"Are you going to be interviewed?" Sylvia asked.

"Of course," Agatha said. "It is my feeling that these surveys are important."

"What's so important about telling a bunch of college professors how many orgasms you have a month?"

"You can't be serious," Agatha said. "I mean, really, these surveys have already done so much to bring women out of the Dark Ages. I mean, we've found out about our inhibitions and all that."

"I found out about inhibitions when I was thirteen," Sylvia said. "That's when I gave them up. Wanta hear about it?"

"Oh, Sylvia!" Agatha seemed on the verge of tears, and Sylvia was becoming bored with the game.

"Okay, Agatha," she said, "what do you want me to do?"

"I thought you might be interviewed."

"Anything for Walkers Ferry," Sylvia said. "Half the town talks about my sex life as it is, I might as well become official. When do the snoopers get here?"

"There's a general meeting at the school gymnasium on Friday morning at nine," Agatha said.

"I'll be there," Sylvia said. She held the receiver a few minutes more until Agatha had gushed her thanks and said a few more things about the historical significance of the survey, then she hung up.

The conversation left her with a feeling of annoyance. Why had she agreed? It had been the easiest way to get Agatha off the phone, she reasoned. Walking to the maple coffee table between the two large sofas, she took a cigarette from a crystal box, lit it with the silver table lighter.

She inhaled deeply, blew the smoke out, then rubbed out the cigarette in the ash tray. It left a bad taste in her mouth. She was getting nervous again. She crossed to the liquor cabinet, half-filled a tumbler with brandy. She took a long, deep drink of the brandy.

Sex, she thought, the story of my miserable life.

Three marriages had left her financially independent at twenty-eight. She had married Harry the year she graduated from Bennington. He was thirty-seven and successful and had been glad to make a handsome cash settlement. Then there was Arthur, and that hadn't lasted very long because of that party and Arthur's brother, but the father had parted with some gilt-edged securities. Then there had been Cal, and she never could understand that one, because she really loved Cal. There had been no reason for the succession of delivery men, the several husbands of friends.

That was when she had gone under analysis, after Cal had called her a 'damned nympho' and had blackened her eye, and broken the mailman's jaw. When the psychiatrist joined her on the couch, she quit going. He wasn't very good, and she objected to paying for it. She told Cal about the psychiatrist, and he moved out the same night.

She had stopped trying to understand it, but she did try to control it. The phone call, for instance, had interrupted her thoughts about the boy mowing the lawn, and she was glad. It wouldn't last, she'd have to have someone soon, but she'd hold out as long as possible. And then she could go to New York and just get someone out of a hotel bar.

She gulped the rest of the brandy and refilled her glass. Then she went up the staircase and into her bedroom. She put the glass down, and removed the silk pajamas.

Standing before a full-length mirror, she scowled. There was the cause of her troubles. She was tall, five-feet-eight, and her body was perfectly proportioned. Except for her breasts. That's what gets them all drooling, she thought. Her breasts were immense. Turning to the side, she viewed her chest in profile with a mixture of anger and pride. Despite their size, she had no need for a brassiere, and the breasts jutted, firmly and proudly;

soft-textured mounds swelling out from her body, and peaked by long, dark nipples.

Looking at herself made her think of Harry, and she had to chuckle. "I don't know why I ever married you," he had said. "You didn't marry *me*," she had answered, "you married a pair of breasts! And anybody damn fool enough to marry a pair of breasts deserves all he gets!" That did it. He had stormed out of the room. It was true, though, that was the irritating part.

Taking a drink of the brandy, Sylvia went into the shower. She let the lukewarm water caress her for several minutes, then switched it to cold and gritted her teeth. She came out of the shower chattering, but her body tingled. She drank the rest of the brandy and toweled herself dry. Then she went to her closet and pulled a white peignoir off a hanger, slipped her arms into the full sleeves and knotted the cord at her waist.

The brass knocker on the front door clacked. She swept out of the room and across the hall to the stairs. She stopped and gripped the railing, suddenly dizzy. Wheeooo, she thought, the booze hit me fast. Steadying herself, she went down the stairs. She felt suddenly warm and drowsy from the brandy, and she promised herself not to drink so fast in the future.

She opened the door and the grass cutter was standing there. He grinned at her, then his eyes dropped to her breasts, the peaks visible under the filmy material. His tongue flicked over his lips and he swallowed hard, jerking his eyes away.

"The lawn's all done, Mrs. Thompson," he said.

"You want to be paid, I guess."

"Yes, M'am, I guess so."

"Come in." Sylvia stepped back from the door and he entered, standing just inside the room. She closed the door and walked away from him. She stopped at the sideboard, opening her purse. Her hands were fidgeting, and she felt the warm sensation begin to spread up through her body. She fumbled with the purse.

He was even bigger than he appeared from the window. He looked like a college football player, and now his eyes harbored excitement.

"What's your name?" she asked.

"Sam Stafford."

"You live around here?"

"No, M'am," he said, shifting on his feet and taking a breath to expand his chest. "I live in Dunkerville."

"Have a drink?" she asked.

"No, thanks, I don't drink."

"No vices?"

"I smoke," he said, smiling.

"That's all?"

He grinned, and suddenly he took on the look of confidence, his eyes narrowing just slightly.

"How much is it?" Sylvia asked.

"Four dollars."

She took the money and crossed the room. She handed it to him. He stuffed it into a pocket of the tight jeans, but he did not move.

"Kiss me," Sylvia said.

He kissed her in a clumsy way, then stepped back, gasping. "Whew!" he said.

"You must have hard hands," Sylvia said. She reached out, took his wrist, turned the hand over and ran a finger over his calloused palm. She lifted his hand and slipped it inside the peignoir, rubbing the fingers over her breast. She felt him tremble.

Pulling the cord at her waist, she let the peignoir fall open. He caught his breath at the sight of her. The warm, prickling sensation was tearing at her, and she pulled him to the sofa. Grinding herself against him, she kissed him hard, arousing him.

He pushed her over, his fingers clawing at his belt.

I've got to stop this, she thought as the eager hunger subsided. *Somehow, I've got to stop this!*

CHAPTER TWO

I t was 9:43 a.m. on June 12th, a Monday morning when Sam Stafford struggled back to his feet, feeling somehow confused and ill-used by the woman on the sofa, who was now completely bored with him. But it was something for him to talk about all summer.

Harley Wayne, a guard on the bridge over the Delaware River which connected Walkers Ferry on the Pennsylvania side to Ferryville on the New Jersey side, noted that the traffic was heavy for a Monday morning, and predicted a heavy tourist traffic for the summer.

At that precise moment at least a dozen people in Walkers Ferry said, "Nice day, but you never can tell. We might get some more snow," and whoever they said it to answered, "I think we had our share."

The sun slanted down over the village which was snuggled in against the hills rolling up from the riverbank, and shafted fat pillars of light through the tall elms and thick, gnarled oak trees.

Walkers Ferry was quaint. It hadn't meant to be in the beginning, it just got that way. In the beginning it had just been the place where the ferry landed. The stage from Flemington crossed there and had rattled off along the rutted York Road to Philadelphia. There was shad running in the river in those old days, and clusters of fisherman's shacks had lined the river bank, and nets dried in the sun. And there were the quarries a short distance up the river where the stone was hammered out for

Philadelphia's cobbled streets. And there was Hoagland's Mill along the river. And damn little else.

But people built houses. Workers at the Mill. Fishermen who figured to stay and raise families. They built the houses themselves of native stone, solid, thick-walled Colonial houses. They built them wherever it suited them, and just left it up to nature for the roads to get around to passing their front doors.

George Washington came along with his bedraggled Army and camped there before the Battle of Trenton.

In time the ferry was replaced by a covered bridge and Walkers Ferry began to take on the appearance of a town. The automobile came, and paved streets followed. But Walkers Ferry was such a hodge-podge of planless thoroughfares it would have been impossible for the road planners to straighten it out, so they paved the narrow, crooked streets, and Walkers Ferry became quaint.

It still wasn't much of a town. Lying there along the river, with the rolling hills of southeastern Pennsylvania embracing it on every side, it had a beauty of quiet dignity.

Some artists found it in the Twenties. It was a quiet place to paint, it was inexpensive, and the narrow little streets and stone houses made excellent subjects for their canvases. And artists are like mice. Let one in and you're soon overrun. Then came the writers and the photographers. Walkers Ferry began to appear in the national magazines.

Walkers Ferry was just 60 miles from New York City, and when it became fashionable to live in the country, and the new radio industry was burgeoning, and advertising was a new trade, the place to live was Bucks County, and the capitol of Bucks County happened to be Walkers Ferry. Houses valued at six hundred dollars went up to six thousand and up and up.

Farmers sold out to the newcomers at fantastic prices, then moved into town and opened hardware stores, lumber yards, grocery stores; and became carpenters and plumbers and stonemasons, to supply and rebuild the houses they had sold.

Chet Parker's father had become a contractor and Chet worked for him as a carpenter, and he was now working on the house in which he had been born. He was in the basement where his mother had stored the home-canned vegetables, and where he had first learned the taste of a cigarette. But now it was a "family room" and Chet was nailing white perforated celotex on the ceiling.

A playwright had first bought the house from Chet's father, and had started the remodeling. A few failures and he went off to Hollywood, selling the house to a radio actor with a yen for young men and a need for seclusion. There was more remodeling, but one day the actor's current companion ran off with a burly ballet dancer, and in a show of grief, the actor decreed never to enter the love-nest again. He sold out cheap to an artist who struck it rich and moved to Europe, selling to the current occupants, Brad Pennington, his wife and daughter.

Brad Pennington was copy chief for a major New York advertising agency. He left the house at seven in the morning for the forty minute drive to the Penn Station in Trenton where he caught an express from Philadelphia and got into New York by nine. He arrived home again at seven each night, except some nights, and then he usually stayed in a New York hotel. These nights had been seldom in the beginning, but they became more frequent, and in the past year Brad Pennington had spent more time in New York than he had in Bucks County.

Chet Parker knew this because he had been working on the house for the past three months, and he wondered how Elizabeth Pennington was taking it.

Standing on the stepladder, leaning back to hammer the nails into the square of celotex, Chet wondered what Elizabeth Pennington was doing at that moment. Probably back in bed, he thought. He knew the bedroom. He had been born there. Of course it was different now, but he knew the house. He could imagine her sprawled out in the big bed, her chestnut hair spilling over the white pillow, her long-legged body mounded in gentle rises under the light cover.

Chet had worked for a lot of these newcomers, had known a lot of the wives. The week, for instance, that he had spent building a breezeway for that Sylvia Thompson. Geezus! He stopped hammering at the thought. Now that one was something. Those fantastic breasts on her, and she could go day and night. It had been almost frightening with that female, but the thing that amused him was that he had been getting three-fifty an hour all the time. But of all the women, this Pennington dame was the real stuff. It made him tingle to think about her, and he had to force himself to go back to the hammering.

Upstairs, sitting at the kitchen table with a cup of coffee before her, Elizabeth Pennington stared out through the window, a troubled expression marring the beauty of her face.

The phone call from Agatha Kelsey had started it, or rather it had brought up the fact that she had to do something about Debbie. It had made her start thinking about sex again and male-female relationships, and what was right or wrong, and she had been over and over that all night. This was coupled with her annoyance with herself for agreeing to participate in the damn Wilson interviews. Her response had been automatic, a result of wanting to participate in community activities, feeling that it was her duty to accept chores pushed upon her by Agatha for the Village Association. Now that she had time to consider it, she didn't see where the Wilson Reports had anything to do with the community or herself.

But it had brought up this other thing again, and she didn't know how to handle it. Damn Brad for not being home. But then she couldn't tell him anyway, because she knew he would be unreasonable about the whole thing. But damn him anyway for staying in New York!

She heard footsteps on the stairs and knew that it was Debbie. She was suddenly nervous. Calm yourself, she thought, we'll just talk this thing out and nothing will come of it. But she knew that she had to be careful, because she did not want to alienate her daughter.

"Hi." Debbie came into the kitchen.

"Morning," Elizabeth said. The tension was broken and she felt sure of herself and a bit foolish for her temerity. After all, this was her daughter. They were close, and there were no secrets between them.

Debbie went to the refrigerator and opened the door, and Elizabeth watched her.

"What time did Carl go home last night?" Elizabeth asked.

Debbie turned, slamming the door and bringing the orange juice to the table. She wore white shorts and a gray print blouse. At sixteen her body was almost fully developed, a youthful replica of Elizabeth's womanliness. The young breasts were high and conical, pressing out taut against the fabric of the blouse. Her waist was narrow and the line of her hips was an easy curve. Her stomach was flat and her long legs tapered to delicate ankles and small feet. Her shoulder-length hair had a reddish tint; Elizabeth's was longer and fell down the hollow of her back. Debbie's brown eyes were larger and there was a sprinkling of freckles over the bridge of the small nose. She sat at the table and poured the juice into a glass.

"I don't know," she said to Elizabeth's question. "Why?"

Was there a note of belligerence in her voice? Elizabeth felt that she had to be careful, had to say it right. Then the thought angered her. My God, she reasoned, this is my daughter. Why am I afraid of what she might think? But the fear still nagged. When Debbie was a small child Elizabeth had determined that she would be a friend to the girl as she grew. But lately it had grown more and more difficult.

"It ... it seemed rather late," Elizabeth said.

Debbie shrugged, but said nothing. She turned her gaze to the window and finished the orange juice. She got up from the chair. "Okay if I take the Volkswagen?" she asked. "I told Marilyn I'd come over and swim today."

"I want to talk to you a minute," Elizabeth said.

Debbie had turned to leave the kitchen and now she stopped and faced her Mother, one eyebrow arched inquisitively. "About what?"

"About Carl," Elizabeth said.

Debbie seemed to brace herself defiantly. "If this is a lecture about being too young to be serious with a boy," she said, "you can save the time. I'm not serious."

A sudden anger swept Elizabeth and she said, "After what I saw last night it might be better if you were serious."

Debbie caught her breath. "What!"

"You and Carl," Elizabeth said, now confused. It wasn't the way she wanted the conversation to go.

"Because we were necking on the sofa?"

"I don't like that expression," Elizabeth said. "And it was a lot more than necking."

Debbie's face reddened as the anger rose in her, stilting her voice. "Are you in the habit of spying?"

"I don't have to spy in my own house," Elizabeth said.

"I thought it was my house, too."

"It is." Elizabeth had the feeling that the conversation had gone wrong. "And that is beside the point."

"We didn't do anything wrong," Debbie said.

"Wrong! What do you call wrong? I came to the head of the stairs and you were spread out on the sofa like a cat in heat."

"Talk about expressions!"

"It fits!" Elizabeth was fighting to control her anger. "What must you think of yourself to let a boy touch you like that?"

"Good Lord, Mother, all the girls do it! It's petting. Don't you read? It's supposed to be good for the emotional balance. We don't go all the way."

"You mean just anyone can come along and slip his hand up your dress? How do you do, Miss, nice day, my, don't you feel nice!"

Debbie giggled and it broke the tension between them. "It's not like *that*," Debbie said. "My gosh, Mother, didn't you do anything when you were my age?"

Elizabeth felt herself flush, and for an instant she remembered the Harbison boy and the night they went to the darkened football stadium. She had been frightened, but she knew why he was taking her there, and she wanted it too. But when it had happened, the awful pain, and his terrible joke—had left her with a feeling of loathing. She had been fifteen, and she hadn't done it again until she was in college. But then it had been wonderful, and Hugh Bascomb had been her biology instructor, and—but that was a long time ago, and she brought herself back to the present.

"We used more control," Elizabeth said.

"Didn't you ever wonder what it felt like to have a man touch you there?"

I nearly went crazy thinking about it, Elizabeth thought, but she said, "That can only lead to serious trouble."

"Not if you're careful. You have to know how to make them stop."

"And suppose you don't want them to stop? I tell you, Debbie, I don't want this sort of thing to go on. I'm afraid I'll have to take it up with your father."

Debbie's eyes widened and the spark of fear appeared in their depths. Her voice was small. "You wouldn't," she said.

"Well, if you don't think there's anything wrong with it, I don't see why you'd mind."

"But not Daddy," she said. "He just wouldn't understand."

"Very well," Elizabeth said, feeling that she had managed to surmount the problem, "but it better not happen again."

"Okay," Debbie said, "but don't be surprised if I break out in pimples." She left the kitchen.

Elizabeth sighed deeply as she heard the front door open and close, but she felt nervous, and it was a feeling she knew well. She used to get it when she'd sit in class and Hugh would be explaining the anatomy of the human body. She would want his hands on her, and the surface of her flesh would seem to be hot. It had always been that way with Brad, and sometimes at parties she would whisper in his ear what she was feeling, and he would chuckle and whisper back that she was a sex maniac. But he would always take her right home, and those were the times when it was the best. The discussion with Debbie had left her feeling that way, and it also had a lot to do with Brad, and the way he was always tired lately. And last week when he had her almost screaming, she was so on edge, he hadn't been able to do anything.

Think about something else, she said to herself. Her thoughts turned to the phone call from Agatha Kelsey, and the Wilson interviews. Sex again! Damn it, she thought, can't you think about anything else? Annoyed, she decided to take a cold shower.

Chet Parker heard Debbie leave the house. He stopped hammering and listened until the sound of the Volkswagen faded away.

He ran his tongue over his lips, making up his mind. If there was one thing that Chet felt he knew about, it was women, and he was damn near sure about this one. He was 28, married with three children, and he was reputed to be quite a local stud.

"I must be part animal," he would tell the drinkers at Kelker's Bar, "because I can always tell when a female wants it. It's as though they have a scent."

He had the scent now, but he was nervous. He knew that he was alone in the house with Elizabeth Pennington, and he had that feeling about her. But she wasn't something ordinary. This was a woman with class, real class. If it turned out he was wrong, he could really have his butt in a sling.

When he heard the creak of the stairs, and knew that she was going up, he put down the hammer and climbed off the step ladder. He was big and rangy with a long, heavy-jawed face. He wore tight levies and a white T-shirt because he knew it accentuated the broad muscular chest, the narrow waist and the powerful legs. His virility was his vanity and he liked to show it.

Taking a deep breath, he squared his shoulders and went up the stairs and into the carpeted living room. He stopped and stared at the stairs running to the second floor. He could stop now, go back to work. But he was determined. He went to the stairs and climbed. He reached the landing and turned to the right. His heart was beating harder and his jaw was set. The bedroom door was ajar.

He walked along the hall, the carpet muffling his steps. He smiled and his confidence swelled as he leaned against the door jamb.

Elizabeth Pennington was unaware of his presence. She sat on the stool by her dressing table. Her nightgown was open down the front. He let his eyes run over her. Up the long legs, over the soft swell of her stomach. Her eyes were closed. She held her breasts in her hands and when her fingers pressed, she grimaced with pleasurable pain.

"A man could do that better," Chet said.

Elizabeth gasped with surprise. Her head snapped around, and her wild eyes fixed on him with disbelief. Her hands grasped the filmy nightgown and she pulled it around her. Her stunned surprise turned to anger. "What do you want?"

"Just looking." There was insolence in his voice.

"Well, you've seen enough. Suppose you get back to your work."

"You sure you want me to leave?"

"Are you crazy?" Elizabeth was on her feet. "I think you better get out of that doorway in the next minute, and get the hell downstairs, or I'll call your boss!"

"I sort of had the feeling you could use a good man." He did not move and the smile stayed on his face.

This can't be happening, Elizabeth thought. She had heard about this sort of thing, and she had heard plenty of stories about Chet, but it couldn't be happening to her. But now the burning sensation was even stronger, and she couldn't take her eyes off him.

"You sure are beautiful," Chet said.

"How dare you talk to me like that!"

"It's a fact," he said.

"Get out of here!"

"I never in my life saw a woman who wanted it so bad," he said.

She gritted her teeth and swore to herself. Damn you, Brad, why did you leave me like this? It's your fault. You know I need it. Damn, damn, why aren't you a husband? Her nerves jumped. She wanted hands on her breasts. Hard hands. Anyone's hands, but not her own.

"I could scream," she said.

"But you won't."

The sonofabitch, she thought, he's treating me like some cheap whore. But that's how I feel. Oh my God, I can't stand this.

He pushed away from the door jamb and came into the room. She stiffened, but she did not move and she did not cry out. Her breath was tight in her throat. He stopped a foot from her. His left hand came up and closed over one breast. Her body shuddered, and a soft moan escaped her lips. He moved to encircle her with his arms, but she pulled away.

"I don't want you to kiss me," she said.

He slipped behind her. His arms went around her, his two large hands joining on the swell of her stomach. He pulled her back against him. He ran his hands down, then drew them up slowly until he cupped her hard full breasts, squeezing them between his thumb and finger.

She squirmed, grinding her teeth against the maddening feeling that was surging through her body. "My God," she gasped, "I can't stand it!"

He released her and she moved away from him. She went to the bed, not looking at him. She could hear him removing the T-shirt. She heard his shoes clump on the floor, and she turned to see him pull the jeans off his legs.

Slipping the nightgown from her arms, she crawled onto the high bed. He came to her, lying next to her, running his hands over her until she shook her head.

When it was over he threw himself on his back. "Whew!" he said. "You're really something."

She regained her breathing and turned her head to look at him. He made her want to retch, and she hated him. She swung her legs off the bed, stooped to retrieve her gown, then padded across the rug to the bathroom. She stopped in the doorway and turned.

"You can get out now," she said coldly.

"What?" Chet sat up, surprised.

"You got what you came after," she said, "now get out."

"Are you kidding? You needed that, Baby."

"That's right," she said, evenly. "I needed it. But I'm no baby. I'm 36 years old, and I don't need it now. I'll thank you to get the hell off that bed and then get off this property as soon as you can gather your tools together."

"Are you trying to say you didn't like it?"

"I'm only saying I want you to leave."

"You liked it, though."

"If it helps your ego any," she said, "you have the prowess of a young bull."

He smiled. "When you want it again just..."

She cut him off. "The only reason I would want you near me again is because I couldn't find a com cob." She had to force herself to say that, but it had the effect she desired. His face fell, the smile gone. "Now get out!" She went into the bathroom, and locked the door.

Leaning on the sink, she stared at her face in the mirror. God, she thought, he *was* good. But it wasn't going to happen again. It made her shudder to think of Brad finding out. My God, that would be the end of everything. She would have to think up a reason for changing carpenters. He'd want to know why, because he had hired Chet Parker himself. She felt the pangs of guilt, and this angered her. Damn him, she thought, if he'd stay home and be a husband it would never have happened. He knows how I get.

She sat on the edge of the bathtub and waited, giving Chet sufficient time to get dressed. She'd pick the next carpenter herself, a nice, old man.

CHAPTER THREE

For a town known for its creativity, Walkers Ferry used no imagination whatsoever in the naming of its streets. There is, of course, Main Street. This is the black-topped road that winds along the Pennsylvania bank of the Delaware River running from Easton in the north to the flat sprawl of Levittown in the south. There is a point where the road becomes Main Street. It curls into the channel of neat white houses with porches and rockers and squares of trimmed lawn. It passes through the two blocks of business establishments: the drug store, the bank, the cleaners, Haber's newsstand, the Chevy agency, the Ferry Inn, the Co-op, the Walkers Ferry Playhouse. It passes over the mill-run, passes Mel's Coffee House, disappears around a corner and becomes River Road again.

The street that comes in from Philadelphia is Route 202 until it suddenly becomes Bridge Street and swoops down the hill, past the post-office and the line of tourist shops, and runs into the bridge. Where John Derry's old stone house stands in named Derry Street. The road running along the old Easton Canal, which cuts the town in half, is called Canal Street. Where the artisans used to have their shops, and where tourists now gather to oggle in windows at the most god-awful collection of high-priced bric-a-brac ever seen, is called Mechanic Street. There are others, about a dozen in all.

Walkers Ferry is a small town, population one thousand. This, of course, does not include the residents beyond the town limit, who live in what is known as the Township. In the Township are the homes of the wealthy, the large fieldstone farmhouses where George Washington is reputed to have slept.

Millie Gerhardt, chief reporter and critic for the Walkers Ferry *Register,* once said: "Isn't it curious that nobody seems to realize that Martha was with George all that time. Everybody in the Township is trying to sleep in more houses than George did, and he was probably the last one around here to shack up with his own wife."

While this was not exactly accurate, it was not without more than a grain of truth, and it was a typical Millie Gerhardt comment. And she would know.

Millie was a copywriter in a New York advertising agency when she first came to Walkers Ferry as the weekend guest of an amorous vice-president. Even then she was more than a match for the average male, and she stayed on as the vice-president's wife. When he gave up the ghost, some say in self-defense, Millie gathered up the stocks and bonds, sold the house in the Township at an enormous profit and moved into town, taking an apartment over the post-office.

At 48, she still had the body for a tight sweater and skirt. "Hell," she would say, "I've had so many passes made at me since I passed 46 that I feel like an aging halfback." Her face had become more femininely handsome and appealing with age.

Her mind was as sharp as her wit, and she had the faculty to dissect the community from stem to stern with an x-ray eye. She liked to rail against what she considered phoney and battle for something she believed in. That was why she wrote for the *Register.* And because she was outspoken and usually right, she had few friends. But her one concrete friendship was with Knox Martin, editor of the weekly newspaper.

On this Monday morning she was slouched in the wooden captain's chair facing the padded swivel which held the spare, angular body of Knox Martin. The steel gray of their hair was the only similarity between the two. Millie was fastidious in her dress. She wore a tweed suit and a cashmere sweater, and even her casual slouch could not detract from the tailored appearance. Knox, on the other hand, was as tousled as a school-boy. He had a long, horse-like face with blue, sorrowful eyes. His hair seemed untouched by a comb. His arms were long, sticking out of his shirt, and they had hands on the ends like spades. He wore rumpled khaki trousers and a pair of heavy, worn brogans on his feet. He had once written a good novel which did not sell, and a bad novel which did. He had bought the newspaper outright with the proceeds of the latter, and had thoroughly enjoyed life ever since. He had the intelligence to appreciate Millie, and together they rode herd on the town's conscience.

The advertising salesman who worked on a fifty-dollar draw and commission was making his rounds, and the girl who did the office work and acted as receptionist was off on an errand.

"Sex," Knox Martin was saying as he stuffed tobacco into his over-sized pipe, "should be relegated to its proper place in society."

"And what is that?" Millie asked, raising an eyebrow.

"It should be treated for what it is. A human function. It doesn't deserve all this publicity."

"I don't know," Millie said. "You certainly didn't miss a trick when Chief Marlowe nabbed those two pansies in the back seat of their car that time."

"That was news," Knox said.

"You wrote it for a laugh and it was sex," Millie said.

"But this is different," Knox said. "This is just straight everyday sex, and these people are distorting it out of shape. I'm not saying it isn't important, but it should be treated the same as any other bodily function like, well, eating."

"Three times a day! My God, Martin, you're a damned satyr!"

Millie laughed hard and Knox screwed his long, homely face into a grin.

When Millie stopped laughing she became serious and said, "Kidding aside, I think you're wrong. This sex thing is a problem. There are too many people goofed up over it."

"That's just it!" Knox exclaimed. "People worry about it. They've made it into some sacred rite. They've made their lives dependent on it."

"That's not the point," Millie said. "You talk as though its something to turn on and off. Hell, it's not just a bounce in the hay."

"What is it then?"

"Oh, brother! If I didn't know you, Martin, I'd swear you were angling for a demonstration. But I'll tell you. Sex with a woman can be the basis for her whole existence. It may be wham-bam-thank-you-ma'am with a male, but the female feels the need and the fulfillment of the sex urge in every fibre of her body."

"But what in hell's name can these surveys do about that?"

"Plenty. When a woman feels something this strongly and all her life she's been told its unnatural or abnormal or indecent, she begins to worry. Some of them get so panicky over the idea that they're latent harlots that they become frigid. These surveys at least show them that they're not alone in feeling the way they do."

Knox puffed on his pipe thoughtfully. "Well," he said, "I'll admit that the Kinsey people are damned sincere in what they do, and they probably do some good with their publications. But this Wilson, now, I can't buy."

"Agatha Kelsey ought to hear that."

"I mean it. I think this Wilson is a fraud."

"Poor Agatha."

Knox squinted his eyes and pointed with the stem of his pipe. "Are you going to be interviewed?"

"Me? You must be out of your mind. My sex life is perfectly adjusted."

"I thought you were a widow?"

"You know damn well I'm a widow and that's what I've adjusted to."

"Don't get angry. Just a question." Knox chuckled and leaned back. "Can't you just see the interviewer with Bertha van Eckman." He changed the tone of his voice. " 'Now then, Madam, do you prefer to look at dirty pictures before or after intercourse?' "

"That's not what they call it nowadays," Millie said.

Knox raised his shaggy brows. "I'll have you know we're a family newspaper," he said.

"It's called coitus."

"I'll be damned," Knox said with feigned amazement. "When I was a kid they called it ..."

"Boffing," Millie said.

"Nope," Knox said, grinning, "it was jazzing."

"Different neighborhood," Millie said.

Knox leaned forward and winked. "Say, old girl, since we're on the subject, why don't we just lock the door—"

"And jazz a little?"

"Boff a little."

"You're a dirty old man, Martin."

"It's in the interest of science."

"Says you."

"Says Dr. Wilson."

"Hah! Look, Martin," Millie said, "do you want me to do a story on this thing or not? I got more to do then trade dirty jokes with old men."

"Millie, my girl, I think that this deserves the deft editorial touch of Knox Martin. The sex habits of Walkers Ferry shall be approached by the mature mind."

A blonde teen-aged girl passed the large window facing Main Street. She wore a light sweater accentuating her young pointed breasts, and tight Bermuda shorts. Her legs were long and tanned. Knox turned his head to watch her pass. "I wonder what they feed these kids?" he asked.

"The mature mind!" Millie rose from the chair and took up her leather purse. "I can see you under the window at Town Hall listening to the interviews."

"In the interest of science."

"I hope they catch you." Millie crossed the office floor. "Have fun. Write it nice." She pushed through the door and was gone.

Knox watched her pass the window, the smile still on his face, then he turned back to his desk and his long brow washboarded. He lifted the press releases pertaining to the Wilson Report. He scanned the printed pages, then dropped them and pushed them away. What would he write about Dr. Ira Wilson? He knew what he should write. He should take the press material supplied by Agatha Kelsey and prepare a simple story for page one that Walkers Ferry was to be honored by a group of scientists intent on adding the intimate details of the suburban ladies sex lives to the mass of material being gathered to release American womanhood from historical prejudices and fears. This would be fine, but Knox did not believe it. He was ready to admit that Havelock Ellis had been an honest and dedicated man, and his *Psychology of Sex* made fascinating reading. He also gave credit to the legitimacy of Kraft-Ebbing, and there was no doubt that the Kinsey organization was honestly trying to discover patterns of human behavior in their surveys. But Wilson was a cat of another stripe. For one thing, Wilson got too much publicity, and most of it smacked of clever press agentry. Knox did not feel that the popular magazines were the place to publish scientific findings. Wilson went after the sensational, just like picking on Walkers Ferry for his interviews. The town was known from coast-to-coast as the hub of a cultural center, a hangout for oddballs. He turned to the papers and glanced at the title of the Wilson survey. *Sex In Suburbia—An American Phenomena.* He wondered what circulation-minded magazine editor had picked that title.

Ira Wilson, Knox knew, specialized in the sensational. The Kinsey people were always trying for a true cross-section of people in their interviews. They had developed a secret method of selection. Not Wilson. He came out in the papers asking for subjects, and it was no surprise that he got a pack of exhibitionists eager to give the details of their life in bed. This, Knox felt, was not only without weight scientifically, it was detrimental if the housewife in Des Moines, Iowa, felt that there was something wrong with her after reading that the "average" housewife had affairs with the butcher, the baker, the candlestick maker.

Knox chuckled and rubbed his chin. Well, he thought, maybe the candlestick maker is a little too Freudian.

He was tempted to turn to the typewriter and voice these opinions in an editorial, but he knew that he would not. There was a better way. He would interview Wilson when he arrived, and he would follow the progress of the interviews. If the man was a fraud, and he was certain he was, it would show in a good deep interview.

Turning to the typewriter, he ran a sheet of yellow paper into the machine. He stopped to scratch his head. Between Wilson and these Bermuda shorts, he thought, a virgin over sixteen will soon be an oddity. He hunched his shoulders over the machine and the big hands began to rattle the keys.

In the living room of the stucco house at the end of Kerwin Drive, Cora Masserly stood with her back to the fireplace, her arms folded. A slender woman of average height, she wore a light summer dress. Her face, though not pretty, was attractive, despite the present look of annoyance. Her hair was black and cut close to her head. There was a sharpness to her features which Sam Masserly had taken as a sign of ascetic intellectuality when he was courting her. It had turned out that it was merely an outward sign of her personality.

Cora tapped her foot impatiently, then she crossed the room, went through the dining room and stopped before the open door of the downstairs bathroom. Sam was standing before the mirror, running a razor over his chin.

"It doesn't make sense," Cora said. "You were planning on studying for your Masters this summer at Penn, and all of a sudden you've decided to teach the summer term. It just doesn't make sense. You'll be teaching one course. Two hours a day. It's ridiculous!"

Sam grunted, but did not answer. It was plain that he had made up his mind and had no intention of changing it, and this infuriated Cora. It wasn't like him to defy her this way.

"Why?" she asked.

Sam lowered the razor and turned from the mirror. He had an intent, serious face, made more so by horn-rimmed glasses, a face befitting his position as instructor of English at Barrows College. He lifted his shoulders slightly in a small shrug. "I decided I'd rather teach," he said in his mild voice.

"Just like that." Cora spoke sharply, nodding her head. "Toss the Master's Degree out the window."

"I've got plenty of time to get a Masters," he said.

"And in the meantime I continue to pinch pennies on your instructor's salary." To Cora the Master's Degree meant a job at State College or better. It meant more money, a chance to climb the social ladder. She had planned on it, just as she had planned everything in their five years of marriage and she did not enjoy the note of rebellion.

Sam continued to shave, and to Cora it seemed that he was deliberately trying to ignore her.

"I'll be damned if I know what you see in Barrows College," she said. "You'd be content to stay there forever."

"It's a good school," Sam said.

"It's a dead-end," Cora said. "Teaching the regular session is one thing. It's a job. But I don't figure this summer session at all."

"Well," Sam said, "it's too late now. I'm signed up for it. I can't back out."

"And I don't understand why I wasn't consulted before you signed the contract," Cora said.

When Sam did not answer, her lips froze in a tight, thin line. She turned from the doorway and walked away. The mixture of anger and frustration was great in her, and behind it was a tinge of fear. Sam's sudden fling at independence upset the orderliness of her existence. It was disconcerting.

Cora had no illusions about Sam's talents or aggressiveness. He was complacent and he was mediocre. She had met him at a Writer's Conference. He was there to attend a poetry symposium. He had ambitions to write. Cora was there looking for a husband. She had ambitions too, but it was to be the wife of a college professor. She knew the path to her goal, and the first thing she needed was the potential professor. She was attractive, she had read a great deal of poetry and criticism. When she met Sam, it was obvious that he was attracted. He was the type she could bend to her will, and she lured him with the pretention of deep interest in his writing.

They were married two months later in the small up-state town where Cora's father was a chalk-smeared high school teacher, a position she loathed.

The honeymoon was abhorrent to her, but it taught her the power of her body. Within a month she had tamed Sam's animal instincts, and he came to her only at her bidding. The whole business of sex was revolting to her, but she did delight in using it as a reward when Sam did as he was told.

Standing again in the living room, Cora wondered where she had slipped. There was something wrong. Of course, there was a way to remedy things. It might not be too late.

She crossed the room briskly and climbed the stairs to the second floor. Entering her bedroom—separated from Sam's by a locked door—she drew her dress over her head and dropped it on the bed. She removed her underclothing and stood nude over her dressing table. It was a slight, but lithesome body. Her breasts were small, evenly moulded and firm. She reached for perfume, dabbed her fingertips and rubbed the scent over the breasts. Going to the closet, she brought out a filmy white gown. She slipped it on, then went to her bed and pulled down the covers.

Sitting on the edge of the bed, she fluffed out her hair, then crossed her legs and arranged the folds of the gown to show the white of her thighs. She had to wait for Sam to finish shaving. It annoyed her, but it had been at her insistence that he use the downstairs bathroom.

When she heard him come up the stairs she took a deep breath and wet her lips. As he passed her door she called in a soft voice, "Sam?"

"Uh?" He stopped. He appeared in her doorway and stared at her.

"Are you in a hurry?" she asked, tilting her head and trying the winsome smile that always worked with him.

There was a long moment of silence. Sam's tongue flicked over his lips and he breathed deeply. "Well, as a matter of fact, I am," he said. "You going back to bed? Do you have a headache or something?"

Rebuffed, she was overwhelmed with confusion. It was a little like having the wind knocked out of her. Unable to say anything, she swung her legs onto the bed and fell back against the pillow. Instantly she recovered. She held her arms out. "Come here, Sam," she said, "I want you."

Sam chuckled. "I'll have to admit its an inviting thought," he said, "but I really don't have time." He stepped back from the doorway and went on to his own room.

Cora knotted her fists and bit her lip to suppress the scream of anger that was in her throat. She held her body rigid until she shook. This had never happened before! Swinging off the bed she stalked to the door and slammed it shut. She stood there a moment, seething, then she went back to the bed and sat. She felt foolish. But maybe he really was in a hurry. With his doltish lack of imagination it would be like him to not realize anything. At least he would know she was angry. Let him sweat it out all day. She could act peevish at dinner, and she'd make him come to her in the evening. That would do it.

She waited until she heard him leave the house, then she got up from the bed and dressed again. There were a few errands to do, then she remembered that she had promised to have lunch with Marcia Storm. This annoyed her because she really didn't like Marcia, but the girl seemed so anxious for her company that it was impossible to refuse. She checked her wristwatch. There was plenty of time.

Beverly Merrick stalked into the kitchen. Her face was flushed with anger and she had her hands clenched until the knuckles were white. Her mother sat at the large round maple table at one end of the large Early American room.

Going straight to the table, Beverly gripped the edge. She spoke in a tight, clipped voice. "Mother," she said, "I'm telling you for the last time to keep that man out of my room."

Claire Roberts took a quick breath and looked up with surprise. At first glance she was a startlingly beautiful woman, but on closer scrutiny the eye penetrated the cover of make-up and the forty-six years were visible. The face was a mask, the vanity of the one-time actress. Claire viewed her daughter's anger with a mixture of dismay and fear. She loved this child of her first marriage, but she knew Mike's lusts, and she feared the girl's youth.

"Whatever do you mean, child?" Claire asked.

"Look, Mother," Beverly said, "that wide-eyed innocent look might have looked grand on the screen, but this isn't fiction. If you want to be married to that big idiot, that's your business. But I can't get dressed or undressed without him standing around watching, and I don't like it."

"I'm sure you're exaggerating," Claire said.

Beverly closed her eyes and took a deep breath. She stood away from the table. She opened her eyes. "Mother. Your husband is doing his best to seduce your daughter. Doesn't that mean anything to you?"

"Bev!" Claire lurched to her feet. "I won't have that sort of talk in this house! How dare you suggest such a thing?"

Beverly swung away from the table. She walked to the center of the room and spun about. "Look at me," she said. "I'm not a little girl. I'm twenty years old. I'm a woman."

Claire looked at the fully-developed girl, and her lips trembled. Her breasts jutted against the fabric of the print blouse. The line of her body swept down to the narrow waist, then flared out over her full hips and long legs. It was a sensuous body.

"You never did like Mike," Claire said, attempting to cover the truth that was within her nagging at the small flame of jealousy. "You were hurt when I married him."

"For God's sake, Mother, talk sense. I got over that sort of thing with your third husband. I admit I don't like him, but not for the reasons you think. He's no damn good, that's why I don't like him."

"Bev! I won't have that!"

"All right! Think whatever you like. I ask only one thing. I want him to stay away from me. If he doesn't then I'm going to move into the dorm at school."

"Now, honey." Claire started around the table, but Beverly turned and walked quickly to the door. "Honey, your breakfast."

"I'll eat in town." She opened the door, went out and closed it after her.

Claire was left standing in the middle of the room. She wrung her hands. Why hadn't Beverly taken that trip to Europe like she wanted her to. It would have been so nice, but she had insisted on taking the summer course. It was nice to have her home, of course, nice that she had chosen to attend Barrows

College, which was so close, but now, right now, with Mike—well, it might have been better.

She was afraid. She stared at her hands. No matter how much hand cream you used, the age showed there. Her life had been built on one thing—beauty. As Claire Carlyle she had been Miss Texas. After that it had been the modeling jobs, and the screen test, and the bit parts in films. My God, she thought, how long ago that was. She had everything then. The beauty, the youth. Men were nothing to her then, because there were always so many. Well, she wouldn't say they didn't mean anything. There always had to be a man. God, she would die without a man. And then there were better parts for her, and although she never became a star, she was well known. There were the marriages. Mark Merrick was the first one, and Beverly had been born, and then divorce. And the others. It got worse with the years, but at least she had enough sense not to marry any more actors like Mark. She had the beauty and the youth, and it was enough for the owner of a hotel chain, a corporation lawyer, and an oilman. She was wealthy. But she was also forty-six, and Mike Roberts was thirty-seven. He was a man, God, he was a man. She knew that he had married her for her money, but he gave her what she needed, and she was afraid to lose it.

But she was afraid to lose Beverly, too.

What could she say to Mike?

The phone rang and it startled her. She went to the wall and took the receiver from the cradle.

"Hello? Oh, hello, Agatha." She half-listened to Agatha Kelsey, her thoughts elsewhere. "Of course," she said. "Well, yes, certainly, I'd be glad to. When is it? Friday morning? I'll be there."

CHAPTER FOUR

David Belson stood at the window staring down at Madison Avenue and 52nd St.

Behind him was the voice of Dr. Ira Wilson. It had a metallic ring, and except for the fact that he knew the man, had spent the past two years with him, it might have seemed like a machine spitting out the words, as cold and impersonal as the IBM machines which digested the facts they fed to them.

But David was more concerned with the flow of walkers on the west side of Madison. They seemed to walk slower after the hunched cold winter, seemed to expand outside of themselves, reaching for the warmth of the sun. From the eighteenth floor the mass was without character. Perhaps it is better that way, he thought. He heard his name and turned from the window.

"It's nice that you're with us," Dr. Wilson said.

The others in the room chuckled at the caustic humor, and David cataloged them. Bill Sharmer sitting on the red leather couch, laughing harder than the rest because he was the least secure. Dr. Hugh Bascomb in the leather chair, his legs crossed casually, the pipe between his fingers, the hair receding from the handsome face, not laughing at all because he did not like Wilson, and because he was a good guy. Howard Denby, Public Relations Counsel, a high-placed pimp, in the chair by the boss, the smirk on his face. Rita Talbot, secretary, recorder of sex histories with no known sex history of her own, trim and efficient, polite chuckle. To hell with you, Rita.

This was the inner sanctum of Research Affiliates, the home office of Ira Wilson, Phd. The room was thickly carpeted, the furniture was masculine and expensive. The windows and one wall were draped to the floor. There was a large Modigliani print on one wall, and behind the vast modern curve of Wilson's desk was a map of the United States, decorated with tiny flags.

"As I was saying," Wilson said, "we will move in force on Walkers Ferry on Friday. That will give us the weekend to set things up, and we can start the samplings on Monday morning. I hope to finish up there by the end of the week."

"The editors of *Argus* are beginning to needle me for some copy," Howard Denby said.

"They'll get it in good time," Wilson said. "David, I want you to run down there tomorrow and see how things are shaping up."

"I'm supposed to finish processing the Scarsdale samplings tomorrow," David said.

"Hmmm. Well, go down on Wednesday then. You can arrange for our accommodations and just stay on and wait for us."

"Does Rita have all the stuff on the contacts?" David asked.

"Yes," Wilson said, "she'll give you the complete dope sheet on the operation. Woman named Agatha Kelsey is lining it up. I want this to come off smoothly so that we can get into Cleveland the following week. That will be the wind-up."

David watched and listened to Wilson with an interest that was new to him. The man was like a General in his planning, but he had the look of a religious fanatic. He had a narrow, ascetic face, the eyes close together with permanently knitted brows giving him the look of perpetual intensity. His jaw was long and determined and his mouth was like two parallel lines, the lips bloodless. He sat on the chair with bird-like readiness, the long, bony hands clasped on the desk.

"That should do it," Wilson said. "We're nearing the end of the present campaign, gentlemen. This next encounter should be extremely rewarding. I know we'll all pull our weight, do our best."

That was the end of it. Rita Talbot scurried to the door and opened it. They filed into the outer office where a dozen typists flailed their machines.

David did not return to his own cubicle. He turned to Martin Bascomb. "I got a date for lunch. See you after."

"After Westport I stopped going out to lunch," Bascomb said. "I stay here and secretly analyze the typists."

David smiled and went through the office. His heels echoing down the empty hall. He turned at the end and stopped at the elevators. He pushed the button that lighted the red arrow.

Before the elevator arrived he was joined by two secretaries from the publicity firm with offices on the same floor. David glanced at the girls, eyeing them both with critical appreciation. How much of the contours they exhibited in their light summer dresses was their own he had no way of knowing, but it was good to look at with an air of absent speculation.

For a moment he tried to remember his impressions when he had first come to this building three years ago. He had been used to the small mid-west college town, the atmosphere of the laboratory and classroom, and he had been strangely affected by the New York office, the Madison Avenue approach to science. It had intrigued him then, but that was a long time ago. Now it was just part of the routine. In his dress, the well-cut brown worsted suit, the striped narrow tie, the button-down collar, the square edge of handkerchief showing, he could have been in advertising or public relations. He had fallen in with the style and attitude of the city just as he had framed his life to fit the large salary he received from Dr. Ira Wilson.

The elevator arrived and he followed the two girls inside. It reached the lobby, the door slid open and the people filtered out, each in his own world, mindless of the sudden and momentary proximity to the others in the small cubicle

David hailed a cab. He climbed into the rear and settled back. "Forty-seventh and Sixth," he said. David glanced at his watch. He was a little late, but not much, and Gwen wouldn't mind.

He turned his thoughts to Gwen. He had to relate her to his current feeling of dissatisfaction. It had nothing to do with her, and yet it did. She was a factor in keeping him tied to New York, and it would be ridiculous to think of Gwen being anywhere else. And what did Gwen mean to him really. He had to face that one, and he didn't like it. Are you in love with her? he had to ask himself, and he had to answer, Dammit, I don't know.

"Here, y'are," the driver said.

"Oh." David paid the driver and got out. He walked a block south and turned in at the American Bar.

The customers here were a strange mixture. At the bar were construction workers from the Time-Life building across the street. There were also several photographers from Life, some people from NBC, several models, a few merchants, a writer's agent with the editor of a girly magazine. David spotted Gwen sitting alone in a rear booth. She smiled as he approached, and as always he was dazzled by the piquant magnificence of that smile. He slid into the booth opposite her.

"Hi. Sorry I'm late," he said, then reached across the table and covered her hand with his.

"I'm the only woman who has to play second fiddle to sex," she said.

David laughed lightly. "We were getting the old pep talk," he said.

"I got one too," she said. There was an edge of excitement in her husky voice, and her green eyes sparkled with anticipation, as they always did when she had been holding something to tell him.

"Ah," David said, knowing that she had attended a reading for a forthcoming play that morning, "how did it go?"

"I got the part," she said.

David was suddenly swept up in her excitement. "You're kidding!"

"I'm not! I got it! I read for Baragren and he leaped up and shouted, 'She's it! That's Emily!' Think of it, David, the second lead in a Baragren show."

He squeezed her hand. "I'm happy for you, Gwen." And then his own problem surged to the front of his mind, and he tried to see her new success in relation to his feelings, his misgivings. In a way, it solved things for him, because it forced him to look at their relationship in a clear light. What were they to each other? He had known Gwen for a year. They had met at a dull cocktail party, and she had left with him to get something to eat. They had fascinated each other from the first, and dinner stretched into a long evening of talk, and while they walked through Washington Square Park and passed the statue of Garibaldi about to unsheath his sword, he had said, "They say that when a virgin passes here he gets the sword out. It's never happened yet." She had laughed lightly at the joke, and by the time they reached the large, circular fountain, he had the confidence to stop and turn her shoulders until she faced him, and kiss her. She returned the kiss, and they went to bed at his apartment that same night. It had been a good relationship. She was beautiful and intelligent. The fact that she aspired to the theater had been a bit amusing to him, but now she had made the grade, and there would be no bringing her back.

And David knew that he could never marry a career girl. He had old-fashioned ideas about home life, despite the years of interviews into the sex lives of Wilson's samplings. He knew that he would never marry Gwen now, and the sudden realization saddened him.

"What's wrong?" she asked. "Aren't you really happy for me?"

"I am," he said. "It's just that I have to leave again tomorrow and I'd rather not." It was easier to lie. In fact, he was glad of the assignment. He wanted time to think about things on his own.

Gwen pouted. "Where to this time?"

"Not far," he said. "Bucks County. A town called Walkers Ferry."

"They have a good summer theater there," Gwen said.

"Well, I'm afraid I won't be seeing much theater," David said. "We'll only be there ten days. Then we go to Cleveland."

"Oh, David! By the time you get back we'll be in rehearsal, and then we'll be on the road. I'll never see you!"

"I'll be out front cheering," he said.

The waiter came to the table and interrupted them. They gave their order, and did not pick up the conversation.

It was a strange meal to David. While neither mentioned it, it was obvious to him that this would probably be the end of their affair. He couldn't pin down exactly what had happened, where this knowledge had suddenly been telegraphed between them, but he knew that Gwen was feeling the same thing. She looked at him rather wistfully, but they had fallen into a silence that was almost reverent, as though each was remembering all the moments that would have to be "them" for all time.

More than ever, he was eager to begin the new project, and some of his dissatisfaction had been submerged.

"David?" Gwen's voice brought him out of the reverie.

Glancing up quickly, David faced her smile. "Yes?"

"Where were you?" she asked, her head cocked.

"I'm not sure." He laughed. "I don't know."

"You weren't with me," she said.

"Actually I was," he said. "I was thinking about us, thinking about ... well ... all the things we've been to each other."

"The summing up," she said.

He nodded. "I suppose that's it. I have a feeling that—"

"Don't say it, David," Gwen said. "I know what you're feeling, but I don't want to hear it in words. As long as it's just a thought I can keep it in the back of my mind and believe that it's not true. I feel so wonderful about the play and I don't want to think that I'm sacrificing one thing to get another."

"Let's have a drink on that," David said. He signalled the waiter and ordered brandy. When the two glasses arrived, he lifted his drink between his fingers and sighted over the rim. Gwen returned his gaze. "Sköl," David said.

He was about to drink when Gwen said, "Wait, David."

Stayed by the urgency in her voice, his eyes widened, bringing a wide smile to her face. "Sköl is not like saying hello," Gwen said. "The English say, 'cheers,' and drink and it means many things, but sköl is very special." As she spoke there was an element of merriment in her eyes. Her words were chosen with care, giving the explanation an aura of excitement, as though she were about to reveal some deep mystical secret. "I'll show you," she said. "You lift your glass like this." She held the glass at chin level, her two fingers embracing the narrow stem. David followed her direction. "Now then, the man looks deeply into the eyes of the girl. They say nothing. They wait until there is a message, something that tells them both that something wonderful is going to happen." Their eyes held, and David began to lose himself in the cool depth of her gaze. He felt his pulse quicken and there was a strange constriction in his chest. "Now," she said.

"Sköl," David said softly.

"Sköl," she whispered.

They sipped the drink and brought the glasses down to the table. Their eyes still held, then Gwen glanced down at her hands. When she looked up her eyes were glistening with the beginnings of tears. "I don't want to talk anymore, David," she said, her voice on the verge of breaking. "Sit there until I leave."

David did not answer. Gwen rose from the booth. She took her light coat from the hanger and draped it over her arm. Reaching for her purse, she glanced at him quickly, then turned and walked away. David watched her go, knowing that a chapter was walking out of his life.

When she had disappeared through the door, David brought his eyes back to the table. He stared at the glass of brandy. Just one sip. The unfinished drink. He began to raise his glass, looked at it and put it down. The brandy at that moment was symbolic of something. He wasn't certain exactly what, but he knew that it must be left. It was tied in with the single sip, the toast, the parting, something left unfinished, left on the note of longing.

David paid the check, took his coat and left the restaurant. He walked north on Sixth Avenue.

Traffic roared in the street. Cabs, buses, trucks fought for position at the lights, spouting fumes and curses, New York on the rush. The sound was a dull roar, leashed beasts straining to run in circles. Store windows glittered in the sunlight. Pedestrians walked on the treadmill of habit, weaving along the sidewalk, avoiding collision, a detached mob brought together for a few moments to move along as a single, surging entity, a current of humanity joined by chance, separately together, moving north or south with the precise intricacies of a folk dance, and soon to be divided by the separateness of mind and purpose. The street was life, the mindless, cacaphonic polyglot of sound and motion.

Turning east on Fiftieth Street, David walked slowly, his thoughts meshing between Gwen and the new project. Gwen's last act was typical of her. She had a knack for taking the commonplace and adding her particular dash of personality to turn it into a ritual of delight. This was, of course, her natural inclination towards the dramatic, but whatever the motivation it added a spice to life that was continually surprising and exciting. David knew that he was going to miss this quality.

Between them both they seemed to have everything necessary for the complete relationship, but something was missing and David could not put his finger on the elusive key. It was natural that he should seek the fault in himself, because he had come close before, but always there was something lacking when he considered a relationship in terms of that completeness that brings a man and woman together for the tenure of their lives.

The difficulty he had faced in himself was that he was left with the feeling of inadequacy, and with the premonition that he was predestined to the single life. Most confusing was the fact that a relationship began with the best of intentions, but somewhere it soured. Why, David thought, why? You meet a girl, you're excited by her, you have much in common. You talk together, share things. For a time this other person is the axis of your existence, your thoughts and movement circling within the sphere of her being. You make love with her, cojoin in the muscling intimacies of the body, blending aesthetic to reality, exploring the cosmos of sensation and emotion. With Gwen it had all seemed complete, but there was always the nagging doubt that could never be justified. This, to David, was the twilight time of the heart's hunger; the cravings inescapably there, but elusive, beyond reach of the mind.

He paused at Fifth Avenue, waiting for the light to change. There seemed to be more pigeons than usual around St. Patricks, wheeling and turning, swooping over the street, weaving their concentric patterns on the warm air. He turned his head to look at a passing girl, one of the sleek untouchables, model-under-glass women. She walked with precise nylon strides, frostily aloof to the construction stiff catcalls from the protection of high girders and the furtive neck-swivels of the earth-bound gentry. David smiled. He stepped off the curb and moved with the crowd. It was a good day, a pleasant day, Spring in the city with the people walking slower, smiling more, heads high and straight as though emerging from coat collars after the hunched and bundled fast-walks of the winter.

The new project took over his thoughts and he felt a surge of excitement and anticipation.

CHAPTER FIVE

Sylvia Thompson prowled the house with the restless anxiety of a cat.

The morning was gone and there was nothing to look forward to but the afternoon. By that time she hoped to be too drunk to give a damn. She held up the tumbler of brandy, squinted her eye, measuring. She snorted and brought the glass to her lips, tilting her head back.

"Sick," she muttered, "God damn sick bitch!" She passed the large mirror in the dining room and stopped. She looked hard at herself with loathing.

"Taking on the God damn neighborhood kids," she snapped to herself. "Rotten, no good bitch. Sex before breakfast and it never means a damn thing."

Castigating herself with the vilest language she could bring to mind, she turned away from the mirror and crossed to the liquor cabinet. She picked up the brandy bottle. "Christ," she muttered, "'did I drink all that?" She emptied the bottle into her glass, then turned and hurled the bottle across the room. It shattered against the stone fireplace. The action did nothing to release her from the feeling of remorse, and she began to pace again.

"Dammit," she railed, "why do I have to feel this way? Why can't I just take them on and enjoy it? But I never do, never do. When I want them they're wonderful, but it's just something to stop the craving."

She was staggering slightly and she felt dizzy. She stopped by the window and stared down towards the pool. "Good christ, why can't I get drunk enough to pass out! I have to do something. I can't just stay in this house the rest of the summer. Maybe I ought to get married again. If I could find someone to satisfy me. Hell, there isn't any such thing. Even that damn Chet Parker wasn't enough."

It occurred to her that she could use new cabinets in the kitchen. But the reason behind the thought assailed her in her mood of self-punishment, and she spun about and hurled the drink away from her.

A sob caught in her throat. She staggered from the window and flung herself down on one of the couches. Her shoulders shook and the tears ran over her cheeks.

"Why am I like this?" she wailed. "Why? Why did they make me like this? I don't want to be like this! I can't stand it! Cal, Cal, don't leave me! I'm sorry! I won't do it again, I swear I won't!"

Sam Masserly was a different man when he stood before his class. His voice was deep and rich and he spoke with deep passion. He stayed close to the rostrum where he kept his notes, moving a few steps to the right or left, but returning to read something, or merely to clutch the sides of the wooden stand for emphasis.

"Lawrence always wrote with a deep love for his native England," he said, "and it is only with sadness that one contemplates that he is known so widely as a pornographer. In 1913 he wrote—" Sam lowered his head to read, quoting from a letter by D. H. Lawrence. "—I break my heart over England when I read the *New Machiavelli*. And I am so sure that only through a readjustment between men and women, and a making free and healthy of this sex, will she get out of her present atrophy. Oh, Lord, and if I don't 'subdue my art to a metaphysic,' as somebody very beautifully said of Hardy, I do write because I want folk—English folk—to alter, and have more sense.' " Sam looked up again. "This was the motivating factor behind his novel, *Lady Chatterly's Lover*, and—"

He was interrupted by the harsh rasp of the bell ending the class. He removed his glasses, smiling. "We'll continue tomorrow," he said.

Chairs and shoes scuffled, chatter immediately filled the room, breaking the mood he had created. Sam gathered his notes together, taking more time than was necessary. He glanced up and she was still sitting, writing in her notebook as the others moved towards the door. He felt his heartbeat quicken. It was confusing the way she affected him. He deposited the notes in his leather brief-case, snapped it closed. He straightened. She was closing her book and rising from the chair.

Sam started for the door the moment she left the chair. The rest were gone and they reached the door together.

"I'm through now," Beverly Merrick said. "I'm going to drive down to the Crossing Park."

Sam did not trust himself to answer. He nodded, and she passed through the doorway ahead of him. He stepped into the hallway and watched her go away from him, enjoying the shift of her body as she walked, enchanted by the way her hair bounced against the back of her neck. His interest in her gave him a feeling of disquiet that was not quite guilt. It was an old story about college instructors becoming involved with their students, but he felt that this somehow was different.

When she was out of sight, Sam went to the left. He stopped at the office to check for messages, then he left the building. He went to the parking lot and climbed behind the wheel of his old Chevrolet.

Driving out of the lot, he made the turn onto Jericho Road, and took his time, thinking about Beverly as he drove.

He hadn't expected to teach the summer course until she had said that she was going to spend the summer in school, and had asked if he was going to teach. His decision had been made in that moment. He hadn't thought about Cora's reaction until later, and by then he had already signed for the course. The Master's

Degree was Cora's idea. It was a good one, practical as all her ideas were, but her motives did not interest him. Even so, it had surprised him that he had made a decision without consulting her. And then he had enjoyed it.

He wanted to be near Beverly. It was as simple as that. There was nothing and everything between them. He had never held her, never kissed her, and yet there was the intangible attraction between them.

Turning on River Road, he drove south. He passed the fields where com would be growing, passed the strawberry fields, the fields already green with alfalfa, the pastures where herds of Aberdeen-Angus grazed.

At Washington Crossing Park, he slowed down. Making a left turn, he drove closer to the river, parked near the cemetery, and got out of the car.

Was it dangerous to be meeting her here like this? There was always the chance of running into someone from town, and it would certainly start a lot of talk. I don't care, he told himself, I honestly don't give a damn.

She was waiting for him, sitting on the grass by the river, her skirt spread out around her. When she heard him approach she got to her feet. He came across the clipped lawn, his steps soundless. There was something different about her, an urgency which communicated to him. She seemed to be waiting for each footfall, and he was conscious of every step that closed the gap between them. It was electric, this knowledge that leaped between them. He stopped several feet from her. Their eyes held and they did not speak. He could not pass the wall that was between them. He was thirty years old, married, her college instructor, and the barrier of convention stilled his feet, throttled his voice.

"Sam!" Her voice was a choked cry. She bridged the gulf, flinging herself towards him, the tears starting in her eyes as she moved.

His arms came up to encircle her as she reached him, and they clung together, mindless of the world about them, feeling only themselves in relation to the other.

Sam held his breath, his heart pounding in his chest, his face burrowed in her hair, savoring the smell of her. He held her tightly, feeling the give of her soft breasts against him, the firm thighs against his. His chest ached and he had to breath.

She lifted her face and tears glistened in her green eyes. She closed her eyes, sighing, and pressed her face into the hollow of his throat.

My God, Sam thought, is it really possible to feel this way?

Cora Masserly parked her 1950 Chevrolet in the lot behind the Ferry Inn. It was not a tourist day and there were only a few cars in the lot.

Slamming the car door and wincing with irritation at the rattle the window made, she walked behind and around the car and entered through the archway into the garden. The tables here were unoccupied. Her heels clacked on the flagstones as she walked to the oak door and pulled it open, releasing the sounds of restaurant. Voices rose and fell, hummed. Glass clinked, plates clattered.

The bartender smiled politely when she entered. The owner, a gray-haired bouncy woman named Mrs. Alston, waved from the kitchen doorway and Cora smiled back.

Five tables were occupied in the somber, wood-paneled room. Marcia Storm was at the end of the bar. Cora went along the bar and stopped next to her.

"I made it," Cora said.

"I'm two up on you," Marcia said. "God, I'm glad to see you. I'm glad to see anybody who hasn't got a runny nose or needs to be changed. I'm especially glad to see *you*." She swung off the bar stool. "Let's sit."

They went to one of the wooden tables and took chairs on opposite sides.

"What's yours?" Marcia asked.

Cora had to consider the price of martinis and lunch. She was careful with money to the point of stinginess, but she suddenly thought of Sam and his new attitude and she thought, the hell with it.

"I'll have a martini," Cora said.

"Two of the same, Nate," Marcia called to the bartender. She settled back and breathed deeply. "Well," she said, "how are you?" And without waiting for a reply, said, "God, you look wonderful. You always look so damn svelte. Me, I always look like I been chasing the hounds without the horse."

Cora smiled, but she had to admit that Marcia did generally look a bit disheveled. Her brown hair was chopped off, not really cut in any stylish way, but chopped, as if she did it herself. Her face was attractive, but it could have been a man's face just as easily. She wore dark slacks and a rough brown sweater, and her only two sure indications of being a female were the lipstick on her lips and the prominent breasts which could not be hidden by the baggy sweater. Her eyes were her most interesting feature and they harbored an intensity which Cora found slightly disquieting. She distinctly did not like Marcia, and she did not quite know what she was doing here, but it was better than sulking around the house.

The martinis arrived. Cora lifted hers and glanced over the rim of the glass. Marcia was staring hard at her, then she smiled. "Here's to birth control," Marcia said.

Cora blushed slightly, and drank a sip of the drink. Marcia's voice was as deep as a bassoon and it carried well.

"I could drink a million of these things," Marcia said. "Christ, after a morning with four kids, I *need* a million."

It was baffling to Cora how Marcia ever managed to have four children. They were all young, all girls, the oldest one was five. She didn't seem to like children, in fact she seemed to detest them. And she seemed to detest her husband, Harvey, just as much. That, at least, was understandable. Harvey was a hulk of a man, the hard, barrel-like, hairy type with the cigar always in his mouth. He looked powerful, like an animal, and Cora could always imagine him in bed with disgust.

"They're beautiful children," Cora said.

"God," Marcia said, "let's not talk about children. Let's talk about doing something after lunch. I'm about nuts."

They ordered another drink, then ate the special of corned beef and cabbage, then drank two brandies, then called for the check which Marcia insisted on paying. "I asked you, baby, remember? This is mine. I gotta make that hairy sonofabitch pay something for all the trouble I seen."

When they left through the garden Marcia walked with Cora to her car. "Why don't we take a drive somewhere?" Marcia asked. "Let's just drive up River Road, maybe stop at the Stagecoach Inn or someplace and have a quiet beer."

"I really shouldn't," Cora said. "Sam will probably be home for lunch."

"Aw," Marcia said, "to hell with Sam for one afternoon. This is our day. Come on, let's drive."

Cora hesitated, but then she thought, it will do him good to sweat it out today, damn good!

They got into the car and Cora backed away from the stone retaining wall. Marcia sat against the door and Cora could feel the intensity of the gaze on her. It made her nervous. She turned the wheel and shifted gears. "God," Marcia said, "you're a wonderful looking thing."

When Beverly stormed out of the house Claire Roberts stood for a long moment staring at the door and chewing her lip. She didn't know what to do. Turning away, she went back to the table and sat down.

Fear nagged at her. She was an attractive woman and she knew it, but she wasn't a girl and she knew that, too. She had to work at keeping the fat off, and nothing could keep the breasts from sagging, and the muscles of the stomach from loosening, and the buttocks from spreading just a bit too much. She needed a man, and she knew that, too, and she didn't need a companion for her old age. She had that man, and she meant to keep him.

Rising from her chair, Claire walked out of the kitchen. She passed through the dining room and into the antique-furnished living room. The stairs were in a corner of the room, the old-fashioned circular type. She climbed the stairs, rehearsing what she would say as she went. She went along the carpeted hallway to the master bedroom. Her husband was in the middle of the floor doing pushups.

He wore only pajama bottoms. He was stretched out, face-down, his body supported on toes and palms. He held himself an inch off the floor, his biceps knotted, the muscles in his back bunched under the strain. He pushed up, snorting, held himself, then lowered his body slowly. His black curly hair fell over his forehead, and sweat glistened on the wide shoulders. He had a juvenile pride in his body, and he exercised daily.

When he completed the push-ups he rolled over on his back, breathing hard. His face was the kind that attracts women. His nose was broken, there was a small scar marring one eyebrow, the chin was heavy, jutting, and the mouth was wide and full-lipped, and could be laughing or cruel. When he sat up he saw Claire and said, "Hi, what's up?"

"Just like to watch," she said.

"Gotta keep it trim," he said, slapping his hard stomach. He got to his feet and started for the shower.

"Mike?"

"Uh?" He stopped and looked back.

"I have to talk to you."

The tone in her voice made him scowl. "About what?"

"About Beverly."

"What's wrong with her?"

"Nothing. Nothing, really, I mean ... well, this morning she was ... well ..."

"She tell you I'm trying to bang her?"

"No! I mean, not really that, but she said ... well ... damn, I don't know how to say this."

"Just say it. Say it plain." He stood with his legs apart and his hands on his hips. "She said I'm trying to bang her!"

"She didn't! It's just that she said you were always looking at her."

"Well, for Christ's sake, we live in the same damn house! What am I supposed to do, keep my eyes shut?"

"I don't mean that. She said you were in her room."

"I stuck my head in the door to say hello," Mike said. "For Jesus sake, Claire, of course I look at her. She trots around half-naked. What am I supposed to do?"

"I ... I don't know."

"You think I need that kid? You think you ain't woman enough for me?" He advanced towards her.

"I don't know. She's so young, so ... so ..."

"Stacked. So stacked, that it? A kid built like a brick out-house, so I'm supposed to be slobbering after her. Maybe I don't like kids." He took her arms in his large hands and squeezed.

"Oh," she said, "that hurts."

"Maybe I like a woman knows what to do with it, you ever think of that?"

"I think of it."

"I ever let you down?" His fingers untied the cord holding her robe together. "I ever make you think you ain't a woman?" His hands closed over her breasts.

"No, no, Mike."

"You ever get enough of me?" He squeezed her breasts until she ground her teeth with the pain.

"No," she gasped, "I never do."

"You want me to show you I ain't after your kid?"

"Mike, you're hurting me."

"You want me to hurt you good? You want me to hurt you the way you like being hurt?" Still grasping her breasts, he propelled her backwards to the bed.

"Yes. I do, I always do."

"You ever get enough of old Mike?"

"Never."

He released her and stripped off the pajama pants with a fast, deft movement. "You want me to tear them things off?"

"No. No, wait." She pulled the robe off her arms, dropped it. She bent over and grasped the hem of the gown and pulled it over her head.

He grabbed her roughly and threw her back onto the bed, pressing her down with his weight. "This what your kid is afraid of?"

"Oh, Mike. Don't talk, don't talk."

"You want it? You want it bad?"

She squirmed and twisted under him. "Yes."

"How bad? How bad you want it?"

"Bad!" Her legs snaked over his flanks and she held him to her.

"You think anybody oughta be afraid of this?" He moved against her, tantalizing her.

"No! No, I'm not afraid!"

"You think that kid oughta be afraid?"

"Oh, Mike, please!"

"Do you?"

"No! No, I don't think she should be afraid."

"You know I'm gonna have her?"

"Mike, please, now!"

"Do you know? Do you know I gotta have that girl?"

"Now, Mike!" She reached down for him with both hands, but he ground close to her and kept her away.

"Do you know that?"

"Yes, yes, I know it! I know it! For God's sake, Mike make love to me! I don't give a damn about her! I don't give a damn! I don't give…a…damn…oh…my God…my God…I don't…don't…oh, Jesus!…Jesus, Mike…Mike!

CHAPTER SIX

It was dusk, and that time of day in Bucks County in the middle of June is a beautiful time.

The sun was gone over Jericho Mountain. The wind was up slightly, but not much, just enough to rustle the trees and bring out the sounds of the cicadas. This was martini time on flagstone patios, get-the-charcoal-out time and start the steaks.

The sloping mounds of hills lay crouched in beginning darkness. Bass leap in the canal, breaking the water. Frogs burp. A speedboat with running lights skims the still surface of the River followed by the frothy trails of a water skier. The single neon sign at the center of town is lighted. It is the slow hour at Haber's newsstand. The lights are on at the Playhouse. There are noisy drinkers in the bar at the Ferry Inn and all over the town are the sounds of supper.

The woman behind the wheel of the station wagon would—to eyes beyond her sphere of life—be envied. She was beautiful. She had the poise that is the special property of the well-bred. She dressed with a natural good taste, and it was obvious that she had the money for the simplicity of cashmere. She lived in a fashionable and expensive section of the country and had no idea or interest in the price of her home. She did not clean her own house, nor was she bothered by laundry or mending. All her problems were promptly attended to with the simple expediency of a telephone call and the signature on a check. Her husband was successful in his business. Her daughter attended an exclusive private school within a mile of their home.

She was typical of the exurban wife. Not burdened by the wealth that could make her a celebrity, but wealthy enough so that she had no knowledge of money.

Her educational background prepared her for a relationship with the arts, and she enjoyed the proximities of intellectualism offered in Bucks County. Her social group included a cross-section of writers, composers and artists. Unlike many of the women in her strata who became addicted to the arts, worshipping the practitioners with a devotion born of their own frustrated desire for expression, she was able to intelligently view the arts with perspective and appreciate her talent for understanding. During college she had shown promise as a poet, but with maturity had come the realization that she did not possess the compulsive neurosis necessary for the full application of her psych in the singleness of purpose. She did not see the goal to which her writing might take her, and not caring to exist in the vacuum of amateurism, she gave up writing. Her talent, she knew, was understanding, and she regarded it as sound and real as the mechanical application in the arts. In many ways her talent was stronger. She was aware, intelligent, emotionally deep, appreciative of the full range of sensory perception. She possessed the vital necessities for writing to a greater degree than many of her successful literary friends, but lacked the knowledge of craft. This craft, she knew, could be learned, but she was content to assuage her curiosity in understanding.

An unusual woman in enviable circumstance driving an expensive, but plain, station wagon over a country road. She did not feel unusual or enviable. She was nervous, frightened; her mind seethed with the imagery of future reality in a fantasia born of guilt and projected against the everpresent backdrop of moral conscience. She was on her way to meet the husband she had betrayed.

Elizabeth Pennington pulled up to the traffic light at the main intersection of the town and stopped. She checked her watch. Plenty of time before the train. She could take it easy down the River Road. The light changed. The Mercury wagon sailed into the turn. She drove onto the bridge and reduced her speed to the 15-mile limit. At the far side the guard nodded to her and she smiled in return. She drove through the three-block business district of Ferryville, turned right at the highway, and upped the speed to fifty.

She was glad that Brad had called to say that he would be home that night, glad to be driving to the station to pick him up. For a moment she had panicked, thinking that he would surely know what had happened in the morning. She had stood looking at herself in the mirror, certain that she looked different, that somehow Chet Parker would have left some stain on her. But she looked the same. She had changed the bed and sprayed the room with scent. Tonight she would have Brad in that bed, and by God, she was going to have him!

Debbie had come home and there was no sign of any argument between them. She hoped that the morning scene had straightened her out. Neither had mentioned it. Everything was all right. Everything was back on the track. Business as usual. Brad would be home and everything would be fine. Never again would there be a Chet Parker. Never! God, how could she have done such a thing?

It was fifteen miles to the Pennsylvania Station. She pulled into the parking lot, then checked her watch. The train wasn't in yet. She shut off the engine, rummaged in her purse for a cigarette.

She was sitting and waiting and smoking when she saw the advance guard of commuters pour out of the station, men and women hurrying, walking with quick purpose. She watched until she saw Brad, then she opened the car door and got out. He stood for a moment looking, then he saw the wagon and started towards it.

What a good-looking man he is, Elizabeth thought. He wore the narrow-lapel lightweight suit with natural ease. He was tall and spare and the new style suited him well. The narrow dark tie was right for the button-down collar of the white shirt. His narrow face right for the short-brim hat. He carried a thin leather attache case and walked with long strides.

He reached the car and Elizabeth had the door open for him on the driver's side.

"Hello, Hon," he said, pecking at her cheek. "How about you drive, huh? I'm beat."

"Glad to," she said. She slid under the wheel and Brad closed the door. Oh, God, she thought, let's hope he's not *too* tired.

Brad opened the door, got in beside her and settled back. He closed his eyes, taking a deep breath, then sat up. He swung the attache case into the back. "Home," he said.

They drove slowly through the city traffic of Trenton, and Brad showed his irritation.

"Tough day?" Elizabeth asked.

"Tough week," Brad answered. "We got a new account, a shoe company. Walker Shoes. Walkers for the walker. You haven't walked until you've walked in a Walker. When a walker is in style."

"Sounds cute," Elizabeth said. She turned down to catch the expressway.

"Only until you've met Walter Walker. A hard, tough bastard with no sense of humor. He wants dignity attached to his product. Refuses to have the word 'walk' in his copy."

"But people walk in shoes."

"He says they don't, and he may be right. He says that Americans move on their asses over a set of wheels. Shoes are a luxury, he says. Oh, hell, screw him, what's been doing?"

"Nothing much. Same old things."

"How's the building coming along?"

"Fine," Elizabeth said. "Fine. But we have to find a new carpenter."

"What's wrong with Parker?"

"We had an argument," Elizabeth said. "I didn't like the way he was doing things. I fired him."

"Jesus, Liz," Brad said, "those guys are hard to find these days. I'll talk to him tomorrow. He'll come back."

Elizabeth started to object, but stopped. She couldn't make too big an issue of it. Maybe later. She'd work it out, but this wasn't the time.

"God," Brad said, pressing his fingers to his temples, "I've got a bastard of a headache."

It had never occurred to Sam Masserly that he was not in love with his wife. It had not occurred to him before this that he had never been in love with anyone. In fact, he really hadn't thought about it very much, and when he did it was merely to excuse love as something created for readers of the *Saturday Evening Post*. Love, he would have said, was a mutual understanding between two people, a plan for getting along together.

Looking across the table at Cora he wondered why in hell's name he had ever married her in the first place. They were eating in the kitchen. The dinner was hastily prepared of frozen foods. They were silent, Cora picking, bird-like, at her food, Sam chewing thoughtfully, wondering.

Here I sit, he thought, in a kitchen eating dinner with a woman I frankly don't give a damn about. The woman there is my wife. She is 29 years old. She thinks sex is something unpleasant that you have to put up with once in awhile to keep a husband in line. She wants me to teach in a bigger college town to give her status. She thinks that I am dull, untalented, easy to handle. She feels that she has married beneath her intellectual level and is therefore a martyr. She thinks children are messy and unnecessary. She hates housework and cooking. She has a sharp tongue and likes to use it like a drill sergeant. She is an unmitigated, god-awful pain in the neck day or night. Then why in hell's name did I ever marry her?

Sam thought back to the time they met. He had wanted to write. Hell, he still wanted to write. He did write in fact, but he would never show anything to Cora. She had been interested then. She had talked writing, writing, writing. In short, he thought, she sold me a bill of goods!

Actually, he had known all these things for several years. But he had merely shrugged and decided that that was the way things went. You got married. You got a job. You learned to live with someone reasonably well. You interested yourself in your work, and to hell with it. That was life!

And now it was as though he had suddenly been led out of the fog and there before him was an exciting land of everlasting sunshine. There was a woman, a young, warm, breathing, human being of a woman, a woman who clung to you, who made your heart hammer and made the blood pulse through your veins, a woman who made you feel young and want to take on the gah-damn world. There was life to grasp, to hold, to savor. There was life to throw yourself into, to wallow in.

He became aware that Cora was speaking to him. He looked across at her. "What?"

"I said I'm sorry I wasn't home this afternoon," Cora said.

Sam took a deep breath. When Cora was sorry about something it meant that she was going to lead him into something or that he was going to be punished for something.

"That's okay," he said, "I wasn't here."

"You weren't? Where were you?"

And now suddenly he realized that he had to lie. It was the first time that he realized that he was an unfaithful husband, and that he was now forced to play a role. He was certain that the lie would be clumsy, and he was nervous. And then he was surprised at his nervousness. If he lost Cora tomorrow he wouldn't miss her a bit. "I had work to do at school," he said. Now why did I lie, he thought, why invent a story?

"Oh," Cora said, satisfied.

It was easy to lie, he thought, and she believed it. I wonder what she would do if I told her the truth, told her that I was with a girl, a young girl, and that I was in love with her. He poked at the fish and smiled.

"What's so funny?"

"Nothing," Sam said, "nothing. Just a story I heard today."

Beverly Merrick was thinking of Sam Masserly. When he touched me, she thought, it was like ... like ... God, there is nothing to describe it. But you can feel it. I felt it, I felt love. Sam, Sam, I love you.

"Penny for your thoughts."

"Wha'?" She looked up and Mike Roberts was smiling at her. He sat at one end of the table, her mother at the other.

"What were you thinking?" Mike asked. "You weren't with your dear old parents."

"Why don't we just get off that parent bit," Beverly said.

"Step-parent," Mike said, smiling. "I am your stepfather."

"The thought makes me ill," Beverly said.

"Beverly!" Claire said. "I don't like that kind of talk."

"Then tell lover-boy to shut up!"

"Really!" Claire said.

"I don't think she likes me," Mike said, grinning.

"Mother, would you mind if I ate in the kitchen?"

"Well ... I ..."

"I'd mind," Mike said.

"I didn't ask you," Beverly said.

"Please," Claire said. "Why can't we just sit and eat like civilized people?"

"Because certain members of the group are not civilized," Beverly said. She pushed back from the table and stood. "Excuse me," she said, "I've suddenly lost my appetite." She turned away from the table and went into the living room, then up the stairs.

Inside her room with the door closing her off from the world she did not like, Beverly put a record on the player, then sprawled on the bed to think.

For the first time in her life she wanted a man, wanted him completely. The depth and ferocity of her feeling frightened her a little. Today, she thought, today on that lawn he could have done anything he wanted to me and I would have helped him. He could have had me on the grass in broad daylight and I wouldn't have cared if there were photographers present.

She was in love. That was the first thought in her mind. She had been attracted to Sam for many months, but today was the first time they had touched. The fact of love was established, and like a woman, she moved on to other facts, cataloging with the reality of a woman. I love Sam, he loves me. Fact. Sam is married. Fact. I must have him for myself. Fact. I don't care how I go about doing it. Fact? Yes, dammit, fact!

There were bound to be complications. Sam hadn't mentioned his wife, but she was there as big as life, and she would have to come up between them sooner or later. What did Sam feel for his wife? Did he ever love her? Why didn't they have children? Could Sam have children? Yes, he must, must! A lot of things were not facts.

She got up to change the record, then paced the room. The important thing was to be near him. That was first. No matter what the complications, she could not stand being away from him. And it had to be more than afternoons in the park.

There was a light knock on the door and Beverly stiffened. "Who is it?" she asked.

"Claire," her mother said from beyond the door.

Beverly opened the door. Her mother came into the bedroom and Beverly closed the door after her.

Assuming that her mother was about to reprimand her for her conduct at dinner, Beverly said, "I'm sorry about the way I acted, Mother, but he baited me. I can't stand that man and he knows it and he baits me everytime."

"I know," Claire said. She went to the window and stood with her back to the room. When she turned her eyes were moist. "I wish I could explain to you what he means to me," she said. She went to a chair and perched on the edge, her hands clasped.

"What do I mean to you?" Beverly asked.

Claire blinked. "You don't know?"

"I'm not sure."

"Haven't I always given you love?"

Beverly was suddenly ashamed of her belligerence "Yes," she said in a small voice. "Yes you have. I'm sorry."

"You said this morning that you might move into a dormitory at school," Claire said.

"I'm sorry, Mother. I was angry."

"That might be a good idea," Claire said.

Beverly stared, wide-eyed. "You mean ... you mean you want me to?"

"It's not a matter of what I want." Her eyes were on her hands. "It's just that it might be better."

Beverly was stunned. It had never occurred to her that she might lose out to Mike Roberts. For a moment she was angry and was about to say that leaving would be a pleasure, then she thought: in a dorm she would have hours to keep. She would be confined to the campus. It was going to be difficult enough seeing Sam without the rigors of the college rules. "I'd rather not," she said.

Claire glanced up quickly and there was a note of panic in her eyes. "It would be better," she said. "Better for you."

"Are you ordering me out?"

"Bev!" Claire was on her feet. "Bev, don't say things like that!"

"What am I supposed to say?"

"It's not like that! It's just that with you and Mike in the same house ... well ... I mean, it just doesn't seem to be working out."

Beverly narrowed her eyes. "You wouldn't be afraid of losing your man, would you, Mother?"

Claire caught her breath and her hand flew to her mouth. "How dare you say a thing like that!"

"That's it, isn't it? You're worried about that bastard!"

"Beverly, I won't have this."

"Just keep him away from me, Mother, and you've got nothing to worry about. The very thought of his touching me makes me crawl."

Claire looked confused. She sat down again. "I don't know," she said, "I just don't know."

"He's your husband, Mother, not mine."

"Do you have to be so cruel? I'm only thinking about you."

"Worrying. That's the word, isn't it? Worrying about me, because you know that hairy sonofabitch is a rapist!"

"He's not!"

"Well, whatever he is, tell him to stay away from me. I'm not leaving this house for him or anyone like him. This is my home and I intend staying right here. If he comes within three feet of me I'll kill him. Just tell him that and stop worrying!"

Claire stood. She walked to the door and opened it. "I'm sorry," she said. She went out and closed the door.

Beverly had the urge to call to her, to bring her back and beg her forgiveness. She knew that she had been cruel. But she did nothing. She went to the bed and sat down.

Sam, she said to herself, Sam, I want you, I need you, I have to have you and forget all this ... all this!

Elizabeth Pennington came out of the bathroom wearing a new shortie nightgown that accentuated the full length and curve of her legs. Brad was already in bed.

Elizabeth stopped in the middle of the bedroom. Was Brad asleep? She had been talking to him a few minutes before. She went to the bed quickly.

He was on his side with one arm outflung. He breathed heavily and his mouth was slightly open. Sound asleep.

Going to her side of the bed, Elizabeth pulled the blankets down and climbed in. She pulled the blankets to her neck, then reached up and pressed the button to extinguish the lights. She lay quietly for several minutes, then she turned on her side and moved closer to Brad. She outlined her body against his, put one arm around him. Her mouth was close to his ear.

"Brad," she whispered. There was no answer. "Brad," she said again. She tugged at him.

"Uh? Wha'?"

"Brad, I want to talk to you."

"Talk? What, what?" He came awake. "What's wrong?"

"I want to talk."

"About what?" His voice was irritated.

"Things. Just things. About us."

"Let's talk at breakfast."

"Brad," she whispered, rubbing her hand over his chest, "I want you."

"Baby, I'm tired. I had a rough day. I gotta be up at six to make the train. Be a good girl and go to sleep."

"That's the way it is?"

"Uh? Oh, look, Honey, don't be like that. Honest to God, I got a rough week ahead. I came home tonight to get away from it."

"That's the only reason you came home?"

"Liz, for Christ's sake stop the hurt-wife theatrics. I'm tired. It's as simple as that. What the hell do you expect after all these years of marriage?"

"I expect my husband to make love to me." She was not whispering now, but speaking in a matter-of-fact manner. "I don't expect it every damn night, but I expect him to be man enough and want to enough to make love to me once in awhile. I expect him to come home more often and spend more time with his family."

"You also expect to eat."

"Other wives eat and their husbands come home and they go to bed with them and they make love to them once in awhile!"

"Lower your voice," Brad snapped. "You want Debbie to hear all this nonsense."

"Nonsense? Is that what this is to you?"

"Oh, dammit, Liz...."

"It's not nonsense, Buster. I just asked you to make love to me and you refused. That isn't nonsense."

"Will you keep your voice down?"

"You afraid Debbie will hear about boys and girls? Well, just listen, Captain of the Advertising Industry, your daughter knows more than you'd ever guess!"

"What do you mean by that?"

"If you'd stay home more often and see your daughter you might not have to ask that." She rolled away from him.

Brad was up on one elbow. "What's this about Debbie?"

"Nothing," Elizabeth said wearily. "Forget it, Tycoon. She was petting with a boy and I had to call her down about it."

Brad was silent a moment, then he stretched out flat again. "Damn," he said, "I certainly don't understand women."

"You sure don't, Buster," Elizabeth said to herself, "You sure as hell don't."

CHAPTER SEVEN

I t was Wednesday, the sun was shining, and Walkers Ferry wore the day like a resplendent cloak.

David Belson parked the station wagon with the lettering, *Research Affiliates,* on the door. He backed into a parking space by a meter in front of Dr. Cogley's house. He got out, locked the door, then fed the meter a nickel. He turned and crossed the street and entered Haber's newsstand where he expected to find a telephone so that he could call Agatha Kelsey.

Knox Martin came out of the drug store while David was parking. He noted the name on the car and stopped. He watched the young man cross the street, then he followed.

Inside Haber's, David decided to put the call off a moment, and went to the counter. A juke box wailed behind him, but the customers did not seem to notice. Four women sitting on the far side of the counter glanced at him, then resumed their conversation. Two men sat further down from him, and one teen-age boy sat reading a magazine. The young, pretty girl behind the counter came to him and he ordered coffee.

"Make that two coffees, will you, Joanie," Knox Martin said, taking the stool next to David. "You must be with Dr. Ira Wilson."

David showed surprise. "Word travels fast in this town. I just got here."

"I saw you park," Knox said. "I'm the editor of the local paper. Name's Knox Martin."

"I'm David Belson. Your name seems familiar."

"I wrote a book once," Knox said. "It kicks around now and again."

The coffee came and they both went through the ritual of sugar and cream.

"When does the great man arrive?" Knox asked.

"Friday."

"And what do you think of the sex possibilities in our little town?"

David smiled, liking the appearance of Knox Martin and particularly his wry comments.

"I haven't checked your night baseball schedule yet," David said.

"No team."

"Then I'd say we ought to do pretty well."

Martin grinned. "I should say you ought," he said. "Where you be staying?"

"We have reservations at the Ferry Inn. I don't know where it is."

"Just a block down the street," Knox said. "I don't imagine you'll be busy for dinner if you just arrived, so how about if I join you there?"

"I'd like it fine," David said.

"Good. How about six o'clock? I never could get used to this dinner-at-eight business."

"Fine."

Knox finished off his coffee and stood. "See you this evening." He turned to leave and bumped into a girl who was passing him. He recovered, laughing, and took the girl's arm. "Dammit, Athena," he said, "If I was younger I would have done that on purpose."

"You're young enough for me any old time, Mr. Martin," the girl said, smiling.

David turned at the sound of her voice. It was a soft voice with just a bit of huskiness. And the voice belonged to a pretty girl. She was small, but her body was perfectly proportioned to her height. She had blonde hair woven into a single thick braid, worn over one shoulder. Her face was round, the eyes blue, the nose small. The full-lipped mouth was laughing, and there was a slight separation between her two front teeth, which, for some reason, made her even more attractive.

"Athena," Knox said, "I'd like you to meet a new friend of mine. David Belson. Athena Wells."

"Hello," she said and the voice was a caress.

"How do you do," David said.

"Athena is one of my very favorite people," Knox said. "Buy her a coffee and I'll tell you all about her tonight."

"Thanks a *lot*," Athena said.

"It'll all be good," Knox said.

Athena took the stool next to David and Knox left. "You must be new here," she said. "I haven't seen you before." She spoke with the open candor of the small town, a comfortable ease of manner that was strange to one from the city.

"About as new as possible," David said. "I just got here."

"Oh. You know Knox from somewhere else."

"No, I just met him."

"But he said that you were a friend."

"That's funny, but I feel the same way about him. There's something about him."

"It's honesty," she said. "It sticks out all over him. You must have it too or he wouldn't have introduced us."

"Oh?"

"Knox is protective," she said. "I haven't any family and he has sort of adopted me. You made a good impression."

David smiled, but did not answer. He stirred the coffee. The girl disturbed him in a pleasant way. Her candor was disarming and he enjoyed listening to her.

"He's really wonderful," she said, "but he ought to be married."

"Why?"

"Because it's a shame to waste such a good man. He could make the right woman happy."

"That sounds like a typical female cure-all for everything," David said.

She laughed. "I suppose you're right. Maybe Knox would be miserable with a woman around him all the time."

David glanced down at her hand and saw that she did not wear a wedding band. She noticed his appraisal and smiled.

"I'm not married," she said.

"I'm sorry," David said. "Curiosity."

"That's quite all right," she said. "I looked for a wedding ring the moment I sat down. Of course, not all men wear them, and that's not fair."

"Why isn't it?"

"Because a girl is generally looking for a man just as much as the man looks for a woman. Very few of us like the roll of being the other woman, and most of us are so wrapped up in the nesting instinct that we really don't want to disturb someone else's nest."

"Contrary to popular belief."

"Of course," she said, "but the belief was started by men."

"You don't like men?"

"Adore them," she said, "but I can still be just a little bit critical of them."

"You don't spend much time criticizing Knox Martin," David said.

"He likes me," she said. "I'm the one the town talks about. Every small town has a girl they talk about. Knox Martin doesn't, except to stick up for me. He shouldn't really, I guess, because I've certainly given them plenty to talk about."

"What?"

"I was in love."

"That's all?"

"Have you ever been in love?"

"Well, I guess I...well, I don't know. I mean, I've thought I was in love, but I've never been sure."

"Then you've never been in love. And neither have most people, and that's why they hate to see somebody really in love. It embarrasses them, because they're always hearing about love, and reading about it, but they don't know what it is."

"What is it?"

"The most wonderful slow death on earth."

David smiled. He had interviewed hundreds of women about their sex lives, but he had never once discussed love with any of them.

"This is pretty potent conversation for two people who met three minutes ago," Athena said.

"I was thinking that myself."

"I guess I talk too much," she said.

"You talk good. I like it. What can town gossips say about someone who just happened to fall in love?"

"Plenty. I had the audacity to also have a baby, and before you feel sorry for me, I wanted it, I love it, and I'm awful glad I got it. Knox knows how I feel."

David wasn't quite certain what to say. He had never met anyone quite like this girl. Her honesty was startling. "Isn't it...I mean...well, in a small town like this, wasn't it kind of rough?"

"Not really. I was scared to death, of course, but it isn't so bad. I was always disliked because I was pretty, so I was used to that. I was afraid the town might be cruel to the baby, but they're not. If anything, they're just the opposite."

"How old are you?"

"Twenty-two," Athena said.

"Why didn't you marry this man you were in love with?"

"He was married, still is."

"You still in love with him?"

"Little bit, not much. He's been nice about it all. How long will you be in town?"

The speed with which she changed the subject and more or less announced her departure took David back. "A week or two," he said. "I'm with the Wilson interviewing team."

"The sexologist?"

"The same."

"We'll have to have a talk."

"We did."

"I mean a long talk. Where are you staying?"

"The Ferry Inn."

"Wonderful. I work there waiting tables during dinner. Let's have a drink when I get finished."

"I'd love it."

"Me too." She got up. "See you tonight." She gave him the full depth of her smile, then turned and walked to the door.

David watched her go. In ten minutes he had met two people who interested him very much, and he had all but forgotten that he had work to perform. He forced his mind back to business, took out his notebook and looked up the phone number of Agatha Kelsey. He left a half dollar by his cup, got up and went to the phone booth.

Sam Masserly felt the pangs of disappointment when he saw Beverly gather her books at the end of the lecture and leave the room with the rest of the class. His eyes followed her to the door, but she did not turn back or make any sign towards him.

Leaving the room, Sam expected to find her waiting in the hallway, but she was gone. The discovery annoyed and angered him, but he chided himself: Why should she be waiting? What have you got to offer her except a lot of trouble? She's just using her head. You're thirty years old. You're married. You don't make hardly enough to support the wife you've got. For Christ's sake, act your age.

He followed the usual route to the office, checked his box for messages, found nothing. He left the office, walked along the hall to the main entrance.

Suddenly he wasn't interested in teaching the summer term, and it annoyed him that he had made the decision. It further annoyed him to realize that only the girl had prompted him to spend the summer teaching instead of working towards the Master's Degree. He would rather it had been some other motive, something a little higher than merely leching after one of his students.

Leaving the building, he crossed the mall to the parking lot.

Beverly was standing by his car and he had to resist the urge to run.

"I've been waiting for you," she said.

"I'm glad."

They stood facing at the side of his car. It was an awkward moment, each wanting to embrace the other, each resisting the urge, the nervousness growing between them.

"Where can I meet you?" she asked.

"Let me take you. We'll drive."

"No. It wouldn't look right. Just tell me where."

"When you left the room with the others I thought you were walking out of my life."

"Where can I meet you," she persisted.

"I have to be with you," he said. "I have to tell you what it was like to think of losing you."

"Tell me when you can touch me," she said. "Tell me then. I can't stand being this close and not touching you. Just tell me where to meet you."

"At the Tower?"

"Right away." She turned and briskly walked away.

Sam watched her until she got into her car, then he opened his own car door and slid behind the wheel. He followed her out of the parking area, then along Jericho Road, then south on River

Road. She drove fast and he followed her, a sense of urgency growing in him to match the speedometer. They turned off River Road and wound up the curling road of Bowman's Hill. At the top was a parking lot and the stone tower marking the lookout post used by General Washington while he awaited the Battle of Trenton. Beverly parked, and Sam pulled in alongside her. He got out of his car. There were no other cars in the lot. He went to her car and got in beside her. They hesitated a moment, then she slid into his arms and they held each other for a long breathless moment.

They separated, sat apart, but their eyes held, and the eyes were filled with longing and loneliness and pain and love.

"Now I'll tell you," Sam said.

She lifted her hand and pressed her fingers to his lips. "Don't," she said. "Don't. It will only make it more difficult."

They were silent again. Beverly turned away and stared ahead through the windshield. Her hands gripped the steering wheel. "We have to talk," she said, finally. "Yesterday, the day before, it didn't matter. Now it does. I know you love me. You never have to say it. I can see it, I can feel it. I want you to love me, but I'll want more. Not now, not right away. Just now it is wonderful being near you. Tomorrow, the day after, next month, then I'll want more. I'll want you, all of you. I won't want to have you go home to your wife."

"I'm going to divorce my wife," Sam said.

Beverly turned and faced him. "Are you? Have you told her?"

"Well, no," he said. "I just never thought of it before. When I'm ready I'll tell her."

"It's never that simple," Beverly said. "A woman doesn't like to give up a man to another woman. It has nothing to do with him. It is just a matter of pride."

"That doesn't matter. I want you. That's all there is to it. I'll tell her today if you like."

"It can't be up to me, Sam. I won't start on the basis of taking you away from your wife. That is your decision to make. I want you with me only because you want to be there."

"And what do we do in the meantime?"

"I want to be with you in the meantime," she said.

"Then it doesn't make sense. You want to be blameless, and at the same time see a married man. It just stands to reason that I'll be leaving Cora for you."

Beverly slid over and leaned against him. "I know," she said. "It's a curious kind of female logic. I must like to worry things. I really don't care how I'm with you so long as I'm with you, but I also know that love has to have sunshine or it will die. It just won't grow in back alleys, and I don't think you've had much experience with deception."

"None, to be exact," Sam said.

"This could be very hard on you, Sam," she said.

"I don't see how having you could be anything but good," he said.

"Again I can only say that you don't know the extent to which a woman will go to maintain her position."

"But Cora doesn't really want me," Sam said. "There are times when I know that she actually despises me."

"But that doesn't matter, Sam. She will lose face in the town if you leave her for someone else. If she is the kind of woman I think she is, she'll fight for this, just for the sake of her ego."

"I don't know, Bev," Sam said, dropping his head against the back of the seat, "I really don't know."

"We have to work something out," she said.

"Like what?"

"We could go away," she said.

Sam twisted his head to look at her, surprised by the determination in her face, realizing that he actually knew little about her. This, in itself, was startling. Was it necessary to know someone to love them, really, deeply love them? There was the worn adage that you never know anyone until you live with them. You married a woman before you knew her. Was it just a matter of chance that two people found themselves able to sustain a love in the embrace of living? Had he loved Cora in the beginning? No, he didn't think so. With Cora it had been a matter of a bored young man feeling that he might find the riddle of the essence of life answered by marriage. Compared to what he felt for Beverly, the whole business with Cora was ludicrous from start to finish.

"Could we, Sam?" Beverly said.

"Actually it's the only way," he said. "I'm certain of one thing right now. I love you and I want you near me. But I also want this feeling to grow into something greater and stronger, something that will sustain. I want to give it every chance of blossoming." He spoke with his eyes on the ceiling of the car. "What we have now is an attraction. It is strong, but essentially it is a physical longing. It's a sexual attraction. Although I have never made love to you I know that the only thing that keeps us apart is that we have not encountered the time or place and we both feel that it has to be a spontaneous mating. So we have sex holding us together and this is good, but there is also more. I think of it as a growing thing. Sexual attraction can be a basis, the roots. It must be real and solid to create an anchor, but then from the roots must grow the plant, the stalk, and from the stalk—sustained and fed by love—grow the blossoms, the beauty for the world to see. I want this plant to have every chance of a full life, and I believe that staying here in this town might stunt its growth. Hatred might keep out the sun, and even though the roots are solid, the stalk might grow gnarled, the flowers weak and colorless. I must admit that I never thought about this until now, but for some reason I know that I am right. If we are going to have anything we'll have to go away." He stopped speaking. He brought his eyes down to hers. She stared at him for a long moment, then she moved into his arms.

"Oh, Sam, kiss me, I love you so much!"

Elizabeth Pennington did not rise for breakfast. She feigned sleep until she heard Brad leave the house, knowing that Debbie would drive him to the station. She stayed in her room until she heard the wagon pull up before the house again, heard the front door slam, and knew that Debbie was home.

She rose then and went downstairs. She said good morning to Debbie and received a cold silence. They were in the living room and Debbie was standing by the picture window staring out over the terraced lawn.

"What's the matter this morning?" Elizabeth asked.

Debbie turned. "You told me you wouldn't tell Daddy," she said.

"Tell him what?"

"As if you don't know. I just received a one hour lecture on the fallen woman and how she grew. I was embarrassed to death!"

"Oh," Elizabeth said, remembering that she had mentioned the petting incident to Brad. "I didn't think he would say anything."

"I'll bet!"

"Now just a minute, young lady, I'm not going to have you speak to me in that tone of voice. I happen to be your Mother, and I expect some respect from you."

Debbie's anger spilled over. "It never occurs to parents that maybe they have to earn respect!"

"Just what do you mean by that?"

"After what I heard last night, I don't think you ought to ask that! You were practically shouting!"

"Now, see here…"

"What you said to Daddy, well, I don't think you have any room for criticizing how I act with anyone!" She bolted from the room.

"Debbie!"

The kitchen door slammed. As Elizabeth hurried to the kitchen, she heard the sound of the Volkswagen starting. She opened the kitchen door and called, "Debbie!" But the small car was already kicking up the gravel in the drive and roaring off.

Elizabeth stood there watching the car disappear, then she saw the pickup truck turn into the drive and approach the house. She caught her breath and stared with a mixture of disbelief and panic. The truck rolled up and stopped. Chet Parker opened the door and stepped down.

"Howdy," he said, smiling.

"What do you want here?"

"Mister Pennington called the office this morning before he caught his train. Asked me to forgive and forget and come back. I told him there really wasn't anything to forgive. And I wasn't kidding."

"Well, you can just turn right around and go back!"

"You sure that's the way you want it?" He leered.

Elizabeth tried to imagine explaining it to Brad again, and she gave up. "I don't care one way or the other," she said. "Go to work if you like, but stay away from me!"

"Yes, M'am. But in case you—"

Elizabeth cut him off by slamming the kitchen door. She heard his chuckle and it infuriated her. She knew that she could not spend the day in the house with him, so she went to her room to change, planning to drive to Jenkintown to shop.

Cora Masserly was in the kitchen drinking coffee when the doorbell rang. She had expected Sam home for lunch, and when he had called to say that he was spending the afternoon in the library, it had left her with a vague feeling of annoyance.

Rising from her chair, she went through the house and opened the front door.

"Greetings," Marcia Storm said.

"Oh, hello, Marcia."

"Well, invite me in. I escaped again, and I need company."
She held up a paper bag. "I brought along some booze to kill the
pain."

Cora stepped aside and Marcia entered. Cora closed the door
and followed Marcia into the living room.

"Home sweet home," Marcia said. "Where can I find the ice
cubes?"

Cora led the way to the kitchen. She did not want to spend
the afternoon with Marcia, but there didn't seem to be much she
could do about it. What she wanted to do was just sit down and
think about Sam. He had changed and the change bothered her,
in fact it frightened her. He acted as though she did not exist, and
this was a threat to her.

"It's scotch," Marcia said. "How do you like it?"

"With water," Cora said.

They took the drinks into the living room. Marcia dropped
onto the couch and Cora sat in the easy chair.

"Where's Sam?" Marcia asked.

"He had to spend the afternoon working," Cora said.

"Wonderful," Marcia said. She lifted her glass. "Mud," she
said.

They drank and talked for an hour. The conversation was
general and gossipy. Cora was beginning to feel her drinks, and
she yawned. Marcia got up from the couch.

"Stretch out over here," Marcia said. "This is the time of day
to take a load off your feet."

"I'm all right here," Cora said.

"Oh, come on, stretch out. You'll feel better."

Rather than argue, Cora got up and went to the couch. She sat
down, curling her legs under her. Marcia paced the room, glancing at the books and bric-a-brac, then she went to the kitchen and
mixed fresh drinks. When she came back she sat on the couch.

"How come you never had any children?" Marcia asked.

Cora shrugged. "We've never been in the position to have children," she said. It was the stock answer. She would never have said that she didn't want children.

The conversation dragged and they drank and Cora was getting drunk. She did not notice that Marcia had moved closer to her until she felt her arm on her shoulder. She turned to face Marcia, not quite sure what to say. Her senses were dulled. When Marcia ran a hand over her breasts she wasn't certain just why she had done it, then Marcia's face was close, very close, and she was whispering into her ear.

Cora stiffened and got to her feet abruptly. Her voice was thick, but she managed to say clearly, "I think that you had better go."

Marcia regarded her coolly. "You don't like me?" she asked.

"I think that you had better leave," Cora repeated.

"Very well." Marcia got up. She stood a moment, then turned and went to the door. She stopped there and turned back. "I'm in the book if you want to see me," she said.

Cora said nothing. She waited until the door had closed behind Marcia, then she slumped down onto the couch, trembling. How is it possible? A married woman with four children. How is it possible? But she remembered Marcia's words in her ear.

I'll be good to you. I'll be gentle with you. I just want to hold you. You'll like it, you'll see. I just want to love you. Let me love you.

CHAPTER EIGHT

The Ferry Inn is an institution in Walkers Ferry. It was at one time a stop for the Easton Stage, and the stone stables still stand in the rear of the hotel, although they are now garages and storage rooms. Benedict Arnold stayed there for a night when he was fleeing the authorities. It is where any notables visiting Walkers Ferry take a room during their stay, and the actors from the Playhouse spend the summer there.

It is an "L"-shaped building of three stories. It faces Main Street and Ferry Street. The ground floor houses the bar and dining room, the kitchen, the living quarters of Mrs. Alston. The second and third floors house the guests, some permanent, most transients. The accommodations are clean and spacious, but there is no room with a private bath. On each floor are two baths. "It was good enough for George Washington," Mrs. Alston says, "and it was good enough for John Barrymore. If you don't want to share a bath with those two gentlemen, I'd suggest you go to a motel."

The Ferry Inn flourishes. The food is good and the drinks are honest. The walled garden is a place of gaiety on warm summer nights. The bar and inside dining room are wood paneled and decorated with paintings of Revolutionary times. The tables are polished wood. The room is warmly lighted and it is generally graced with considerable laughter and good conversation. This is the watering place for Walkers Ferry, the right place to be seen.

David Belson and Knox Martin had finished dinner and were now drinking sour mash bourbon on the rocks. They sat at a table parallel to the bar. They had talked a lot and had established a mutual liking and respect. In the afternoon David had looked up Knox's books in the local library, and they had discussed his writing. Local topics had been disposed of, and they were now on the subject of Dr. Ira Wilson.

"Fraud is a pretty strong word," David said. "Just because you don't like Wilson's methods is not reason enough to accuse him of fraudulence."

"It's fraud, plain and simple," Knox said. "It is moral thievery."

"I don't get that."

"Well, take our town for instance. You people come in here. You interview women who have some sort of problem with their sex lives. You have methods for getting them to talk about it. For years they may have kept it to themselves. Maybe they're afraid of it, maybe they don't know how to handle the situation or themselves in respect to the problem. You act as a psychiatrist. You as much as put them on the couch and let them bare the problem. To the troubled person this is like opening a nerve to the air. You take down all the facts. You have a case history. Now what? As far as you are concerned, that's all there is to it until those facts are processed by a machine. But what about the victim, the patient? What about the woman who has bared her secret, laid it open for the world to see? Now is the time she needs help, and you people simply pack your bags and head for the next town. Have you ever stopped to think of the number of wrecks you have left in your wake?"

"I never looked at it like that," David said.

"Never?"

"Well, maybe I thought something like that."

"You're too sensitive not to think about it," Knox said. "I think I know you, David, and I'm sure you see some evil in these surveys."

"Not evil," David said. "I'll admit I have certain dissatisfactions with the methods, but it's not evil. The scientist does not effect cures. He examines, he probes. The cures are up to other people. We're scientists."

"The people who invent the thermonuclear bombs take the same stand," Knox said, "but you know damn well that it is merely a rationalization for guilt."

"With your attitude there wouldn't be any research," David said.

"And maybe we'd be better off."

"Now you're rationalizing."

"Yes, I guess I am. But I still think that your boss is a fake. Just take the matter of all his publicity. If he is such a pure scientist, how come he publishes everything in the national magazines instead of in scientific journals?"

"He wants to reach the masses with his information."

"That's a grand thought, but does he take the money from the magazines?"

"Of course," David said. "That's how he finances the surveys."

"That I don't like. A program like this should be financed by a university or a foundation."

"Wilson wants a free hand in what he does. He feels that an organization would inhibit his findings."

"His methods would be a better word," Knox said. "Don't you think that the fact he is being paid by a big circulation magazine dictates his methods? Isn't he deliberately sensational for circulation reasons?"

"I don't know," David said, "I honestly don't know."

Knox took time to rekindle his pipe. David lit a cigarette. The conversation was hitting David too deeply. It brought to the surface much of what he himself had thought about Wilson and his Madison Avenue approach to science. But he had to defend the man's motives, because if Wilson was a fraud then he, David Belson, was also a fraud.

"What did you do before you went with Wilson?" Knox asked.

"Taught biology."

"You didn't like it?"

"Teaching? Yes, I liked it. But it seemed like a rut. I wanted more. I wanted to be doing something more important, something with more purpose."

"You mean you wanted to taste the big time," Knox said. "Now don't get sore. I'm an older man. I've had some desires of my own. There was a time when I wanted to win the Pulitzer Prize. But I settled for less, or I might say I went after more. I found that sailing along on top of the pile you soon forgot to look down. And only looking down can you find the real essence for life. I came here to start a paper, a small paper, and I stayed here for a lot of reasons. One of them is that I see as much life right here, and have a chance to see it closer and better and have more time to try to understand it than I ever had in New York."

"A lot can be said for the big time," David said.

"Not by me," Knox said. "But of course, I'm a small time guy at heart. Let me ask you a question. Were you a good biology teacher?"

"I don't know."

"Did you love it? I mean did you love the idea of having a part in developing other minds?"

"I guess I thought more about developing my own mind."

"Have you done that with Wilson? Have you really had more time to develop your own beliefs? Or are you actually too busy doing the bidding of the great man?"

"How come I'm getting the third degree?" David asked.

"Because I like you," Knox said. "And also because I'm a damned meddler and I like to have the people I like doing the things I think they'd like to be doing."

"I thank you for that. I'll tell you the truth, Knox. I'm not entirely satisfied with what I'm doing, but I'm not against it either. Something about it bugs me, but until I know for myself what it is exactly, I'll go on with it. The premise is healthy and good. Sex is a bugaboo and has been for generations. We presume to prove and convince that it is a natural function and should not be an area of fear."

"Have you ever been in love?" Knox asked.

"That's the second time I've been asked that today," David said.

"I ask that because in your position it is something you should know about. And you should also wonder why these surveys of yours have nothing to do with love. That word never enters into your questions. There must be a reason for that. I don't know what it is, but it is something you ought to be thinking about. It just might make your computing machines blow a gasket."

"I'll think about it," David said.

"Do that," Knox said. "And now I've got to get back to my office. The paper gets delivered tonight and the boys will be coming back with last week's rejects. This has been real enjoyable. Come by the office tomorrow and we'll talk some more." He pushed back his chair and stood.

David got up. He extended his hand and shook with Knox. "I don't know when I've enjoyed talking to anyone more," he said.

"Another thing you might do tomorrow," Knox said. "Take a run out to our college here. Barrows College. It's a pleasant set-up. Small, but active. You might like it here, and I'm sure they could use some good new blood. Matter of fact, I could fix the deal myself. Take a look."

"I'll do that."

Knox Martin crossed the room. He spoke to several people as he left, then disappeared through the doorway into the hall, then the door closed behind him.

Settling back in his chair, David took a sip of his drink, then checked the clock over the bar. It was eight-thirty and he wondered what time Athena Wells finished work. She was working in the garden and he had only seen her briefly in passing, but he had noted that the waitress uniform had failed to subdue the wonderfully exaggerated curves of her small body. He thought to go into the garden and ask her, but decided to simply sit and wait. A waitress came to his table and he ordered another drink.

It had already been a full evening. The talk with Knox Martin had left him moody. There was an awful lot of truth in what Martin had said, and David recalled his feelings of despair when one of the interviewees had committed suicide. That was six months ago, and it had been in Florida. He remembered her name, remembered that he had interviewed her, and he remembered that at the time of the interview he had sensed some root to her problem, had wanted to talk to her more, to help her. But he had kept his silence, had recorded her, let her go. He recalled the words of Cain. *I am not my brother's keeper.* Wrong! Wrong! Just as surely as Cain smote his brother, you failed that woman. You are your brother's keeper, just as everyone is his brother's keeper. To deny this is to deny your existence as a human being. For some time he had wanted to discuss this feeling with Gwen, but had never been able to. In some recess of his mind he knew that when he fully admitted this feeling of guilty inadequacy he would be finished with Dr. Wilson. Instead he kept it to himself, hoping that something would happen to reassure him. It never did.

Athena came to his table a little after nine. She had changed and was again wearing the skin-tight tapered slacks and a harlequin poncho. She sat across from him, bathing him in her smile. "You're a patient man," she said.

"Not unless there's something good to wait for," he said.

"And a gentleman, too. Keep it up, David Belson, I need flattery tonight."

"Facts, M'am, nothing but the facts."

"I feel better already. Let's get out of here and log some walking time."

"I should think you'd have walked enough for a week."

"It's a different kind."

"Suits me. I used to be the athletic type myself."

David signed the check and they left. Athena led the way, and they went along Main street, crossing the bridge over the mill-run, then turned right on Mechanic street. They walked without speaking as though through some prearranged agreement that talk was not necessary.

The night was warm. A light breeze carried flower scent. Clouds scudded across the sky, illumined by the brilliance of a half moon. The street was a short hill. It was narrow and uneven with crazily placed brick sidewalks. They walked along slowly, pausing to look at the displays in the shop windows. An old-fashioned wooden bridge crossed the canal at the top of the hill, and they stopped to lean on the railing and look down on the dark glass surface of the water. Willows bowed over the towpath below them, the delicate, ragged leaf-laden limbs brushing the water.

"This is a place for thinking," David said.

"Peaceful. I love it."

They were silent, both gazing at the water. Athena straightened and moved off. David followed. They went on along the street. The row of shops gave way to houses and TV seen through front windows, and dark shadows of people sitting on porches and the sporadic hum of summer night voices, and the houses gave way to open field. Now it was a country road with dense woods rising on the left, the yellow lights of distant houses, the moon defining the ragged outline of the dark hills. They walked along in the middle of the road, not touching, but close, feeling close, closer still because of the silence and the night.

"Are we going someplace special?"

"Yes," she said.

"Where?"

"Someplace. You'll see."

"It's a secret?"

"Yes. My special place."

They walked for half a mile, then Athena stopped. "We go down here," she said. "Just follow close behind me."

David followed her down a narrow path. They crossed a single railroad track, walked along the bed of the railroad, then descended along another path. The weeds were waist high. David heard the sound of falling water. "Here we are," Athena said.

The moonlight glowed on a grassy clearing. They crossed to the edge of a steep bank, and below was a large pool. A creek ran level with the clearing, then tumbled over a waterfall and boiled and danced in the pool below.

"God, what a wonderful place," David said.

"The kids swim here in the daytime," Athena said. "I have it all to myself at night. I come here a lot."

They sat on the grass at the edge of the bank and listened to the musical sound of the falling water. The multitude of night sounds, the myriad million bugs chirping and sawing, joining in one continuous sound.

"Want to swim?" Athena asked.

"I'm a little unprepared," David said.

"Not really. God gave everyone a waterproof skin for a good reason. It's the only way to swim. I'll show my maidenly modesty by moving over there to undress." She got up and moved off into the shadows.

David was still undressing when he heard the splash of her entering the water. He removed his clothing, then scrambled down the bank and dived into the water. It shocked him at first, but his body adjusted and then it was exhilarating. He looked about for her, saw her head, and swam to her.

"Now you know I'm shameless," she said, laughing.

"Nothing of the kind. This is wonderful. I'd forgotten what it was like to swim in the moonlight."

"Now you're young again."

"You think you're kidding. I feel young. I really do. I feel as though I've missed this, but never realized it until now."

She went underwater. He stayed where he was, treading water, waiting for her to come up. When she did not appear he felt a wave of panic touch him. "Athena!"

"I'm back here."

He turned and she was behind him, a few yards away. "For a minute I thought—"

"I wanted to see what you looked like."

He swam to her. "I was a bit startled."

"I know. I'm sorry. I liked what was in your voice though." She kicked her legs up and swam across the pool with easy, even strokes, then she went underwater and came up under him, grasping his legs. He went under and they both came up sputtering and laughing. They swam, ducked, tumbled in the water until they were both breathless, then Athena swam for the shore and he followed.

The water dripped from her as she climbed over the rocks. The moonlight shadowed and highlighted the flawless contours of her body, and David was awed by her child-like grace. He came up after her and they stood together on the grass. She accepted her nudity with a natural innocence that stilled anything that might have been remotely carnal, and as David looked down upon her, his eyes covering the shoulders, her firm, dark-tipped breasts, he saw only the simple beauty of her.

"The air will dry us in a few minutes," she said.

"You know," he said, "it's a strange thing, but I feel as though we've swam here before, as though I've known you a long time."

"I know," she said.

"You know?"

"Yes, I feel the same way. It's like that with two people some-times. Not often, but sometimes. It's the only way it should be, really. It's just a waste of time to be with someone unless you know, feel that you're supposed to be with him."

"You know an awful lot for a little girl," David said.

"I don't know anything, I just feel things. If I had brains I'd be different, but I don't so I have to just go along with what I feel."

"What do you feel about me?"

"I feel that you're nice, that I'm comfortable with you. We can be silent together and that's important."

"That's all?"

"That all for now."

"I have the feeling I'm going to be in love with you," David said.

"Maybe," she said. "I know that you want to be in love. You want to love someone and I'm here with you and it's comfortable and we've had fun and I bring out a knightly instinct in you. I'm the pretty girl with an illegitimate child."

"That's not very kind," he said.

"Ah, but it is. I want someone to love me. The things I mentioned are just part of the good I see in you. But I want my man to fall in love with me in the daylight. It's not a game with me. It's a day and night affair. And I know that you have the kind of mind that has to weigh things from all angles. You might be in love with me, but it will take time."

"Do you mind if I tell you that you're wrong?"

"Of course not, I want you to. I won't believe it, but I want you to."

"You're wrong. I'm going to be in love with you."

She took a step forward and pressed against him. He encircled her with one arm and tilted her chin back with his hand. He kissed her, the heat surging through him as her lips responded to his and her fingers dug into his back.

When she took her mouth from his she was breathing heavily. "We'd better get dressed," she said, turning out of his embrace. "Then we can talk about falling in love, and you can walk me home, and I'll make you a cup of coffee."

CHAPTER NINE

Folding chairs had been set up in the high school gymnasium facing the stage. The chairs were filled with women, some brought by Agatha Kelsey's efforts, others present in answer to the story in the *Register*.

"...really such an honor," Agatha Kelsey was saying. "I'm sure that there is no need to say..." And she went on at great length to say what there was no need to say.

David Belson stood in the rear. He did not bother to listen to the woman speaking. His eyes strayed over the crowd, and he wondered why they were there. Were they all exhibitionists, as Knox Martin had said? They couldn't all be. Were they all women with problems? Certainly not if they compared to other sampling groups. He had interviewed hundreds of them and there were many women with a good healthy outlook on sex and life in general. But he had to admit that the balance was certainly in the other direction.

He knew that a lot of the women had not come to be interviewed. Many of them were there just because they went to things. They would just as soon attend a hanging or a PTA meeting or a movie on the life cycle of the tsetse fly. Others were there to see the notorious Dr. Wilson in person and hear him speak. Some were there because they thought the proceedings might be a bit racy and they hated to miss even a tinge of smut. A few would be genuinely interested in the scientific purpose of the samplings, and some would be seeking some answer to their problems, and some would be there for the vicarious thrill of getting their perversions into the record.

"...and I might say," Agatha Kelsey said, "that this is an historical moment for Walkers Ferry. It gives me the deepest pleasure to present to you, Dr. Ira Wilson."

Wilson got up from his chair and walked to the rostrum. He smiled down at the women and for the moment his narrow, cold face was friendly and warm. "That introduction makes me feel like a celebrity," he said. There was desultory laughter. They were at ease. Here was father beaming down at them. They could be safe with him. He would listen to them. "I am sure that you all know the nature of my work. I have come here to Walkers Ferry for a sampling of the sexual attitudes inherent in your female population in an effort to categorize your community in relationship to the widely divergent communities in the rest of the country."

David had heard it all before, but he was always fascinated. Wilson had a studied way of making the women feel that their sex lives were important to the course of history, that the way they jumped into bed was going to affect the force of gravity. He went over the history of the surveys, hammering away at the science angle. After all, this was the age of sputnik and science was respectable.

"Our methods are revolutionary," Wilson said. "There are other surveys, of course, and they use all sorts of methods. We at Research Affiliates have worked out a system which we feel gets to the heart of the subject, keeps things on the human level, but also insures anonymity."

Elizabeth Pennington did not have her mind on the lecture. She was glad to be there, glad to be anywhere but inside her house where Chet Parker was working. She looked about her at the assembled women, idly cataloging what they were wearing, trying to recall some who were familiar, but not known. She looked at Sylvia Thompson, marveling at the girl's beauty, wondering if all the stories about her were true. She noted that Claire Roberts looked tired. No wonder, she thought, with that husband of hers, then she added to herself, sister, you should talk.

Looking up at the figure on the stage, she brought her mind back to what he was saying.

"...indeed, you might well find the experience of discussing the most intimate portions of your life with total strangers a bit difficult. These are your innermost secrets and it is understandable that you should be reluctant to tell the absolute truth. But I can assure you that my three colleagues and myself are not sitting as judges. You must think of us only as statisticians. We will not see you when we talk to you, although you will see us. We have worked out a list of questions. For these questions we seek answers, nothing more. What you tell us is simply part of the record, a portion of the whole."

Elizabeth wondered what she would tell them. Would they want to know about the episode in the football stadium? Would she tell them about that? And the affair in college, would she want to discuss that with this stranger? She was certain that she would leave Chet Parker out of it. He couldn't be important. It was just that she had been in a weird frame of mind and he happened to be there. The whole thing was disgusting and could not possibly have any bearing on her real life.

"I want to impress upon you that while we wish to investigate into your lives it is not our place to advise you. We are here to do nothing but record. We are not doctors, we are not marriage counsellors. We are here on a scientific mission to collect a portion of your lives, and that is all."

Cora Masserly listened attentively, twisting a handkerchief in her hands. She knew that Marcia Storm was in the room, sitting somewhere in the rear. The thought made her nervous. Marcia had not come near her since that afternoon. When was it? Was it only two days ago? It seemed like a month, or as though it never really happened.

In her limited world Cora had heard about women who loved other women, and in Walkers Ferry there were a number of women of whom it was said they were lesbians. She had always wondered about them, specifically wondering what they did to each other, but it was an area of experience that she would never, *could* never bring into conversation. Somehow, she could not reconcile Marcia with this type. After all, the woman was married and she had four children. That she was a lesbian was unthinkable. What then? What?

"When we assemble our records," Dr. Wilson was saying, "we feed our findings into a complex electronic computing machine. They are digested and through a series of parallels we are able to establish certain trends about the sexual habits of a variety of different types of women. When you are talking to our interviewers you must remember that he is not a man, that he is merely the voice to ask the questions and the hand to inscribe the answers. His approach will at all times be completely clinical, and just as you do not feel shame when disrobing your body before your doctor, you should not feel shame when disrobing your mind before us."

What on earth will I tell them, Cora thought, and what can I say to them about Marcia? Is it necessary to talk about her? It wasn't anything sexual. Perhaps it was just the drinking. But she did have her hands all over me, handling me the way Sam used to before I put a stop to it. When she thought about Sam her brow wrinkled. He was certainly acting strange lately. He had left the house in the morning without waking her or having breakfast, and he hadn't shown the least interest in coming to her room with his disgusting proposals as he used to. She brought her attention back to the speaker.

"I think that about explains our mission here," Dr. Wilson said. "We will begin the interviews on Monday morning. On the way in you were all given a card to fill out. Those of you who will be so kind as to help us in our work here, please present the card at the large table in the rear. Be certain to include your telephone numbers and tomorrow you will receive a call telling you the time of your appointment. While some of you may be seeing me again, I will not be seeing you. And so, I thank you very much for listening to me, and I thank you in advance for your assistance in our project."

Cora lifted her hands and joined the applause as Wilson stepped back. She glanced down at the card in her lap, then lifted it. It contained her name, her telephone number and the day she would prefer the interview. She had written "Monday" on the card. She wanted to get it over with, but she was also curious about the interview.

Sylvia Thompson had not been particularly interested in what Dr. Wilson had to say, but sitting watching him, she had become interested in him as a man. She knew that whatever he might say would be prepared in advance and would in essence be meaningless, but she was intrigued with the way he said things. He spoke as though his voice was divorced from his mind or body. He mouthed a series of platitudes, but his eyes covered the assemblage like the eyes of a hawk. There was a fierce dedication that was written in his face, a fanatic quality that belonged to a traveling preacher. And there was a hardness about him. She imagined that if you could see his heart it would be solid granite with the blood merely piped through.

And the thing that Sylvia found most fascinating was her instinctive knowledge that the man had never been with a woman physically. It was something she would never have ventured to explain, but she was certain that this was the truth. There are some things that a woman who is almost completely physical can feel about a man simply by observing his mannerisms, and Sylvia had made this decision about Ira Wilson.

It was a fascinating incongruity. The idea that the man most noted for his knowledge of the sex habits of women had never had intercourse was thoroughly intriguing to her.

Perhaps out of her constant state of boredom, perhaps because of a feeling of dissatisfaction with men, perhaps she was a scientist in her own way; whatever the reason, Sylvia knew that she had encountered something challenging.

David Belson was waiting by the staff car when Ira Wilson scurried out of the door in the rear of the gymnasium. He said what was expected of him. "It was a good talk."

"Tiresome but necessary," Wilson said. "I guess we better get back."

They got into the car, David behind the wheel, Wilson next to him. They drove down the lane past the high school, paused at the highway, then turned left onto the pavement.

"The newspapermen will be waiting at the Inn," David said.

Wilson nodded. He brought the long, bony hands up to press against his closed eyes, then he rubbed the craggy forehead and trailed his hands down over the thin, drawn face and rubbed the prominent chin.

"Well, David," he said, opening his eyes, "a few more weeks and we'll be finished. Another survey complete." He smiled tightly and there was a note of satisfaction in his voice.

"Then the work begins," David said.

"Yes, but the really tough part will be over. Then there is only the pleasure of seeing our field work come together, see all these bits as a greater work, see all the timid jabberings, all the hesitant little half-truths, all the dirty bits of female perversion summed up in facts and figures. There is a purity in the finished product that you don't find in the interviews. The final result is the thing!"

David was remembering the things Knox Martin had said, also recalling his own disquieting thoughts about the true meaning of the interviews, wondering what Wilson would say if the questions were brought to him. He found himself anticipating with relish the questions that Knox would have for the good doctor.

They turned into the parking lot behind the Ferry Inn and David parked the car near the garden entrance. They got out, slamming the doors, and walked around to the front.

"I asked Rita to have the newsmen gather in your room," David said.

"Good. I called Howard and told him to come down," Wilson said. "He should be here."

David had hoped that Wilson would face Knox Martin without the Public Relations man, Howard Denby, present, and he now wondered why Wilson always insisted that Howard be there. If the man was really sincere, why did he need someone to run his interference?

David and Wilson went up the stairs. Rita Talbot was waiting for them on the landing. She was looking nervously efficient.

"The newspapermen are in your room, Doctor," she said in her dry, officious voice.

"Howard here?"

"Yes, Sir. He's with them."

Wilson led the way down the hall with Rita dogging his steps and David bringing up the rear. The door to Wilson's room was ajar and there were voices from within. Wilson swept into the room.

"Good morning, Gentlemen. Hello, Howard, good to see you."

There were five men in the room. They were seated, but they got to their feet when Wilson entered. When David got into the room, Howard was making the introductions.

"Reed Pernock of the *Philadelphia Bulletin,*" he said. "Milton Barnes, the *Trentonian;* Harry Sachs, *Philadelphia Inquirer;* Bill Marris, *Trenton Times;* Knox Martin, the local paper."

"Pleasure to meet you," Wilson said. "Let me get comfortable." He stripped off his jacket and dropped it onto the bed, then he sat down on the edge of the bed, crossed his legs and gripped one knee with both hands. He looked at Knox Martin. "I wondered what ever happened to you," he said. "I read your book, *Tomorrow's Dawn,* while I was in college. It was a fine book. And then you dropped out of sight."

Knox was visibly taken back by the statement and the man's knowledge of his work. The other reporters were obviously impressed. But David had a moment to glance at Howard Denby, saw the relish with which the press agent took the statement, and knew that Howard had done some research on Walkers Ferry and that Wilson had been briefed beforehand.

"Now, then, I suppose you have a few questions," Wilson said. "As you may know I always try to be candid with the press. I fully realize the importance your reports have on the continuance of my work. So, just fire away."

The reporters looked at one another, then Harry Sachs of the *Inquirer,* asked, "Dr. Wilson, could you give a brief summary of your survey to date?"

"It is much too early for that," Wilson said. "The results must be processed."

"Can you give us an indication of trends," Milt Barnes asked.

Wilson smiled. "I seem to get the same questions everywhere we go," he said, "and they're always impossible to answer."

"Well, Dr. Wilson," the reporter from the *Trentonian* said, "You have been on this survey for almost a year, and in that time you have stated that your findings have indicated something revolutionary in regards to the sex habits of the American female. Can you give us a hint what these findings show?"

"I think that I can tell you something," Wilson said. "This is our next to last sampling, and with the results already processed we have come up with something which you might find a bit startling." Wilson paused for a moment to give his words the feeling of portentous decree. The reporters held their pencils poised. "In the past," Wilson went on, "it has always been thought that the sexual desires were more sublimated. In the samplings we have taken thus far, we find indications that this is not true. This is not definite, you realize, but there are indications. The mass of females whom we have interviewed have shown far more aggression than one might have supposed. This is particularly true of married women. It has always been assumed that the woman merely waited for the husband to approach her physically, but our samplings show that in seven out of ten cases, it is the wife who is the instigator of the sex act."

"Is there a reason for this?" one of the men asked.

"It is a matter of interest," Wilson said. "The husband has other things on his mind, business pressure, bills, and so forth. Sex becomes a secondary thing with him."

"Do you mean that women have sex on their minds more than men?"

"That is precisely what I mean," Dr. Wilson said. "With a man it is a physical act of pleasure. With a woman it is a way of life."

The reporters wrote in their notebooks, heads bowed to the page. David saw Wilson glance at Howard Denby and saw Howard wink slightly. Tomorrow's headlines were set. It was certain that the pronouncement made in this hotel room would be on the news wires, and tomorrow would be read in every city and hamlet of America. It was a million dollars worth of publicity for the series in *Argus* magazine, a tantalizing prediction for the sensation-hungry press. In the past months David had listened to Wilson drop hints about this and that to reporters, giving them just enough to make the story interesting, but this was the first time that he had heard Wilson issue a deliberate falsehood.

"If this is the case," Harry Sachs said, "then what about the widely spread idea that the vast majority of women never achieve an orgasm throughout their lives?"

"Pure nonsense," Wilson said. "We have found that women on the average achieve much greater pleasure from the sex act than men, that their sex lives are much happier, and that they often experience not only one orgasm during coitus, but several."

David scowled and looked at Knox. A wry smile played about the mouth of the elderly editor. He knows, David thought, at least he knows. This is all a goddamned lie. David saw that Knox was about to speak, but Howard Denby also saw it. The press agent stepped in front of Knox and cut off the question.

"Well, fellows," Howard Denby said, "let's wrap it up with that. I told you the Doc would give you something to make the city editors sit up and take notice, now, didn't I? That's front page copy, and you're the first to get it. Now, I know you've got deadlines and these boys have got a lot of sex problems to tangle with. Let's go downstairs and the drinks are on me."

It was a clever maneuver, and David knew that Howard had earned his week's salary. The reporters got up to leave. Knox shrugged and got up with them. They shook hands with Wilson, then went through the door and into the hallway, Howard Denby herding them away.

Rita Talbot came into the room. "Dr. Wilson," she said, "Mrs. Kelsey is downstairs. She has the cards."

"Well, take them away from her, Rita. Then begin working on the schedules. Have Bascomb and Sharmer arrived?"

"Only Dr. Bascomb," Rita said. "Mr. Sharmer is still tied up in the City."

"Very well. Have Bascomb start to work with you."

"Yes, Sir." Rita left.

Wilson got up from the bed. He paced to the window, pulled the curtain aside and looked down at the street. "Quaint little town," he said. "We ought to get our share of screwballs here."

"Sir," David said, "I don't understand that statement you made to the press."

Wilson turned slowly and one shaggy eyebrow was cocked. "Don't you?"

"No, Sir, I don't. I don't think we have the facts to back up that opinion."

Wilson pursed his lips and nodded thoughtfully. "Opinion," he said. "Now that is an interesting choice of words. Opinion. You mean by that, I presume, that I made those facts up, took them out of the air."

"I didn't mean to be rude, Sir, I just—"

"You were right," Wilson said, "absolutely right. Not a word of truth, but excellent newspaper copy." Wilson turned back to face the window. "David," he said, "this is a tough, competitive world in which we live, remember that. I have worked with you for three years, watched you, lived with you. You have one fault. You are an idealist, an idealist in a time when ideals won't buy you a cup of coffee. What I told those newspapermen offends your scientific purity. Forget it. It has no bearing on our work. No matter what they print, our work goes on as usual, and the results that come out of the machines will be the truth. By that time the story will be dead, and the newspapers will be happy to see me contradict myself. In the meantime we keep our work in the public eye. The end, David, the end justifies any means."

"But what has a newspaper story got to do with the 'end?' "

"What do you think our 'end' is, David?"

"What? Why, to complete the survey," David said.

"No, David, that is only part of it. The important thing is to continue our work. To do this we need money, the money, incidentally, that pays your salary. This money comes from publications, and the publishers are eager to underwrite our work only so long as our results sell their publications. You may not like these facts of life, David, but they are facts nevertheless. What I said today will help sell magazines." When David did not answer, Wilson turned from the window. "Would you give Bascomb and Rita a hand with the schedule?"

"Yes, Sir," David said. He turned and left the room. There was much realistic truth in what Wilson had said. If you want to dance, you must pay the piper.

He walked along the hallway and turned into the stairs, went down slowly. Wilson was no doubt correct, he reasoned, but it left a bad taste. He reached the bottom of the stairs and stopped. Howard Denby was saying goodbye to the last of the newspapermen at the front door. The screen closed and Howard turned, a scowl replacing his usual smile.

"Oh, hi," Howard said. "How about a drink? I really need it."

David did not like the public relations man, but at the moment he was curious about him.

"Fine," David said, "I'd like it."

They went into the bar and took chairs at a corner table. Howard leaned back, rubbing his eyes. "This is too early for me," he said. "I had to get the seven o'clock train out of the city." He blinked and yawned. "Brother, what a burg," he said. "I get on the other side of the Holland Tunnel and I might as well be in the Aleutian Islands. The Great American Desert." He lifted his arm and waved his hand in a circle. "There it is," he said. "Land of the Great Unwashed. From the Hudson River to Golden Gate Bridge, the vast intellectual vacuum, stronghold of the *Argus* magazine mentality."

"Some of the best universities are out there," David said.

"Oasis," Howard said. "An occasional watering spot. And besides that there aren't any universities in this country anymore. They're just big high schools. Believe me, when they applied democracy to education they ended learning. Our ideas of mass education had to account for the incredible stupidity of all the buffoons out there, so we just gave up on education. The college student of today has been sold a bill of goods. He goes through those cretin level grammar schools for four years and gets a piece of paper written in Latin that he can't even read and believes that he's a scholar." Howard laughed and slapped a hand on his leg. "Pure public relations, the whole thing. One of the great con jobs of all times."

"You make it sound pretty grim," David said.

"Don't ever think it," Howard said. "I'm just a realist. I can appreciate a con man because I know where I stand with him. You take the Doc. He's got it knocked, because he knows just how stupid the people are. He's selling sex, but he's also got enough sense to play up to the illusion that the Great Unwashed are also scholars."

"You don't think that our work is honest?"

"What's honest got to do with it? What's honest? Wake up, man. The one thing you got to get used to in this racket, or any racket, is wearing the mantle of pure crap. Public relations is just a matter of trying to make the crap smell sweet. They can write books about it and teach it in journalism schools and it still remains crap. Now you take me, I can get up a press kit, write a release, run interference with a bunch of newspaper guys. Any idiot can do that. But I know one thing better than anyone else. I know one thing, and you want to know what this is?" He did not wait for an answer, but winked and said, "I know everybody in the business. I know what everybody drinks. I know what they like and what they hate. I know a little dirt here, a little there. I know who has to get paid off with a jug and who gets paid off with a hooker. I know if they like blondes or brunettes, a leg man from a chest man. That's all I know. Everybody in the business. And believe me, in a tower built of crap you don't find any bricks."

David smiled. "Madison Avenue wouldn't agree with that," he said.

"Agh, honk them," Howard growled. "Look, boy, listen to the old man. This is the big clip-job, the biggest carney on earth. That Madison Avenue, hell, a couple thousand gray-flannel barkers pushing the old shell game. And the midway is all the pre-fab split-levels from Hackensack to Sheboygan. They're all marks, the same country bumpkins who have been crowding the carneys since Barnum went legit. Dress 'em up, give 'em big cars, send the kids to college, and hell, they haven't changed a bit. Sell them hope, give them a look at the future, make their sex lives legitimate, tell them they're gonna get something for nothing and you own them. But don't ever try telling them the truth. Jesus, that would really panic them!"

"I take it you don't like the beautiful common people," David said.

"Like 'em? Me, like 'em?" Howard blinked and his eyes widened. "They make me want to throw up."

"Then how can you stand doing what you do?" David asked. "How do you face each day?"

"What am I supposed to do, drop dead? I gotta eat, and my tastes run to first class fare."

"Do you think Wilson feels this way?"

"Hell, what do I know what Wilson feels. You saw that little act up there this morning. Pure crap and the marks bought it."

"Maybe not," David said. "Knox Martin didn't go for it."

Howard chuckled. "I had to do some fast broken field running around that one," he said. "There's always an exception and he happens to be one of them. But that's just another example of why the con artists will always come out on top. I checked Martin out before I came down here." He grinned. "We really threw him a left hook with the nonsense about his books. He was a threat, but once we had him off balance it was easy. I tell you, boy, the road to success is littered with the bones of sincere guys. Do you think the rest of those newspaper guys gave a damn what we told them? They don't care. They got to get a story in and if we can give them something sensational they're happy. People like Knox Martin don't count. They're always small-time. Hell, let's have that drink and forget it." He turned and signalled the bartender.

David did not say anything. His opinion of Howard Denby was strengthened. Not only did he think that the man was wrong, but he also saw him as typical of the New York success mind. They see the world in the capsule of their own frustrated designs, their minds ingrown to the point where they see the rest of the world in the image of themselves. They had to be wrong! People like Knox Martin and Athena might be in the minority, but the very fact that they existed gave the lie to Howard's conception.

And what about Ira Wilson? Seen from Howard's point-of-view, Wilson was unsavory. David was still undecided, but the wheels of his mind were spinning and facts were clicking into place.

CHAPTER TEN

Agatha Kelsey's parties, according to the hostess, were as democratic as the Fourth of July. A widow of invested wealth, she practiced the new democracy—the belief that anyone who belonged to the Village Association was welcome to her home. Her guest list was the roster of the Association.

If one wanted to spend the evening drinking and talking with the same people they met at the post office that morning, or encountered at the newsstand or hardware store, or rubbed elbows with in the Ferry Inn, they came to one of Agatha's parties. As a general rule the majority ignored her invitations. Even suburbanites can tire of one another, and to be in the same room with Agatha, drinking her whiskey, was an open invitation to serve on the next committee for the Horse Show or Children's Bazaar or one of her dozens of activities. The conspiracy between Agatha and the telephone company was bad enough.

But this Saturday night her guest list was out in force. It wasn't every day that Agatha had a famous sexologist on tap.

The party filled the ground floor of the huge stone house and spilled out onto the flagstone patio where Paul Cortland's Dixie Five tortured the *Muskrat Ramble*. The pool was lighted and several knots of people stood around its edge, but there were no swimmers. Agatha's parties were never that democratic. A buffet lunch covered a long table at the edge of the patio. Two white-jacketed bartenders sweated over the drinks at the portable bar set up in the TV room.

Dr. Ira Wilson was backed up against a bookcase by a press-ing group of admirers. Even a studied smile could not dislodge the grimace on his face.

Conversation surged like incoming waves, a rolling mass of words crossing like tides to crash on ears and die out, to be replaced by still more waves, high-low, rising, falling, more words and more words until the overall sound was like the rush of a strong wind. Two hundred people talking and nothing being said.

Exurbia on Saturday night, different from Scarsdale or Westport only in that Bucks County parties seldom have themes; no costumes, no Japanese lanterns, no charades. Everyone pres-ent was either part of a couple, the resident half of what used to be a couple before Reno, the adult children of couples. Husbands and wives arrive together, then go their own way. It is considered bad form for couples to stay together at parties. It might be a bit embarrassing, when the booze takes hold, to make a pass at your own wife. There is generally live music at a Bucks County party, but seldom any dancing, unless a few guests stray in from Princeton. The chief sport at a Bucks County party is to stand close to someone's wife, close enough to smell her perfume, close enough to gaze into the valley of her breasts, and talk. The talk might lead to a casual ramble across the lawns and some blurred lipstick, and occasionally a neighbor's wife might be cov-eted in the bushes, but for the most part it is all talk. There is the usual quota of moral dereliction in Walkers Ferry as in any other healthy suburban community, but not at parties. Parties are for talking, drinking, accidentally nudging breasts to check for resilience, getting someone's wife to pour out the woes of her marriage while you listen sympathetically and arrange to meet her in New York for lunch. An unwritten divorce law—one that is as intractable as tempered steel—in Walkers Ferry decrees that Mother keeps the homestead and Dad shambles off to New York to live in near poverty. This has a heartening effect on the moral discretion of the male.

David Belson and Hugh Bascomb stood together in a corner of the library. They had drinks in their hands. Hugh smoked his ever-present pipe. They watched the changing of the throng around Ira Wilson with interest.

"This is the first time we ever gathered socially with our victims," Hugh said. "I thought it was against the rules."

"I guess Wilson makes up the rules as he goes along," David said.

"You sound a bit chagrined, my lad," Hugh said. "Something bothering you?"

"Oh, nothing much. Idol with feet of clay, that sort of thing."

"Gods must be made of stone to endure," Hugh said. "And even they get tumbled from time to time."

"Guess you're right. I was called a foolish idealist yesterday."

"Munitions makers call pacifists idiots. It's only according to what side you're on who the bigger idiot is. It's an art to be an idealist, boy, don't knock it."

"How do you feel about the surveys, Hugh?"

"Best salary I ever had," Hugh said.

"That's all?"

"That's something when you're forty-seven years old, that's a lot. I spent ten years dissecting frogs for college girls, and after that Mr. Wilson is a joy to behold."

"Do you think he's really dedicated?"

"In his way," Hugh said. "He's dedicated to Ira Wilson. Senator McCarthy flew high on Communist witch hunts, Wilson intends to fly high on female hormones. He's got a good thing and he won't let go."

"But what good are the surveys? Do we really do any good?"

"It's easier reading than Chaucer. It's sex, boy, pure and simple. Women lay in bed wondering how other women are doing it and we're there to tell them."

"What do you think Wilson really thinks about sex?" David asked.

"You ain't the only one wondering that," Hugh said with a chuckle.

"What?"

"That girl there, the one in the black dress. She's been standing there for a half hour letting him get a good look. The others come and go, but she just sticks there. Jesus, what a pair on her! She's giving him the full treatment, like dangling a fly near a trout."

"She's a beautiful girl," David said.

"Yep, and hot as a cracker. I spent ten years in the area of that kind of thermal radiation, and I'd know that look anywhere. Methinks Dr. Wilson might just become one of his own statistics before we leave this happy town."

David laughed. "You know, Hugh," he said, "you've always amazed me with your outlook on things. Nothing seems to bother you. Life seems to fit you and you wear it like an old shoe."

"I have my bad moments," Hugh said, "but mostly you're right. I believe in a lot of things, but mostly I believe in my own insignificance. Because of its relative size and density the human being displaces a certain amount of the earth's atmosphere for a certain amount of time. During this short duration of vegetation it busies itself with the creation of superfluous bric-a-brac like building bridges and the like and feeling superior to other forms of life. I find it impossible to take anything that simple too seriously. I'm here, I live, I busy myself, that's all."

"Do you believe in God?"

"In my own ridiculous way."

"How come you never married?"

"I did when I was much younger. It was disaster. The moment I turned away from the altar I felt mummified. Six months later I arose from the tomb."

"Were you ever in love?"

"Once, when I was teaching, but she was..." Hugh paused and stared. "Well, I'll be damned," he said, "that's her."

"Who?" David followed the line of Hugh's stare, saw an attractive auburn-haired woman in a white dress.

"The one I was in love with," Hugh said. "Well, I'll be go to hell, imagine that." His face broke into a broad grin. "I never thought that *I'd* be one of the statistics." He jammed his pipe into his pocket. "Keep the home fires burning, old pal," he said, winking. He started off through the crowd, leaving David to stare after him in astonishment.

Sylvia Thompson was aware that a good percentage of the husbands in the room had difficulty keeping their eyes off of her. A number of them had given up trying and were just staring. It amused her, but did not interest her.

The black cocktail dress she wore was designed specifically on the premise—If ya got 'em, show 'em. The skirt billowed over a series of crinoline petticoats, but the bodice was skin tight and constructed to push the breasts up. The square neck was cut back on the sides to exhibit as much of the breasts as the law allowed. On Sylvia's extraordinary development the effect was startling.

She had positioned herself on the fringe of people paying homage to Ira Wilson. She made certain that he saw her. Her occasional glances in his direction told her that he had gotten the message, but he was bridling against the obvious. This served to support her earlier theory about him, and she enjoyed the thought.

For a moment Wilson was standing alone, so she moved in. She stood before him and said, "We haven't met, Dr. Wilson, my name is Sylvia Thompson."

Wilson reddened slightly and kept his eyes up with effort. "My pleasure," he said.

"We never had an expert on sex with us before," she said, "even though most of the men here might disagree." When Wilson smiled, but did not answer, she said, "Do you practice what you preach, Doctor?"

"I'm not a preacher, Mrs. Thompson."

"Miss," Sylvia said.

"Sorry," Wilson said.

"So am I," Sylvia said. "Are you married, Doctor?"

"No, I'm not."

"Well, how fortunate," Sylvia said.

A new group of worshippers moved in around Sylvia. She smiled. "I hope to see you again, Doctor," she said.

Wilson smiled nervously and nodded. Sylvia backed out of the group and moved away. So far, so good. He's scared to death of me, but the fact that he had to keep his hands behind his back means something. She felt smugly sure of herself. It was a new experience for her, having a man within a mile who wasn't ready to leap. She went towards the TV room to have her drink replenished.

Elizabeth Pennington stood alone. Brad had been taken in tow by George Bedlow, an account exec for a rival agency, and he was in the kitchen. She noticed the man coming towards her. He was a stranger, and since she knew the complete roster of the Village Association, he must be one of Dr. Wilson's associates. He certainly looked the part with the gray hair and the tweed suit that could stand a pressing. But there was something familiar about him and it was obvious that he was making a direct line towards her and he had a broad smile on his face.

"Elizabeth!" he said when he was close enough. The voice was deep and warm and her puzzlement turned to surprise. Her mouth opened and she caught her breath.

"Hugh," Elizabeth said in a whisper.

"What a wonderful surprise," he said. "Eighteen years."

"I'm stunned," Elizabeth said. "I don't know quite what to say."

"I was right," Hugh said. "Remember the time I said that you were a pretty girl, but you'd grow into a beautiful woman? Well, by God, you've gone and done it."

"Oh, Hugh," Elizabeth said, "This is so wonderful. Are you with Dr. Wilson?"

"Yes, indeed. When you left school to get married I just gave up."

"That's not true."

"Almost. Except that I took ten years to get up enough nerve to leave."

"You haven't changed a bit," Elizabeth said.

"I have retained my wit," Hugh said, "but everything else is changed. The hair is gray and my daily diet has changed from red meat to pills and vitamins, blood builders, gas relievers, lining soothers and tranquilizers. In short, young lady, I have become an old man."

"You were an old man then."

"Thank you."

Elizabeth laughed. "I mean, really, you were all of twenty-nine, a man of the World."

"Twenty-nine. My God, was I ever only twenty-nine?"

"How about me? I was eighteen."

"You make me sound like an aging lecher."

Elizabeth laughed again. "Oh, Hugh, there has never been anyone else since who could make me laugh the way you used to. I mean happy laugh, good-feeling laugh."

"Or cry?"

Elizabeth sobered and her expression was wistful. "I did cry, didn't I? No, I never cried like that again, either. I've cried because I was hurt or unhappy, and then I've felt foolish about it. It was different, somehow."

"The sweet sadness," Hugh said. "To cry for something that should be, but isn't or can't be, is like pleading. It has a deeper meaning than the crying of self-pity. It has a place, and it merely soothes instead of making you feel ridiculous."

"The sweet sadness," Elizabeth repeated. "I like that, Hugh, because that's the way it was. It was just saying goodbye to something that had been very beautiful."

"I've never forgotten it," Hugh said.

They were jostled in the press of the crowd and Hugh spilled his drink. "Damn," he muttered.

"Let's get out of here," Elizabeth said. "There's breathing room down by the pool and I want to hear everything about you."

They angled towards the door, finally made it to the patio, then walked slowly across the close-cropped lawn towards the pool.

Sam Masserly did not like parties, nor could he see how they could have any bearing on his job. It was Cora's idea that participation in community social life was an absolute necessity for a college instructor. Bucks County parties were the easiest for Sam because he did not have to participate beyond having his body in attendance and a glass in his hand. But this particular party held a strangeness for him.

On one side of the room Cora was in animated conversation with Farley Dunham, the writer. On the other side of the room, sitting on a sofa and talking with a young French artist named Emile, was Beverly. It was the first time Sam had seen them at the same time.

Beverly, Sam imagined, must be getting the better conversation. He glanced at Cora, noticed that she was doing more listening then talking. That figured. Despite his own inclinations towards writing, Sam disliked writers. Farley Dunham was tall and thin and he slouched. His hair was short-cropped and a heavy, untrimmed mustache covered the upper lip under the thin, long nose. Dunham, Sam knew, affected a rough, ungrammatical speech that went with the biography notes on his books.

He talked about his railroad days, his construction days, the period of finding himself, and he was an incredible bore. Beverly, on the other hand, was laughing and sharing the conversation about—well, whatever it is that French artists talk about.

The comparison between the two women was interesting. There was Cora, a complete phoney, a shrewish bitch, talking with that paperbacked creep just because he was supposed to be successful. And there was Beverly, being herself, her wonderful, sincere, beautiful self.

Sam felt that he was looking into a shop window. There was his wife, who was not going to be his wife for damned long, and there was the girl he wanted. He wondered how he would tell this to Cora. He had thought about it the night before as they sat in the living room. He had even put down his book and was about to speak, but when he looked up at her, he couldn't say it. It had occurred to him that she would merely laugh at him and refuse to get a divorce. What would he do if she refused? He had been doing what Cora said for so long that he wasn't certain how to go about defying her. So he had picked up his book and resumed reading. When he was with Beverly it seemed too simple. He was quite brave about it then, felt like a man. In Cora's presence it was a different matter, and he hated to admit to himself that he was actually afraid of her.

I'll work it out, he said to himself, it will take a bit of time, but I'll work it out.

Claire Roberts was afraid. She stood listening to Morley Callahan extoll the artistic merits of his latest industrial film, but her eyes were on her husband.

Mike had intercepted Sylvia Thompson as she crossed the room and he was staring with unabashed interest at the brazen female's decolleté. There was certainly nothing subtle about Mike. From the variety of facial expressions, Claire could pretty much figure out what he was saying. But the proposition received a disinterested reception and whatever it was that Sylvia had said, it wasn't flattering. When the girl moved off, Mike was left with a deep scowl marring his face.

Claire hoped that it hadn't been some insult regarding Mike's physical prowess. Like most men who are narcissistic about their bodies, Mike was secretly afraid of impotence. To them brute strength is maleness. It would never occur to Mike that a woman might respond physically to tenderness. He was never interested in mating with a woman. His pleasure was to have her ecstatic because of his stimulation. Mike was surly and difficult if anything seemed to threaten this male worship, and a remark from a woman to suggest that she might not be eager to submit to him would make him morose.

And now Mike was staring across the room at Beverly, and the look on his face made Claire afraid.

When Hugh Bascomb walked away, David was left alone. He went to the bar for a drink, then walked out to the patio and stood for a few moments listening to the Dixieland. He decided that the musicians would be better off playing fox-trots. Their interpretation of Dixie was too polite, and he liked more "gut-bucket" on the slide trombone.

He went back inside and watched the guests with a sense of detachment. Since Agatha Kelsey had been the main recruiter for the interviews, David felt that he could safely predict that most of the women in the room would record their sex histories in the next week. Here in public, in the safe area of the crowd, the drink, the platitude, there was no indication of the private hells they dwelled in. The cocktail dresses were brave armor. How many of them faced the nakedness of the marriage bed with the trembling horror of the victim being led to the guillotine? Which divorcee, now laughing, cried herself to sleep? Which one was the frigid wife who would stammer through the story of the uncle who crawled into her bed? Which one was the perfect wife and mother who dreamed of an affair with a truck driver?

By the end of the week it would all be recorded, and David would once again leave a town wondering how in hell's name so many people could make such an ungodly mess of their lives through the simple device of choosing a mate. If only a man and woman would mate for the simple reasons of desire and love it might be different, but there were so many other factors involved. A woman might feel she was in love with a man, but it was impossible to see the man through the forest of social adornments. A woman married a social position, a career, security, a salary, many things, but seldom a man. These were the accouterments of the "good" marriage, but even on bedsheets of finest damask linen the sweating gyrations of procreation boiled down to basics of naked man and naked woman, and without the sanctity of pure love it is animal rutting.

Against this background of social marriage, a girl like Athena Wells was a paragon of virtue. She would be ostracized by polite society, but only because she threatened the structure of anti-love with her honest acceptance of love. She had knowingly taken the seed of love into her womb and nurtured it there, walked heavy-bellied through the love-hostile town safe in her world-woman knowledge of love, suffering gratefully the body-wracking pains of birth necessary to bring the screaming reality of love fulfilled from her loins. The frustrated whore-wives would hate her when they should envy her and emulate her. She was woman, the symbol, as natural as the earth is the mother birthing the Oak.

The jabbering, gesticulating scene in the room before him took on the appearance of mummery and David saw everyone wearing a mask, talking to suppress their real anxieties, hopeful that the masks would contain the real selves beneath. He felt closed-in and nervous, and he had to get away.

Putting his glass down on a table, David left the house. He had come with Hugh, but he assumed that his friend would have little trouble getting a ride back to the Inn, and he did not want to bother trying to find him. He crossed the patio, went up the flagstone walk to the swooping driveway. Cars lined the drive-way on both sides. He walked along in the darkness, feeling a sense of relief.

He had difficulty getting his car out of the parking place, and when he had it on the drive, decided to back out to the road rather than chance a jam of cars at the circle near the house. It was a hundred yards to the road, but the moon was up and he maneuvered without difficulty.

When the car was heading away from the party he felt a sense of purpose and urgency, almost akin to escape, and he had to chide himself to keep the speed down.

Entering the town limits of Walkers Ferry, he cut off the highway and swooped down the narrow channel of Ferry Street. He braked hard and turned into the parking lot at the Ferry Inn.

There were two tables of late diners in the garden and Athena stood on the fringe of the dining area. David went to her, walked into her smile.

"When do you finish?" he asked.

"They're the last two tables," she said. "A half hour, I guess."

"May I wait for you?"

"I'd be disappointed if you didn't," she said. "How was your party?"

"Grim," David said, "absolutely grim. I missed you every minute."

"Hmmm, pretty words. You probably couldn't take your eyes off Sylvia Thompson."

"Who?"

Athena laughed lightly. "I forget that you're new around here," she said. "Sylvia has the record bust in Walkers Ferry."

"I saw her," David said.

"You can't miss her."

"Do I hear a purr?" David asked.

"You do indeed. A purr of envy. Pardon me." She left his side and walked to one of the tables where a stout man was signalling for his check.

David turned and opened the door behind him. He entered the barroom and went to the bar, taking a stool near the end. He ordered Irish Whisky on the rocks.

The tables in the garden emptied on his second drink and he saw Athena clearing away the dishes. He glanced at the clock, toyed with his drink, lit a cigarette, killed time.

Athena came into the bar. She wore a full cotton print skirt that lashed about her legs as she walked, a simple short-sleeved blouse and leather thong sandals. Her thick coil of honey-blonde hair was doubled and fixed atop her head. She wore no lipstick and her eyes were ringed with a thin line of black, making them stand out startlingly blue against the cream texture of her skin. David slid off the stool, nodded to the bartender, and took her arm. They smiled together without speaking, went to the door and out into the night.

"Do we walk tonight?" David asked.

"Not tonight. Let's just go to my place and we'll listen to music."

"We drive?"

"It's only a block," Athena said.

They walked up Ferry street, crossed the canal bridge. They passed the office of the Justice of Peace, a bookstore named "Lefty's", a Tea House that catered to the girdled gluttons who came in bus groups to browze through the town like locusts, two shops operated by respectable homosexuals, a barber shop for French poodles.

As they walked David suddenly realized that Gwen had completely left his mind. It was less than a week since he had seen her, had seriously wondered if he was in love with her, and already she was out of his life completely. Well, not completely, he reasoned. It is impossible to touch upon someone without taking something of them to heart. Even the casual acquaintance has an influence on your life, but for the future, there was no Gwen, and it seemed that he had been some other person, some stranger whom he had known.

He glanced at Athena, was taken as usual by the elfin beauty of her, but seeing her as a woman was even more exciting to him. Just the thought that he loved her filled him with a feeling of delight. It was a wondrous warm sensation that made him glad, made him want to shout. It was like finding a treasure, like suddenly deciphering a map that he had pondered over for years. Love was like a riddle. It is baffling until you find the key, then it is astoundingly simple. Love was simply a case of finding the girl capable of receiving it.

They turned into a short side street and at the end was the small house where Athena lived with her child. Athena rang the bell and the baby-sitter came to the door.

"Hello, Martha," Athena said as they entered, "you remember Mr. Belson."

A few words about the behavior of the child and Martha gathered up her school books and left. Athena was in the kitchen making coffee, and David kneeled on the floor by the record player, shuffling through the records.

"Feel like some Bartok?" David asked.

"Not tonight," Athena said. "There's a record there of Debussy. Some of his lesser known things. Play that. It was given to me by a wonderful guy named Ed Staley who knows every note Debussy ever wrote. Come to think of it, you'll have to meet Ed. He's a rare and wonderful person."

"You're kind of rare and wonderful yourself," David said.

"Thank you, Sir."

David found the record and put it on the turntable. He listened a moment, enjoying the lyricism, then he stood up and prowled the room. It was a small house. The living room, a small kitchen, two bedrooms on either side of a narrow hall. The living room contained a modern sofa, two sling chairs, a long coffee table and a number of cushions for sitting on the floor. David sat on the sofa, tapped a cigarette from the pack, lit it.

"I like your house," David said.

"You said that the other night."

"And you said it was too small."

"Yes," Athena said, coming in from the kitchen, "and it is. One small boy can make it very small in about five minutes."

"When am I going to see that boy?"

"One day, maybe."

"Maybe? Don't you want me to see him?"

"I'm not sure," Athena said. "Little boys are impressionable, David. I don't want Dougie to have a series of 'Uncles'. If I date someone, that's one thing. I know that one day whoever he is won't be coming back, and that's all right. It might not be so easy for Doug."

She was sitting on a cushion in front of him, her legs curled back, the skirt spread around her. He leaned towards her. "I love you, Athena," he said.

She returned his steady gaze. "Don't joke, David, that's not something I take lightly."

"I'm not joking, Athena, I love you." There was gravity in his voice and he did not take his eyes from hers. She looked at him for what seemed like an interminably long time.

"I think I love you, too, David," she said. "I'm not sure, but I think I do." She got to her feet and went to the kitchen. In a moment, she came back. "The coffee can keep," she said.

Pushing a cushion around, she dropped on her knees before him. "Have you ever had the responsibility of having someone deeply in love with you?"

"I make—"

"I'm not talking about money, David. There's a much more difficult responsibility. You're a good person, I know that. There is an emotional responsibility you accept when you accept love.

It hangs in a delicate balance, but it can become awfully heavy. When I love, I love for keeps."

"I love you," David said, "I want to marry you."

Athena looked up at him with questioning intensity. "I don't know, David," she said. "I think that you know that you want to marry, but I'm not certain that you want to marriage. The distance between marrying and marriaging is wide. One is the impulse of the moment. It is simple. The other is two people being so close that they lose their indentities as individuals and exist as one mind in two bodies."

"Are you certain that's the way it should be?" David asked.

"It has to be," she said.

"I'm not sure. I like to think of marriage as two ships traveling separately to the same destination. If the ships were lashed together a rough sea would destroy them."

Athena mulled his words in silence. She glanced down at her hands. "I don't know, David. Putting this into words gets it all confused."

"I love you, Athena. You can't be confused about that."

She looked up. "I asked you once if you had ever been in love," she said.

"I can't answer that," he said. "At the time I thought that I was. It was never like this, but maybe it is a matter of degree. I could have been in love, but not deeply enough."

"Do you know what the feeling is?"

"Yes. You feel it in the heart."

"But the heart is just an organ, a part of the body for pumping the blood through the body."

"That's true, but there's something else. It defies science to explain it, but it exists. Athena, let me try to explain this with an example. I have this friend, a good, close friend. He's an intellectual, somewhat of a cynic. But not too long ago his wife died suddenly. I was with him when it happened and afterwards we were driving away from the hospital and he was talking. One thing he said really hit me. It was about the heart being just another organ of the body, but he also said that the pain hit him squarely in the heart, a heavy ache that made him grimace. Why the heart? Why not the liver or the kidney? I know that psychologists scoff at the existence of such a thing as the soul, but there must be something to the poetic premise that love exists in the heart, just as there must be a soul in the human body that is divorced from the mind. I love you, Athena, and at this moment it is as if a wire noose is being pulled tight around my heart. That's all I can say. I love you."

Athena swallowed and her eyes misted. "David," she said, "I'm going to stand up. I don't want you to kiss me. I want you to lift me and carry me into the bedroom. I don't want to walk there as though this were a prearranged assignation, I want you to take me there, to carry me. I want to lie next to you in the dark with nothing between us. I want to hold you, listen to your heart beat. I want you to make love to me, make love *with* me, and then we'll know." She got to her feet.

David was trembling as he stood and lifted her into his arms.

CHAPTER ELEVEN

ora Masserly parked her car on South Main Street and walked to the Town Hall. She checked her watch and noted that she was on time for the appointment.

Cora stepped into the musty hallway where a desk had been placed and where a tidy, officious woman now sat. "I'm Cora Masserly," she said, approaching the desk.

"You're here for the interview," Rita Talbot said, glancing along her list of names.

"Yes."

"Hmmmm. Here you are." Rita made a check after the name on the list, then got to her feet. "Come with me, please."

The hallway was uncarpeted and their heels clacked on the hard wood. There were two closed doors on either side of the hallway. Rita went to the last door on the right, opened it, and stood aside for Cora to enter.

The room was square and small. Just beyond the door was a small table holding a pad and pencil and an ashtray. A wooden chair with curving arms faced the table. On the ceiling of the room hung a portable light fixture which contained four bright spotlights. The lights shone on the young man who was seated behind a table on which were a pile of forms and a number of pencils stuffed into a jar.

"You will sit right here, Mrs. Masserly," Rita said, indicating the empty chair. "This is Mr. Belson who will interview you."

"How do you do?" Cora said.

"How do you do," David said.

Rita held the chair until Cora sat, then she turned and left the room, closing the door behind her. There was a moment of tense silence, a shuffling of the chair while Cora got comfortable.

"Your name, please."

"Cora Masserly."

"Age."

"Twenty-nine."

"Married?"

"Yes."

"Children?"

"No," Cora answered.

David nodded, then took a deep breath. "You may wonder about the spotlights, Mrs. Masserly," David said. "They are a special innovation of Dr. Wilson's. While you can see me plainly because of the intense glare, you are sitting in darkness. This gives you perfect anonymity while at the same time you will not experience the terror that generally comes with talking to a screen or a microphone. I would like to say that the questions I ask are of no interest to me personally, they are just part of the questionaire I have here in front of me. I will try to help you with any answers you find difficult. Are you ready?"

"Yes."

"Fine. Now, we'll begin with the series of questions on pre-adolescent heterosexual sex play. When did you have your first experiment with masturbation?"

Cora gasped and her eyes widened. "Are you serious?"

"Most children masturbate, Mrs. Masserly."

"Well, I certainly never did!"

David marked the answer on the form. "Did you engage in sex play with other children?"

"Never!"

David glanced up and Cora had the feeling that he could see her. This whole thing is thoroughly disgusting, she thought.

"When was the first time that you were aware of the sex act? What age?"

"What age?"

"Yes, how old were you?"

"I'm not sure." Cora scowled, and the memory came back to make her shudder. She had been spending the week at Uncle George's farm and there was that beautiful sorrel mare and then that day that she had stood by the fence and had seen the stallion chase the mare and the way the mare screamed and kicked, but the stallion stayed there, and she had run back to the barn to tell Uncle George that the stallion was stuck to the mare and he had laughed.

Her face reddened and she felt the same disgust as before. "I ... I'm not sure," Cora said. "I suppose it was when I was ten."

"What were the circumstances?"

Cora's hand trembled. She had inched the chair forward unconsciously and her breasts touched the edge of the table. "A girl in school told me," she said. That was Gladys. What was her last name?

"In what way were you told?"

"In what way?"

"Yes, how did this girl explain it?"

Cora swallowed hard. What could this have to do with her sex life? "She ... she said that she knew where babies came from," Cora said. "She said that boys urinated on girls and this made babies." And that same week Cora had gone with Gladys to the old Canby house and Jerry Graham was waiting and they had crawled under the house and she watched Jerry do it to Gladys and then they said that they would tell her Mother unless she let Jerry do it to her and she was so frightened that she let him and she didn't feel anything even though Gladys said it was fun and then she thought sure that she would have a baby and she cried in bed that night because she didn't want a baby and she told her

Mother and she was beaten with a strap and told that she was filthy.

"Did you experiment with any boys at this time?" David asked.

"Really!" Cora said in a shocked voice. "What a thing to ask. Why that's a positively filthy thought!"

"I'm sorry," David said. He made notations on the form, wondering what made this woman frigid, feeling a bit sorry for her husband, but also feeling sorry for her. "We'll go on now to premarital sex," he said.

While Hugh Bascomb could not see the woman, he remembered her from the party when Elizabeth had pointed her out, and he also remembered seeing her in a number of movies. He looked at the form, surprised that she was forty-six because she had looked much younger, still beautiful, but in a more sedate way. He had been through a number of questions. Claire Roberts had been an early experimenter in the rites of sexual pleasure.

"Did you have sexual relations with the opposite sex prior to marriage?"

"Yes," Claire said, twisting her handkerchief. Damn, she thought, why am I nervous?

"At what age?"

"I was..." She thought a moment. "I believe I was thirteen." My God, she thought, I was just a baby! Beverly is twenty and I think she's still a virgin.

"Did you experience pleasure at that time?"

"Yes." Did I? God, it was wonderful. I thought I was going to go crazy. It was that big guy who worked on the same drilling gang as Dad. I was scared to death at first, because he was so big and all, but after that first terrible hurt, it was wonderful. That was the end of playing with dolls for me!

"Have you always received satisfaction in the sexual act?"

"Yes." Well, not always. There was that time with old man Ruebens when I was fourteen and had to have that party dress in his window. But, of course, that was a different kind of satisfaction when I realized I could have anything I wanted if I was smart about it.

"Between the first time and your marriage, how many partners did you have?"

Claire took a deep breath. "I'm not certain," she said.

"Take your time," Hugh said, "try to recall."

Claire picked up the pencil on the table before her and made scratches on the pad. About a dozen before she entered that first beauty contest. There had been four judges and she had to take on three of them. And then there had been other beauty contests and agents for modeling jobs and photographers who would make up your portfolio without charge if you were friendly. What could this man know about being hungry and poor and wanting to be somebody important? What else do you do when you're a girl and all you've got to get ahead on is the fact that you're a girl and beautiful and men want you? Dammit, what else do you do? You flop on your back and spread your legs, that's what! She had to suppress a giggle when she remembered the famous actress who once said to her, 'I'm just damn glad we're not like those old time western gun fighters. If I had a notch on my ass for every man I had to knock off to get where I am, they'd call me the Corduroy Kid.' There must have been more than a hundred men, she thought. It never occured to me to count them before. It's almost sickening when you think of them in numbers like that. I never thought of myself as being immoral. I had to do it, that's all. I had to do it, just like Beverly will never have to do!

"I'm not sure," she said in answer to the question. "I'd guess about twenty-five." Then she felt that she could explain. "I wanted to be an actress," she said.

Claire twisted the pencil in her hands. He must think I'm an awful slut, she thought. Well, let him. I had to do what I had to do. I got where I wanted to go. I did it for my baby, and she'll never have to do it for anybody except for love.

The interviews broke off for lunch, and David walked down Main Street with Hugh Bascomb.

"How was your morning?" David asked.

"Just dandy. I'm now qualified to write the Girl's Guide on How To Be An Actress."

"Maybe you should open a school."

"I'm afraid I wouldn't have the strength. Those schools must use the couch more than a psychiatrist. How did you do?"

"Two happy, bovine housewives and one mixed up enough to make your blood run cold."

They laughed together, and when they reached the Ferry Inn, David said, "I won't be lunching with you, Hugh, I have to see someone down the street."

"That cute little blonde?"

"No, but a friend of hers."

"Well, good luck, Don Juan." Hugh turned up towards the entrance to the Inn, and David continued along Main Street.

When he reached the office of the *Register*, David went up the steps and through the door. There was no one in the office, but he heard a chair scrape behind the screen at the far end of the room. "Knox?" he said.

"Yes." Knox came from behind the screen. "Ah, David," he said, "good to see you."

"I thought we might have lunch together."

"Wonderful. I was just going to lock up and eat. I live upstairs and cook for myself. Come on, we'll open a can of soup."

They left the office, went to the side of the building and up the steep flight of stairs to the tidy three-room apartment.

"Make yourself at home," Knox said. "I'll do the kitchen chores."

David dropped into the depths of a large leather chair. He settled back and tapped a cigarette from his pack, lighting it and inhaling deeply.

Knox came from the kitchen and dropped silverware and napkins on the table. "Is this strictly a social call, or do you have something else on your mind?"

"I've decided to leave Dr. Wilson," David said.

Knox nodded his head thoughtfully. "I have anything to do with this decision?" he asked.

"A little," David said. "Mostly you've just been the catalyst to set a lot of thoughts into motion."

"You thinking of staying here?"

"I've thought of it. I want to marry Athena."

Knox raised his eyebrows, then he smiled and chuckled. "Well," he said, "this has been a week of decisions for you."

"I'm in love with her," David said.

"I would assume you'd have to be in love to marry anyone," Knox said. "Does she know this?"

"Yes."

"Have you met her child?"

"Yes."

"Then she must believe that you want to marry her," Knox said. "And you know about her past."

"She told me."

"She would. She's quite a girl."

"There's one thing I don't understand," David said. "She never says anything about this other man, but she still seems to be in love with him in some way."

"Only because he was a good man," Knox said.

"A good man? My God, Knox, he got her pregnant and didn't do anything about it! You call that a good man?"

"He didn't deny her, David. He didn't marry her, because he didn't want to marry her. He was honest with her. Marriage isn't everything. You should know that better than anyone, you who must have recorded the hundreds of lives made miserable by the simple institution of two strangers sharing bed and board when they should have had their little tumble in the hay and gone their happy ways." Knox went back to the kitchen to tend his soup, but he raised his voice to be heard. "His name was Frank and he had a business here in town. He also had a wife who hated the way a jealous woman can, and she refused to give him a divorce. But that is beside the point. He wouldn't have married Athena anyway, because they weren't suited to live together. Anyway, when Athena was pregnant with his child he recognized the fact. Most men would want to hide her or deliver her to some dirty backroom to be aborted by a rusty spoon. Frank stood by her while she had the child, and he made her walk open in the street and keep her head up. He lost his business over it." Knox came back into the room and put two bowls on the table. "What would you have done in his place, David?"

"Something stupid, I suppose. Maybe something cowardly. I don't know."

"It's hard to know," Knox said. "But he did what any man would like to think he would have the courage to do. He kept that girl's love clean. That would mean a lot to a woman, and Athena is a woman." Knox waved at the table. "Come eat."

David went to the table and they ate in silence. When Knox was finished, he asked, "Have you told Wilson?"

"I'm going to do it this evening."

"Have you given our local college some thought?"

"I drove out to see it," David said. "It's very nice. I didn't make any inquiries, though."

"If you're interested, I'll have you meet the President. He's a bit stuffy, but a nice enough person."

"I'm interested."

"The pay won't be great."

"There are other things," David said. "And now I have to get back."

"No coffee?"

"No thanks, I need steady nerves."

Sylvia Thompson smiled with pleasure when she saw that Dr. Wilson was handling her interview. She allowed Rita Talbot to seat her, then toyed with the pencil and pad and examined the man while he made his usual preamble about the lights and secrecy and his own clinical disinterest.

"May I smoke, Doctor," she asked.

"Of course, Mrs. Thompson."

"Miss," Sylvia said. "Remember, I said the same thing at the party."

Wilson coughed and made no answer, but Sylvia could see that he was remembering, not what she had said, but what she had looked like.

Wilson recorded the facts of age, marital status, education.

"Would you like my measurements, Doctor?"

"That won't be necessary," Wilson said, a look of cold disdain on his face.

Sylvia had looked Wilson up in *Who's Who* and knew his age to be 48. She liked his long hands, his wiry, sturdy build. The leaner the horse, the longer the race, she said to herself, smiling.

Wilson was asking his questions pertaining to preadolescent sex and Sylvia was answering with relish.

"The first orgasm was self-induced at the age of eight," she said. "I used my father's best meerchaum pipe. I hated the sonofabitch and it made me laugh every time I saw him smoke it after that."

Wilson scowled and his fingers whitened on the pencil, but he kept his voice steady and asked, "How would you define foreplay?"

"Does that mean having someone finger you?"

"Is that what it means to you?"

"I guess it means all the stuff a man will do to get you hot. Frankly, Doctor, I've never needed any. When I'm ready to go, I go."

"Have you ever achieved satisfaction through petting?"

"Not me," she said. "I always had to have the real thing. I guess you might say I was precocious."

When Wilson reached the section dealing with premarital intimacies, Sylvia leaned back in the chair and lit another cigarette.

"Look at it this way, Doctor," she said. "I got bounced the first time when I was fifteen and I had to use will power to wait until then. I always needed it. I was a healthy young girl. I never thought it was bad and I still don't. It's a function like anything else. I have no idea how many men I've tumbled. I took them whenever I could get them."

"Were any of these affairs of a sustaining nature?"

"No. After a bout with me they were usually scared to death."

"What was your relationship with your father?"

"I couldn't stand the righteous bastard." Now there is an understatement, Sylvia thought. But how could you really explain that much hatred? Her father was more than stern, he acted as though the devil walked the halls of his house. Sylvia remembered the night that her mother had been thrown out of the house. She had heard angry voices from her bed, had gotten up and rushed to the hallway. At the bottom of the staircase her father stood over her mother, who was sprawled on the carpet. He was calling her foul names, then he kicked her and she screamed. That was the last time Sylvia had seen her mother, and later she learned that her father had found his wife with another man. She had been lectured and lectured on sin, but it only served to make her hate the man more. I paid him back, Sylvia thought, I paid that bastard back in spades. I became the worst slut in that damn town. And every boy and man she knew was the image of the father, and she relished the hold she had over them in their lust.

"Have you been married?" Wilson asked.

"Three times." And everyone of them was as righteous as that bastard.

"How often did you have intimate relations with your husbands?"

"Every night at first. Sometimes in the mornings. But they generally begged off after awhile." God, the way she used to taunt them—anything to make them realize that they weren't men. The worst part was when it was over and she couldn't stand to have them near her, and she didn't make any bones about telling them. How she avenged her mother! How she hated them, how she hated them all!

Elizabeth Pennington was startled when she entered the room and saw Hugh Bascomb sitting behind the table under the bright lights. She took her chair and saw Hugh stiffen when Rita Talbot announced her name.

When Rita left the room, Hugh said, "You don't have to go through with this, Liz. I'll have one of the others interview you."

"No," Elizabeth said, "I have nothing to hide." She added to herself, not from you, anyway.

Hugh went through the questions about preadolescent sex, recorded a natural sexual interest. He had to chuckle over the incident in the football stadium.

"It wasn't funny at the time," Elizabeth said.

"I'm sorry," Hugh said.

"I hated sex until I met you."

"Hmmmm, yes, well." He cleared his throat. "Am I next?"

"Yes."

He smiled. "This is a bit irregular," he said.

"Well," Elizabeth said with an edge of irritation, "I don't do this every day myself."

Hugh sobered. "I think I'll just skip on to your marriage. But I do want to say, off the record, that I made love to you with love. There hasn't been any love since." He coughed. "Okay, on to marriage. What is the frequency of love-making in your marriage at present?"

Elizabeth bit her lip. She hadn't thought about it so coldly. Putting love into figures made it distasteful. When was the last time with Brad? Three weeks. And before that? "It's … its about once a month. I mean, it's because Brad is away most of the time."

"He's home on week-ends?"

Elizabeth realized that this was not one of the printed questions, but she felt compelled to answer, to make some rational excuse for her marriage. "He's very tired most of the time." It was a lame excuse. Hugh had met Brad at the party and he was certainly lively enough, and Hugh had been to the house for Sunday dinner and Brad had spent the afternoon playing tennis with Debbie. But later, in bed, he had again begged off on the excuse that he was tired.

"Do you reach a climax in your love-making?"

"Yes … usually … I mean, well, sometimes I don't."

"Do you know why you don't?"

"I don't know … I mean … that's a difficult question. How should I … well, yes, I know. Dammit, it's because I know he's not interested. That he's just doing it to keep me quiet!"

Hugh looked hard at her, then he bent back to the questionaire and tried to keep his approach more clinical.

"Since you have been married, have you engaged in any extramarital relationship?"

"Once." Elizabeth bit her lip because she saw the surprise register on his face.

"When was that?"

"Last week."

"Last week?"

Elizabeth swallowed hard and clenched her fists. She had no idea that this was going to be so difficult. "Oh, Hugh," she said, "it was horrible." The tears spilled from her eyes, running the mascara down her cheeks. In jerky sentences she related the incident with Chet Parker. Before she could finish Hugh was at her side, holding her arms. She rose from the chair and leaned against him. "Oh, Hugh," she cried, "what am I going to do? I'm so miserable!"

CHAPTER TWELVE

David stood in front of the closed door. His tongue flicked over his lips and he squared his shoulders. He lifted his fist and knocked.

"Come in."

Opening the door, David stepped into the room. Dr. Wilson was standing at the table which had been put into the room, and Rita Talbot was shuffling questionnaires into an orderly pile.

"Hello, David," Wilson said. "That will be all, Rita."

"Yes, Sir," Rita Talbot said. She nodded at David as she left the room, closing the door after her.

"Well, David," Wilson said, rubbing his hands together, "It's been a productive day. I always feel good at the end of the day, as though another brick has been cemented into an important monument."

"There's something I wanted to speak to you about, Sir," David said.

Wilson's expression changed, as though he was suddenly thrown on the defensive, and his eyes were wary. "What is it?"

"I want to submit my resignation," David said.

Wilson pursed his lips. One hand came up and rubbed the side of his face. "I see," he said. "You have the offer of a better position?"

"No, Sir, it's nothing like that. It's just that ... well, Sir, I just don't believe in the work any longer."

Wilson looked as though he had been struck in the face. "I don't understand," he said with effort.

"Well," David said, "when I first began this work I felt that we were doing something important, something good. Now I don't believe that."

"What *do* you believe, David?"

"I believe that what we're doing is destructive. I think we're little better than peeping toms. Everytime I complete a questionnaire I feel as though I have just opened an ugly sore, not to cleanse the wound or heal it, but just to open it to see the color of the puss inside."

Wilson whirled abruptly and went to the window, his back to David. The muscles stood out in his neck like thin rope and his hands were clenched. "That's clear enough," he said. "I accept your resignation." His voice was cold.

"I'll complete the survey here," David said.

"I'd rather you didn't. I don't believe I could trust your work, David, after what you've said."

"I'm sorry, Sir."

"Don't be sorry for me, David, only for yourself and your obviously narrow vision." He turned and his eyes glistened. "It is our *duty* to expose the puss, as you put it! If there is evil locked in the breast of women, and we have proved that there is, then it is our duty to show it to the world!" His jaw jutted. "Goodbye, David."

David watched the man turn his arched back away, ending the interview, and for a moment he felt that he was in the presence of a madman. There was nothing more to say. It was done, over with. Turning, David went to the door and opened it. He stepped into the hallway and closed the door.

Going down the stairs, David peered into the bar. He saw Knox Martin alone at a table. He entered and went to the table.

"David," Knox said.

"Hello, Knox, may I join you?"

"Please."

David took a chair on the opposite side of the table and sat down. "I just told Wilson I was resigning."

"How did he take it?"

"Not well."

"A general hates to have his lieutenants desert him," Knox said. "He'll get over it."

"Knox," David said, "there's one curious thing. In the conversation up there just now I had the feeling that Wilson hates women. I mean really despises them."

"That's possible."

"But if he's conducting the surveys on the basis of hatred the whole program is vicious. How could he get into this line of work?"

"It compensates," Knox said. "Beethoven wrote militant music and he was a coward. Nietzsche believed in the super race and he was a physical misfit. All things are relative. The Marquis de Sade wrote that a sadist gives extreme pleasure to a masochist."

"But if that's the case then something should be done about it."

"You've done all you can," Knox said. "You got out of it."

"But—"

"David, don't fight it. Have a drink, have dinner, be glad that your ideals are intact. Evil has a way of destroying itself. There are those who believe that good always triumphs. This is never the case. Morality is steady and complacent and safe and it lasts. Evil is born in passion and it rages until it has run the gamut and is consumed in its own flames. Good has nothing to do with it."

The heavy chords of Beethoven's Fifth Symphony rumbled through the house. Hugh Bascomb seated on a divan in the living room, looked up as Elizabeth came into the room.

"I guess Debbie isn't going to get home for dinner," Elizabeth said. "We may as well eat."

Hugh gulped the last of his martini, put the glass down and got to his feet. He followed Elizabeth into the dining room where three places had been set at the long, rectangular table.

"Sit at the end, there," Elizabeth said. "I'll bring everything in."

Hugh busied himself with uncorking and pouring the wine while Elizabeth brought the several dishes to the table, then they sat facing each other. Hugh lifted his wine glass. "To old times," he said.

Elizabeth smiled. "Which is now a matter of record."

"We were going to forget all that," Hugh said.

"Yes, but I can't."

"No, I guess not. We never ever forget the things we do. They pass out of the mind for a time, but they're always there, lurking for the inopportune time to come popping up."

Elizabeth did not answer and they ate in silence for some minutes. Finally, Hugh asked, "Do you eat alone often?"

"Quite a bit, but you have to realize that Debbie is a teenager. She has friends of her own and she spends a good bit of time with them."

"Brad couldn't commute?"

"He did for awhile," she said, "but it was awfully hard on him."

"In other words, he would rather stay in New York."

"Really, Hugh, this doesn't concern you."

"Have you thought of getting a divorce?"

"No," she said abruptly.

"Why not?"

"I don't know why you ... Oh, I don't know." She put her fork down and took a gulp of the wine. "I know my marriage is a failure, but I don't want to admit failure. And I have Debbie to think about."

"She doesn't know about you and Brad?"

"She ... well, I'm not sure."

"Then she does know."

"She knows something is wrong, yes, but ... Oh, Hugh, what is the point of all this talk?"

"No point, I guess. It's just that I'd like to see the woman I've always loved in a happy situation."

Elizabeth lowered her eyes to her plate and her voice was small when she said, "Thank you, Hugh."

Hugh stared at her in silence, then he lifted his glass. "Another toast," he said. Elizabeth looked up. "To keeping my mouth shut," he said.

"I'll drink to that," Elizabeth said.

Claire Roberts was still disturbed by the morning interview, and now, at dinner, Mike was taunting her.

"How did the scientific mind react to all the shocking details?" he asked.

"I don't know what you mean," Claire said, toying with her food.

"How about positions? Did you tell them your favorite?"

"Mike, really!"

"The Roberts family at home," Beverly said. "Frank discussions at the dinner table. Do you think you might get your mind out of the gutter while we eat, Mr. Roberts?"

"The gutter?" Mike said. "I was talking about your Mother."

"You don't have to twist what I say, Big Man. I was talking about your mind."

"How come you didn't get interviewed?" Mike asked.

"Because I wasn't interested," Beverly said.

"Afraid they might find something out?"

"That's none of your damn business!"

"Please," Claire said. "Mike, talk about something else. This is really very dull."

"Sex is dull? Since when?"

"I don't mean that," Claire said. "I mean—"

"She means she'd like to eat her soup in peace," Beverly said. "It's bad enough sitting and looking at you without having to listen to your gutter tongue."

Mike dropped his fork on the plate and his eyes narrowed with anger. "You think I'm out of the gutter, huh?"

"It shows, Buster, I don't have to think," Beverly said.

"You figure you're better than me, huh?"

"That's a laugh!"

"And better than your Mother," Mike said.

"I didn't say anything about my—"

"I said it!" Mike snapped the words through his teeth. "You're a gutter kid, and don't you forget it! If I walked in the gutter, your Mother laid in it!"

"Mike!" Claire cried.

"Shut up!" He pointed his finger at Beverly. "You're the same flesh and blood as your Mother, girlie, and your Mother ain't no angel!"

Beverly leaped to her feet, the tears had started in her eyes. "I won't listen to this!"

"You don't have to because you know it's true! You wanta hear how I met your Mother? You wanta hear it?"

"I don't want to hear anything from you again!" Beverly shouted. "Your voice makes me sick! You've got a rotten mind, and I can't stand being under the same roof with you!" She turned and ran from the room.

Mike Roberts sat back. He was breathing heavily and his mouth was twisted into a snarl.

"You didn't have to say that," Claire said.

"It's the truth!" Mike snarled. "You're a tramp! I know it, just like everybody else knows it! I'm sick of that damn kid of yours treating me like dirt!"

Claire got up from her chair. "You are dirt," she said softly.

Mike spun out of his chair. A constricted cry of rage rose from his throat. He lurched forward, swinging his arm. His open palm cracked against the side of Claire's face, snapping her head back. She cried out in surprise and pain. She was knocked off balance, and Mike swept his arm around again, back-handing her across the mouth. She staggered away and fell to her knees. Mike came to her. He jerked her head up by her hair. "Don't say that to me, you two-bit whore!" He smashed his fist into her mouth and let her drop to the carpet. "That'll teach you," he growled, "and I'm gonna teach that kid, too."

Claire whimpered, but she did not move. The blood trickled from the corner of her mouth.

Sam Masserly could not get his mind on the book. The page was a blur of gray. He looked across at Cora who was knitting. How was he going to tell her? It had to come out, sooner or later. He knew that he couldn't go on meeting Beverly without the town knowing about it, and there was always some helpful soul who would be on the telephone to let poor dear Cora know about it. Beverly was right. What they felt for each other had to be exposed to the sun. But how could he tell Cora? Damn, this was a helluva lot more difficult than he had thought it would be.

The telephone rang, startling him, and he began to get up.

"I'll get it," Cora said. She put her knitting aside and went to the hallway. She felt uneasy for some reason she could not fathom, but she had decided that it was because of Sam's strangeness, and while she had sat knitting, she had been plotting some method of making him tell her what it was all about. She lifted the receiver and held it to her ear.

"Yes?" she said.

"Cora? This is Marcia."

"Oh."

"Still mad at me?"

"I hadn't thought about it," Cora said.

"I'm glad. Look, Hon, I've missed you, and I wanted to apologize for the other day. I guess it was the brandy."

"It doesn't matter," Cora said.

"Good. I knew you'd understand. Look, Cora, there's a party on tonight up on Temperance Hill."

Cora frowned. She had heard some wild stories about Temperance Hill—the name given to an area North of the town where a group of New Yorkers owned houses and did considerable drinking. She had never been on the Hill, but she knew that the houses were expensive and extremely private. "I'm sorry," she said, eager to end the conversation, "Sam and I are staying in tonight."

"Come on," Marcia said. "Don't be a sober-sides. This is strictly a hen party. You'll love it. Let Sam stay home. I'll come by and pick you up."

"No thanks," Cora said. "I really don't feel like it."

"Okay," Marcia said, "suit yourself. But I'll be here until nine. Give me a call if you change your mind."

"Goodbye," Cora said. "Thanks for calling." She cradled the phone and went back to the living room. She hadn't told the interviewer anything about Marcia. When the question had been raised she had felt a moment of panic. She didn't know why.

David turned the car off River Road and the headlights swept up the steep incline of Jericho Hill.

"It was nice of Knox to loan you his car," Athena said. She sat against the door with her body turned so that she could look at David.

"Now that I'm unemployed I don't have the use of the company car," he said. "How does it feel to be with one of the vast army of the unemployed?"

"Feels fine to me," Athena said. "How do you feel about it?"

"I feel the way a catholic must feel when he has left the confessional, lit six candles and said twenty Hail Marys. If I have sinned, and that's possible, I at least have the feeling that my sins have been neatly bundled, that as far as that set of sins is concerned, they're finished."

"That's not very scientific."

"You're right. It's a complete rationalization, but it makes me feel better, and tonight I want to feel better. Do you realize that this is our first real, official date?"

"I realize it. That's why I'm taking you to an expensive place to buy my dinner."

"And me without a job."

Athena laughed. "That's my luck. I meet a successful man, and the minute I fall in love with him he quits his job."

"Then you *are* in love with me?"

"Didn't you know?"

"Yes, I knew, but I've never heard you say it."

"Do you need reassurance?"

"Hey, now, I'm the expert at questions."

"About sex," she said. "I'm talking about love."

"You're talking about reassurance."

"I have the feeling we're not always going to agree on things," Athena said.

"We'll scandalize the neighbors with our fights," David said.

"Do I take that as a proposal?"

"You may, indeed."

"I take it and I accept. David! Watch the road!" She laughed lightly, a warm, happy laugh.

CHAPTER THIRTEEN

Sylvia Thompson made tunafish salad and ate it alone in her kitchen. She washed the meal down with brandy, left most of it on her plate and went to the living room and switched on the television, trying all the channels. It bored her and she turned the set off and went to the hi-fi set, took a handful of jazz records without looking at the titles and put them on.

Returning to the kitchen, she took the brandy bottle off the table and brought it back to the living room. She filled her glass and dropped onto the wide divan. The phonograph was turned too high, but she didn't move. The throaty baritone sax of Gerry Mulligan filled the room, seemed to make the air tremble with sensuous sound. She leaned back, closed her eyes, drank slowly.

Before the record ended she was on her feet pacing the room. God, how she hated being alone in the big house! Maybe it would be better if she sold the place and got an apartment in New York. At least she wouldn't have to be alone. The nervousness took hold of her and her skin seemed to itch with restlessness. She stopped and gulped the brandy.

She went back to the divan and dropped down. The feeling she knew so well was beginning to spread through her. She poured more brandy and gulped it. Maybe a tranquillizer would help, she thought, or a cold shower. But she knew that neither would do her any good. How long had it been since that kid cutting the grass? A week. She cupped her hands over her breasts. They felt swollen and painful.

Springing off the couch, she ran to the door and flung it open. The record continued to blare. She slammed the door after her and ran down the stone steps. Her low-slung Mercedes was in the driveway. She jerked the door open and slid under the wheel. The engine roared and the tires wailed against the macadam as she tramped the accelerator.

She kidded onto Bradley Road, shifted gears, enjoying the feeling of motion, the driving power the car gave her. She knew Wilson was staying at the Ferry Inn, and she knew that she had to have him. The righteous bastard, she'd make him crawl!

I really shouldn't drink this much, Elizabeth Pennington thought. There had been martinis and wine and now bourbon, and she was feeling the relaxed glow that always came to her with drinking.

Hugh was sitting in the easy chair adjacent to the sofa where she sat, and he was talking, but she wasn't listening to the words. She was thinking how comfortable it was to sit in a room with a man who loved you, just sit and listen to someone who was not looking at you with critical eyes. You could just relax and not give a damn about how the argument was going to start or had you said the right thing or were you really at fault or had it been a bad week at the office. And how nice that it could be Hugh. She was remembering those other years and how gentle he had been with her and how she had loved him. She recalled the ache she always felt just before she saw him, and the terrible depression she felt when he told her that he would not marry her because she was too young. And now here he was and they were in the same room and it was just like wiping out all those years between. She suddenly realized that Hugh was asking her a question.

"I didn't hear you," she said.

"I know," Hugh said. "I asked you what you were thinking."

She tilted her head and gazed at him. Yes, it was the same Hugh. "I was thinking," she said, "that if you didn't come over here and kiss me I was going to scream." Now why did I say that? she wondered.

Hugh's hands gripped the arm of the chair. "I …" he stammered. "I mean, well, Liz …"

"Now," she said.

He got to his feet, not sure of himself, gazing at her with consternation, wondering if she meant it or was joking or was drunk. "Hell, Liz, I just don't—"

"You don't want to?"

He came to the sofa and dropped next to her. He looked into her face without speaking. His hands came up and he touched his fingers to her face. He leaned over her. She closed her eyes, offering her lips to him, and he brought his mouth down on hers, lightly at first, just brushing her lips. She opened her mouth. He kissed her hard. She dug her nails into his back and pulled him against her.

When they parted she was breathing heavily. She opened her eyes slowly. Nothing had changed. He was still Hugh and she was still herself and they were holding on to one another and there was the same bliss.

"I love you, Liz."

"Yes." She pulled him to her. "Yes."

"I never stopped."

"I thought about you," she whispered. "I never stopped thinking about you."

"I've found you again. I want to keep you. I don't want to let you go again."

"Just hold me. Kiss me."

He kissed her again. Her heart pounded and her skin was burning. His hand moved along her arm and shoulder, along her back. His finger brushed lightly over her breast and she shuddered with pleasure. She pressed against him, her senses reeling.

"I want you, Liz."

Like before. Wipe away the years. Wipe away the unhappiness. Wipe away everything. "Yes," she said, "yes."

His hand caressed her. His lips touched her eyes, settled over her ear. She squirmed against him. "Not here," she said.

He released her, got up and pulled her to her feet. She leaned against him. He swung her into his arms and carried her to the stairs, then up, slowly, a step at a time. Her face was nuzzled into his neck and she felt peaceful and wanted and protected.

Moving along the hall, he peered into the bedrooms, found hers, knowing it because it was the largest. He carried her to the bed and put her down carefully. He pulled her shoes off, then reached to unzipper her dress.

"I'll do it," she said. "Your hands are shaking." She got to her feet and undressed.

He was waiting for her by the side of the bed. She dropped the last of her clothing and went to him, curling her arms about him, pressing herself close to him, leaning her cheek against the hair on his chest.

"Mother!" a shrill voice screamed from the doorway.

Elizabeth snapped erect and spun away, stunned by the shock in the voice. She faced the horrified expression of Debbie. Stepping back, she cowered and tried to cover her nakedness with her hands. She fought for something to say, some way to explain, anything to take away the growing look of hatred on her daughter's face. "I didn't hear you come in," she said.

"That, I'd say, is pretty damned obvious!"

Elizabeth began to shake. The sudden shock and shame on top of a nervous system brought to fever pitch by a mounting passion, coupled with the dulling effects of the liquor, erupted into sudden hysteria. Elizabeth buried her face in her hands and began to laugh.

"Mother!" Debbie screamed. "How can you laugh?!"

Elizabeth fell back against a table. The laughter shook her body, rose in frenzied peals. Her face was contorted with the mirthless, wracking laugh and tears ran down her face.

Frozen into immobility, Hugh came to his senses. "She's hysterical," he snapped. He reached out and grasped Elizabeth's shoulders and shook her. He slapped her face and the laughter stopped as suddenly as it had begun.

"Oh!" Debbie cried. She turned away from the doorway and ran, the sobs of anguish and anger trailing her.

"Debbie!" Elizabeth screamed. She tore loose from Hugh's grasp and ran to the doorway and into the hall. "Debbie!"

The front door slammed. Elizabeth sagged against the railing over the stairs. She began to cry and dropped to her knees in the carpeted hall. Hugh knelt beside her and held her shoulders.

"She's gone!" Elizabeth wailed. "She's gone!"

"She'll be back," Hugh said, trying to gentle her.

"What have I done, Hugh? What have I done? My own daughter to see me like that! Oh, my God, it's horrible! I've lost her, Hugh, I've lost her!"

"You can never lose a daughter," Hugh said.

"But I have! How can I ever face her again? What could I ever say to her?"

"I don't know, Elizabeth."

She leaned against him and cried until there were no more tears. Then she got to her feet. She turned and walked back to the bedroom and picked up her clothes. She dropped into a chair, her shoulders slumped with weariness. "I suppose she'll call Brad," she said. "Well, it had to happen sooner or later. First it was Chet Parker—"

"Don't, Liz."

"—then you, then it would be someone else."

"You know that's not true," Hugh said.

Elizabeth buried her face in her hands, then she lifted her face and she felt a numbness. "My life as I know it has ended," she said. "Just like that. And I'm sorry. I'm truly sorry."

"I'll make you a new life, Liz."

She shook her head. "No," she said, "however it works out, I'll have to try to pick up the pieces of this one. I felt young again with you, but that's just my age, I suppose. I'm thirty-six, and my mind fights against it. For a moment I thought I could be eighteen again. But we can't. We have to be what we are. I've never had to beg before, but I'm going to beg them to forgive me. I know they never will, and I know I'll suffer, but I have to try."

Hugh stared at her for a long moment, then he began to dress. "We had better find her," he said. "I think she'll need someone."

Mike Roberts paced the thick carpet of the bedroom with the restless fury of a caged animal. The hour since dinner had only served to heighten his anger.

"Dirt," he said over and over again. "They got the damn nerve to call me dirt!"

His hands were balled into tight fists and buried in the pockets of the silk robe. Back and forth, back and forth he paced. The muscles in his neck bulged and his anger was like a tight ball in his chest.

It's that kid, that damn snooty kid. Figures I ain't good enough for her. Not good enough. There ain't the woman been born that I can't make crawl. They're all the same, every damned one of them.

Claire hadn't said a word after he hit her and she was still downstairs. The other bitch was locked in her room. He knew her kind. Tease you and then lock the door. Yeah, he knew that kind all right. She'd find out. She'd damn soon find out!

He went to the door and jerked it open. He strode along the hall until he reached Beverly's room. He gripped the door knob and shook it. "Open this door!" There was no answer from within. "You hear me? I said to open this goddamn door!" Still no answer. He turned away and went to the head of the stairs. "Claire," he shouted.

Claire came to the base of the stairs. "What do you want?" she asked.

"Come up here!"

"No."

"You just better get up here, Baby, because that fancy kid of yours is gonna get it."

"You leave her alone!"

"I told you, didn't I? I told you?"

"Don't you lay a finger on her!"

"I'm having her, see!"

"Don't touch her!"

"You coming up here? You gonna watch?"

"I'm calling the police!"

"Call 'em! Call the goddamn Marines! Call the National Guard! You're gonna need them!" He swung away from the stairs.

"No!" Claire screamed. "No!" She turned from the stairs and ran to the kitchen.

Mike went to Beverly's door. He felt exhilarated. He hammered on the panels with his fists. "Open up!" He jigged back to the far wall, bent and hunched his shoulders. He flung himself forward and hit the door. The hinges groaned. He danced back, then drove forward again. He was laughing. He fell back against the wall, then threw himself into the door. The top hinge tore out of the woodwork and the door canted. He danced back, then drove forward, toppling the door and bursting into the room.

Beverly was crouched against the far wall. She held a letter opener out before her. "Don't come near me!"

Mike laughed. He stripped the bathrobe off his shoulders and paraded naked, making a half-circle around her. "Like what you see? All muscle, Baby, and all yours."

"Stay away from me. I warn you, I'll use this!"

"You got it all wrong, Honey. I ain't the one's gonna get stabbed." He grinned and came towards her, crouched, wary, his eyes on the letter opener. "I'm gonna take that away from you, and you're gonna be glad I did. This is gonna be a big night for you, Kid." He was a foot away from her outstretched hand. He feinted to the left and she stabbed at his arm. His right hand whipped up and closed over her wrist. She screamed as he jerked her forward. The letter opener clattered to the floor. She swept her nails out to claw him, but he grasped her wrist and spun her around. He grabbed her robe and jerked her to her knees in the process of tearing it from her.

"No!" she screamed. "No! No!"

He swung the back of his hand and cracked her across the mouth. She gasped in terror. He reached down and tore away the buttons of her pajama blouse. He closed his hands over her breasts and pulled her to her feet, laughing at her cry of sudden pain. He flung her back onto the bed.

Beverly's hands flew up instinctively to cover her breasts. Mike grabbed the legs of the pajama trousers and jerked them down over her hips. Beverly kicked, screaming, fought him with her fists, but he stripped them from her legs and flung them aside.

"Now, Baby!"

Claire burst into the room. "Mike! Stop it! You're mad!"

"Wanna watch, huh? Okay, just stand aside!"

Beverly tried to crab away from him, but he grasped her ankles and dragged her back. She sat up to fight him off, but he slapped her hard across the face, stifling her scream.

"Leave her alone, Mike!" Claire screamed.

Mike pushed Beverly's shoulders back to the bed. She clawed her nails over his chest, leaving angry red lines. She crossed her legs, locked her ankles. He kneeled over her.

"Mike! Get off her!" Claire shouted.

Beverly raked her nails over his eyes and he bellowed with pain. He tried to force his knee between her legs, and she strained against him. He doubled his fist and punched her in the stomach. She gagged and her legs relaxed.

"I swear, Mike, get off her!"

"Shut up!"

He pressed down against her, butting her with his knees. She whimpered and shook her head from side to side as her strength left her.

Claire ran to the bed and stood behind him. "Mike, stop!"

"No, damn you!"

Beverly screamed and her body recoiled and arched with pain as he forced himself toward his goal.

Claire's face was twisted with torment. A sob strangled in her throat. Her arm swept over her head. The long blade of the butcher knife glittered for a second in the light before she plunged it into his back.

He expelled the air from his lungs in a single gasp. He was dead the instant the knife entered his heart, but his body jerked with nerve spasms. Beverly's eyes were wide with shock and horror.

Claire had dropped to her knees. She was sobbing. "Mike, I told you not to. I couldn't let you."

Beverly touched the lifeless shoulders. She twisted and cast the body away from her. She slithered from the bed, backed away until she reached the doorway. The shock was still great upon her and she trembled, unable to make a sound. She saw the blood beginning to spread, saw the handle of the knife protruding from his back. She clasped a hand to her mouth and ran from the room. She flew down the stairs and grabbed the telephone. She dialed the number automatically.

When the telephone rang Cora Masserly knitted her brow with annoyance, thinking that it was Marcia calling back. She went to the hall and lifted the receiver, her mind forming the words of refusal.

"Hello," she said.

"Let me talk to Sam," the female voice said. It was a voice edged with panic.

"Who is this?" Cora asked.

"Let me talk to Sam," the voice insisted, then added with emphasis, "Please!"

"I'm afraid I'll have to know who is speaking," Cora said, the frown deep on her face. The woman on the line was crying and it baffled her.

"What is it?" Sam asked from the living room.

"I'll handle it," Cora said.

"I must talk to Sam," the voice shrilled.

"What nonsense is this?" Cora asked. A knot of fear was growing within her, born of the urgency in the voice. What could Sam possibly have to do with—.

"Who is it?" Sam asked, coming into the hall.

"Some female," Cora said. "I think she's drunk."

"Give me it," Sam said.

"I'll handle it," Cora said.

Sam reached out and wrenched the receiver from her grasp. "Sam!" she said. Sam ignored her and Cora caught her breath. He turned his back on her and said into the phone, "Hello, this is Sam."

"Sam!" Beverly cried. "Oh, Sam, I need you!"

"What's the trouble?"

"Sam, come here right away! I need you! Now!"

"All right," he said, "but tell me what's wrong." He felt his pulse begin to throb.

"It's Mike," she said. "He's ... he's dead!"

"What?"

"He's dead!" She began to cry. "Mother killed him," she wailed. "Oh, Sam, please! I need you!"

"What happened?"

"I can't talk about it! He tried to rape me! It was horrible, I don't—"

"I'll be right there!" Sam said. He dropped the phone in the cradle and started for the door.

"Sam!" Cora barked. "Where are you going?"

"Out. I have to go out."

"What do you mean, out? Who was that woman?"

"Beverly Merrick," Sam said, his hand on the door knob. "She's in trouble."

"Why would she call you?"

"I can't talk about it now," Sam said.

"This is preposterous, Sam! You can't run out into the night for some stranger! I forbid it!"

"You forbid it?"

"Yes! I'm your wife!"

"Cora," Sam said, "let's get one thing straight. You've never been my wife. You've been my advisor, my guiding light, but you've never been a wife."

"Sam, if you go out of this house, don't come back!"

"Cora, stop threatening me. I have no intention of coming back to this house, this palace of frigidity. I'm in love with this girl. Does that surprise you? Does that dirty word shock you? Love! It's a four-letter word, Cora, and you don't like four-letter words. Well, they exist, whether you like them or not. Love, Cora, think about it sometime. Something you've never known. It hasn't anything to do with Masters Degrees or social position or letting someone have sex with you to get what you want. But it's real, Cora, and I love this girl, and that's where I'm going!" He jerked the door open.

"Sam!" Cora screamed. "Don't go!"

The door slammed and she heard the sound of his footsteps running down the walk.

CHAPTER FOURTEEN

So that's what I get for five years of waiting on him, Cora thought. I might have known it. They're all alike. I give him five years of my life and he runs to the first little harlot who waggles her finger.

Cora had stood by the window, her hands shaking with anger. Then she had wandered through the house, denouncing him. She went to the kitchen and mixed a drink. An hour and four drinks had passed and her ashtray was littered with cigarette butts, crushed and twisted stumps of unabated frustration.

He'll pay for this, she said to herself. He'll come crawling back here, begging me to take him back, and he'll pay dearly for what he said. I know him, he's weak, he'll be back.

She sat quietly, listening to the sounds of the house in the stillness. She got up and paced nervously, then went back to the kitchen to mix another drink. She glanced at the clock and it was almost nine. She stopped pouring and put the bottle down. She gulped what she had in the glass, then turned abruptly and went through the living room and into the hall.

Her nerves were on edge. I can't stand being in this house alone, she thought. Not tonight, not after what he said. Men are beasts, damned ungrateful beasts. She picked the telephone receiver up and dialed.

"Hello," she said, "Marcia?"

"Cora," Marcia said. "You've changed your mind."

"Yes. Is that party still on?"

"I'll say it is," Marcia said. "I was just about to leave. I'll be by in five minutes."

"I'll be ready," Cora said. She put the receiver down. I'll show him, she thought. I'm not going to sit around here while he goes chasing his trollops. She hurried up the stairs to change her dress.

Sylvia Thompson sat at the bar in the Ferry Inn. She was nursing her scotch and soda.

Don't want to be drunk, she thought. Want to know what's going on.

She had sat in her parked car watching his window when she had first arrived at the Inn, sat there smoking for a half hour. When the light went out she had come into the bar. This was her second drink. She had been in the bar for a half hour.

This has to be done just right, she thought, just right. Her mounting excitement made her fidgety. This will be like winning the Grand National, she thought. They ought to have a trophy for this one. She chuckled. That's what I need, a damn trophy room. Subconsciously, Sylvia sought the Holy Grail of sex, the conquering of the urge. She sought the hated father image, her tormented psyche believing that through seduction and subsequent shaming of the image she would be released from the obsessive demands of the libido.

She twisted her glass, making rings on the bar. She glanced about her. A couple sat at one of the tables, their heads together in smiling conversation. A single man sat at the end of the bar and kept his eyes on her chest. The door to the garden was open and there was the drone of conversation from a large dinner party. This was punctuated by the meaningless, sporadic chortles of laughter from a drunk who sat alone at a table near the stone wall.

Sylvia slipped from the stool and left the bar. She went up the stairway to the second floor, then along the hallway, the carpet muffling her steps. She stopped by his door and listened. From within came the sound of snoring. She smiled and her hand rested on the door knob. There were no locks on the doors at the Ferry Inn. She turned the knob carefully, nudged the door with her shoulder. A hinge creaked, but she slipped inside and closed it quietly. She stood by the door letting her eyes become accustomed to the semi-darkness. The diffused light from a street lamp filtered into the room.

Moving to the foot of the bed, she stared at the mound of covers. She slipped off her shoes, then padded to the side of the bed and began to unbutton her blouse. She dropped each garment onto a nearby chair. Finally she stood nude in the half-light, trembling with excitement, anticipating his reaction. She leaned over, took the edge of the covers in her fingers and pulled them down slowly.

The bedsprings creaked with the addition of her weight. She slid her legs down, careful not to touch him, then she moved up to his back and wrapped her left arm about him.

Ira Wilson came awake with a start. He was confused for a moment, then, realizing that someone was in the bed with him, he cried out with alarm and leaped from the bed. He fell against the wall, groping for the light switch, assailed with terror. He found the switch and flooded the room with light.

Sylvia was kneeling in the middle of the bed and her arms were outstretched to him. "Come back," she said.

"What do you want?" His eyes bugged at her nakedness, at the voluptuousness of her body. He pressed back against the wall, as though trying to get farther away from the vision.

Sylvia read the fright in his eyes. She had to resist the impulse to laugh. He wore an old-fashioned night shirt of striped cotton and his appearance was comical. "Come back to bed," she said, tilting her head to the side and smiling. "I want you."

"Get out of here!" His voice was a strangled whisper.

"I have to have you," Sylvia said.

"Whore!" he said, spitting the word, as though it was too distasteful to speak.

"No," Sylvia said. "I'm your lover. Come." She began to edge off the bed.

"Filth!" Wilson rasped. "Filth!"

Sylvia came off the bed and advanced slowly, her hands out to him, moving with seductive precision. Wilson's hands came up to ward her off. A tick started in his right cheek. Sylvia stopped before him.

Wilson's teeth chattered and nausea gripped his stomach. It was coming over him again, the burning hatred. His mind was revolving back in time to the week-end with Uncle Arthur when he, Ira, was fifteen and Uncle Arthur said that he should be a man, and Uncle Arthur's friend, the woman with orange hair named Sarah. The memory made him shake. Uncle Arthur making him undress and the woman with the red laughing mouth standing in front of him compounding his shame with her nakedness, her breasts shaking, and her laugh making the mound of her stomach tremble, and Uncle Arthur behind her, laughing, urging him on, and the woman enveloping him, clutching his head and pressing his face into the sweat-perfume of her until he screamed and beat at her with his fists and the woman shouted, 'Crazy little bastard,' and Uncle Arthur pulled him off her, and then he had vomited, and Uncle Arthur had knocked him to the floor.

It came over him now, the panorama of never-forgotten horror, and before him, twisting and smiling, was the incarnation of wanton evil, the symbol of woman's innate depravity. Her features were blurred by his mounting fury, but he saw the form of her, saw the evil gestures.

Wilson lunged away from the wall and fell upon her with the wrath of an avenging angel. He pummelled her with his fists. Sylvia cried out, but more in pleasure than pain, and threw herself against his chest. Her hands gripped the nightshirt. Wilson flung her from him and the shirt tore down the front. Sylvia grabbed his legs, tripping him, and they rolled on the floor together. She crawled onto his back and he threw her off, but she carried away the rest of the shirt. He sprung to his feet, naked now, his face twisted with anger.

"Filth!" he shouted. "Vile, dirty thing!" He kicked at her and she sprawled, but she came to her feet quickly and rushed at him, her arms flailing. He swung his fist, hitting her in the face, and she staggered back to the bed. He fell upon her, beating her, cursing with each blow. She twisted from the bed and gripped his thighs with her arms. He pulled away, dragging her with him, beating upon her back and shoulders with his fists. He kicked her away from him and reeled across the room, staggering drunkenly, waving his fists, bellowing curses.

Sylvia could not get up. Her mouth was split and bleeding, and her front teeth were broken. One eye was swollen closed and the pain shot through her head. She laughed, gagging on blood. She was being punished for her sins, the punishment she wanted. She dragged herself to her feet, saw Wilson through one eye. She knew that she had to finish it. She went after him.

Wilson's tortured mind was teetering on the edge of sanity. His heart pounded and his breath came in gasps. He saw her approach. A savage cry gurgled in his throat. He leaped at her, smashing her down. Wild laughter burst from his mouth, and he ran to the door and wrenched it open.

There were people in the hallway, a small knot of terrified and curious faces gathered around the doorway, attracted by the sounds of violence within. They fell back as Wilson rushed from the room, startled by his sudden appearance and the onslaught of maniacal laughter. He rushed past them and down the hall.

"He's nuts!" A man exclaimed.

"He's going downstairs naked as a jaybird!"

They watched Wilson's flight, then turned and pressed against the open doorway, eager to view the carnage. A woman gasped and one of the men whistled through his teeth.

"It's that Thompson woman."

"Beat the hell out of her."

"My God, would you look at that. What a pair on her!"

"A real looney!"

Wilson rushed down the stairs as though pursued by the Devil. He burst into the bar. A woman screamed. He stopped and shook his fist at her. "Filth!" he shouted. He bounded across the room, leaving the bartender with his mouth agape, and ran out into the garden. He leaped onto a table next to the large dinner party and pointed his finger at one of the women. "Harlot!" he screamed. "You're all alike! Harlots!"

The drunk at the table by the wall straightened in his chair and blinked. "You tell 'em, Buddy," he shouted, clapping his hands.

The woman screamed at the sight of the naked wraith on the table and buried her face in her hands. The men kept to their chairs, too startled to move.

"Vessels of evil!" Wilson shouted, shaking his finger. "Hoydens of perverted lust!"

"You tell 'em, Buddy!" the drunk shouted.

"Bitches! The wrath of God will descend upon you for your wickedness!"

"Give 'em Hell, pal," the drunk shouted, gleefully leaping up and down in his chair.

"The evil in your bodies will be purged by the fires of everlasting—"

The bartender ended the sermon with a flying tackle that sent Wilson tumbling into the bushes, bellowing with rage. The two men wrestled, the bartender finally twisting Wilson's arm behind his back. Two men from the dinner party helped to hold him down.

"Somebody call the cops," the bartender said. "This baby needs a strait jacket."

Sam Masserly skidded to a stop before the house. He ran up to the front door and turned the knob, entering the house unannounced.

The living room was empty. "Beverly," he called, advancing into the room. There was no answer. "Beverly," he called again, baffled by the silence. He went to the stairway and stopped. Dr. Willard Curran was coming down the stairs.

"Hello, Sam," Curran said.

"Where is she?"

"I got her to sleep," the doctor said. He reached the bottom of the stairs and stopped.

"What happened?"

"Sit down over here and I'll tell you as much as I know." He went into the living room and Sam followed.

"Is Beverly all right?"

Doctor Curran shrugged. "I don't know," he said. "I administer drugs, set bones. Physically, she's fine."

"On the phone she said—"

"She was raped," Doctor Curran said. "But it won't kill her. Sit down."

Sam sat on the edge of a chair and faced the doctor. His hands were clenched. "How about Roberts?"

"He's dead. Died instantly. Claire stabbed him in the back while he was still on top of the girl."

Sam grimaced. "That's murder."

"Homicide," the doctor said. "I imagine the coroner's jury will pronounce it justifiable. That remains to be seen."

"And Beverly—"

"She's still in a state of shock, but she's fine as far as I can tell. Tomorrow it may be different. She called me, and she told me that she had called you. I had to insist that she take the sedative because she was waiting for you. I take it that you're involved with the girl."

Sam wasn't prepared for the statement and the word 'involved' made it sound illicit. He nodded his head.

"Seriously?" the doctor asked.

"Yes."

"Your wife know about it?"

"Look, Doctor, I don't see that this is any of your—"

"It is my business, Sam, because now that girl is my patient, and I want to know anything that might have an effect on her recovery."

"I'm in love with her," Sam said. "Cora knows it. I'm going to get a divorce."

"The fact that Beverly was attacked isn't going to change your mind?"

"Certainly not!" Sam snapped angrily. "Why should it?"

"I only asked. But it might make a difference. Rape is a strange crime, Sam. In actuality it is only a case of forced copulation, something that happens to millions of women every night, and the victim is seldom injured physically. What it does mentally is a different story. Sex to a young girl is generally associated with love. She sees herself giving herself to a gentle, desiring lover. She sees it as the union conceived in loving. It has a poetic quality, a beauty. With this picture in mind, if she is forced through brutal lust her femininity is shamed and she is repelled by the act. It suddenly takes on only the vilest aspects. It is a shock to the mind more than the body or the nervous system.

"Is Beverly—?"

"Beverly is still in shock, but I can say this for certain, she is going to need patience and understanding and a lot of tenderness. You'll have to realize what she's been through. It will take time before she can ever make love with a man and not bring back a memory of horror. And you'll also have to understand that a man was murdered on top of her. Are you sure that you're big enough to undertake this?"

"I don't know," Sam said. "I know I want to try."

The doctor smiled. "That's all any of us can do, Sam. I have a feeling that it will be worth the effort."

A car pulled into the drive and stopped.

"That will be the Township police," the doctor said. "I called them."

"Will they arrest Claire?"

"As a formality, yes. But they can't take her tonight. I put her under sedation, too."

"Is it okay if I stay here? I'd like to see Beverly when she comes around."

"That will be good." He went to the door to admit the policemen.

Hugh was driving. Sitting beside him, Elizabeth Pennington was thinking about God. They had been to the homes of two of Debbie's friends and were now on the way to a third. The Township Police Car had passed them on Bradley Road and its red lights had been blinking and she had wondered where it was going, and who could possibly have more trouble on this night than she did. And then she thought about Debbie and the police car and her heartbeat had quickened, but no, Debbie was not that foolish. And now she was thinking of God.

He makes us the way we are, she thought. He gives us all the desires that must be satisfied and it is always the desires that destroy us. If Greed, for instance, is evil, why didn't He just create us without it? It only took Him six days to create the world, she said to herself, but He might have done a damned sight better job if He had taken more time. Pretty haphazard job if you ask me. It's almost as if He has a great diabolical sense of humor, as if he created man for His amusement, filled us with urges and needs and moral codes, and just watches to see us fall on our collective faces. Brother, I'll bet He's getting a chuckle out of the mess I've made. And why is God always *He?* Why masculine? Well, why not, He's God isn't He? Capital *He,* a man's God, the man's world. If Brad wants a woman and tumbles some New York floozy, so what? I'm supposed to shrug and say, "Well, that's the way it is. A man will always be off slaying dragons. That's their nature." But just let *me* do it and I'm a leper because I'm a woman. And all because God is a He. Could this be the reason that most of the church-goers are women? Is it possible that they're really in there worshipping Men, not necessarily Him, but the whole concept of Male? Who knows, she mused, who knows?

They were approaching the Blakely house. "It's the first drive on your right," she said and Hugh nodded. What will I say to her? What can I say?

Hugh turned the car into the drive and stopped. "Want me to ask? The car isn't here."

"No," Elizabeth said wearily, "I'll ask." She got out of the car and walked to the front door. It was already being opened by Susan Blakely. "Hello, Susan," Elizabeth said. "I was wondering if Debbie had been here."

The girl gripped the door and her eyes were wide. "She was, Mrs. Pennington, but she's gone."

"Oh." Elizabeth felt the relief of not having to face her daughter in front of strangers. "Did she go home?"

The girl shook her head. "She came to use the phone. She called her father in New York. She ... she was crying ... and ... well, she went to Trenton to take the train."

"I see," Elizabeth said, trying to keep the despair out of her voice. By the girl's expression she knew that Debbie had been explicit in the phone conversation to Brad. "Well, thank you." She walked back to the car and got in.

"Was she here?" Hugh asked.

"Yes."

"She go home?"

"Yes, she went home," Elizabeth said, then added, "to her Father."

Hugh said nothing as he started the car and drove away. Elizabeth spoke only to give directions. Finally Hugh said, "I'm sorry, Liz."

"It's over with," she said.

"Nothing ends, Liz," Hugh said. "A life that nourishes on another life is part of that life."

"The intellectual approach won't help, Hugh. I've lost my baby, and that's a fact!"

"She's a grown girl with a mind and will of her own," Hugh said. "She grew within you and was yours, but the moment she was ready to come into her own life, she was no longer yours, you had no recourse but to let her come down through your body and be herself. You were there to care for her, but already her will was being formed. You were given her care and only ego makes you believe that she was yours, that you possessed her!" Hugh took a deep breath. "And in the same way that you do not own her, she does not own you! And if she will forsake you for loving when she knows the circumstances, then she's not worth bothering about! Damn it, Liz, I love you! I'm glad of what has happened because I want to marry you!"

Elizabeth stared at Hugh. It was the first time he had ever spoken sharply to her. She saw him with an added dimension. He was no longer just Good Hugh, Gentle, Wise Hugh—he had a stern, forceful side on which a woman could lean. She liked this.

Hugh turned the car into her drive and parked. "Want me to come in?"

Elizabeth shook her head. "Not tonight, Hugh," she said. "I think I want to be by myself. I want to think."

"Think about what I said."

"I will." She got out of the car. "Will you call me tomorrow?"

"First thing in the morning. I love you, Liz."

"Thank you, Hugh," she said. "I think I need that." She closed the door and walked to the house.

Cora was too drunk to think clearly, and she did not know what she was doing in the bedroom, or why Marcia was fighting with the big woman named Clara. She was on the large bed and her head was spinning, Marcia said. "I brought her here!"

Yes, she thought, Marcia brought me. I wanted to get away from the house, away from the things Sam said. Just wanted to get drunk, forget everything, called Marcia.

She had known immediately upon entering the house that it was a strange party. Her first reaction had been one of panic. She had heard about the parties on Temperance Hill, not really believing the stories of wild orgies, thinking that nothing like that could really go on just a mile above a town like Walkers Ferry. Her next reaction while she was being guided into the room by Marcia had been curiosity.

There were about two-dozen women in the room, many of them dressed like men. Cora recognized several of the guests, having seen them on the street, but the rest were strangers. It took her several minutes to realize that the women were paired into couples, and she stared in confusion at a square-shouldered woman kissing a pretty blonde girl.

Marcia pressed a drink into her hand. "Surprised?" Marcia asked.

"A...a little," Cora said. Nervously, she gulped the drink, asked for another. Marcia laughed and pointed to the stairway. Cora looked and caught her breath. A nude woman was coming down the stairs. She was big, with a square face and short brown hair swept back over her ears. She could have been a man except for the large breasts that flopped with each step. There was a crudity about her, and the way she managed to mimic a man was grotesque and horrifying to Cora.

"That's Clara," Marcia said. "This is her house. She's a real card, you'll have to meet her."

And now, lying on the bed, unable to collect her thoughts, Cora heard Clara snarl, "That's just tough. You brought her and I got her. This is *my* house, see, *my* house, and in *my* house I damn well do what I want."

Marcia protested, but Clara forced her out of the room and slammed the door. Cora giggled. They were fighting over her and it was funny because she wasn't a lesbian. She wanted to tell Clara, but the words would not form. Drunk, she said to herself, too drunk. Clara settled on the bed beside her and began to stroke her with her hands. Then Clara was kissing her and she wanted to laugh and tell Clara that she had made a mistake, but she was going to sleep. Yes, go to sleep and then Clara would take her hands away. She felt her dress being unbuttoned as she slipped into darkness, a deep, drugged sleep.

The door slammed open and she came awake. She was sober, and her mouth felt thick and she was sick at the stomach and her head ached. There was shouting and she shook her head. She sat erect in the bed. Clara was standing and Marcia was framed in the doorway.

"Come and look at it!" Marcia screamed. "Come and look at your goddamned house!"

Female screams, high and shrill and filled with panic, came from the floor below.

"It's on fire!" Marcia shouted. "And I hope that the goddamned thing burns to the ground, and I hope you burn with it, you damned bull dyke!"

Cora scrambled from the bed. Clara bellowed with rage and rushed from the room in pursuit of Marcia. Cora found that she was only half-dressed. She could see the flickering shadows of flames. Marcia had said the house was on fire. She could not find her shoes. She fumbled with the buttons of her dress, gave it up. She looked for her purse, found it on the bedside table. She ran from the room and into the hall. From the top of the stairs she could see the fire raging in the kitchen and spreading into the living room. She ran down the stairs. The front door was open and she rushed out into the night.

The women stood on the lawn and in the driveway, some danced about in confusion. One girl was wrapped in a blanket, another was clothed only in a pair of brief panties.

"Call the fire department!" Clara bellowed.

"I did," someone said. "Listen, you can hear the siren."

Cora ran across the lawn. She had to get away, she couldn't be there when the firemen arrived. What would the town say? Her, a respectable woman, at a party on Temperance Hill! She started up the drive, the small stones cutting her feet. She heard Marcia call to her. She ran faster. Not the road, no, not that way! They would come up the road. She veered off across the lawn, stumbled and fell. She dropped her purse and started to grope for it, then she heard Marcia coming after her. She lurched to her feet and ran, crashing through the brush. She had to get away! Had to! She fell down a small bank, got to her feet and ran. Briars tore at her arms and hands. Her body ached and her breath came in tight, strangling gasps. She plunged through the dense brush in the dark, falling and stumbling, picking herself up and running, pushed on by her panic, the terrible fear that brought wracking sobs from her throat.

She stopped to catch her breath. Turning, she saw the flames rising against the dark sky, a billowing pillar of red. She heard the approaching siren. Her fear grew anew. She turned and ran again. Get away! Get away!

CHAPTER FIFTEEN

Athena sat close to David with her head on his shoulder. He drove with both hands on the wheel, turning his face at intervals to kiss her forehead.

"I feel swept off my feet," Athena said.

"That's how we Belsons always get our women," David said.

"You mean you don't club them and drag them away?"

"Grandfather did that. Nowadays we sweep them."

Athena laughed lightly. "David?"

"What?"

"I'm happy. I'm very happy."

"I'm glad," he said.

They drove in silence for a time, then Athena said, "David, when are you going to make an honorable woman of me?"

"We'll get the license tomorrow."

"Hmmmm, good. I think I'm going to like keeping house for you."

The headlights probed the darkness of the road before them, outlined something moving in the near distance. David leaned forward and blinked, easing off on the gas pedal. "What's that?"

Athena sat up and looked. "It's someone walking in the road," she said.

"He looks drunk," David said.

He slowed the car. The headlights picked up and held the figure that staggered in the middle of the road, the arms flailing for balance. The car drew closer.

"It's a woman!" Athena said.

The figure staggered and fell. David pulled up and stopped. He leaped from the car. Athena was getting out the other side. David ran to the crumpled figure in the road. It was a woman. Her legs and arms were cut and scratched. Her dress was torn and covered with mud. Her hair was a mess of tangles and briars. He turned her over and her face was a cross-hatch of cuts and bruises. He began to lift her, and she suddenly came to life. He saw terror leap into her eyes. She snarled, the broken lips curling back over small white teeth. She squirmed, kicking, and lashed out at him with her nails.

Taken by surprise, David released her and stepped back. The woman whirled and ran across the road.

"Hey, wait a minute," David said. "Wait. We'll help you!"

The woman plunged off the road and ran down the embankment and into the thick brush and darkness. The sounds of her flight were evident for several minutes, then there was silence.

"Who was it?" Athena asked. "Why did she run?"

"I don't know," David said. "She suddenly looked at me, and was frightened and fought to get away. She was like an animal. I had the feeling I had seen her before."

"Wonder what happened?" Athena said.

"I guess there's no point trying to find her," David said. "She obviously doesn't want to be helped."

"Running around out here in the dark," Athena said. "Brrr, it gives me the willies. Maybe she was someone's date and decided it would be better to get out and walk."

"She was all scratched up," David said.

"I'm glad I have an honorable man," Athena said. "Come along, honorable man, I'm beginning to feel the call of home and hearth."

David wrapped his arm about her and they went back to the car. When she got in he closed the door and went to the driver's side, casting a glance into the darkness at the side of the road. He got behind the wheel and drove off.

Crouched in the brush, Cora waited until she saw the car drive away. She smiled with appreciation of her own cunning. Can't take the chance of anyone seeing me like this. When I get home it will be fine. She got to her feet and climbed back to the road. She walked along slowly, letting her strength gather. Her feet hurt and her body was a mass of burns from the cuts. She saw the lights of another car approaching and she scurried off the road and hid in the bushes until it went past.

She got up again and walked. It was all his fault, all Sam's. He would pay for this! When she got home and there would be no way of anyone knowing, then he'd pay.

The fire was extinguished and the firemen were gathering up their equipment. There were three trucks and a number of cars. It was a volunteer fire company and the firemen were the townsmen of Walkers Ferry, mostly the sons and grandsons of the more permanent residents, the unsophisticated portion of the town.

"Queer party," one of them mumbled. "All women. Damndest thing."

"How did it start?"

"One of them got jealous because her girlfriend was with another woman."

"Jesus."

"Crazy damn thing."

"She poured kerosene all over the kitchen and put a match to it."

"She did a good job. That joint ain't worth ten cents now."

"I can't understand that kind of thing with women."

"You see them two blondes? God, they're nice stuff."

"Damn waste of female, you ask me."

A young fireman wearing a pair of rubber boots folded to his knees came up to the first truck where the Chief was talking with the men and directing the reassemblage of equipment. He held a woman's purse in his hand. "I found this in the grass over there," he said.

The Chief took the purse in his hands, turned it over, pursing his lips. "Guess it belongs to one of them," he said. "It ought to have a name in it."

He opened it and held it to the light and peered inside. He reached his hand in and brought out a wallet. Opening the wallet, he extracted a driver's license and read the name. "I'll be damned," he said. He handed the license to one of the men. "Look at that."

"Cora Masserly," the man said. "Well, I'll be go to hell. Imagine that. I never figured her to be one of them."

CHAPTER SIXTEEN

oward Denby, public relations man, angled across Sixth Avenue in New York City, cutting a straight and true course for Moriarity's Steak House.

It was after the lunch hour, but he did not have food on his mind. He was preoccupied with his recent state of unemployment.

He paused at the entrance to Moriarity's, gripped the door handle and pulled it open. He went in, nodded at the headwaiter, and went to the long bar. He saw people he knew. There were several public relations men at the bar, a press agent for a Broadway show, a famous columnist, and a clutch of freelance writers for the bigger magazines.

Howard Denby took a stool and ordered his usual scotch on the rocks.

"Hear your boss went off his chump," the press agent said. "Tough luck."

"That's the way it crumbles," Howard said. He knew that everyone had heard about Ira Wilson. It was perfect tabloid material and the *Daily News* had two-decked the front page banner: *Sexologist Runs Amok!*

"It's a lousy life," one of the public relations men said. "You figure you've got the golden egg and zippo, it goes through your fingers."

"The secret," Howard said bitterly, "is to make sure that your golden egg don't get laid."

The men laughed and Howard felt better. It was a good line and he'd be quoted at Sardis and some of the better joints. A little talk around might bring up a good client.

"What you got cooking?" one of them asked.

"A few irons in the fire," Howard said.

One of the magazine writers came down the bar and took the stool next to Howard. "You were close to Wilson," he said. "Why don't you write a book about the survey business."

"*Argus Magazine* owns all the reports," Howard said.

"I mean a novel."

"Nah," Howard said. "Nothing there. Statistics, that's all. Figures. How many times you do this, how many times you do that. Just figures. It looks jazzy in the magazine article, but in a book you gotta have people. Conflict, man, ya need conflict. A bunch of scientists talking to women, that ain't nothing. It's all statistics."

"I don't know," the magazine writer said. "I'm sure there's a story there somewhere."

"Look, Pal," Howard said, "take my word for it. Nothing there. Like this last time. A little jerkwater town that folds up at nine o'clock. Dullest damn place you ever saw. A parking ticket in that burg is a major event. Believe me, I was there. Genuine squaresville. Nothing could possibly happen there."

"Wilson happened there," the writer said.

Howard groaned and held his head. "Wilson ended there, and that oughta prove that nothing happens there. Wilson never touched a broad. He hits that town and it's so damn dull that even he goes off the deep end."

The writer laughed. "Maybe you're right."

"I know I'm right," Howard said. "Bartender, make that a double."

THE END

JUDGE NOT
MY SINS

If it was love, it was also fear, and we might have huddled behind a rock while the night wind devoured the plain.

"Save me," I heard her cry.

—Norman Mailer
Barbary Shore

PROLOGUE

This is David Markam.

A young man of 34, he walks along 31st Street in New York City. He has just left a cab at the corner of Third Avenue. It is a spring night and he wears a light trench coat. He has a mustache outstanding amidst gaunt features, and a pipe juts from his outthrust jaw.

The girl with her hand folded into the crook of his elbow is blonde, four inches below David's six feet height, and easily the most beautiful girl he has ever seen.

"This is it," the girl said, tugging his arm.

David stopped, surveyed the brick building with a quick glance. The girl had loosened her grip and was rummaging in her purse for a key.

"Damn," she muttered, "I can never find anything."

David peered closely at a brass plate next to the door of the building. He read the two names to himself. "Is this an office building?" he asked.

The girl looked up from her purse, followed his eyes to the brass plate. "Photographers," she said. "I have the top floor." She returned to her search.

David watched her. She was intent on her task, muttering, shuffling the contents of the overburdened purse. He wondered if he was going to make love to her. It was obvious that she was going to ask him in. He wanted to make love to her. Well, that was nothing new. She was a woman. She was beautiful. And he couldn't remember her name. The perfect ingredients for wanting to make love to a woman.

"Here it is," she said, lifting the key between her fingers, and flashing a small smile of triumph.

David took the key from her, climbed the two steps, inserted it in the lock. He opened the door and she stepped in ahead of him. He followed, let the door close.

The girl started up the stairway and David followed. For the first time he saw the fine lines of her full calves, the slim ankles. She wore a raincoat that rustled against her legs. She had worn the raincoat since he had first met her, and it was difficult to tell about her body, but it looked good, and the face was perfect—angelic.

"Wait," the girl said. She had reached the first landing and turned. She stopped David's approach, resting her hands on his shoulders. Her expression was suddenly pensive. "Are you certain you want to do this?"

"Do what?"

"Come with me like this."

"Why not? What's wrong with it?"

She bit down on her lower lip and stared at him with luminous blue eyes for a long moment. "Nothing," she said, "come along." She turned and walked along the hall, turned into the next flight of steps. David followed. At the next landing she stopped and turned again. "I don't know," she said.

"About what?" David asked, beginning to weary of whatever it was she didn't know.

"I'm afraid you'll be in love with me," she said.

"Try me," he said.

"I mean it," she said. "I wouldn't like that."

"I promise not to."

She chewed her lips and her eyes narrowed thoughtfully, as though she were seriously considering the validity of his promise. "I'm certain that you will," she said.

David sighed. Just his luck. A beautiful girl. She asks him home. And she has to be a nut. "Scout's honor," he said.

The eyes changed. They were smiling, and she asked, "Were you a scout?"

"No," he said.

"Then why did you say . . ."

"Are we going to stand here and talk all night?"

She caught her breath, then she smiled, and David's pulse quickened as he was caught in the radiance of the most beguiling smile he had ever seen. "I'm sorry," she said. She turned again, and went heel-clacking along the hall and into the next flight of stairs.

"Another flight?" David asked.

"This is the last," she said.

"Point of no return," David said.

She stopped suddenly and whirled. "Why did you say that?"

"I . . . uh . . ." There didn't seem to be a reasonable explanation. "I don't know," he said. "It just seemed like something to say. I mean, after all your talk about . . ."

"You're making fun of me." The eyes had changed again and now they were sparkling with quick anger.

Damn, David thought, and we're not even up the steps yet. "Look," he said, wearily, "I'm not making fun of you. I said it because I think it's idiotic to think I'm going to fall in love with you just because I'm going to your apartment. I don't even know you."

The anger subsided. "I'm sorry," she said, her voice subdued. "I guess I'm nervous." She turned again and started up the stairs. David shook his head and followed.

They reached her door, the only one at the top. "Use the second key," she said.

David fumbled, trying to remember which key he used in the downstairs door. She pointed. He put the key in the lock and began to open the door. A dog snarled, startling him.

"Fang!" the girl snapped. The growling ceased, and David opened the door. The girl stepped in ahead of him, pushing the large Doberman ahead of her. The dog was black, lithe, powerfully muscular. He danced backwards, nuzzling at the girl's hand, making whimpering sounds.

David closed the door and followed her along the short hall. He gazed at the dog, clucking his tongue against the roof of his mouth. Nothing like being well-chaperoned, he thought.

The hallway opened onto a huge rectangular living room. The floor was black, the walls white. It was psuedo-Japanese with low tables, cushions on the floor, a white screen across the far end of the room. One wall was white brick with an austere fireplace. There was a long, black, ornately carved chest against one wall. Lights were suspended from the ceiling and contained in large, balloon-like Japanese lanterns. It was unusual for a New York apartment, but effective.

"Quite a room," David said.

"I like space," she said, shrugging out of her coat, and draping it over the chest.

"You've certainly got it," David said. He was looking about the room, but now his gaze stopped on the girl.

"You'll have to see the rest of the place," she said. "There are three more rooms."

David was only half listening. He stared at her. If it was possible to fall in love with a body, the girl's fears were justified. She wore a black dress that clung to her, a startling contrast to the corn-colored hair. Everything about her seemed to be in the right proportion. She was tall, her neck was arched, perfectly formed; the undulations of slightly sloping shoulders, high breasts, waist and hips were distinctly feminine, womanly; a mating of sophistication and earthiness.

She had stopped speaking and when David looked up at her face the eyes were shaded with sadness, the expression of the mouth wistful. "You're staring at me," she said.

"I'm sorry," he said. "It's just that I hadn't seen you before. You're beautiful."

"Don't," she said, a slight note of pleading in her voice.

"What?"

"Don't be like other men."

"I'm a man," he said. "That's all I am. I was just looking at a beautiful woman."

She turned slowly and walked the length of the long room. She slid a portion of the screen aside, exposing a large window that looked out upon the lighted skyline of New York. She stood with her back to David. The room was charged with silence. The black dog lay in the middle of the room, relaxed and tense at the same time. Its head was arched, and the wary eyes moved between David and the girl. David stood at the far end of the room, near the small kitchenette, watching the girl, listening to the silence. When she spoke her voice was distant. It was almost a whisper, but its resonance carried and filled the room. It had a dirge-like quality, a voice speaking from the lonely depths of the soul. "I wanted to be ugly," she said. "I wanted to be ugly on the outside. I wanted a mask to cover beauty; to have all the beauty inside where people could not see it. I wanted it so that one day a man would feel the beauty and he would be strong enough and tender enough to accept the beauty and his love would transform the ugliness to loveliness, but for his eyes alone."

She stopped speaking. The plaintive anguish of her voice seemed to echo in the still room. David glanced at the dog and it seemed as though the animal were listening and understanding. It was a strange experience, and David found that he was conscious of his breathing, being careful of it lest he make a sound.

"Once," the girl said, starting again, "I thought about using acid on my face."

David waited, but she said no more. He was uncomfortable, nervous, and he had the feeling that he should not speak, that if he once mouthed words he would suddenly be enmeshed in an emotional web. He sensed that a door had been opened to him, and beyond the threshold was a frightening darkness, and he felt that once he stepped into the void the door would close behind him, never to open again. "Why didn't you?" he asked.

The girl stiffened and turned. Her eyes blinked as though she was only now aware of his presence, as though she had just returned from some distance place. One hand fluttered to her throat. She smiled suddenly, breaking the reverie. She slid the screen back into place and started across the room. "Let me show you the rest of the place," she said.

David scowled, his curiosity unabated, but the mood of the moment was gone. She stopped next to him, still smiling, and raised a finger to his brow. "Don't look so fierce," she said. David lifted a hand to stay her, the words forming to question her, but she had already moved away, her step light, her mood changed. He dropped his hand and shook his head. Then he followed her.

They entered a room that was as large as the living room and painted the same colors. It contained a desk, a typewriter, a filing cabinet. Nothing else. It was bare, austere, businesslike.

"This your office?" David asked.

"Yes."

"You're in business?"

"I was," she said. "I gave it up."

"What business?"

"I was a manufacturer's representative," she said. "I bought aircraft parts. Very dull."

"What do you do now?"

"Nothing."

David was about to ask further questions, but she was gone again. He bit down on the words and followed.

The next room was smaller and it was impossible to get past the door. The walls were painted a dull, lusterless gray. It was a storage room, jammed with a collection of chairs and tables, lamps, boxes of books, straw hats, paintings, a seedy racoon coat, suitcases, paper boxes. It was a disordered clutter. Everything seemed to have been hastily thrown in from the doorway.

"I hate this room," she said. She turned away quickly and David followed her back to the living room. She opened a door to the right of the kitchenette and ushered him into the bedroom. It was a room slightly larger than the storeroom. The walls were pastel green, the ceiling a warm shade of peach. The wall-to-wall carpet was beige. There was a tall chest of drawers, a large dresser with mirror, two wing-back chairs. The bed was large and the headboard was a bookcase. The furniture was in dark maple and the chairs were covered with a cotton print material.

David was startled by the room. It had a warmth, a lived-in quality that was lacking in the rest of the apartment. He turned to the girl and caught his breath. Except for the obvious physical similarity, he was looking at a different person. She was relaxed. She moved across the room as though she belonged, as though she had just arrived home from some far place, and she exuded a radiance that complemented the decor of the room.

Standing in the middle of the room, David watched her turn and come towards him. She stopped before him, stood there saying nothing, her arms at her sides, looking into him. He felt his nerves tremble. He wanted to reach for her, but he was afraid to break the mood. The beauty, the warmth of her, created a constriction in his chest. He looked back into her eyes and he saw longing there, saw the bottomless depths of loneliness.

She rose on her toes and leaned forward. Her lips grazed his for an instant, then she moved away. It was the mere suggestion of a kiss, but his heart leaped and he felt the sudden wave of emotion strike the deep core of his senses. She turned and moved away, going to the dresser to turn on the radio. He watched her, a scowl marring his forehead, the deep furrows gathering at the bridge of his nose.

He saw again the odd decor of the entire apartment and knew that he was looking at the girl. The austerity of the living room was the face she turned to the world, impersonal, unemotional, devoid of feeling. The office was even colder. The drab gray of the storeroom was her past, all the clutter of what she had known and cast away from her. The bedroom was the woman, the beauty, the warmth, the love that crouched, waiting with the trembling rabbit-heart of the woman-within-woman.

Static, the dissonance of voices hastily changed, then music came from the radio. She flicked a switch that transferred the speaker to the living room, turned the volume down.

"Coffee?" she said, turning to face him.

"I'd like that," he said.

"Good, I'll make it." She walked past him and through the door. He followed, closing the door after him.

She watched him close the door and the smile left her face. She stood at the end of the bar which separated the kitchenette from the room. "Now *you're* afraid," she said.

David glanced back at the door, then at the girl. He hesitated a moment. He came and perched on one of the stools facing the bar. "Not afraid," he said. "It's something different. I'm not certain exactly what, but it is more like caution. I mean I've never met anyone quite like you, and I . . ."

"You think I'm crazy?"

She had interrupted his train of thought and he had to pause a moment to consider her new question. "No, I don't," he said. "Different, but not crazy."

"Do you want to make love to me?"

He looked hard at her. Her questions came too fast. It was not repartee, there was no flippancy to it, and he knew that he had to answer with serious conviction and honesty, knew that she expected it. He swallowed and one hand gripped the other.

"I'd like some coffee," he said.

She smiled, then reached under the counter for a pan and moved to the sink and the water tap. She filled the pan and placed it on the stove. She came back to the counter and stood opposite him.

"You promised not to love me," she said.

"I know." His eyes dropped to his hands. "I. . ." He paused. It was difficult, confusing. "Look," he said, lifting his head, "couldn't we talk about something else? I don't think I like this?"

"But you came here to make love to me," she said.

He stared at her with an even concentration for a long moment, then he spoke. "That's right. You were a girl. A girl I met in the night."

"And now I'm not?"

He took a deep breath and his eyes dropped again. He nodded. "And now you're not," he said. He looked up at her again and there was the wistful little-girl expression again. He lifted his fist and bit on his knuckles, not taking his eyes from her face. "That's too bad, isn't it?" he said.

She nodded. She was standing with both hands touching the edge of the counter. Impulsively, David reached out and gripped her wrist. Her lips parted and her eyes flashed.

The dog came to his feet and a deep growl built in his chest. The teeth were bared and the animal was poised, taut as a bowstring.

"Down, Fang!" the girl snapped.

David released her wrist and drew his hand back. He looked at the dog, watched it settle down on the floor, embarrassed, but watchful. David turned back to the girl.

"Strange name for the dog," he said.

"Funny," she said. "Amusing funny. Nobody really expects a dog to be named Fang." She turned to the stove where the water was boiling. She turned off the gas, then brought down cups and a jar of instant coffee.

"I used to have a dog," David said. "A mongrel type dog."

"You managed to change the subject," she said.

He shrugged and smiled with a mock rueful expression, but did not answer. This was definitely not the kind of girl who spent the evening in small talk. She had a way of slicing through sham and insisting on direction. It was not evident in her appearance or in outward movement, but in conversation she was incisive and purposeful. There was an enigmatic quality to her that was disconcerting.

They drank their coffee in awkward silence. David could not speak. The subject matter was limited and he was afraid to pursue the obvious. He had the feeling, knew for some inexplicable reason, that the only thing they could talk about was each other, one in relation to the other. It was a subject that he might have entered with relish had it been with some other girl. It would have been a gambit. He knew the things to say that a girl would want to hear who needed reassurance for what was already decided in her mind. It was a game, a method of putting love-making on a civilized or intellectual basis. It was something you indulged in, regretting the shallowness in a deep recess of the mind, but admitting—and even believing—that any means justified the end. With this girl the concept of such self-deception was ludicrous.

"I think I'd better be going," David said.

The slightest suggestion of a smile passed over her face. "You're being afraid again," she said.

"Stop it!" David snapped, coming to his feet abruptly, slamming his open palm down on the counter. "Just lay off! I'm afraid. All right, I'm afraid. But don't rub it in." His facial muscles were taut and he gripped the edge of the counter, leaning towards her, the words coming fast and clipped, because he was incensed with a sudden anger. "I came up here for one thing. You know it and I know it. You were a pretty girl I met at Galligans. That's all. I figured you for a fast roll in the hay. That's all it was." His voice rose and he trembled as he spoke. "But that's not enough now. I want you, but not that way. I don't know just how, I don't really know what this is all about, but I do know that a one-night stand isn't it. You know that it's wrong and so do I. I feel it, I honest-to-God know that I ought to get out of here."

"Don't go," she said.

"Shut up! I want to finish. I feel something for you. I don't know what it is . . ."

"It's love."

". . . I said, shut up. I don't think it's love. I damn well don't know what it is, but it bothers me." His voice was tense. "It makes me afraid, I'll admit it, but don't bug me about it."

"I can tell you what it is."

"I'm leaving."

They were both silent. There was the sudden void. The background of music, the quick breathing, the expectant rustle of the dog moving on the floor.

The girl took a deep breath and bit down on her lower lip. Her eyes dropped and she swallowed. "I'll get your coat," she said.

David watched her come around the end of the counter. He relaxed, removed his hands from the counter and turned to her. She lifted the trench coat and held it up for him. He turned his back and slipped his arms into the sleeves, shrugging it up over his shoulders. He jammed his hands deep into the pockets and turned to her.

"Look," he said, "I'm sorry if I sounded like . . . well . . . you know."

"It's all right," she said. She attempted a smile, but it didn't quite form and there was a hesitant coolness in her voice.

He took a deep breath and was about to say something, somehow explain to her the way he felt, but the words did not form in his mind, and he pursed his lips and shrugged.

"If you're going to go you had better go," she said. There was a crispness to her tone.

David felt the reluctance to move, but there was also the feeling that it was the right thing to do. Why, he didn't know, but a feeling had passed between them, a rapport. It happens all the time. A man is in a room. He looks up and there is a woman. Their eyes meet and something happens. It cannot be explained, but it exists, it happens. It was like that with David. He knew that the feeling was there.

Stepping back, he took a deep breath and nodded his head. He bit his lip, then he said, hesitating over each word, "yes … yes … I … had better … I …"

"Please," she whispered, her voice suddenly fraught with pleading, speaking to him with the frantic loneliness of her eyes.

He clenched his teeth to stay the trembling within him. They stood in silence, separated by a veil of fear, two people poised on the brink of a crevasse, decided, but frightened of the dark void into which they knew they must plummet.

Their eyes held. She took a tentative step forward. He waited, but his eyes told her to come to him. She paused for a second that seemed interminably long, then she caught her breath, and fell against him, burrowing her face into his chest, encircling him with her arms, holding on with relief and desperation.

The gap was closed. He sighed aloud. His right hand burrowed into her hair. His left hand settled in the small of her back. He bent his face to her hair, savoring the combined scent of cologne and rain. A galaxy of emotion spun and exploded within him, and he held her tightly.

She lifted her face and tears glistened in her eyes, but her expression was happy, secure. "I don't want you to go," she whispered.

"No."

"Stay."

"Yes."

"Oh . . ." Her voice trailed off and she closed her eyes, pressing herself against him.

He lowered his lips to hers. They touched gently, a furtive brush. She did not speak, but her lips formed words against his.

"Love me." He moulded his mouth to hers and then he was lost in the cataclysm of longing. His heart thudded painfully. His nerves responded and sensation of touch, the awareness of her, spread over him. He felt with new clarity the press of her breasts against him, the frantic grip of her hands against his back, the pressure of her thighs against his. She moved her head, increasing the force of the kiss. Her hands left his back and encircled his neck. She clung to him, kissing him with new hunger. Their lips parted, teeth clicked in clumsy anxiety, then David's tongue touched hers, the contact electrifying him.

She pulled her head away. She arched against him, her head back, her eyes still closed. She moved her head from side to side. "Yes," she whispered, as though she were speaking to herself. "Yes … oh … yes." She gripped him more tightly, and her lips returned to find his and she kissed him with renewed fervor.

The dog shifted on the floor and whimpered.

She moved her lips away and the fraction of an inch separated them. "Love me," she whispered.

"I do," he said, and he tensed suddenly with the realization that he meant it, that it was madness, but that he did mean it, that he wanted her, wanted to love her, wanted her.

Her voice was a strangled plea, the voice of a small girl. "Take me to bed," she said.

He awoke in the confusion of love. The radio alarm came on and he sat up in the bed. The room was strange and dawn streamed through the window facing the street. He rubbed his eyes, listened to the street sounds of morning. He turned his head and stared down at the sleeping girl.

Her blonde hair sprawled over the pillow. She cradled the pillow with one arm and her breathing was slow and even. In sleep her expression was placid. She wore no makeup, but there were the slight traces of lipstick on the perfectly formed lips.

He felt strange, remembering what did not seem real. He took a deep breath and shook his head. He leaned forward to peer at the clock. It was early. He lay back, his hands joined behind his head. He turned and gazed at her. The light blanket and sheet were pulled up to her neck. He turned on his side, supporting his head with his right hand, and reached out to touch her with his left.

She stirred, mumbling, and he smiled. He moved closer to her and blew softly against the nape of her neck. She squirmed, moving her head. He blew again.

She was beautiful, more beautiful in the daylight. Defenseless in her sleep, angelic.

He leaned over and brushed her lips with his. He moved his hand over her waist, stroked the velvet skin. She came awake suddenly, spun about and stared at him with surprise widening her eyes. She bit down on her lower lip, as though stunned to find him there.

"Oh," she said, "you."

"You expected maybe, Lassie," he said, scowling.

She pursed her lips and her eyes smiled. "You're funny, too," she said.

"Too?"

Her head was nestled in the crook of her elbow, both imbedded in the pillow. "My funny lover," she said.

"You remember, then."

"Of course."

"Good memory?"

"Wonderful," she said, the eyes still smiling. "You look nice in bed."

"You too."

"Even in the morning?"

"Especially in the morning."

They lay facing each other, separated, but held together with their eyes. They were silent, looking, judging, then he reached out and touched her shoulder. She moved her hand from her head and covered his hand. The smile had left her eyes and now she was serious, probing his face.

"You frighten me," she said.

"Still? I thought we finished that last night."

"More than ever now," she said. "Looking at you I fall apart inside. When you touch me—" She didn't finish.

"It must be good," he said.

"You don't know me," she said.

"I will," he said.

She bit on her lip and closed her eyes as though some painful thought had just fluttered across her mind. She opened her eyes, taking a deep breath. Pulling his hand away from her arm, she moved it, turning the palm up. She brought his hand to her lips. She held it there, lingering, then she moved it down and covered her breast.

There was an element of quiet desperation in the move, and David found it vaguely disturbing.

She moved cat-like, sliding close to him. She pressed her face against his chest, moulded her body to his, holding on to him. There seemed to be more fear in the movement than passion. She clung to him as though seeking refuge, as though she was placing him between her and something beyond them both. David brought his arms about her and held her close to him. He felt the slight tremor in her body, felt it became still as she nuzzled close.

He furrowed his brow. There were so many moods to her. She smiled, laughed, then suddenly she was serious, and in the next instant she was caught in the abyss of terror. He kissed the top of her head, and she lifted her face. She was smiling again. The moment of fear had passed.

"You're very strong," she said. She squirmed against him, bringing her face to meet his. He kissed her, turning her head, pressing her into the pillow. His desire for her began to spread. He was aware of the body pressing against him, moving against him. He forgot to breathe and his eyes were closed, sharpening his sense of touch. He loved her and he wanted her. He moved his mouth from hers, gasped for breath, kissed her face, moved his lips into the hollow of her throat, savoring the lavender taste of her, moved his lips down to brush lightly over her breast. She grasped his head and pulled him into the breast-soft flesh, holding him so that he could hear the pounding of her heart.

Thigh to thigh, breast to breast, belly to belly, they became one entity, one breath-held, teeth-clenched, lip-touched being, divorced from reality, plummeted into the depth of soul. Swaying, clinging, they led each other into the beauty of love-passion, mindless of the world that moved beyond the window, creating their own world that was a galaxy of multi-colored light beating against the iris of closed eye.

They clung together even as the passion subsided and their breathing was ragged, forcing strength into dissipated muscles. They lay together for long minutes, then she said, "That's what frightens me."

"It shouldn't," he said. "It's beautiful."

"That's it!" She jerked away from him, startling him. She tossed her head and sat up. She pulled her legs up, hugging her knees. She stared out into the room. "That's exactly what's wrong."

"How can beauty be wrong?" David had twisted and he gazed at her pose, so like the classic simplicity of an Edward Weston nude, the unbroken line of back and thigh and leg.

"It's not just that," she said, "it's me. I can't love!" She spoke the words evenly and softly, but they were issued with impact, an outcry against the frustrated image of self.

David did not move or speak. He watched her face, saw the sudden despair. She closed her eyes and lowered her forehead to her knees.

"I'm not sure I understand," David said, after a long pause. "I won't try to give you a lot of crap about how I can change the way you feel." He spoke with gravity, and she lifted her face to look at him. "Something bothers you, I know that. I also know that we have found something. Even there I'm not sure what it is. I feel that I love you. I know that. I want to see you again, and I'd like you to give me the chance to be something to you." He stopped speaking and their eyes held.

She bit down on her lip and her eyes misted. "I knew it when I saw you," she said. "Later I was sure of it."

"What?"

"That you're nice," she said.

"I know some people who would argue the point," David said.

"They don't know you."

"Maybe not."

She watched him silently, then she smiled. "Go away," she said. "Get dressed and go away. I have to be alone with myself. You've gotten me confused."

Their gaze held, then David nodded. He slid from beneath the sheet, swung his legs off the bed and stood. He went to the chair where his clothes were draped. He kept his back to her as he dressed, and when he was finished he turned. "Do you want me to come back?"

She shook her head. "No," she said, "I don't want to see you again."

"You're sure?"

"Yes."

He nodded, gazed at her, then he squared his shoulders and went to the door. He stopped, looked at her again, then he opened the door and went into the living room. The black dog eyed him with suspicion, but David ignored the animal. He went along the hallway and let himself out of the apartment.

Going down the stairs he had the feeling that he was leaving something vital and precious. He shrugged, knowing that he had to go. At the bottom he paused by the three mailboxes, and it occurred to him that he had never learned her name.

Leaning over, he peered at the name on the middle box. The other two were the names of the photographers. He looked closely.

"Leslie," he said aloud. "Leslie Darrow." He rummaged in his coat for a pencil and wrote the name on the inside of a matchbook cover.

Opening the door, he stepped out into the clamor of the street.

CHAPTER ONE

W ho was I that morning? I asked myself the question as I
walked into the morning sounds of city. Who was I? What
did I think, believe, know, feel? My name was David Markam,
but that was a yesterday label, a tag, the identification for a certain body of a certain size. I had a past, thirty-four years of it.
But now who was I and what did I really think and where was I
going?

I moved along thirty-first street with a buoyancy that I had
not known since youth. It was a strange combination of feelings.
Confusion and this other feeling of lightheartedness, the way I
felt one time during high school when I had kissed a girl for the
first time and I ran through the night, elation bursting from me,
and I had to leap up and swing on the limb of a tree. Like that.

Second Avenue was spread with the bright newness of morning sun. Traffic released by a change of lights charged across
the intersection, expelling grey-blue exhaust, grinding out the
sounds of impatience.

I turned the corner and walked into the tide of go-to-work
faces, impassive, flaccid, vacant, grim. No smiles for the worka-
day. Heel-stilted bouncing girls, nylon legs dropping from folds
of crinoline, tight-waisted and pert-breasted; happy swinging
bodies and bored last-night faces. Wide awake legs carrying
sleepy bodies. Lately risen brains still fuzzily pillow held.

There was no rush for me, no determined purpose to my
stride, so the morning-march went past me, broke and eddied
about me as water cleaves past a rock, leaving me with the stigma

of curious glance and angry glower. I was out of place. I was not office-bound, not a worker, and their eyes chastised me for my indolence.

I smiled in return. I pulled my tie loose and unbuttoned my collar. I jammed my hands deep into pockets and slouched for all their indignation. I felt good.

I had met a girl, an unusual, incredible girl, a beautiful girl. I walked the street under the bright sun with the smells of love still upon me, and I felt good.

Leslie. Her name was Leslie. I saw it on the mailbox when I left. A chance meeting in a bar. A glance, eyes meet. The moments of indecision, then the opening gambit, lighting her cigarette. A joke, a word about the weather. The hesitant gulf between man and woman, wary for fear of being rebuffed, staying the palpitating eagerness to protect the veneer ego. Her smile saying, I am willing to speak with you, and then the flow of conversation.

A pick-up in a bar. Strangers in a large, soft bed, brought together by city loneliness and the hunger for human touch. A cheap one-night grappling of sweating bodies, the casual debauch, the dregs of immorality. But then there was something new, something different. As our bodies met in passion there was an awakening, the birthing of something strange and unknown, a feeling of such depth that it defied casual explanation.

And so, as I walked the street that morning I was not the same David Markam who had climbed those stairs with a strange girl. I had achieved a new dimension that bordered on the metaphysical, a sharp delineation of love—not the meaning of the word, but the feeling. I felt like an explorer on the threshold of a strange and wonderful land. I had no idea then that it would be a savage land.

The Second Avenue bus roared into the curb ahead of me. I ran and jumped aboard, swung from an overhead strap until it reached Fourteenth Street, then shouldered my way to the door and the sidewalk.

I walked east passing through the channel of seen-better-days brownstones. It was early, but the street was awake, alive. The East Side is always alive with the harsh, frantic sound of poverty. This is the social cellar of New York and only the language changes. It was Irish once, bawdy and musical with the rolling gaelic vowels; it was Jewish once, hard-pressed dignity and the somber chant of a; was Italian once, an eruption of sound, a virulent stacatto of language. Now it was Spanish, hopefully musical.

I walked along Fourteenth Street, the social barrier. On the left was the towering maze of the housing project, red brick respectability, angular proper buildings of careful conformity, the sheep pens. And on the right was the east side, the stinking lop-sided spawn of architectural abortion, the fire-escape girded cold water walk-ups, mean low-rent buildings permeated with the rank stomach-turning smell of poverty. Here live die new Americans, the new strong blood, the individualists just waiting for their chance to get across Fourteenth Street and clean conformity.

I turned down on Avenue A and crossed the street to the discolored brick building where I lived. I walked through the brown-walled, trash-littered hallway of the front building, out into the small square courtyard, and stopped. Clotheslines created a colorful design of waving faded underwear. Women were already leaning from the windows, fat bosoms on fat arms, shouting across at other women, comparing the evils of husbands, bemoaning the lost dream.

My building was in the rear, smaller than the front, but more cheerful. Flowering window boxes embraced the windows, classical music blared, five floors of tired, cramped apartments, a tiny center of aspiring artists. Three writers, like myself, two unpublished. A dancer who worked as a waitress. Two actors, one a homosexual, one sculptor, two painters. My place, my friends, all aspiring to success, all living here for one reason—it was cheap.

A sign over the door said: *Dunghill Manor.* My roommate's sense of humor.

I walked into the smell of age and bad plumbing and clorox. Dreams of tomorrow growing in the dunghill of today. I climbed the stairway to the top floor, pushed open the door and I was home.

A kitchen with a large round table and a daybed that served as a couch, a small studio where Claude painted, two cell-like bedrooms.

Claude looked up from his coffee and smiled. "Home from the wars," he said.

I shrugged out of the trench coat. "Scored again," I said. It was the thing to say, but even as I spoke the words I knew that it was too flippant.

"For an old man you do pretty well."

I hung the coat, went to the stove to heat the coffee.

"Who was she?" Claude asked.

"A girl."

"Something new?"

"Different," I said. "Something different."

"Your wife called," he said.

"Oh?" I looked up from the stove. "What did she want?"

"Talk to you."

"She say anything?"

"Wants you to call her. I told her you were at a party with some editor."

I nodded. The coffee was hot. I poured a cup, brought it to the table, pushing my typewriter aside to make room. "Any other happy tidings?"

"Martha called."

"Big night for the phone company."

"I told Martha the same story. She didn't believe it. You were supposed to see her last night."

My past. Part of it. A wife in Connecticut, a girl named Martha. The story of my life—ten years of it. A wife in Connecticut, and always a girl named something. The girls changed in appearance, but that's all. But that was David Markam yesterday. I knew that I had something now, something important, different, real.

"Nice girl, that Martha," Claude said.

"The world's full of them. Nice girls. Too nice."

We talked. We drank coffee. I didn't say anything about Leslie. Generally we would talk about a girl, male talk, comparing her with other girls, talk that would lead into anecdotes of other girls, sometimes funny, sometimes tragic. But I didn't talk about Leslie. I didn't want to compare her, to bring her down to the level of conquest, casual lovemaking. I don't know why. I just couldn't do it. I should have, I suppose. It might have been easier. But hell, there were a lot of things I should have done.

"You think you'll ever get back with your wife?" Claude asked.

I shrugged. "I don't know," I said. "I doubt it. There's nothing there."

"Too bad. I like her."

"So do I. She's a nice girl. But I'm not in love with her." That word again, that damned four-letter word that has no meaning, no definition, and means everything. Love. I must have said it a thousand times. I love you. And every time I said it I knew that it meant nothing. I might have said, I want to touch you, I want to touch a woman. I might have said, I want to lay with you, want to feel the woman-soft of you against me, want the woman-smell in my nostrils, want your voice close to my ear. It was easier to say, I love you.

"Why did you marry her?" Claude asked.

"I don't know. I honest-to-God don't know. I guess I was just ready to get married, and she was there."

"Sounds like a helluva reason to get married."

"Oh, there's more to it than that." It wasn't the kind of thing I wanted to discuss early in the morning, not the kind of thing I wanted to discuss at all, but there was the question, and I had to struggle with the answer. "You can say that you're ready to get married, and that sounds like a reason, but there is always more. With me, I guess I was tired of sleeping around. I knew that I didn't want a lot of women. I wanted a woman I could talk to, someone to share things with. I had one thing and I went to the opposite pole to get something else. I was looking for an intellectual companion. I found her and married her."

"And it wasn't right?"

"No," I said, "not right. The reasons were wrong. The girl was fine, but my motives were wrong. You just don't marry a girl for those reasons. You marry a girl because you want to touch her, because you want to be with her. You marry a girl because she is a woman, because she has warmth. You marry a girl whom you want to lay close to in the dark, not just to make love with, but someone who feels good to hold close to you. I didn't have that. I had someone to talk to, but then I wanted someone soft, someone feminine, someone to understand what I felt, not what I thought."

Claude had a deeply serious look on his face, so I laughed and said, "Ah, screw it, c'mon I've got work to do and my wife problems aren't that interesting."

"She's a nice girl."

"You're right, buddy, and don't think that doesn't make the problem a rough one."

Claude pushed back from the table and stood. "I'm thinking about getting married," he said.

"Think hard about it," I said. "It's not a joke."

"It's very difficult," he said.

"Amen," I said.

He shook his head, then turned and went into the studio. I was alone in the kitchen, alone with thoughts that should not be early morning thoughts. A wife I didn't love; a girl I didn't love; both of them asking me to commit myself to them, and the girl I wanted was almost a stranger.

I got up from the table and took the dishes to the sink. I came back, sat down, pulled the typewriter over, and rummaged through the papers. I checked the writing schedule, saw what I had to produce that day, then leaned back in the chair, rubbing my chin, thinking how nice it might be just to have a job and stop writing garbage.

It was a tough morning. It was getting tougher all the time. In the beginning, when I first began to write for the men's adventure magazines it was a breeze. I was thrilled about being published, I liked the idea of being a professional, and I felt that I could grind out blood and guts without having it affect me. I enjoyed the freedom from the time clock and I got a charge out of concocting the nonsensical plots for the hairy-chested magazines. But lately it had begun to bother me. There was the feeling that I was in a rut, that I was selling myself down the river as a writer. There was the time—a long time ago—when I wanted to be a playwright. But those were hungry days, and I was never sure of my talent. I had hit it as a hack writer. It paid the bills, and I enjoyed it. ... but lately ... damn, I knew that it was going to be one of those days.

I stopped for lunch and talked with Claude. It was light talk, mostly about writers and painters, and where we were going to live when we cut the mustard and would have the checks rolling in from the agent. It was dream-talk, wishful thinking in a slum apartment to still the ever-present frustration of failure.

The afternoon was an agony. I tried to work and could not. I smoked until my mouth was raw, drank coffee until the taste of it made me nauseous. I was caught between two machines—the typewriter and the telephone. Perhaps I should have called my wife, or Martha, but I didn't really want to talk to them. The girl. I thought of the girl. I couldn't remember her clearly in the light of day, and there was a dream-like quality about the night before, but I knew she was real, knew that she was there.

I gave up the writing and left the apartment. I walked south along Avenue A, past the one-block concrete excuse for a park. I walked west to First Avenue, drawn by the color and clatter of the street markets, the heady smells of strong spiced meats and cheeses; the European smells of good food and the animated hawking of the merchants. I walked for a long time and when I returned it was growing dark. I stopped for Ravioli at a small place on Second Avenue, then went home for a long evening of pacing the small apartment, and when I could stand it no longer, I walked to 31st Street and stood on the sidewalk in front of her building.

It was a warm night with just the suggestion of a breeze. There was a procession of men and women walking their dogs, typical New York, the lonely cave-dwellers with their lost country youth on a leash.

The windows of her apartment were dark. I crossed the street to the doorway and rang the bell. I waited, but there was no answer.

Strange, but I was elated. It was as though I were compelled to be there, that I had walked the twenty blocks knowing that whatever awaited me, it would not be good, but unable to resist the attraction the girl held for me.

While this may be difficult to accept with credence, one must realize my state of mind at that time. I was completely at odds with myself in matters of love. I honestly believed that it was impossible for me to feel this emotion. There had been many women in my life, and I had felt something for all of them, but it had always paled and each time I knew that I had not touched upon the magical formula of love—whatever it might be. As in any case of frustration the search for love was greatly magnified in my mind until it became inflated beyond importance and was able to overshadow reason. The girl, Leslie, had touched me more deeply than anyone previous, and I had to know what lay beyond the threshold of this emotion called love.

But I was also timid in the possible presence of the unknown, and thus it was a relief to turn and walk away from her doorway.

I walked to Third Avenue and started south, but I stopped before covering a block and turned back. I had to see her. I had to know. I went back to her building and sat on the steps to wait.

The time went slowly. I dislike waiting for any reason. My mind had flights of fancy and I imagined many things, all of them concerned with the girl, all of them bad. I convinced myself that she was a tramp, that she was even then in someone's bed. I decided that she was a hopeless neurotic, a nymphomaniac who picked her men in bars, then got rid of them as quickly as possible. I was mentally castigating myself, successfully soiling my thoughts of her.

I was sullen by the time I saw her come along the street with the man on her arm. Her laughter rippled through the dark, quiet street, and the sound was grotesque to me. I sat unmoving. They reached the steps and stopped, then she saw me. "Oh," she said with surprise. "What are you doing here?"

"Waiting for you," I said.

"Oh." She was at a loss for something to say. I turned my gaze from her to the man at her side. He was middle-aged, somewhat paunchy with a pleasant face that was now furrowed with concern.

"What's up?" he asked.

"Oh," she said, "this … this is a friend of mine."

I stood. "I have to see you," I said, ignoring the man at her side.

"I told you not to come back," she said.

"I know. I had to. I had to see you."

"Say, look," the man said, "I don't like to butt in . . ."

"Then don't," I snapped. I came down the steps and stood before her. I stared at her, tried to erase the set lines of anger on her face.

"What is this?" the man said to her.

"Keep out of it," I said. "It doesn't concern you."

"I told you not to come back," she said, and now her voice was tense.

I reached out and took her arm. She wrenched herself free. "Leave me alone," she snapped.

Her companion's voice hardened. "I think that you had better leave," he said.

My anger rose in a flood of frustrating despair. I wanted to speak with the girl and I had not included this third person in my thinking. His interference was annoying. I tried to ignore him. I reached out again and gripped her wrist, holding her tightly. She cried out in pain.

"Just a damn minute, buddy!" Her companion said. He grabbed my arm.

I released her, then turned, dropping into a crouch. I drove a fist into his mid-section. He grunted, surprised, and backed off, doubling over. I raised my hand over my head and chopped down against his neck. He began to go down. I stepped in close and drove my knee into his face, snapping his head back. I chopped him across the throat, then grabbed his lapels, jerking him upright. His face was contorted with surprise and pain. I held him with one hand and drove my fist into his face. He gasped, gagging. I hit him again. I was furious, not at him, at the girl, but I had to strike out at something and he was there. I drove a fist into his stomach and released him. He staggered away, reeling, and clutched a lamppost. He retched, hanging limply, his anguished groans the only sound on the street.

I turned back to the girl, about to speak, but I stopped. She was smiling. It was a strange, gleeful smile. Her forehead glistened with sweat. My voice, when I spoke, seemed to bring her out of a reverie.

"Sorry," I said. "I had to see you."

She recovered and looked at me. Her tongue traced a circular pattern over her lips. She nodded. "Come in," she said.

The man had pushed away from the lamppost and he started up the street, clutching his mid-section and muttering. I watched him go, feeling badly about what I had done. He had done what any man should have done. He hadn't deserved the beating. My conscience was beginning to gnaw, but I shook off the feeling of guilt and followed her through the door.

Inside the narrow vestibule, she stopped and turned to me. "You're strong," she said.

"I know some tricks," I said. "I'm not strong."

She was standing against the wall looking up at me with a mixed expression of awe and pleasure. "He didn't even have a chance to touch you," she said.

"Look," I said, "I'm not proud of that. I was angry. I don't like anger, I don't like fighting. It doesn't prove anything. It never has."

"You won," she said.

"When you win you lose. That's probably a decent guy, I don't know. But because I fight with bastard tactics he lost. But I know how I won, so I lose just a little bit of myself."

She did not answer. She stood there waiting. I leaned forward and placed my hands on her shoulders, holding her lightly. I kissed her, gently placing my lips upon hers, bringing no pressure to bear, treasuring the moment of sensual contact. I moved my lips over her cheek, savoring the perfume smell of her. I pulled her close to me and her arms went about me and we clung together in silence. I felt the soft womanness of her, rejoiced in the way her breasts flattened against me, the pressure of her thighs against mine. I ran my hand along the hollow of her back, listened to her murmur of pleasure. It was a strange feeling at that moment, a feeling of complete relaxation as though I had been searching for something for a long time and had at last come upon it, the kind of feeling you might get after a long, long drive in the desert when you finally reach a destination and know that you can stop.

I released her and stepped back. She continued to look at me for a long moment, then she turned and started up the stairs. I followed. She stopped once and turned and I braced myself for her warning conversation, but she said nothing, turned and continued.

At the top she paused by her door, spoke to the restless dog inside, then opened the door. I followed her as before, along the hallway and into the large room.

I stood by the bar, the big doberman sniffing at me. She went into the bedroom. I leaned over and patted the dog's head. I find something sadistic about keeping dogs in a big city, but what the hell, I could still be nice to the dog.

"Come in here," she said.

I went into the bedroom. She was standing by the closet and pulling her dress over her head. She hung the dress on a hanger, then came across the room in her slip. She passed me, shooed the dog from the room and closed the door. "He's jealous," she said, smiling. She crossed the room to the closet. I sat in a chair and began to light my pipe, watching her.

There was beauty in the way she undressed, a grace that few women possess at such times. I noticed it for the first time that night, but in the months that followed it was to become a ritual that never failed to move me with the natural beauty of her. It was almost like a dance, not the gauche movements of a strip-tease or an exotic, but simpler. The beauty was in the movements of her body and her arms as she removed each piece of clothing.

She turned. "Stop staring," she said.

"I've never seen anything quite so beautiful," I said.

"You make me feel naked."

I smiled and she laughed. "You have a dirty mind," she said, then she moved from the closet and walked, naked, to the bed. She pulled the covers down, slipped beneath the sheets. She sat against the pillows and held the sheet over her breasts. The laughter had left her and her expression was sober. "I wanted to see you again," she said. "I knew that I shouldn't, but I wanted to."

Leaving the chair, I went and sat on the edge of the bed. "I love you," I said. "I want to be close to you."

"But you don't know me!" Her voice was a wail.

"I can only know you by being with you," I said. "I want to know you."

"You don't even know my name."

"Leslie," I said. She looked surprised. "I read it on the mailbox," I said.

She leaned back against the pillows. Her panic was replaced by a smile of intense warmth. "You're too clever for me," she said. "What's your name?"

"David," I said. "David Markam."

"What do you do?"

"I write."

"Under your own name?"

That is never a flattering question for a writer, but I was used to it. "Sometimes," I said.

"What do you write?"

"Magazine stuff. Stories, articles, mostly junk."

"It couldn't be junk," she said.

"Take my word for it," I said. "It's junk."

"But why write junk?"

"It's a living. It beats getting up in the morning, and maybe one day I'll write something good."

"David Markam," she said. "It's a good name. Come to bed, David."

CHAPTER TWO

It was an idyllic week. There was nothing in my life but Leslie, I could think of nothing else, I wanted nothing else. Had it been in my power I would have stopped time, I would have shut us off completely from the rest of the world.

We were together, we found one another, we explored a pathway of love that was new to both of us.

It was a strange newness. It was common-place, something that happens to thousands of men and women in the world every day; they meet, they are attracted to each other, and something grows between them; common-place. And yet, this relationship—just as every relationship—was unique. It was strange and beautiful. A man and a woman are moving through their lives, traveling two distinct paths, and then suddenly they are moving along a single line.

What startled me and delighted me was the uniqueness of the physical relationship. I had known many women, and I had come to expect and accept certain things. While they would all be different, there was also a sameness about them. You could expect certain attitudes from a woman simply because she was a stenographer, or a college graduate, or from the midwest or from a large family. They fell into general moulds in their thinking and only the embellishments made them individuals. This was particularly true in making love. There were patterns, and to me the patterns reduced love-making to boredom. I could be aroused, of course, and I performed the physical act of love with relish, but afterwards it was always a let-down. In a way, it was like buying a glittering object and then finding it tarnished and green and cheap.

It was different with Leslie.

I discovered feelings with her that I would never have believed possible. It was not something I was doing or thinking consciously, and I would not have put it into words if I had not had to make an explanation to Martha.

The meeting was accidental. I was crossing Third Avenue on Fourteenth Street. It was late afternoon, and I was walking east towards my apartment. Martha came out of a drug store just as I stepped onto the curb. We were face-to-face; it was impossible to avoid her. She was as surprised and embarrassed as I.

"Hello, David," she said.

I hesitated a moment. I'm certain that my expression was sheepish—the boy with his hand in the jar of jam. "Hello, Martha," I said, almost with a note of apology.

"I—I haven't seen you," she said.

"I—uh—I've—"

"You've been busy," she said, smiling.

"I don't know quite what to say," I said.

"You don't have to explain yourself to me, David," she said. "You never promised me anything."

It would have been easier if she had been angry. I felt like the original bastard. It was such a damned fool thing. I should have called her, seen her, talked to her; I should have done something, at least. But dammit I hadn't, and now I was facing her. She wasn't just anybody. For christ's sake, two weeks before I had shared her bed, professed a love for her, and now I was wishing that I had been able to avoid her. Damn an understanding woman!

"Are you in a hurry?" I asked.

"You want to get rid of me already?"

"No," I said, embarrassed. "I just thought we might get a cup of coffee."

"I'd love it," she said.

"There's an expresso place on Seventeenth."

"Fine."

We walked to the curb and had to wait for the light. It was a tense and annoying moment. It might have been easier if we could have kept moving, but the pause brought up the necessity for conversation. I wasn't in the right frame of mind to make street conversation. I had dumped this girl without even a phone call, and whether she was going to be big about it or not, I just couldn't get over the feeling of guilt.

"How have you been?" I asked.

"You don't have to make polite talk, David," she said.

I bit on my lip. I was on the verge of anger. Was she trying to make a fool of me? No, I had done that myself. I broke into a smile, and it spread to a guilty grin. "You're a mind reader," I said.

The light changed. "I think I know a little about you," she said. We crossed the street.

Walking along we said nothing. The routine of walking with her had a disturbing influence upon me. It was so natural. I must have covered half the damned city at her side, walking and talking. What had we talked about? God knows. Just about everything, I suppose. Writing, a lot about writing. Usually, *but, David, it seems like such a waste for you to be writing the type of things you do. You have so much more to offer.* And me saying, *I have to eat. I've got a wife and kids to feed.* And her answer, *you could get a job.* And me saying. *I'm a writer, dammit, that's my job. I do the job. It's crap, but so are most jobs.* And she says, *It's not just a job and you know it. You can write, David, and it's a shame to waste it.* And then I would be annoyed and angry because I agreed with everything she said, but was too damned afraid to really try to write something decent, and then I would bring up the kids again as the buffer against my own frustration, *Look, I'm a hack writer with kids to feed. Let somebody else write the pretty prose. I know my limitations. I'm a hack and I'm proud of it.* But always afterwards, when I would be alone at the typewriter, the dream would grow out of her chiding, and I would find myself writing harder, looking for the elusive phrase to make the story better, stronger, more concise. And on those walks we covered other subjects: Marriage, love, parenthood, art, politics—name a subject and we worried it in agreement or argument. Yes, I guess Martha did know a little about me.

"Penny for your thoughts," she said.

"What?...oh . . ." I laughed, caught unaware. "You're the mind reader," I said.

"Sometimes I wish I were," she said.

"Do you, Marthe? Would you really like to always know what people are thinking?"

"No, I guess not," she said, frowning. "I'd hate it, really. There are too many times that you want to fool yourself into believing that they're thinking something else. There are times when you want to be beautiful and you make yourself feel beautiful. It would be terrible to know that you weren't."

I started to answer, then checked myself. Damn! It was too easy to fall into this. Martha was the kind of girl you talked to. She was a pretty girl with a full, shapely body, and you could be initially attracted to her physically, but within an hour, she became a girl to talk to. I remember her saying once: *I'm the sister type, every mans sister, and just once, just one time I'm going to be someone's woman.* Even with me. It was a week before I kissed her, and even though I could sense the longing in her, a latent power of unexplored womanness, I pulled back, wary of her. I often tried to say that I was being decent, that she was too nice to be hurt, but it was an excuse. With Martha it would be important and a man would have to be one hell of a lot of man to match her womanness. And I was unsure of myself. So we talked, and it was comfortable and good. I liked her and in time this grew into a kind of comfortable love. I don't know what it was. It seemed good at the time. There were no problems with her, and when we slept together, made love, it was as though we had been married for years. It might have gone on if I hadn't met Leslie.

We reached the coffee house and took a table in the rear. It was quiet. Classical music formed a soft background and the light was dim. We sat, looking, uncomfortable, trying to find the level of conversation.

"Is she nice, David?"

I didn't answer immediately. It was the kind of thing she would say. I wasn't surprised. "I don't know," I said, finally.

We were silent again. The waiter came and went. I was wishing that I were somewhere else. I didn't really want to talk about Leslie, but now that it had been brought up, there didn't seem to be anything else that I could do.

"I figured that there was someone else," Martha said. "I called a few times and Claude was too evasive."

"He likes you," I said.

"Yes."

The waiter brought the coffee and now there was something to do. A spoon to fool with, coffee to stir, a place for the eyes that did not want to meet hers.

"You want to talk about it, David?"

"I'm not sure," I said.

"It's none of my business, really," she said. "It's just that . . . that . . . well, I guess I'm basically . . ."

"Marthe," I reached across the table and covered her hand with mine. She looked down and bit her lip. "Marthe, I don't know quite what to say. I feel a little rotten about . . . well, about things. Seeing you, I realize how shabby I've been."

"You're not," she said. She smiled, but her eyes were misted. "You could never be anything like that, David. If you did anything wrong it was only because you couldn't bear to hurt anyone."

"But I hurt you more."

"You didn't mean to," she said. "I'll admit, David, that I was hurt that you wouldn't talk to me, but I know that it was only because you were afraid of the tears and recriminations. You're a very nice man, David Markam."

"You're making me feel worse," I said.

"Of course," she said, smiling, "that's what I'm trying to do."

We laughed together, then I sobered. "Marthe, you know . . ."

"If you tell me I'm a nice girl I'll scream," she said. "I don't want to be a nice girl!"

We were silent again, thoughtfully quiet for what seemed a long time, then Martha asked, "David, what is she like?"

"What do you mean?"

"I mean what is there about her, whoever she is, that I don't have? I'm a girl, I know I'm attractive, I have warmth. I was good in bed with you. Why couldn't I hold you?"

"It's hard to explain. I know that it's not a matter of holding someone. It's . . . well . . . dammit, Marthe, I don't know."

"Chemistry?"

"The time-worn explanation," I said. "But it's something like that. I met her in a bar and three hours later I was in bed with her. It's the sort of thing you'd expect from a tramp, but that's not it. I'm in love with her, Martha, that's all I can say. I never knew what it was like to be in love before. I mean, I thought I was in love, but now I know that I wasn't. This girl throws everything else into focus. I'm not sure just what it is with her, but being with her makes me realize that everything before her fell short of the mark."

"She's a lucky woman," Marthe said

"Maybe."

"Did you . . . did you ever feel anything for me?"

"I felt a lot. I felt an awful lot. But, Marthe, with this girl it just isn't like anything else. If I could just explain it. It's . . . it's like . . . oh, damn, I don't know. It sounds foolish in words. Sometimes I'm standing in a room and she is there, maybe reading a book, and she looks up, and I hold her eyes for a moment, and I'm suddenly filled with this feeling of great elation, as though I own the whole damned world."

"Are you going to marry her?"

"Marry?"

"I mean, if you love someone...well...I suppose you want to marry them."

I stared into my coffee, perplexed. Marriage. It had never occurred to me. Why not? Why had I never thought of Leslie in terms of wife? "I don't know," I said.

"It's something you don't like to face, isn't it?"

"Wouldn't say that. It's...it's just that...well, it hasn't come up."

"She doesn't want to get married?"

"I don't know."

"Would you marry her?"

The conversation was running along the wrong tack. I scowled, not liking it. Martha had a way of driving into the core of a thing, peeling away protective coverings to expose nerves to the air. She forced you to look into yourself, to examine the motives behind your actions, and this is seldom pleasant. What she was really saying was: *Are you sure about this, or are you creating a romantic image of what you want a woman to mean to you? Are you willing to place this woman on a scale balanced against your two children, or are you afraid to face the ultimate decision of this choice?*

"It's something I'll have to face when the time comes," I said.

"You're evading it, aren't you?"

"No. I've known this girl for a week. She's like nothing I have ever known. It's important, but I don't believe that you have to have marriage to sustain love. I've been married; I am married, and it has nothing to do with love."

"You love your children."

"Yes, and I'm not married to them."

She smiled. "You win," she said. "Oh, David, please don't think I'm trying to belittle what you feel. Believe me, it's a wonderful thing. I'd give anything to have you feel that way about me. It's just that I . . ." She paused, a slight catch to her voice. She glanced down at her folded hands, then looked up. "Oh, David, I just want you to have what is right. You have so much to give, so much feeling, and I hate to think of anyone soiling it." She stopped abruptly, swallowed and closed her eyes. She opened her eyes and smiled. "I'm sorry," she said.

"Marthe," I said, caught up in the absolute honesty of the girl. "Marthe, if I . . . I . . . oh, hell, there's nothing to say."

"I know what you mean, David. I'm a good friend."

"No, it's not that. You're more than that. You're . . . oh, dammit, Marthe, I feel so goddamned ineffectual. I want to say things to you, want to reach out and touch you with words, and I don't have them."

"David," she said, spacing her words carefully, looking closely into me, "I love you. I'm not a martyr, but I do know that there are times when you love someone you can only express that love by sending them away from you. The love I feel for you will be stronger in knowing that you have something you want, knowing that you have a contentment. For a time I filled a gap in your life. You were sincere, I know that. We made some plans, looked ahead when we should not have, but that doesn't matter. A relationship must always look ahead, it's the way people are, but it doesn't mean that it is anyone's fault if the future ends with the present. It had to end sometime, and no matter when it ended it would have been the present and there would still be a future unfulfilled. I loved you, David, and you brought a great deal into my life, and out of it all I have only one regret." She paused, waiting for me to say something. I kept quiet. "Do you know what I regret?"

"What?"

"The weekend we were always going to spend together. We never did it. I would have liked to have had that weekend."

There was nothing I could say. Damn! How does a man get so fouled up with people? It never starts off that way, but it grows and grows, and then you're up to your clavicle in problems. Why can't it remain simple and uncomplicated. Every year of your life you get deeper and deeper in people until there comes a time when you feel swamped, and out of the maze of people you find yourself struggling to find yourself, trying to establish the identity that is your own, and with each pull away from the peopled past you only sink into the morass of more people. If only you didn't have an effect on others it might be easier, but a man walks hand-in-hand with the world and whenever he goes off the path he has to pull; someone else out of line. There are times when you wish that you were just a damned vegetable.

I was angry with myself and angry with Marthe for the contrast she presented against my self-indulgent son of a bitch attitude of being concerned with number one.

"We'd better go," she said.

"Yeah."

We left the coffee house and walked back to Fourteenth Street. We said nothing. It was all said. It was over, so what can you say? *Happy Days? Good Show? Nice to have known you?* It would all sound like so much crap. Better to say nothing.

We parted at the corner. She held out her hand and I pressed it. Thank God, there were no brave smiles; Just, "Goodbye, David," and she turned and walked south. I stood for a moment watching her, then I crossed the street and headed for Avenue A.

I was on my way home. I had spent the afternoon uptown talking to editors. I had several assignments for stories and I was going to work. But my mind was filled with Martha and Leslie. I stopped at the corner of First Avenue. I had to see her. I had to see her against the background of Martha, see her in the new light of having tried to put her into words.

And I found another side to Leslie.

The First Avenue bus let me off at her street and I walked west to the apartment house and pushed through the door after her answering buzz. I climbed the stairs, reached the top breathing hard, and lifted my hand to knock. The door opened. Leslie stood there.

"Hello," I said.

Without a word she flung herself across the threshold. My arms came up automatically and she fell against me, clinging, burrowing her face into my chest. Behind her, in the hallway, the dog whimpered.

I was stunned. I held her close and her body trembled under my hands. Her shoulders shook and her crying was muffled. I stroked her hair. "Leslie," I said, "Leslie, what's wrong?"

"Don't leave me, David," she said. "Please, don't leave me."

"But I'm here," I said. "I'm not going to leave you."

"David, I'm afraid." She lifted her face and deep within the pupils of her eyes I could see the terror there, an unmasked horror that obviously lurked in her mind, an inconsolable loneliness. "Don't leave me, David. I don't know what I'd do without you now, David. Please, please say you won't leave me."

"I have no intention of leaving you, Leslie." I turned her back into the apartment, closed the door, and led her along the hallway. She stopped suddenly, turning and shoving against me so that I was backed against the wall. "David," she wailed, "I'm frightened!"

I gripped her shoulders hard. I did not know what to say. The outburst was confusing and erratic and I wanted to shake her and tell her to get hold of herself, that I had no intention of leaving her, and that she was imagining things. I said nothing. I held her close, actually welcoming and enjoying the Strength she thrust upon me, feeling my importance to this girl's wellbeing.

In time she became quiet. She sighed deeply and straightened. She shook her head, fluffed the blonde hair, then suddenly she gave a short laugh.

"David," she said gaily, as if nothing had been said, "how nice to see you." She took my hand in hers and preceded me along the hallway and into the large living room.

I was scowling, wondering what in hell's name the hysterical scene had been about, getting just a bit angry. I had the feeling that the whole bit had been an act, some sort of weird joke that she had put on as a whim. I didn't like it.

Leslie went behind the bar. "Drink?" she asked.

"Scotch," I said, still trying to contain the anger that was gradually building.

"Have a martini with me," she said.

"All right."

I turned and walked the length of the room. I stood by the window looking north to the Empire State Building. I watched the searchlight sweep over Manhattan. The dog came and nuzzled at my leg. I dropped my hand and scratched its head.

It was disturbing, this feeling that the scene had not been a whim at all, but genuine hysteria suddenly forgotten.

"Drinks are on," Leslie said.

I went back to the bar. We drank several martinis and talked. It went on for several hours, then I remembered the work awaiting me at home, and said that I had to leave.

A flash of panic appeared in her eyes. The conversation faltered. She attempted to ignore the fact that I had to go home, then said, "Get something on the radio, will you, David."

I nodded and slid off the bar stool. The radio was on the dresser in the bedroom. I was there working the dial when she came in, passed by me and went to the closet. She was hurrying and I watched her. She began to undress, slipping the sweater over her head, unzipping the tight slacks and pulling them off her legs. It was all too obvious. She had no intention of having me leave and was about to offer what she knew would keep me there. It was too planned, too exacting. It was the first weakness in our relationship. It was too desperate. It gave me a feeling that is impossible to explain, a kind of foreboding.

"David?"

I had turned to the radio, but I was aware of her movements as she pulled back the covers and climbed into the bed. I turned at her bidding.

She was smiling. I was annoyed, not so much at her as with myself. I had the feeling that there was a flaw in my character, a weak spot, and that she knew about it and could play upon it. But despite the annoyance I was struck by her beauty; the blonde hair, golden under the warmth of the bed lamp, spread on the pillow; the nakedness of her shoulders, and the slight swell of the beginning of her breasts.

"Come here, David."

I went to the bed and sat on the side away from her. She pouted and patted the bed at her side. "Over here, David, I want you to be close to me for just a moment before you leave."

There was no point in showing reluctance. I wanted to be close to her. I knew that I should not move, that I should have left then, but I wanted to be close to her. I got up and circled the bed. She held up her arms. I sat down, then leaned into the enclosure of her arms and buried myself and my doubts and my thoughts in the woman scent of her.

"Stay with me, David," she whispered, "please stay with me."

I did not answer. It was not necessary. I wanted to stay within the mind-consuming warmth of her. I knew that I would. It was inevitable.

But as I held her to me in the later darkness of the room, our bodies sated of desire, but clinging, feeling her breath upon my neck, feeling the press of her from neck to thigh, I was frightened; frightened for myself, because I knew that I was lost.

CHAPTER THREE

It was the end of the month and I was making the duty call to wife and children. It shouldn't be called that, I suppose, but that is what it generally amounted to.

The idea that a man can be a parent two days a month is pure nonsense. Becoming a father is one thing. You're a father biologically and you remain so through your life. No matter what happens, you are still the father of the children you conceive. It is a meaningless thing. Being a parent is quite another activity. This takes time and effort, and is something that one does by choice. You don't make it as a parent on two days a month.

These monthly trips never failed to increase my bitterness towards the situation with Marion. The kids were great and I honestly loved them both. I just couldn't take their mother. So, I always came out of these trips the complete bastard. Why? Because I could not stand to be in the same room with that damned female—as simple as that.

The train swayed and labored through the Connecticut countryside; postcard pretty on both sides, the rolling hills, the neat farm clusters, the stone fences that always made me think of the Revolutionary War and Minute-Men crouched with blunderbuss waiting for the Red Coats. It was Saturday, a warm, sunny day. The car of the train was filled; it was stuffy; I wished that I had rented a car.

I sat by the window, bored, counting telegraph poles as they swept past, glancing at disinterested cows and horses; I tried to place myself back in the suburban life, compared it to the way I was now living, found the whole thing unreal and depressing. I had the usual trappings of the visiting father; the flowers for Marion, the two books and two toys for the children; the bric-a-brac of a man's guilt, the payoff.

Where is it that a man's life gets screwed up? I could remember back to childhood and it all seemed so simple. There was high school and the biggest problem was how to get the family car for the week-end. The real problems, the kind that were like ice in the guts, started and ended with sex. There was that girl, Clara, the hot number in town. I went for a walk with her one summer night, walking and talking, and nervous, knowing what I was after, knowing that Clara knew what I was after, being led by her to a special place she knew about. I was scared, but excited. This was it. This was what the guys talked and laughed about. I was frightened because I had given Clara a lot of big talk, and I had not the remotest idea of what I was supposed to do. I could have saved myself the worry. Clara knew where she was going and what she was going to do, and she was a patient teacher. I'll admit that it was quite a letdown, but then I had a full month of feeling certain that the girl was pregnant. It was plenty to worry about, but it didn't stop me from taking other walks with Clara.

Finally you get married. Why? What is there about one girl that makes you marry her? In my case I say that it was boredom. I was simply tired of sleeping around and wanted to settle down to the full, complete relationship with one woman. And when I had that feeling I happened to be going with Marion. Maybe it was more than that. I don't really know, but I do know that the moment I turned from the minister and faced Marion, seeing her as my wife, I knew that it was a mistake.

The conductor came down the aisle announcing East Trumble. I watched the train roll into the run-down cluttered outskirts of the town, and when I knew that we were near the station, I got up from the seat and went to the door.

I took a cab at the station. In another age, another life, Marion used to meet me. The smiling, suburban wife, the peck on the cheek, the drive home—a complete bore.

There was the street. The neat, identical houses; the neat, identical patches of lawn; the neat, identical cars in the neat, identical driveways; the neat, identical wives; the neat, identical children. East Trumble. Home is where the heart is. The cab stopped, I paid the fare, got out and walked into the squeals of two children eager to get their gifts.

The week-end, as expected, was a disaster.

I went through the motions of parenthood. The children reacted to the routine visit with the exuberance of a holiday, and the old feelings of responsibility assailed me.

To whom or what does a man owe his life? Should he be true to himself or should he live a lie? Does he owe his life to a marriage? These are questions I had asked myself a thousand times and there were no simple answers. I had two children. They were young, just beginning their struggle with life. They were the innocent victims of a broken home. Did I owe these two children my life? Would it make a difference to them whether or not I lived with them? Questions, Questions, the damnable unanswerable questions that beat against the mind with the numbing persistance of a metronome.

The children wandered off to play and I was alone in the house with Marion. We were in the living room, amidst the usual time-payment furnishings, the trappings of the stifling suburban conformity. I sat on the divan and Marion stood by the fireplace that was never lighted.

"Care for a drink?" she asked.

"Have scotch?"

"I think there's a little," she said. "On the rocks?"

"Fine."

She left the room to fix the drink. I leaned back and looked about me. There was my chair. *My chair.* There had been a big production about making certain that I had my own chair, the unassailable throne, the symbol of the head-of-the-house. That was a long time ago. I was a stranger here, now. I was still making the payments on the house, but it had nothing to do with me. But then, it had always been Marion's house. The chair, that cubicle had been reserved for me.

Marion returned with the drink. She sat on the chair across from me.

"How have you been?" she asked.

"So-so," I said.

"How is the city?"

"Warm, crowded. You know, 'the usual rat-race."

"Yes."

The conversation died. I twirled the ice cubes in the glass. Marion went to the record player. Background music to relieve the tension.

"I saw Dick Berger," Marion said.

"Oh?"

"He was a bit concerned about you."

Berger was a magazine editor and he had rejected my last two stories. The hell with him, I thought. Like all editors, a frustrated no-talent writer. They had to reject just to assert themselves. He lived in East Trumble.

"Nice of him," I said.

Marion ignored my sarcasm. "He seems to think that you might have written yourself out."

"What would he know about writing?"

Marion shrugged. "He was genuinely concerned," she said. "He seemed to think that maybe something was bothering you."

"Look, Marion," I said, keeping my voice low and steady, "I don't give a particular damn what Dick Berger thinks."

She was silent a moment, then she said. "You have the same old reaction to criticism."

"Meddling, not criticism." There was an edge to my voice now. Damn! I didn't want to get into a hassle with her.

"Are you eating right, getting enough sleep?"

"Oh, for christ sake, Marion, get off it." I was annoyed now. Marion sincerely believed that the ills of the world could be cured with enough wheat germ and vitamins. There is nothing more irritating than having an estranged wife firmly believe that a balanced diet could save a marriage.

"Well, you don't take care of yourself."

"Don't worry about it, Marion. I won't fall apart and not make it to the typewriter. I'll get the money in, don't worry." It was an unfair thing to say, but it had the usual effect.

"I'm not concerned about that," she snapped.

I closed my eyes and spread my hands. "Okay, okay. Let's just forget it."

"I still happen to be your wife," she said.

"Let's forget it, Marion."

"It's easy for you to forget it," she said, the edge of hysteria growing in her voice. "You have your little nest in the city and your entourage of females."

"Let's forget it."

"No, I won't forget it. David, those children out there are yours. When are you going to grow up and accept your responsibilities?"

I got up from the divan and went to the window. I was already thinking about the train back to New York, eager to get away. Escape? Yes, but what; what was I escaping? Was Marion right? Was I really running from responsibility? I accepted economic responsibility with ease. I might live in near poverty myself, but Marion and the kids had all that they needed. But I knew that I could not face the emotional responsibility for wife and kids, and this bothered me.

"Marion," I said, "it won't work. Let's not fight about it. I've tried and it won't work."

"You never give it a chance."

I felt suddenly weary. "I have tried," I said. "I have tried more than you know." I turned from the window and walked to the center of the room. She was waiting for me to speak, and I would try to explain it again, even though I knew that it would have no effect upon her. "Marion," I said, "I'm truly sorry about this situation, believe me. You feel that I'm juvenile in my thinking. You may be right, but that still does not stop me from feeling the way I do about things, and I have to live with die way I feel. It is important to me that I feel love for the woman I live with. You don't seem to realize that my life would be a simpler thing if I could live here with you. But I can't. I'm not in love with you."

"Your grade school idea of love."

"Let me finish."

"I don't see what you—"

"Please, Marion."

She was silent, but there was a grim determination about her that I knew would refuse to accept the truth of anything I might say. It was hopeless, but I felt that it had to be said; for myself as much as for her. "Love to me is a lot of things, but one of the basic necessities is an unspoken tenderness between two people."

"You've been reading your stories again."

"Dammit, Marion, shut up and listen!" I paused, waiting for my irritation to subside, then I went on. "This love thing I have to have is wanting to reach out and touch the person. I suppose that seems too simple, but it is a basic truth. Just to suddenly want to cover her hand with mine."

"I think I hear violins."

I stopped after her sarcastic interruption. "Okay," I said, "just forget it."

"That doesn't solve anything," she said.

"It can't be solved the way you want it," I said. "Marion, for God's sake, get it through your head that I cannot live with you."

"Because you have to have some slut!" she snapped. "Oh, brother, don't think that I don't know what the real problem is. You just have to have those cheap tramps around you!"

What was the use of talking. There was a wall between us that could not be penetrated. Marion was a wife first and a woman second. She saw everything from the peculiar attitude of American Wife. To her a girl like Martha would always be a tramp; a girl like Leslie would be even worse. It has to do with fear, I know, but more than that it is the product of the mythology of husband and wife. The American girl is trained from childhood in the art of securing a husband. This is her insurance, her personal retirement plan. She supports the cosmetics industry in this quest, spends hours dancing or talking or indulging in sports activity to give the appearance of the perfect mate. But when she succeeds, she feels that she can at last relax, that the battle has been won. Even when she suddenly realizes that her mate is disenchanted, that the marriage is drifting, her thinking is dictated by what she feels are the inalienable rights of the wife. She got her husband, her meal-ticket; let other women get their own the same way she did, just so long as they stay out of her territory. The fact that this attitude collides head-on with the basics of human nature mean nothing to her; she wears emotional blinders. What is hers is hers, and that's all that there is to it.

"Well," she said, "who is she this time?"

"Let's just forget it."

Forget it, forget it. Is that all you can say?"

"Marion, I don't want to fight about this."

"I have a right—"

"You have no rights over me!" I was angry then, and I went on with a rush of words. "You lost any rights to me when I left your bed! You won't realize it or accept it, but that's where a marriage is made."

"You've got a—"

"Dirty mind! Yes, that's what I've got! I believe that the relationship between a man and woman must be largely physical or it can't exist. I don't only think that sex is important, I think it's a damned absolute essential! When a man first looks at a woman it is physical; when he touches her it's physical. A man wants his wife to be wanted by him, goddamit, and if that's having a dirty mind then I've got it! Everytime I ever touched you I felt that you were giving up that jewel more precious than life itself!"

"Don't be funny!"

"It's not funny, Marion, it's damned well not funny!"

There, at last, was the problem, and I suppose it was mine. Marion was quite willing to carry on a polite separate-bedroom marriage and I could not. Sex. The world revolves and evolves on it. Show me a problem, a frustration, and at the bottom of it all will be sex. There was nothing more to say.

CHAPTER FOUR

The days piled one upon the other; the city became warmer
and warmer as if the concrete held back a portion of each
days heat and added it to the next day.

It had been a particularly hot day, but the sun had gone down
and now a thin breeze was stirring. It was the kind of day that
people rush from air-conditioning to air-conditioning, the dull
shock showing on their faces during the interim.

I was in the Mansfield Bar on 44th St., drinking beer and
listening to my agent.

"You've got to make up your mind, Dave," he said. "You're
either a writer or a lover."

"C'mon, Sam, it's not that bad."

He narrowed his eyes. He ran a hand over his balding head,
then brought the hand down and pointed one finger. "Dave," he
said, seriously, "I'm not kidding. I've met this girl, and I say that
she's bad news."

"It has nothing to do with her. I'm in a bit of slump. It happens to all writers."

"Call it what you want. Say you've got writer's cramp. I happen to know different. It's that broad."

"What have you got against her?"

"I got against her that she's hurting one of my writers, that's
what. Dave, I know you. I been handling you from the start. You
can't do anything half-way. You're impetuous, you throw yourself into things. This has been good for your work, but it's minder
when you tangle with a broad."

"There have been other women."

"Yeah, but you always dumped them when they got into your hair. This broad is a kook, Dave, and she's gonna have you on your butt."

"You're wrong, Sam. If anything, she always wants to help me with my work."

"I'll bet," he said, "and I know just what kind of help. She want you to be a better writer, to stop the commercial stuff and write something great. That's right, isn't it? Agh, don't answer. I know these broads. Kid, that kook will have you so far out in left field on the Great American Novel that it will take ten years to get back."

"What have you got against quality?"

"Ah!," he snorted. "Ah … ah-ha! I hit it didn't I. So she wants you to write quality." He grimaced, shaking his head. "Kid, for christs sake, will you get it through your head that you write quality. You write blood and guts, but you're better than average because you always put more into it. You're growing, and each day you get better, but, boy, keep your head. There are a lot of steps on this ladder. You're climbing them one at a time, and each time you take a step you're sure of yourself because you've got damned good footing on the rung under you. You suddenly take a leap at the top and you're gonna fall on your ass."

"You think I'm not good enough."

"Agh, for christs sake, cut out the temperament. You're not talking to some art nut. I'm your agent. I own ten percent of your future."

"Ten percent of nothing."

"Stop looking for sympathy. David, boy, you've got talent. I know it and you know it, but your talent is a special kind. One guy comes along and writes a book, and wham, it's a hit. He happens to have been ready to write a book. You're a different kind of writer. You have to grow by writing, and that's what you're doing.

You started out on newspapers, then moved into pulp fiction and articles, and now you're moving into a little better market. In a while you'll do some paperback books, and in time you'll move up to better things. In the meantime you keep meeting the challenge of what you're doing."

"That has nothing to do with the present problem," I said.

"Right. The present problem is that dame."

"The present problem is the fact that I can't seem to write this garbage anymore."

"Crap! It's tlie broad!"

"Lay off her, Sam!"

No, dammit. Besides being your agent I'm also your friend. I'm going to tell you something and you're going to listen, because I'm the boy who has to go to bat when you foul up on an assignment, and you happen to have missed five assignments this month, and I've got five angry editors." He took a deep breath, and I kept silent. "I'm going to tell you something about that girl. She may be a sweet looking thing, but she's a witch. That's a girl who likes trouble, and another thing she likes is to castrate a man. You say, she wants to help you; I say she wants to ruin you. If you can't write, and that happens to be the one thing you do well, then she has complete control over you. Take my word for it, Dave, that girl wants you to fall on your face."

"Sam, I'm happy with this girl."

"Happy! What the hell does happy have to do with it? I'd rather have you miserable and working. For christs sake, if the world was happy the damned place would fold up in a week!"

"You'd rather have me back with Marion."

"Right! That's exactly where I would like to see you. At least you got some work done, and the writing was good."

"I know that, and I know why. I stayed in my work room because I'd rather be there behind the typewriter than in the room with her. I was driven to that damned machine out of a frustration, and I wrote in anger."

"Good! Thank God for miserable marriages, or nothing would get written!"

"I couldn't go back to that, Sam," I said. "I'd rather give up writing."

He was silent, then. He knew that I meant it. He wrinkled his round, homely face, and shook his head. I knew that he was genuinely concerned about me, but I also knew that he could never understand the way I felt about things.

"Life gets fouled up sometimes, don't it?" he said.

I smiled. "Amen," I said.

"Look, kid, I don't want to make you sore at me, but take my advice and get rid of that girl."

"I can't."

He took a deep breath and sighed. "Do you realize how much money you kicked this last month? Seven hundred and fifty dollars. That ain't peanuts. If Marion don't get her check there's going to be hell to pay."

"I'm thinking about it."

"You better do more than think about it."

"I've been thinking of getting a job."

"Is that gonna help your writing?"

Sam was too right and I didn't like it. The money monster was perched on my shoulders. I glanced at my watch. "I better be rolling," I said.

"Get rid of her, Dave."

I got up from the table. "Yeah. Well, thanks for the drink."

"That story for Berger is due tomorrow," he said.

"I'll have it done," I said. "I'll work tonight."

"See you in the morning," he said.

I said goodnight to Andy, the night bartender at the Mansfield, and pushed out into the heat. It was like walking under a heavy blanket.

I hailed a cab, settled back against the leather seat, and gave Leslie's address. The cab crawled down Fifth Avenue, then across to Third, and down. I got out at 31st and walked east.

She was standing in the open doorway, the dog at her side, when I labored to the top of the stairs.

The radiance of her welcoming smile nullified anything that Sam might have said against her. It was ridiculous to imagine that Leslie could be anything but good for me. She made me feel that it was important that I be there, that I was an integral part of her existence. I had never known a girl before who did not bore me after a time, who did not become a drag as she stupidly wheedled her way into my life. With Leslie it was always as though I were meeting her for the first time. There was always the intrigue, the mystery, the vicarious pleasure that you get from the chance meeting; everything is new and challenging, an uncharted sea.

"Hi," she said in the soft melodic tone that always said so much more than the simple word. "How did it go?"

"Terrible," I said. "The editorial world doesn't like me."

"They don't know you," she said. "Come, let me get you a drink."

She clutched my arm and leaned against me as we went along the hallway to the living room, then she broke away and went behind the bar. She made martinis, maintaining a running commentary about nothing as she went through the motions. I have always hated small-talk, but coming from Leslie, it was pleasant.

The apartment was comfortably air conditioned and it was a welcome relief from the street, and I was thinking ahead to my own stuffy, hot apartment.

We sipped the drinks against a background of a Franck symphony.

"Let's go to a movie tonight," she said.

I was slightly startled. We had never been to a film before. As a matter of fact, we seldom went out. I hadn't thought about it before, but our entire social life consisted of meeting occasionally at the Mansfield or a small party with friends of mine. It occurred to me then that I had never met any friends of Leslie's. As far as I was concerned she had no past. There were many telephone calls, and it was evident by what she said that most of the calls were from men, but there was never any mention of anyone, and we never met anyone she knew. It was strange, but I had never thought of it before. And now, suddenly, she wanted to go to a movie.

"I can't tonight," I said. "I've got work to do."

"Ohhh," she said, disappointed.

"I'm sorry," I said, "but this is important. It's a firm assignment and I need the money bad."

"I think I hate those editors," she said. "You ought to be working on a novel anyway."

"That's a nice thought, but novels pay very little money. And right now I need money or I'm going to have two starving children."

"Ah, well," she said, cheerfully, "another time."

That was the end of it, and we talked about other things. It grew dark, and I checked my watch.

"I've got to go," I said. "Duty calls."

"Work here," she said.

"No, I think I'd better go home. I have to get this thing completed by tomorrow, and I'll be working all night."

"I promise not to bother you," she said.

I was skeptical and it was obvious. "I don't think so," I said. "I don't think that I could stay away from you all night."

"I'll lock my door," she said. "It will just be nice to have you in the house. You can work in the office. Everything is there. Paper, carbon, everything."

"Well...I...uh..."

"Oh, c'mon. I promise. I won't bother you, and if you leave the typewriter I'll send you right back. If you go home you'll just die of the heat."

She had a point and a good one. I dreaded the thought of the hot apartment awaiting me. It was under the roof and would be like an oven.

"Okay," I said, "but seriously, I really must get this damn thing written."

She was childishly delighted, as though I was doing her some great favor by agreeing to work in her apartment. I could only think that Sam could not have been more wrong, that if anything would get me out of my writing slump, it would be Leslie's enthusiasm.

I followed her into the office. She rushed about turning on lights, clearing away the clutter on the desk, swinging the typewriter into position, getting paper from the desk. Her production was making me feel foolish.

"That's fine," I said, "that will be just fine."

"Try the chair."

I sat down. She fussed about. "Is it comfortable?" I nodded that it was. "You're sure? I can get another chair."

"It's fine," I said.

She stood back and looked over the scene; me sitting at the typewriter, ready to go to work. She tilted her head, smiling, as though she was gazing at a flower arrangement of her own handiwork.

"How do I look?" I said.

"Like a writer," she said.

"Then let me write."

She bowed, still smiling, then left the room. I filled my pipe and lit it. I leaned back in the chair, stared at the blank paper. I knew the story that I had to write. Hell, I had already written the same damned story fifty times. All I had to do was change the characters. But a story, even the same tired plot, has got to start somewhere. I sat for a few minutes, then I began.

It went slowly, but I kept at it steadily for several hours. Leslie brought me coffee, favored me with a kiss on the forehead and left the room. I had the feeling that she was playing a game; a charade in which she was cast as the typical helpmate to the struggling artist.

By midnight it was obvious that I was right, and that she was now tired of the game. She came into the office.

"Aren't you finished yet?" she asked.

I looked up from the typewriter. "I'll be here all night," I said. "It goes slowly."

"Why don't you let it go until tomorrow?"

"Because it has to be turned in by tomorrow," I said.

She scowled, turned and left the room. I went back to work, but then she returned. "Why don't you take a break," she said. "I don't have anyone to talk to."

"Leslie," I said wearily, "I have to get this thing finished. I told you when I agreed to work here that it would take all night."

"I know that, but I'm bored."

"You promised not to bother me."

She walked the length of the room and looked through the window, then she turned and paced the room. The dog came into the room and joined her in her pacing.

"Look," I said, "I'm trying to work. Would you mind going into the other room?"

"I'd mind," she said.

"But I can't work with you walking around in here."

She stopped and scowled and was about to say something, then she changed her mind. She left the room with the dog at her heels.

I heard the television suddenly turned on, and a few minutes later it went off. The radio came on next. I heard her humming, then she appeared in the doorway. "I want you to come to bed," she said.

"I can't. I have to work." The irritation was honing the edge of my words.

"Work! All you want to do is work!"

"Leslie, for christs sake, I've got to get this done."

"Well, I want you to come to bed."

I ignored her and concentrated on the page in the typewriter. She came into the room and stood in front of me. "Are you coming to bed?"

"No."

The expression on her face then was—how can I explain it?—it was mischievous and malicious. It was as though she had accepted a challenge and was delighted with the prospect of combat. She smiled just slightly and there was a smouldering insolence in her eyes. Perhaps the maliciousness was in my own mind, I don't know, but I was angry with her, because I knew at that moment, whatever it was she had in mind—I was going to lose.

She stood before me, just beyond the circle of light from the overhead lamp. She was wearing a white cotton blouse and skirt. Without taking her eyes from me, she lifted her hands and slowly began to unbutton the blouse. I said nothing. I sat and watched her.

Her movements were deliberate. She unbuttoned the blouse and pulled it off her shoulders. She dropped it to the floor. Her hands went to the skirt and found the zipper. She removed the skirt, then stood for a moment, motionless, her eyes boring into me; the eyes harboring excitement. I was determined that I would not move.

She reached behind her back. With die lithe, dancer-like motions that always characterized her, she undressed completely. She spread her arms. The light cast deep shadows across the flawless perfection of her body, an aureole glow about the tawny blondness. She stood unmoving, inviting, her head tilted slightly towards me and to one side, the smile of conquest disfiguring her beauty. My hands were knotted into fists in my lap.

"Are you coming to bed?" she asked in a voice that was barely audible.

My stomach churned and a desperate cry of rage gathered and strangled in my chest. I came out of the chair and stood facing her. I slapped her across the face.

The sound was like a shot in the dead silence of the room. Her head snapped back and an expression of surprise and shock replaced the smile. But she did not lift her hands, and she recovered quickly and smiled.

"Are you coming to bed?" she repeated.

I slapped her again. This time she took a step backwards, but she still smiled.

My heart was beating rapidly, and I was weeping inside myself. I had never struck a woman before. It was a complete denial of a code of ethics that had been drilled into me as a child; a negation of my environment. A man, in order to survive as a distinct personality, must be true to the roots that anchor him and sustain him. Each man is—in effect—but a sequence in a chain of life. While his personality may be the sum of his own experiences, his code of behavior springs from the past and the indelible teachings of his ancestors. I had struck this girl in anger and frustration, and in that instant I slipped from the confines of a tradition. I had performed a cowardly act against a background that decreed: *Above all things, a man must live as a man.* In the short space of a hand traveling through the air and connecting with the flesh and bone of that woman, I had lost something of myself, and I could never again be the same person I had been the moment before. It was a frightening and distressing revelation.

Leslie lifted her arms and held them outstretched to me. "David," she said, as though I had done nothing, "come to bed with me."

"Let me alone," I whispered.

"You want me, David."

"I can't."

"Look at me, David. I'm yours. I only want to be with you." She spoke the words, but behind each word was a deeper meaning. *I possess you,* she was saying. *I control you through your hungers, your lust, your weakness.*

I wanted to turn away from her at that moment, to leave then with the remains of my failing dignity. But I could not move away from her. I hated her as I loved her, my emotions an admixture of loathing for myself and longing for her. I knew that if I left I would have to crawl back; I knew that I would crawl back, that I would submerge any feeling of pride to be with her.

Stepping forward, I reached for her and lifted her into my arms. Her arms encircled me and she clung tightly. I carried her to the bedroom and put her down upon the bed. She lay there, unmoving, and I undressed.

No words were spoken. I came to the bed and stretched out next to her. We were close, but untouching, holding, talking with our eyes.

A sudden pained expression appeared in her eyes. It was as though she were awakening from a sleep. "David," she said, an edge of panic in her voice, "what have I done to you?"

I closed my eyes and swallowed, unable to speak, an unfathomable misery clutching me.

"Oh, David!"

We came together, a breathless impact of longing. We clung together as though in fear of being lost. My love for her flooded me. The blood throbbed against my temples. She began to cry, softly, quietly, a muted sound of terrible anguish, her body shaking under my touch. "David," she said, "why do I do that? Why?"

I nuzzled the hollows of her neck and kissed her. Her crying ceased as physical desire began to take hold of her senses, blotting out the loneliness and pain. I caressed her body and our mutual passion increased until we were blended in the dizzying paroxysms of physical emotion.

Afterwards, when the jangling nerve endings were numbed, we still clung together, silent now in our new separateness. Then

Leslie drifted into sleep and I was alone in the room with my thoughts, my doubts.

I reviewed what Sam had said earlier in the evening, hearing his words with a new perception; I thought about my conversation with Martha, thought about Marion and the children. And against this panorama of people with whom I was involved in one way or another, there was my career as a writer. In a way it all blended in confused patterns. Was Leslie a detriment to my work? She had certainly negated my activity that night. Would I consider marrying Leslie? I shoved this question away from me. It was a stark reality that I did not want to face. Could I ever reconcile my problems with Marion? Never. How much of myself did I owe to my work? All of me, I suppose.

Questions with sketchy, unrealized answers; what every man faces every day of his life in his own way. The simple, insurmountable problems of a man's life. A man travels a straight, predestined path to a hole in the ground. There is no avoiding birth, and with the first awareness of the developed mind, Man realizes that his inevitable goal is the grave. Nothing could be simpler to understand and accept. It is baffling that Man seems to apply his superior intellect towards keeping the period between beginning and end as confused and fouled-up as possible. I really did not know where I was going or why, but I did know that I could not—at the moment—be without the girl who lay beside me.

When I awoke in the morning I was immediately faced with the problem of the unfinished story. I got up and dressed, then I went to the phone and called Dick Berger. It was a difficult thing to do. I didn't like Berger as a person, and he would carry the word to Marion that I was having trouble with my work. I don't know why this bothered me, but it did. I called, made excuses, suffered through Berger's condescension, and got a one-day reprieve. I went into the office and began to work on the story.

I worked through the morning with Leslie coming in for occasional snatches of conversation. She seemed a different person, and I felt that she was genuinely sorry for the scene she had caused the night before. Her cheerfulness was a form of repentance. I felt better about everything. I knocked off for lunch and then went back to it.

In the middle of the afternoon Leslie came into the office. Her attitude was different and she seemed restless.

"Is that story going to take forever?" she asked.

"I'll be done in a few hours," I said.

"I haven't even read it, and I'm bored with the whole thing," she said.

"So am I," I said, "but I need the money."

"I have money," she said. "You don't have to work."

I stared at her. "I'm a writer," I said.

"It takes up too much time," she said, turning and walking the length of the room to the window.

"Men work," I said. "My work happens to be writing."

"It would be more fun if you didn't work," she said. "We don't need the money."

"You forget I have a wife and two children," I said.

She turned and faced me. "I don't forget it," she said. "I think about it a lot. Sometimes I hate them."

"I still have to support them," I said.

"I don't care about that. They take up too much of your time. You're always thinking about them."

It was difficult to know what to say. I was used to Leslie's changing moods, but I had never encountered this naked animosity before. It was obvious that beneath her chagrin was the desire not to share me with anyone or anything; this was basically flattering. But now the division of my loyalties was being challenged.

"They happen to be my children," I said.

"I don't care!" she screamed. "I'm sick of it! Your children, your work! I'm always playing second-fiddle to something!"

I had to remain calm. "That's not true," I said. "I've only mentioned the children once, and—"

"You go to see them!"

"I've been to see them once since I met you," I said.

"And I'll just bet you went up there to sleep with your wife," she snapped.

"Now, wait a minute!"

"It's disgusting!"

"Leslie, what are you—"

"Why don't you divorce her?"

"I—uh—"

"Because you have no intention of divorcing her, because you go up there once a month and jump into bed with her!"

"Let's get off that!" I got up from the chair and crossed the room to her.

"Hit me! Go ahead! You're good at that sort of thing."

"Leslie, for God's sake, what's wrong?"

She grasped the window and slammed it upwards. The afternoon heat poured into the room. She whirled away from the window and stalked away from me. "I'm sick of just being on call," she said.

I didn't answer. Her accusations were too wild, too irrational to be based on any fact. I watched her walk to the desk. She picked up die copy that I had written. With quick movements, she tore the pages in half.

"Leslie!"

She threw the torn pages into the air. "That's what I think of the damned story!"

"Are you out of your mind?"

"Yes, dammit, yes! I'm sick of having you spend your time with everything except me."

"This doesn't make sense. Dammit, I've got to get that story in by tomorrow!" I was angry. I crossed the room and bent down to pick up the scattered pieces of paper. I glanced up.

Leslie went to the typewriter. She grasped it and lifted it from the table.

"What are you—?"

Her face was contorted with anger and the strain of lifting the heavy machine. She staggered with it across the room.

"What are you doing?"

She threw the machine through the open window. "There!" she cried. A moment later it crashed into the courtyard below. "That takes care of that."

I stared at her, horrified by the act of wanton destructiveness, unable to correlate my thinking. It was impossible to identify the girl I had known for a month with the creature by the window. I gathered up the torn papers, folded them and stuffed them in my pocket. I started for the door.

"Where are you going?"

I didn't answer. I was out of the office and into the hallway.

"David!' she screamed. "David, don't go!"

I opened the door and slammed it closed after me. I knew that I had to get away from there. This was too sick. I loved her, there was no doubt of that, but there comes a time when the love has all the properties of a malignant cancer, and that is the time to cure it. I ran down the stairs. I heard the door open behind me.

"David!" she screamed into the hallway, her frenzied voice echoing. "David, don't go! Don't go!"

I closed my mind to the anguished plea in the voice, made myself run. Her voice was a distant, plaintive moan, and then she began to cry. I slowed my steps. A part of me said: *Go back to her. You can't afford to lose this.* I forced myself down the remaining stairs and bolted into the street. I ran for half a block as though I were being pursued. When I reached the corner I slowed to a walk, but I did not stop.

My feelings at that moment were a mixture of fury and self-pity. It was a situation beyond reason. I walked fast. I wanted to cry and there were no tears. I wanted to wail and I did not utter a sound. I was seething with the desire to do violence. I wanted to lash out at something, to destroy. I kept walking. I had been hurt and I wanted to inflict pain in return. I had had an image shattered; I had seen what I did not want to see, and I was furious with this new knowledge. I wanted to wipe out the memory of what had happened in the past day, and knowing that I could not, I snarled and cursed my misfortune. Where was the girl of the first night? God, how could I have been so stupidly blind?

I surged along the street, seeing nothing, hearing nothing. I ignored the insufferable heat. I walked fast, flagellating myself for my soiled dream. It was a terrible revelation. The girl was human.

By the time I reached my apartment I was exhausted, but my anger had also dulled, and now there was only the sense of loss, the disappointment.

Claude came out of his studio when I entered. He was wearing bathing trunks, and he had two paint brushes on his hand. There were smudges of oil paint on his face and body. I dropped into a chair at the kitchen table.

"What's with you?" Claude asked.

"I've been walking hard," I said.

"You look terrible."

"I feel terrible."

"Too damned hot for that sort of thing," he said. "Too hot for anything. How about a beer?"

"Great."

He went to the refrigerator and removed the beer. He opened it, placed a can before me. "'Welcome home," he said.

We drank. The beer was cold and good. I was beat and drenched with sweat. I unbuttoned my shirt and pulled it off. I leaned back and sighed heavily.

"How's Leslie?" Claude asked.

"Ended," I said. "Finished. Kaput."

"Oh?" He was surprised, but he smiled. Then he lifted his beer. "To true love," he said, grinning.

God, it was good to be home, good to just sit in the casual, uncomplicated atmosphere.

"She throw you out?" Claude asked.

"I ran," I said.

He chuckled. "The battles of the sexes," he said.

"When you win you lose."

"Amen."

"You really cut out for good?"

"It has to be," I said. "Everything just went haywire. It's too fouled up. I don't know what happened, but I do know that the whole thing is too screwy to be good."

"Do you think she'll let you off the hook that easy?"

"It's not a matter of that. I left, that's that."

"Well," he said, "it's too bad in a way. I mean you really seemed to be hooked on her."

"I was. I am. But, hell, I suddenly saw the whole thing destroying me as a person."

We drank in silence. I pulled the torn pages from my pocket and spread them on the table.

"Ann and I are going to get married," Claude said.

I looked up to make certain that he was serious. I saw that he was, and that he was waiting for me to say something. I knew the girl, Ann, well, and I liked her. She and Claude had met at a party and their attraction for each other had been immediate. Their situation was typical for New York. They had dated briefly, then slept together at her apartment, and gradually their relationship became an affair. This is an accepted pattern among the New York expatriates.

"I think it's a good idea," I said.

"Do you really? I mean, I'm still a little edgy about it. I guess it's because I've never been married."

I knew that I had to be careful about what I said. I was ten years older than Claude and he reacted to me as though I were an older brother. I knew that out of the shambles of my own marriage he expected me to come up with the pattern for the perfect marriage.

"Well," I said, "you can either get married now or just forget the whole thing before it gets unbearable."

"What do you mean by that?"

"Just what I say. Let me ask you this: Have you and Ann been having little disagreements?"

"Everybody has disagreements," he said.

"But have these arguments come up for odd little reasons that you never seem to understand?"

"Well … uh … as a matter of fact, Ann has been acting pretty strange."

I laughed. "She's acting like a woman," I said.

"Are you going to give me the double standard bunk?"

"No, I'm not. I'm just saying that Ann has more time to think about the future in terms of herself as a wife and mother. You're more concerned with the future in terms of success as a painter. Both of you are thinking of the future, it's just that her future is dependent on another person."

"You make it sound as though she's working some angle to get me married."

"Not at all. It's just that she cannot be fulfilled as a woman without marriage."

"We could live together."

"Maybe," I said, "although I doubt it. You've both shaken off middle-class morality to a degree, but it is still there."

"That's nonsense. I don't have American problems. You forget, I'm French."

"With a stronger moral sense than any American. If you don't get married now you'll be denying the necessity for continuity in life. It's a basic fact where the relationship between a man and woman are concerned. You must always have movement; the relationship must always be going in some direction. A man and woman meet and are attracted. Each is actually seeking a mate. The preliminary love-making is merely testing for the compatible mate. The next step is the affair, but the relationship cannot stop there or it will be destroyed. It has to go on to marriage, lawful or unlawful. The next step is children and then the marriage of those children and then grandchildren. The mating instinct is only the primary factor in this natural continuity. Now, you and Ann could live together and it would be a marriage, but you would force her to deny her background. And anyway, if you're going to go that far, if you feel that this is right for you both, marry her and alleviate any chance of her feeling guilt. The only reason that she has been acting strangely is that she is beginning to feel the hopelessness of the static quality of the relationship. It must have a future, and she's sensing it."

Claude sat quietly mulling over all that I had said. He nodded finally, then smiled. "It figures," he said. "I was beginning to feel pretty hopeless about it myself."

"It'll work," I said. "She's quite a wonderful girl."

"What bothers me about it," he said, "is that I'm sure that everyone thinks that their marriage is right when they marry, and then so many end up in divorce."

"Because our customs say that we must take the biggest step of our lives in the blindest possible way," I said. "How the hell these rules were ever established is beyond me, but they have been. I'm sure that it has to do with the basic puritanical morality of the American. They absolutely deny the existence of sex, and if they accept it at all, they refuse to admit that it is the natural and basic reason for the attraction between male and female. If you could get to the root of every divorce, I'm certain that you would find the couple sexually dissatisfied. I never knew a married couple who agreed on everything and I know a few who don't agree on anything, but they make it together in bed, and that overshadows everything else. The magazines, the churches, all the do-good consultants can preach forever about the ways to hold a marriage together; play together, pray together, all nonsense. A marriage is made in bed, and that's that."

"Hear, hear!"

I laughed, but then I sobered. "I mean it. A guy who marries a sweet little virgin is doing about as stupid a thing as a man can do. Good Lord, it's the same as buying an automobile without starting the engine. They call it morality when it's actually complete imbecility."

"I don't feel immoral," he said.

"Well, you are. In the eyes of society you are, and so is Ann and Martha and myself, and just about everyone else you know. And because you are immoral you've got a better than even chance for a successful marriage. The average person in the Midwest could never begin to understand the standard of morality that exists in New York, and it's their loss, because they also deny the natural impulses of mating with their blinders of morality, and that's why they keep the divorce lawyers busy. Agh, I could keep on about this for an hour."

"Go ahead, you look fine when your face gets purple."

We laughed together, then I shuffled the torn pages of the manuscript on the table. "I have to get to work," I said.

Claude stared at the torn pages. "What happened there?" he asked.

"Leslie didn't like it."

"She has definite ways of expressing herself," he said.

"Yeah. Now, get out of here and let me get to work."

"Okay, then I take it you'll be my best-man."

"That, old buddy, will be a pleasure."

He went back to his studio and I went to work. It took me four hours to retype the torn pages. By that time Claude had dressed and left to see Ann, and I was alone. I had a sandwich and beer for dinner, and kept working.

The telephone rang several times, and each time I stopped and waited for the ringing to stop. I had the feeling that it was Leslie and I had to struggle to resist the impulse to answer. It was disturbing to me that I could talk to Claude about love, and morality, and marriage, and the general relationship between man and woman, and still not be able to apply the same rational thinking in my own life. I knew that with Leslie I would retain nothing of myself, but I wanted to be with her; every moment that I spent at the typewriter was an agony of wanting to forget my own existence as a human being and submerge myself in the aura that was her.

But there was a part of my mind that retained its clarity and saw Leslie as a sickness, and kept me from the telephone.

It was after midnight when I completed the story. I was tired, but I also felt relief. The bills were paid for another month. I drank a final beer and went to the bedroom. It was still hot. I lay on the bed in the dark for a long time. I was exhausted, but restless.

I have no idea when I slept, but I was suddenly awakened by the crash of the apartment door being slammed open. My immediate reaction was fright, but I recovered and leaped from the bed. There was a long groan and a body crashed to the floor in the kitchen. I fumbled for the light switch and turned on the bedroom light. It gave me enough light in the kitchen to find the lamp. I turned it on.

"Leslie!"

She was sprawled face-down on the floor. My reaction to her was anger. *Damn her for busting in here, preying on my sympathy to get me back into her self-indulgent net. I would have none of this nonsense. I was through.* I stood over her. "What do you want?" I barked.

"David," she whispered. She turned on her side and lifted her face to the fight. "David, help me."

I caught my breath. "Leslie." My voice was barely audible. "My God, what happened to you?"

"David, help me."

I was unable to move. I could say nothing. Her left eye was swollen closed. Her blonde hair was spattered and matted with blood. The left side of her face was a purple-red bruise, and her jaw was misshapen. Her lips were split and bleeding.

I dropped to my knees and gathered her into my arms. I lifted her and carried her to the bedroom and laid her on the bed. I turned to leave.

"Don't leave me!" she screamed, clawing for me. "David, don't leave me!"

I pressed her back onto the bed. "I have to get some ice and water for your face. I'll only be a minute."

She would not release my arm. "Save me, David. Don't let him hit me again! Don't leave me, David. I love you. I love you, David!"

I held her close to me until she quieted, then I was able to go to the kitchen for water and ice cubes. I came back and washed the blood from her face, then made an ice pack for the side of her face. When the last traces of hysteria had gone I asked, "Leslie, how did this happen?"

Her voice was like that of a little girl. It was strange to hear her whimper. 'I'm not sure."

"But you must know."

"I don't know...I...I didn't do anything."

"Leslie, where did it happen?"

"In the subway."

"The subway?" I could hardly believe it. I glanced up at the clock. It was 3:30 a.m.

"Whereabouts?"

"I was down by the Brooklyn Bridge. I was taking the subway back up-town. A man grabbed me and just began beating me."

"But what were you doing down at the Brooklyn Bridge at this hour? That's *asking* for trouble."

"I don't know. I was just there. I don't know how I got there. Don't ask me anymore questions, David."

A moment later she was asleep. I stood by the bed looking down upon her. Was she telling the truth? There she was, beaten, and I could only think that she was lying; and I knew that I would never be able to believe her again. There would always be doubts, and so long as there was doubt of her veracity, there could be nothing for us. I knew then that she walked in the shadow of violence, that wherever she was there would be the seed of disturbance. In her way she loved me, but her nature decreed that this love must be torn and dragged in the mud as punishment for whatever it was that lurked in the untouchable recesses of her mind. Our love affair had been too constant, too pleasant, and she intentionally created the breech. Could she possibly have gotten herself beat up just to make certain that I would go back to her? It seemed unbelievable, but just the fact that I could think such a thing was reason enough to stay away from her.

But I knew that I would not; that I *could not* for as long as she would want me near her.

I pressed my fingers against my eyes. Where would I end in this?

CHAPTER FIVE

My affair with Leslie had a defined pattern.

In the month following the mysterious beating I came to accept certain facts. Leslie, I was certain, had a definite schizoid personality. She was not acting her various roles. When she was charming and understanding, she meant it and felt it; when she was the complete bitch, she was just that. It is always difficult to accept a mental abberation in a beautiful woman, but I had to force myself to realize that there was a Leslie who loved and needed me, just as there was a Leslie who hated my guts.

It was difficult, but during that month I was able to sense the subtle changes, and I did my best to stay away from the side of her that rebelled against me.

I was able to do my work in a haphazard fashion, managing to get just enough accomplished to keep going. I knew, of course, that something had to give ... and it did.

If I remember correctly, it was near the end of July. It was mid-morning. I had not seen Leslie for three days. I had been working steadily on my most promising writing assignment to date—the treatment for a low-budget movie. While the pay was not astronomical, it was an assignment that could lead to better things, and I was bearing down on it, anxious to pull it off.

I was finishing coffee when the telephone rang. It was Sam, my agent.

"How goes it, Kid?" he asked.

"Fine," I said. "Just fine."

"You're not crapping me, are you?"

"I mean it. Why would I lie?"

"All writers lie," he said. "That's what makes you writers. You're respectable liars."

"Well, it's going fine," I said.

"That broad leaving you alone?"

"If you're referring to Leslie," I said, annoyed, "I haven't seen her for three days."

There was a moment of silence, then he said, "I hope you're not crapping me, Dave."

When he called me Dave like that I knew that he was really concerned. "You have to trust me," I said.

"You, I trust," he said. "But that broad is bad news. I won't relax until that baby is gone."

"Forget it, Sam. I'm doing the treatment."

"Okay, okay. Just checking. You know how important this thing is."

"Believe me, I know."

"This can be the big one, Kid. For you and for me. I don't get that treatment, I'm dead with Carmine. He's gonna be big, Kid, and we'll have the inside track on all his work."

"It'll be done," I said, beginning to weary of Sam's trepidation.

"Tomorrow morning, right? We got a meeting for ten o'clock, right?"

"It will be finished. It will be good." I emphasized each word.

"Okay, okay, don't get sore. It's you I'm thinking about. I'm your agent, you know."

"I know."

"Okay, I'll let you get back to work. Goodbye."

"Goodbye, Sam." I waited for his click, then hung up the phone. I finished the coffee, and went back to the typewriter.

The day went slowly. It was hot in the apartment and I was working in my shorts. Claude had gone to the Cape for the week, so it was as quiet as a building can be in the Lower East Side. The sweat ran. I drank orange juice, and every damned sip made me think of Marion. *The vitamin C will keep you going.* Christ, couldn't I ever do anything on my own? I paced, I sweated, I worked. There were those moments when I knew with clarity that the movie would be a piece of garbage, that what I was sweating to put into words would then result in the labor of a hundred pages of more words, and then the group labors of dozens of technicians and actors and the employ of tons of equipment and the use of thousands of feet of expensive film, and all this for the production of a movie designed for the puckered navel mentality of the Great Unwashed. It was distressing to realize the amount of effort that was pouring into the creation of crap, but I managed to shake myself off the self-righteous pedestal by saying over and over again: *Money, money, money, money.* And I followed this with: *Shit, shit, shit.* But I was able to keep working.

The phone rang. I ignored it. It persisted. I answered it.

"Were you sleeping?" Leslie said.

"Working," I answered.

"Still?"

"Still. It's going good."

"I haven't seen you for days," she said. I noted the slight petulance in her voice. "Will I see you today?"

"I can't," I said. "I have to finish this thing."

She sighed deeply and I got the danger signal. "Well," she said, "I just wanted to know. There's an old friend in town, and I guess I'll have dinner with her."

I felt relief. No scene, no recriminations. I was off the hook. "I'll call you as soon as I'm done," I said. "It really is important."

"I'm sure it is," she said. "Well, work good."

I was about to say more, something sentimental, about how much I missed her, something, but she hung up and I didn't have the chance. I stood holding the phone, staring at is as if I could learn something from it. Was she angry? Dammit, why did it bother me? She had moods. I accepted this fact. She was as nutty as a Mars bar. Then why did it bother me?

I went back to work with less relish than before. She kept getting in the way of my thoughts. What the hell did I want? If she had created a scene on the phone I would have been annoyed, accused her of interfering with my work, and when she accepted the fact that I wasn't going to see her with casual indifference, it still bothered me. Damn!

More orange juice, more sweat, and I was into the fifth draft when I knocked off for a dinner of peanut butter sandwiches. I relaxed by composing an unsolicited testimonial to the inventor of peanut butter, then I picked up my ragged and dogeared copy of Norman Mailer's *Advertisements For Myself.* I read for a half hour, then tossed the book across the room and slumped into the chair, scowling, the dead-weight of conscience nagging me.

Mailer is not for a hack. He says too much, opens up too many windows of the mind, and when you look out you see yourself. I had always known one thing to be an unassailable truth. Every time a man compromises himself, no matter how many excuses he may invent to give his compromise the air of nobility, he loses a little of himself. This is a frightening thing to a writer who started out with a dream of putting something significant into print, a sentence, a paragraph that would raise him above himself; it is frightening when you are 34 and you haven't done it. I could agree with Sam that I was developing in my own way, but in the twilight hours of the heart's hunger I was afraid. I lost something of myself each time I wrote what I knew was trite before I started, and I wondered if there would be anything left of me when I reached that place—wherever it might be—when I *wanted* to put myself into the work.

Mailer on Mailer was an outcry to all writers—I still thought of myself as a writer—to cut out the low whoring and cheating and to be honest unto themselves. He said point-blank that you can't walk through shit without getting the stink on you, and while you may be *tip-toeing* in the gutter, you're still in the gutter.

A writer who whores, he said in effect, is emasculating himself not only as a writer, but as a man.

I mention this because it is important. To read Mailer on the tail-end of a three-day labor on a screen treatment was like pausing for a chat with Christ on the way to a whore house. I was sick with myself. Was this it? I asked myself. Was this my place? Was I merely a word flunkie, the esteemed author of two-syllable imbecility to keep the cameras grinding for a producer with the sensitivity of a gorilla and the brains of gnat?

The dinner break stretched into several hours. I was sitting in the dark. My depression had flowered into a brooding anger. I was no longer merely reviewing the failure of my work, I was also seeing the failure of my life. My weaknesses stood out in the darkened room in technicolor, a leering panorama of cowardice and ant-size insignificance. If I had an ounce of guts I would go dig ditches and write. If I had an ounce of guts I would divorce my wife. I would seize my life and live it.

I turned on the lights and went back to the screen treatment. I cursed Mailer and his book. Later, I said, later. Get this job done and worry about who you are later. Right now you're a hack, so be a good one.

The phone rang and I snarled and knocked the chair over getting up. It was Leslie.

"Hi," she said, too brightly.

"Hello," I said. "How was dinner?"

"Wonderful." She slurred the word. "What are you doing?"

"Sitting here thinking about you," I said.

"Aren't you sweet."

"Are you drunk?"

"Of course I'm drunk," she said. "Beautifully drunk. Wonderfully, beautifully, sensationally drunk."

"That's fine," I said. "Why don't you go to bed and sleep it off."

"I might just do that."

There was music in the background and over this I heard a male voice. I had been depressed, then annoyed that she was calling me drunk, and now the sound of that voice, knowing that she was with a man, infuriated me. I had been feeling mentally cuckolded, and now I was feeling physically cuckolded. It was an unbearably constricted feeling, a type of anger I had never experienced. It was jealousy compounded with fear.

"Is that your friend?" I said.

"What?"

"Your old friend," I said with sarcastic emphasis. "The *she* you were having dinner with. Her voice is awfully deep."

She laughed. "Of course not, silly. That's … oh, dear, I've forgotten his name. Just a minute." She spoke away from the phone, asking the man his name, then she came back to me. "It's Murray," she said, "and he's very sweet. He bought me a drink at the Embers, and he says I'm beautiful. He's very nice, and he's a gentleman, and he's not stuffy and working all the time like some people. He bought a beautiful bottle of scotch and we're going to drink it all up."

"Leslie, why don't you cut this out?"

"I don't want to cut it out. I'm sick of just sitting around waiting for you. Goodnight, Mister Big Writer."

The phone clicked and went dead. I took a deep breath, bit down on my lower lip.

I was angry, but more than that, I was afraid. I had to have her.

Don't try to rationalize this, don't ask me why? Someone once told me that it was because of a Christ complex, born of guilt; that I sought atonement for my sins, and Leslie was my cross, and that symbolically, our matings were the spikes being driven into the hands. I don't know, I don't try to explain things in that way. I had to have that damned female, that's all!

For the past two hours I had sat in the sweating self-doubt of my position in life, feeling as necessary as an extra pimple in a field of acne. And now I was about to cuckolded by that impossible, neurotic bitch. Damn women! Damn me for being such a simpering, frightened, ineffectual bastard!

I slammed the telephone receiver upon the cradle. I kicked the fallen chair out of my way and lunged out of the apartment. I ran down the steps, across the courtyard, through the front building and into the street. There were many people on the street, but they did not slow me. I weaved and shouldered through them, running. Voices shouted behind me, but I paid them no heed. I dodged the traffic on Fourteenth Street and cut through the housing project.

It did not occur to me that it would have been simpler to take a cab. The primal rage was upon me. I ran, my anger like a ballooning cancer. It was difficult to breathe. My side ached. My face was contorted. I ran. My feet slapped heavily on the concrete. For long moments of tortured fury I forgot my objective and felt myself pursued, and did not know why I was running away. And, of course, as I ran towards Leslie I *was* running away—from myself, my failure.

I pushed too hard and I had to stop. I clutched the side of a building and gasped for breath. I choked. My senses blurred and nausea gripped me. I retched, spewing the building with vomit. I heaved until the pain was unbearable and the tears ran down my face. I pushed away from the wall and lurched across the sidewalk. People shied from me as though I were a leper. I took great swallows of air and began to run again.

The last two blocks I walked. Suddenly I did not want to rush. I was hesitant to realize the truth of my fears. I reached her building, stopped and looked up. Light showed in the bedroom windows. I used my key to open the downstairs door and climbed the stairs without haste.

I stopped before her door. I held the key in my hand. I waited. My anger seemed to have disappeared. I was chilled and I was calm—too calm. I slipped my key into the lock, and this was a contradiction, because I turned the key carefully so as not to be heard. One moment I did not want to believe that she would be in bed with the stranger, and now I was trying to catch her unaware. I opened the door and closed it softly. I listened a moment. There was no sound but the record player on low volume. Then I heard Leslie's husky laugh, and suddenly the fury raged in me once more. I walked along the hall at a natural pace. I came into the living room.

They were on the divan. They had heard my footsteps and they regarded me with surprise. The dog trotted over to me and nuzzled my hand. There was a bottle on the table before the divan and two glasses. The bottle was half empty.

"David!" Leslie said, still reclining against the cushions. Her fingers fumbled with the buttons of her blouse, attempting to close it.

The man was still leaning towards her, but his head was turned in my direction. He had a nondescript face, the expense account poached egg look, that faceless face that floats along all the streets of the country. I knew that I had nothing against him, but if I was going to be replaced I wanted it to be by more man than that, so it galled me. He did not say anything, but he registered surprise and confusion.

Leslie struggled to her feet. The initial surprise over, she acted with nonchalance. She weaved just a little, and her voice was a little too stilted. She exaggerated all movement when she was drunk.

"What are you doing here?" she asked. When I did not answer she turned to the man who was now sitting stiffly. "This is my friend," she said. "Murray, this is David."

Murray attempted a weak smile. He was not a happy man. He had picked up a live one in a first rate ginmill, she had all the marks of a sure lay, and now angry young man was on the scene. I couldn't dislike the guy.

"Have a drink," Leslie said.

I crossed the room and stood by the table. I still had not spoken. I looked down at Murray. He was looking back unhappily. "See you around, Pal," I said.

He glanced quickly at Leslie, then back to me. He got to his feet and tried the smile again. "I don't want any trouble," he said.

"You're not going to get any," I said.

He took several steps away. "I don't want to be involved in anything."

"You're not."

"I mean, I just met her," he said.

"I know how it is. See you later." I had control of things now and I was able to ride on his fright.

"She asked me up here." He took another few steps, waiting for me to pull the gun.

"Where you going?" Leslie said, finally reacting to what was happening.

"Murray has a previous engagement," I said, keeping my gaze upon him.

"He does not! He's staying right here! Were having a party!"

"Button your shirt," I said, turning to look at her. She blinked and shook her head. She looked down at the open blouse, and pulled it together, bunched in her fist.

"I'm going," Murray said. "I don't want any trouble. I'm just a quiet, friendly guy."

I nodded. Murray was seeing his name on a police blotter, a tough thing to explain to the boss and the wife. A frightened little man. A big stud if the mare had strayed from the herd, but no challenger for the right to mate. He was more secure in the safe prepaid arms of a whore.

"Don't go!" Leslie shouted. "Don't let him push you around."

"Don't listen to her, Pal," I said. "She likes the sight of blood. Just blow."

"I'm going. Don't worry about me. I don't want any trouble. Christ!"

Leslie's face was twisted with the numbed, uncomprehending look of the booze-fogged brain trying to assimilate, and losing the struggle. But she was coming around fast and her eyes were taking on a glitter. "What is this? What is this?"

"Cool it," I said.

Murray had his hat and was making for the doorway. He gingerly skirted the dog lying by the bar. The whole scene was almost funny.

"Wait just a goddamned minute!" Leslie blurted, and now she had a grasp of the situation. "Don't you leave" she snapped.

Murray stopped dead in his tracks, and I knew who was the boss around his house.

"Just who the hell do you think you are?" Leslie said to me. "You don't own me. You can't come around here messing up my life."

"Stop acting like a two-bit tramp," I said.

"You son-of-a-bitch!"

I hit her. The back of my hand caught her across the right side of her face. Her scream followed the sudden impact. I had put some weight behind it, and she staggered off-balance, hit the edge of the divan and fell to the floor.

Murray was out of it. I heard the door close and the quick rattle of his steps going down the stairs. I could almost hear his sigh of relief, and I knew that before he reached the bottom he would already be editing the story for telling to the next group of salesmen. The American hero.

Leslie was coming to her feet. I started to walk away. She was standing, then suddenly she was on my back and there was a hellish bum as her fingers raked my neck. I whirled, flinging her off. Her eyes burned with fury. She rushed at me. I feinted away and grasped her wrist. I spun her off-balance, shifted my weight and flipped her. She sprawled, but she bounced to her feet with the grace of a cat.

"Cut it out!" I said. "You'll get hurt!"

There were tears of anger in her eyes. She rushed me again. This time I spun her about, holding her arm behind her. I placed my foot against her buttocks and sent her flying harmlessly across the room.

The dog was up and milling nervously. He knew that something was damned wrong, but he was used to me and did not know what to make of it. He whined and barked.

Leslie was leaning against a chest. "I'll kill you!" she screamed. She grabbed a vase and threw it, a wild throw. It shattered against the brick wall. I walked towards the window at the end of the room. "I'll kill you!" she screamed again. I laughed and I shouldn't have, because it triggered her rage beyond reason. She pushed away from the chest and moved to the bar. The dog nuzzled her hand, whimpering. She stood straight, and it was startling to me to see such a beautiful face show so much hatred. She was calm, smouldering. She lifted her right arm and pointed at me.

"Fang!" she snapped. "Get him!"

I caught my breath, stunned with terror by the implication of the harsh order. My muscles stiffened and the fright churned in my stomach. It was a split-second reaction, just as much time as it took the big Doberman to register the order. That was a highly-trained dog and the master had pushed the button that changed me from friend to enemy. I could almost see his muscles coil, and then he leaped from her side.

For a fleeting second I knew that I was going to be torn to shreds, but I had no intention of going out easy. I dropped to a crouch, fists out at my sides. I held my breath, muttering to myself, *Come on, you son-of-a-bitch.*

The dog attacked, a snarling black streak. I hated to put my life on the line with something I had read by Carl Akeley about his African adventures and a particular encounter with a leopard, but there was nothing else I could do.

I gauged the animal's strides, and in that instant that he left the floor to go at my throat, I turned, bracing myself to take the blow on my back. The dog landed, jarring me, but the animal was surprised and I was not. I twisted, spinning him off. In the moment of his confusion I slammed him across the nose. He backed off a step and snarled. The teeth were bared. He bunched up and leaped, but just before he left the floor I stepped in, my fist cocked. His mouth was open wide, but he was off target, knew it too late. I aimed perfectly and slammed the fist into his mouth and down his throat. Before he touched the ground I swung my free arm under his chest, holding his front feet off the floor, and hugged him to me, keeping the fist lodged in his throat.

The animal went crazy. He could not bite down, but he writhed and jerked, kicking with his powerful hind legs. I could only compare it to the first time—at Air Force gunnery school—that I had stood up behind a swivel-mounted twin-.50 machine gun, gripped the handles tightly and pressed the triggers. But, at least the wildly bucking gun was not trying to devour me.

I held on, bent over, my legs spread wide. My face was close to the dogs. He was strangling and I saw the panic and new terror in his eyes. *Die, you bastard!* I gasped to myself, straining every muscle to hold on.

"You're killing him!" Leslie screamed. "You're killing him!"

I glanced up. She was still standing at the end of the room. Both fists were clutched at her throat. She leaned slighdy forward and her face was a picture of anguish.

The dog was losing strength. The strain was telling on my muscles. The dog's eyes were beginning to bug. I thrust the fist deeper.

"Don't!" Leslie wailed. "Don't kill him!" I watched her fall to her knees and begin to beat the floor with her fists. She lifted her face. The expression was tortured and tears streamed over her cheeks. "He's ... all ... I ... have!"

I jerked my fist free and flung the animal away from me. Leslie gasped, leaned forward on her hands and knees, poised expectantly. The dog scrabbled about, gasping for air. He lunged to his feet, staggered and fell. But in a moment he was up again, and this time he came at me. I had to admire the relentless courage, but it was my fight by then, and I was tired of the crap. I hooked a right to the dog's jaw. The animal yelped and fell back on his haunches.

"Come on, you bastard!" I snarled. I advanced a step and hit him again. He backed off, confused and frightened. I hit him again.

"Stop it!" Leslie screamed. "Stop it!" She was still on her hands and knees.

I cocked my fist again and this time the dog dropped to his belly and groveled, whimpering.

"Stop it!"

"Maybe you'd like it!"

"Yes! Yes! I don't care, but don't hit him!"

I crossed the room and stood over her, looking down. She lowered her head. I dug my fingers into her hair and jerked her face up. "Look at me, you goddamned miserable little bitch!" I looked down into the nightmare behind her eyes. "That damned dog would have killed me!" I still held her hair and I shook her head. I shouted about the dog, but my real anger sprang from my soul-sick sense of loss; she was gone from me. I wanted to beat her into loving me. "Why? Dammit, why?" She did not answer. I had lost her, I loved her. I took my hand from her hair and slapped her across the face. "Tramp!" I snarled. "Damned whore!" Her expression had not changed. "I love you, damn you!" I shouted. She covered her face with her hands. "Why, dammit?" I repeated. "Why did you turn that dog on me?" I punished her with the words and I wanted to take her into my arms. "Goddamn you, answer me!"

"I don't know," she said, her voice muffled by her hands. "I don't know." A tight sob choked off anything else.

I stood away from her. I looked down upon her and I ached with longing for her. "You're not worth the space you take up on that floor," I said. "You deliberately called me to get that poor guy beat up tonight. You damned near got that dog killed. Why? What makes you think you're worth all that?"

She pulled her hands away from her face and I winced at the look of hopeless, terrified agony. She opened her mouth to speak, her lips moved, but it was several seconds before she could say, "I . . . I . . ." She shook her head wildly. "Oh, my God!" she moaned. "Oh, my God!" She twisted to one side and sprang to her feet. She held one hand to her mouth, her head down, and ran into the hallway. She ran into the bathroom and slammed the door. I followed, walking slowly. I stood by the door.

A bottle clattered against the metal of the medicine cabinet, fell to the floor. I cocked my head, wondering. I heard her gasp. My heart-beat raced with the nerve-numbing new panic. I held my breath. "No," I whispered. I slammed against the door. It was not locked and it flew open. I stumbled into the room.

Leslie leaned over the bathtub. One wrist was bleeding and she held a razor blade poised to slash the other. I lunged for her and grasped both arms. She screamed and fought to free herself. "Let me go!" she screamed. "Let me go! I don't want this!"

"Stop it!"

"No! Leave me alone!"

"I'll have to hit you!"

"Let me be!" She twisted and squirmed, tried to slam me with her head. I worked my hand around her left arm until my thumb was near the armpit. I found the artery and pressed it tightly against the bone.

"Leslie, you little idiot, stop it."

Gradually I quieted her. She settled into a lethargy of despair. I was able to release one arm and remove the razor blade from her fingers. I held the left arm in both hands and released the pressure on the artery. She watched with disinterest. The blood flowed again, but it was not arterial.

"It's not deep," I said. "You'll be all right."

"I couldn't even do that right," she said.

"Leslie," I said, "don't talk like that. It was my fault and I'm sorry."

She said nothing more. I put her wrist under the water tap and washed the blood away. I probed the wound with my fingers. It was not deep enough to require stitches. I cleaned it with alcohol and bandaged it. She sat through it all like a sleepwalker.

I led her out of the bathroom to the bedroom. She sat on the edge of the bed. "Feel better?" I asked. She nodded without answering. I went to the chair and sat down facing her.

"I told you not to love me," she said.

"What?"

"That first time," she said. Her voice was weary, a dull monotone. She stared at the wall ahead of her. Her shoulders were slumped. "That was so long ago," she went on. "I told you not to love me.

"Leslie, don't—"

"What's wrong with me, David?"

"There's nothing wrong with—"

"Yes, there is," she said emphatically. "I do these things and I don't know why." She looked up at me. "You should just let me die, David."

"That's pretty selfish," I said. "You don't seem to realize that part of me would die with you. I want you, Leslie. I need you."

She stared at me and our eyes held for a long moment. She swallowed and I watched her eyes fill with tears. We said nothing, but the pull between us was strong.

I got up from the chair and went to the bed. I put my hands upon her shoulders and pressed her back upon the bed, lying beside her. I kissed her gently, but she received the kiss hungrily and pulled me to her, clinging with a trembling desperation.

We parted and our eyes held. We said nothing, but we both stood and undressed. We returned to the bed. We were side-by-side, not touching, silent, letting the feeling that was in both of us communicate. I reached out and placed my hand on her arm. The move was timorous, exploratory. She moved closer and our bodies touched. It was difficult to breathe. We came together with the ardent expectancy of first mating. Tenderness gave way to the pure physical desire that was like a hard fist in the guts. This love bloomed in the bowels and spread white-hot through the body. There were no words of love. Our breathing was sharp and tense. Arms and legs clutched and intertwined. Our bodies ground together. Every sense was sharpened and brought into play, touch, smell, taste—everything building towards the intensification of this lust.

I opened my eyes to look upon her face. She grimaced, her teeth bared, and she shook her head from side to side as the need for release enveloped her.

In that moment I decided to master her. My brain seemed to take over and my body calmed. I made love to her methodically, sensing her through movement, watching her face. I brought her near to climax, then carefully calmed her; brought her back again, stopped her, soothed her. When she could not stand it I let her ride over the crest, but minutes later I aroused her again, brought her to the crest and eased her over. I repeated this again, and then she was staring up at me with fatigued eyes. Her look was confused, but I smiled down upon her, saying nothing, and began to slowly, carefully stroke her body. She knew, it was in her eyes. I was using her, but there was nothing that she could do about it. Her nervous system was in control of her and I played upon that nervous system. I moved against her, stroking her, kissing her, until she once again twisted and lunged towards fulfillment, and then I began to speak into her ear, whispering intensely, coaxing her, uttering the guttural sounds of passion, adding the sense of hearing, telling her, "Now! Now, baby, now!" Telling her in those terse bombarding words that all before had been anti-climactic. She twisted and writhed beneath me. Her mouth was open, gasping, and her eyes were begging. I ruled her. Exalted, I grasped her, and released my body from my mind.

Strangled sound rattled in her throat. She kicked her legs. Her heels dug in and she arched her body. A piercing scream exploded from her. I glanced at her face. Her eyes were wide and they rolled back into her head until only the whites were exposed. I shuddered with convulsive spasms. For a long moment we soared into the fourth dimension of time and space, weightless, disembodied. Then we collapsed together, returned to exhausted reality. We lay unmoving, wordless, the sweat cooling on our bodies.

I had won. I had lost. It served my ego to know that no other man had brought her to that point before, that no matter with whom she made love in the future it would be a failure, that there would always be the subconscious remembrance of this night. But I had also reduced her for myself, and knew that the only thing that would bind us now would be this compulsive mating. I have said before that a relationship between man and woman is welded in bed, that the physical mating must be strong and reciprocal. But I must add; when there is nothing else, when a man and woman exist for each other only in the hot sweat of lunging bodies, it is dual masturbation.

I slept and was awakened by the ringing of the telephone. I glanced at Leslie, but she did not stir, so I left the bed and answered it.

"David?" It was Sam. My pulse leaped and I turned quickly to look at the clock. It was almost ten o'clock.

"Yes," I said, my stomach churning.

"I been trying to get you," he said. "You sound like you just woke up. I might have known you'd be with that damned broad."

"Look, Sam, I—"

"Ten o'clock," he said, interrupting. "I told you ten o'clock. You got that thing finished?"

I paused too long with my answer and I heard him muttering curses away from the phone. "I have an unpolished draft, but it ought to—"

"Balls!" he growled. "That broad, that damned broad! I counted on you for this."

"I've got—"

"You've got nothing!" he shouted. "This isn't a two-bit piece of crap for a girlie book, this meant some real dough. You blew it, boy, you did it good. I've had it! You can get yourself a new agent!"

"Sam, look, just give—"

"I've had it!" he shouted. "Go back to bed, lover, and this time you better put the boots to that tramp, because it's going to be the most expensive lay you ever had." He slammed the phone down.

I stared at the dead instrument in my hand. I replaced it in the cradle and stood there clenching and unclenching my fists. I had loused up again and I was boiling with self-pity and loathing for myself. If there was one bit of pride that I had always had in myself as a writer, it was the knowledge that I was a real pro; I could be depended upon to produce damned near anything. I was cautious not to let this become an end in itself, but it had sustained me. And now I didn't have that.

In the bathroom I splashed water on my face, then gazed into the mirror, cursing the image. I went back to the bedroom and began to dress.

Leslie stirred. I turned to look at her. She opened her eyes and smiled. "Good morning," she purred, stretching.

I glared at her with vehemence. She lost her smile. I turned away.

"David," she said, "what's wrong?"

"Nothing."

"But there is."

"It's nothing. It has nothing to do with you." I said those words to shade the issue, to avoid a discussion, but as they were spoken I recognized their truth. It had only to do with me. The whole damned thing had nothing to do with anyone but me. I was destroying everything that was me for reasons of my own, and any contributing factors—Leslie included—were merely catalysts in this willful self-destruction. But, of course, this realization did not stop me. It never does.

CHAPTER SIX

Two weeks later I saw Marion again.

She had called me and insisted that I meet her in New York. There was an urgency in her voice that I could not deny, and I agreed.

We met for lunch at Costello's on Third Avenue. I was there first, standing at the bar when she came in. I saw her in the mirror. She paused inside the doorway. I did not move for a moment, but stared at her image, viewing her with detachment.

She was an attractive picture. Her dark hair was cropped and curled close to her head. She was not as striking as Leslie, and she did not have the conscious flair of most New York women, but she dressed and carried herself with the self-assured air of the suburban wife.

I turned from the bar. She saw me, relief and recognition lighted her face. She smiled and came towards me. "Hi," she said, "my train was late."

Her smile, her greeting, everything about her put me on the defensive. The attitude of meeting a date was a little much. I said, "Nice to see you."

A white glove fluttered to her face and she brushed aside a strand of hair. "Warm today," she said.

I signaled the head waiter. He nodded and I led her to a table in the rear. When we were seated she ordered a gin and tonic. I asked for my usual beer. The waiter left. Marion looked about her, taking in the dark wood-paneled walls, the collection of junk hanging behind the bar, the original Thurber drawings, the musical chatter of the lunch crowd. She smiled, obviously pleased. "We haven't done this for ages," she said.

I had been prepared to counter her punch for punch, but she was feinting, it wasn't her usual style; I was thrown off balance, but I was wary.

"How are the kids?" I asked.

Her face clouded, but she brightened quickly and said, "Oh, they're fine."

The bait was irresistible and I had to fight to ignore it. "That's good," I said.

"They miss you," she said.

"I miss them."

The drinks arrived, ending that line of conversation. We proposed a silent toast and drank.

"God, that tastes good," Marion said. "It's the only nice thing about summer."

I didn't answer. My curiosity was whetted. I knew she had an angle, but I couldn't figure it. I could have asked her point-blank, but I decided to go along with the game.

"I talked to Sam," she said.

"Oh?"

"He told me you weren't with him anymore."

I knew that he had told her a hell of a lot more than that, but I only said, "We had a falling out."

"I was sorry to hear that. You were so close."

"That's the way it crumbles," I said. "He acted as if he owned me."

"It's because he's so fond of you," she said. "He called me. He's worried about you."

"You'll forgive me if I don't appreciate that. He dumped me, I didn't leave him."

"He's sorry about that."

"He told you all about it, I guess."

She looked down at her hands. She nodded. She looked up and there was hurt in her eyes.

"Do you want to talk about her?" I asked.

She shook her head slowly. "No," she said in a low voice.

There was an uncomfortable silence. I reached for a menu for something to do. The waiter came again and we ordered, then we had to come back to us.

"Did Sam ask you to talk some sense into me?" I asked.

"No," she said. "I suggested something like that, but he said that it wouldn't do any good. He said that you would bounce back when you hit the bottom, and that you—like any man—had to fight your demons in your own way."

"Then why did he call?" I was scowling. I didn't like Sam's philosophy.

"He … he wanted to know if I needed money."

I was stunned and annoyed. "Just who the hell does he think he is?"

"He's a friend," Marion said, her voice hardening slightly.

"Of yours," I said.

"Yes. And yours too."

"Some friend. I'm capable of supporting my own family." That was a lie, but the old puritanism was up waving the flag of male superiority.

"He knows that. It's just that he didn't know how you were doing."

"He figures I'm starving without him. What crap. It took me one phone call to get a new agent."

"He couldn't be a Sam." There was a deep, deep sincerity in her voice that made me pause. I sobered and stared down at my glass. I took a deep breath and sighed.

"No," I said, moved to honesty by die tone of her voice, "it's not Sam."

I looked up and our eyes met and for just an instant time raced back and she was that girl I could talk to until five in the morning, the one who could argue with me on a good level, who could put her finger on my moods, could perceive my thoughts with a glance. Then I sensed that she was feeling sorry for me and I bridled. I was saved from saying something cutting by the arrival of our lunch.

We ate quietly, then, over coffee, I said, "Marion, you didn't come all the way into town to talk about Sam. What's on your mind?"

She stared, then looked down at her coffee. She looked up, took a deep breath, and said, "I want you to come back."

I was shaking my head even before the statement fully registered. "It wouldn't work," I said.

"You could try."

"It won't work, Marion."

"I'll make it work."

"No, we've tried it and tried it."

"I came here prepared to beg," she said.

I passed a hand over my eyes. "I wish you wouldn't," I said. "I don't feel good about this, believe me, but it just won't work."

"Why? Why won't you try?"

"Marion, I've told you before. I don't love you. I'm sorry, but I don't. I like you. I respect you. And that's why I can't live with you. It's a lie. Every minute I act like a husband towards you I am insulting you, because I don't believe it or feel it. If I didn't like you it might be different, but I can't cheat someone I respect. Have you any idea what I go through every night when I'm with you? It nears the time that sooner or later we have to go to bed, and I get nervous. I know that I'm not going to sleep with you, but I also know that you'd like to be slept with. I know that I'm going to have to turn my back on you, insult you once more as a woman. It bugs me because I know that you're just waiting. And if I did sleep with you, just went through the motions, I'd feel worse. I'd be making a whore out of you, and I can't do that."

"You won't have to come near me, I promise you that," she said.

"But you'd welcome it if I did," I said. She made no answer and it was answer enough. "You see? I'd still be turning my back on you."

"You're turning your back on me now," she said. "Just because you live in New York doesn't change that."

"I know that, but I don't have to live with it. That's selfish, perhaps, but I'm not a masochist."

"David, it's not merely for myself. The children need their Father."

"I'm sorry."

"You owe them something, David. They're your flesh and blood. You created them."

"I know that I owe them something, Marion, you don't have to tell me that. I think about it enough. But do you really think that it would do them a damned bit of good if I were living there against my will? Don't you realize that they would sense that I was martyring myself in their behalf? And don't you think that it would do them a hell of a lot more harm when they realized that their parents were merely tolerating one another to keep up appearances?"

"They need your love, David."

"And they've got it. For God's sake, Marion, I know that I'm a failure as a parent. But that has nothing to do with loving my children. Being with them doesn't mean that I will love them more."

"But you'll lose them, David."

"I don't think so. I don't know, I may be wrong, but I don't think I will. I do know that if I lived in that house there is a better than even chance that they will learn to hate me. What I am doing now is honest, at least, and if they have any feeling when they grow up, they will understand it."

"David, I'm thinking about them *now*. What happens to them now can warp their lives forever. Make them feel wanted, David. Now, make them feel that their Father wants them now."

"And have them hate me later?"

"Yes," she said, "yes. You owe them that. They are *your* children, *your* genes, *your* cells, *your* blood. They are your life after you and it is your responsibility to yourself to sustain the continuance of that life, even if you have to give up your own life in the process."

"I can't."

"You mean, you won't."

"All right, then, I won't. Marion, the psychoanalysts are kept in business by people whose troubles can be traced right back to what you want to create. This way they won't feel that I don't want them unless you make them feel that way, and I know that you wouldn't do that. If I'm going to do them any good it will be by staying away from that house."

She didn't answer. She slipped into a posture of defeat. I felt like hell. I wanted this ended. I wanted to get away from there. Right or wrong, I had made up my mind.

"It's that girl," she said.

"It has nothing to do with any girl," I said.

"Sam told me about her."

"I know that."

"He said that she's hurting you, that she's no good."

"That's a matter of opinion, and Sam doesn't know her. I don't think you'd like her."

"On the contrary, David, I might admire her. I couldn't possibly like her because she has you, but I could probably admire her. It takes a certain amount of courage to be the *other* woman. If she knows you at all, she must know that she will never marry you, because you will never get a divorce. So, she has to deny many of the basic instincts of woman. Her nest is temporary, at best; she cannot legitimately have children by you; the unknown wife is always a threat to her. She has to give up the future, and the number of fortune tellers and astrologists certainly bear testimony to a woman's instinctive interest in longevity and the future. I'm sure that you'll agree that the average working man would not be insurance poor if women were not compelled by nature to think in terms of future stability. She has you, David, but she can never be certain that she will have you for a week or a month or a year."

"This has nothing to do with—"

"But it does, David." She was on her intellectual plane, calculating, unemotional. "I want you to come back to us. I accept the fact that I cannot arouse physical passion in you, and this would not be a part of our life. I want you to come and be a father to your children. I also want you for myself. I can do without sex; I cannot continue without a man in the house. I want this, and I will accept the obvious drawbacks with it. I am quite prepared to accept this girl as your mistress."

"Are you out of your mind?"

"No, David, I'm not. I'm being logical. This is nothing new. It has been going on for centuries in Europe. I want to protect my family unit, and if I must make concessions, I'll make them."

"I couldn't do it. I couldn't do it to her. Marion, I happen to love this girl."

"Then think of her, David. As a mistress she has a position, a clearly defined status. I would have you legally and she would have you sexually, as she does now."

"It's more than that."

Marion gathered up her gloves and purse. She stood up from her chair. "Is it, David? Are you certain of that?" She turned and walked away.

CHAPTER SEVEN

Claude's wedding party was unforgettable. It had the elements of drama. There were two young people in love, and a crowd of friends eager to wish them well, happy in their happiness; the the families of both, opposed to the marriage, now in a state of frozen-smiled traumatic shock. It was a night of humor, pathos, gaiety, drunkenness and near-tragedy.

The wedding was small. I was Best Man. Leslie did not attend. She was moody, depressed, when I called for her to take her to the party. I asked her what was bothering her.

"Nothing," she said.

"Are you sure?"

"I certainly ought to know," she said curtly.

I shrugged, realizing that she was too moody for conversation, and let it go. We went to the party.

There had been a light rain in the afternoon, but it was still hot, the atmosphere close. The small apartment was already crowded when we arrived. It was warm. The men were in shirt sleeves, ties were pulled aside and collars were open.

A concentrated babble of sound rolled through the open doorways, music and laughter and loud talk and singing and shouts, a blend of high-pitched cacaphonic sound that rose and fell with erratic frenzy.

Leslie stopped as we entered the doorway. My hand was on her arm and I felt her stiffen. I glanced at her face. She was holding her breath and she stared wide-eyed.

Seen objectively, the room resembled a mad house. It was a sea of faces glistening with sweat. The noise was a communal thunder. Faces smiled and laughed, mouths moved without the distinction of individual sound. A trumpet blared from the next room. A girl shrieked above the roar. Hands fluttered, seemingly divorced from bodies.

"Quite a crowd," I said to break into her sudden terror of the human mass.

She smiled, a fleeting, timorous contraction of muscles. "I ... I ... don't know if I can take it," she said.

"We won't stay long," I said.

Someone shouted, "There you are!" We were confronted by Carl Sacks, a jazz musician. "Come on in! Jesus, Man, what a scene." He was staring at Leslie. I introduced them. "You need a drink," he said. He took Leslie by the arm and propelled her through the crowd. She glanced back at me, her eyes fearful, but then she was lost in the press of people.

I moved into the room. The heat was unbearable. I struggled to the bedroom and left my coat. I pulled my tie loose and unbuttoned my shirt. I went back into the melee and found a drink.

Claude was pressed into a corner, still in a state of confusion, realizing that he was married, but waiting for some metamorphosis to take place. Ann was on the far side of the room, her face radiant with triumph.

I gulped the drink and refilled the glass. I shouldered my way to Ann and embraced her.

"Big day," I said. "How do you feel?"

"Like a woman," she said.

I smiled and looked towards Claude. "He still doesn't know what has happened," I said.

"Oh, the poor thing," she said. "He's terrified. I almost wish I hadn't done it."

"He'll get over it," I said.

"I hope so." She pressed my arm. "David, when I have a moment I want to thank you for the apartment."

"My pleasure," I said. Claude and I had spent a week painting and cleaning the apartment. I was going to move out when they returned from their wedding trip.

I was pushed out of the way. I finished the drink and got another. I found a spot against a wall and watched the throng. It was the same crowd you would find at a gallery opening on 10th Street, or at the Cedar Bar or at Dillons. They were artists and writers, composers, actors, musicians; most of them young. And their women; some of them talented, most of them just the cockroaches who dog the footsteps of talent, eager to fall on their backs and feel the thrust of future greatness. It was a mixed crowd of white and negro, the democracy of the outcasts.

Sweat ran. Smoke billowed and clung to the low ceiling, a blue-white haze. Shirts were open, hanging free. Hankerchiefs were knotted at necks. The air was strong with the evidence of low-rent cold-water walk-ups, odors free of soap scent or deodorant. It was strong, but in the press of humanity, not unpleasant. It was the heavy musk of man-woman sweat and smoke and whiskey, an earthy, sexual stink.

I listened to the snatches of conversation, the disembodied dialogue:

"... and he'll never learn to use color. I don't ..."

"So I said, screw, who needs it."

"I quit the damned job. I get unemployment for five months and I'll be able to paint. It's like a Federal Scholarship."

"—the shots didn't work, so he had to get up the dough for an abortion. Poor bastard."

"Christ, it's hot!"

"—and she wanted to move in. I had a hell of a time getting rid of her."

"—but, Baby, you just can't compare Ginsburg with Robert Frost. I mean, like, you just don't."

I swallowed my drink and turned them off, threw the switch on my mind, turned the dial to mob scene. I had heard it all, all, all; all the crap of the nonconformist conformity, all the squeez-ings of the liberal sponge minds, the bullshit bleatings of the zero talents; all the talk, talk, talk of the evergreen review rabble; all the psychotic gibble-gabble of the vagina-oriented Bronx bagel-babies with their costume-jewelry pearls of Hunter College wis-dom. I turned it off and the collective stupidity made a nice hum.

A bongo exploded in the next room. I shoved away from the wall and pushed towards the booze. The heat and the crowd helped, and I was getting high. I jostled breasts and begged the pardon of stranger-faces with mascara masks dribbling clown-fashion down steaming cheeks; with dark-stained armpits. I passed an up-town statue looking for a hole to crawl into and said hello to Ann's brother, one unhappy square toasting little sister into hell. I found the bottle and shouted, "No ice!", and got no answer, and took my medicine straight. I was getting bombed out of my skull.

Leslie. I had to find Leslie. There was drumming and trum-peting and screaming in the next room. I pushed through the crowd. "Give the ball to Rockne!" I shouted. What a crowd! I never knew Claude had so many friends. I was shoved against a girl, thigh and breast. She said, "Hi," and I said, "Low," and she laughed, and I rested my drink on her shelf of sweating, freckled breast, and she said, "Oh," and I said, "P-Q-R," and she said, "What do you do," and I said, "Seduce girls," and she said, "Always in a crowd?", and I laughed, and I lifted my glass and bent my head to kiss the exposed swell of both salty breasts, and she said, "Hey," and a male voice growled, "What the hell are you doing?", and I said, "Seeing if its a girl," and angry voice said, "Wise guy," and I said, "Farewell." I pushed on and made it through the hallway and into the crowd fringe of the dancing people. I wiped the sweat from my face. I had to blink my eyes into focus. I saw Leslie. She was dancing with a negro painter. I knew him slightly, a one-man integration movement. She was laughing and her body responded to the beat with joy.

The music stopped for a moment and I got to her. I said, "Hi."

She faced me. "Oh," she said, the smile leaving her face, "what happened to you?"

"I got caught," I said. The music started. I took her in my arms and we danced, but she wasn't swinging with it. "What's wrong?"

"Nothing."

"You want to leave?"

She didn't answer, but she stopped dancing and removed my arms. She turned and went over to the negro painter. He glanced at me, then grinned, and took her in his arms. They swung into the beat of the music and the smile was back on her face.

I backed off the floor. Something was bugging her and this was her way of putting me down. I had the feeling that everyone in the room was staring at me. My muscles were tightening and the anger was beginning to flow like a poison, pumping through my system at the insistence of my quickened heartbeat. Bitch! I muttered. I turned and went back to the booze. I drank to extinguish the anger. I wouldn't go back in there. To hell with her. I drank and the room reeled, the smiling faces became grotesque. I pushed my way back to the other room. She wasn't dancing, but she was still standing with the negro—I couldn't think of his name—and he was writing her phone number on a matchbook cover, a party game peculiar to New York. Those matchbook covers deliver premiums that could put Green Stamps out of business. I was making a personal contribution towards integration—and I didn't like it. I caught my breath. Damn her! Damn that impossible bitch!

I have no memory of the next moments. I did nothing outlandish or I would have heard about it. But it was a complete black-out.

I found myself standing on the roof. I have no idea how long I had been there. I know that I must have left the party and walked up the one flight of steps. I was standing close to the twelve-inch ledge that fringed the roof. I stepped back. I was drunk. My mind was functioning clearly, but the body wasn't. I sat down and leaned back against the ledge. I closed my eyes. I did not hear her come onto the roof, but I heard her voice.

"David?" she said tentatively. "David?"

"What?" I said.

She rushed over to me. "David, I was worried. Someone said you were staggering around up here."

"Beat it," I said. "Go back to your spade."

"David, come along now." She reached out and touched my arms.

The contact triggered an incomprehensible rage that burst upon me, enveloped me; I came up from the sitting position, my hands went out and I had her by the throat. She gagged with surprise. I swung her about and bent her over the ledge. I put pressure on my thumbs. I was thinking with absolute clarity and I knew that I was going to kill her. She did not resist. Her body was limp. I wanted to see her die. I leaned over to peer closely at her face. I saw her look of triumph and I jerked my hands away.

I turned and staggered away. I could hear her gasp of breath. I found the stairs and started down. I heard her call, "David!" I ignored it and kept going, clutching the railing for support. "David!" I heard the clatter of her high heels. I reeled into the courtyard. She was at my side. She took my arm and I knocked her hand away. I staggered through the front building and onto the sidewalk. The buildings seemed to tilt and the world reversed itself on its axis. I remember her hands on me and the yellow blur of a cab.

I remember, next, her voice coming to me from a great distance. The words were unintelligible, but gradually they cleared. "David, get up. Come on, now, get up."

My awareness returned. I knew that I was lying on the ground, I could feel the grit with my out-flung hands. I was face down. I did not open my eyes.

"David, get up! You can't lie here." She tugged at my shirt. "David, wake up!"

I breathed deeply and I knew something was wrong. My face was lying in something wet and foul-smelling. My brain was operating at half-speed and it took several seconds to realize that I was sprawled in my own vomit. I raised my head and opened my eyes. I was in a vacant lot.

"David, you're awake. Get up, now."

When had I ever been so drunk? Many times. Plenty times drunk and I had never fallen to the ground to lay in the stink of my frustrated stupidity. How could I get lower than this? I turned my face to look up. Leslie was leaning over me. I coiled my body in a continuing movement, bringing my legs up for leverage, and I swung my right arm. The back of my hand cracked against her mouth. She cried out in pain and surprise and fell backwards. I got to my feet.

She stood three feet from me. The moonlight gave her blonde hair a mysterious glow. The deep shadows accentuated the contours of her body. Her face was raised to the light and her angelic beauty was marred only by the trickle of blood from the corner of her mouth.

"Where are we?" I asked.

"On First Avenue," she said. "You were sick. I had the cab drop us here."

"Got a handkerchief?"

She produced a packet of tissues from her purse. I wiped my face. When I finished I looked at her. "Sorry I hit you," I said.

She did not answer. I used one of the tissues to wipe the blood from her mouth.

"It has nothing to do with you," I said. "I'm really sorry. C'mon, let's go."

We walked across 31st Street and stopped before her building. She climbed the steps and fitted the key to the lock. When she realized that I was still on the sidewalk she turned. "David," she said.

I turned and walked away. "David," she said again. I went on. I heard her say my name once more without raising her voice. I did not stop and I did not look back.

I walked down Second Avenue, the night air cool against me. I was returned from a long trip. I bore the stink of my degradation. Where I had been I had to go. What I had done I had to do. I knew that I walked through the night city with new knowledge. I could not analyze it, but I knew that in some way it would be made known to me. I walked with a strong, sober stride, one of the eight city-bound million, a unit, a single entity lately distracted from the true course of birth to bury-hole; distracted for reasons as yet unknown. I touched upon people during this incident, but cause and effect are judged from point of view, and thus you may have noted that I have examined myself only, leaving the others in one dimension in a field of gray. From Leslie the story would be truthfully different. We are each of us alone in this world. If I have sinned, it has been against myself.

EPILOGUE

This is David Markam.

A young-old man of 37, he walks south on Seventh Avenue in New York City. It has been a difficult day for him and he is tired. Four hours were spent in conference concerning sponsor-required changes in a new TV series; two hours were spent haggling over the movie option for his new book. He wonders if Sam, his agent, really fought hard enough for his price before he backed down.

At Sheridan Square he stops and enters a small coffee shop. He sits at one side of the horseshoe-shaped counter and orders coffee. When it is brought to him he sits stirring it, his thoughts elsewhere.

A man and woman enter and sit at the counter opposite him. He looks up at them. The man is balding and his face is red and flaccid. He is rotund in a conservative gray suit. His hands on the counter are pudgy and he wears a ring on each hand. He has the look of a tired salesman. The woman is younger by twenty years, a blonde. Except for the tired, lackluster eyes, she would be beautiful. David returns his attention to his coffee.

"I gotta go to Washington tomorrow," the man says.

"When will you be back?" the woman asks.

David looks up, startled, remembering that voice. He stares hard at the woman. She looks at him, frowning as she notes his interest, and turns away.

"I'm not certain," the man says. "A few days."

"We have those tickets for the theater," the woman says.

David stares at her, memory bringing her into focus. He leaves his coffee untouched and hurries from the restaurant.

"What's with him?" the man asks.

"I don't know," the woman says.

On the sidewalk, David turns for a last look at her through the window. Leslie, he says to himself. My, God, I remember that voice across the distance of a pillow. She's hardly changed and I didn't know her. He crosses the street enmeshed in thought.

How is it possible to be that intimate with a person and not remember her? He cannot realize that she was too much the catharsis to exist as a woman for him, that as he purged himself of his guilt, she too was purged from his memory. *Christ, I remember everything about her, and I couldn't recognize her.* An ideal has no human form.

He walks east on Washington Place and turns in at the entrance to an apartment building. He takes the elevator to the sixth floor and lets himself into an apartment with his key. A female voice greets him from the kitchen. "Is that you, David?"

"Yes," he says.

A girl enters the room. She is young and dark-haired. Her face has a sloe-eyed, sensual beauty. She wears a sweater and tight slacks that display the generous femininity of her body. She holds a martini in each hand.

"Your wife called," she says. "She said to remind you about the drapery material."

He nods, saying nothing. The girl brings him the martini and he sits on the divan. "Your wife must be a strange one," the girl says. "I can't understand her accepting this kind of relationship so casually."

David does not answer. He stares at the girl. She frowns. "What's wrong? Why are you staring at me like that?"

Will I forget this girl? Will I forget that face, that body that responds to me?

If there is more than the face and body, he will. And justly so. The flesh disintegrates and it is the experience that remains.

My God, doesn't it mean anything? Is there nothing to cling to? Do I retain nothing of this?

The yesterday you is a stranger today. A life is like skipping a flat stone across still water. The stone is air-borne, carried by momentum; it touches briefly, again and again until natural law brings it down and it sinks from sight. What exists are the ripples made upon contact, and they spread and dissipate, and what remains of the flight of the stone is the memory of the ripples. A man is only the total of his experience.

"Say, what's wrong with me?" the girl says.

David laughs. "Nothing," he says. "I was thinking of something else. Come here and sit next to me."

THE END

In those forever ago army days, when I was suspended in the vacuum of middle-class arrogant ignorance, I met an artist, a rebellious giant of incorruptible integrity. He gave me a novel to read—my first—and thus opened a world to me; and a hunger to see, to feel, to understand—to write. In the interim years, while I prowled restlessly in that world, exalting its beauty, damning its injustice, pondering the miracle of its seed, doggedly trying to shape thoughts into words, there was always the hovering shadow of my friend and that booming voice to say: BE HONEST! I have written other books, but this is the first I want him to read. It may not be good, I don't know, but I labored hard upon it; I used no cheap tricks, followed no formula, tried to appease no one. If it is a bad book, it is also an honest book. He'll have to accept that.

to
Bill Scharf
a painter

AFTERWORD

Judge Not His Genre:
The Knowable Yet Mysterious Stuart James
by David Spencer

I t's only hackwork if you approach it like a hack. Otherwise it's problem solving; meeting expectations. And when you do more than *merely* solve the problem—when you *exceed* expectations, when you transcend craft, mechanics and readability to achieve *transformation*—you wind up with art.

And it doesn't matter how it's packaged.

But it may matter who knows it.

Hold that thought.

As what I'll call an anecdotal corollary:

At the end of *Judge Not My Sins*, Stuart James wrote a deeply personal dedication to what would seem to be his most deeply personal novel. You'll find it on the page just prior to this one. If you haven't read it, check it out; if you have read it, it's worth reviewing. I'll wait...

Welcome back. I don't know about you, but when *I* reread that dedication, in the novel's original edition, I was at a loss to understand how it applied; there didn't seem any false modesty to it. I'd devoured the three books that would be collected for this omnibus, and they seemed to me *suffused* with the kind of honesty his pal Bill Scharf had urged him toward. *What shortfall could Stuart James have been talking about?* What I had yet to learn was that he had written two *other* books whose "honesty" may have been at issue. For him at least.

Hold that thought too. We'll get back to it.[1]

On the subject of my introduction to—and, if I may be so bold, rediscovery of—Stuart James, the timeline is important.

My gateway to some of the great veteran American authors we aficionados affectionately call *pulpsmiths*—when what we really mean, what we're often too coy to say out loud, is *masters of contemporary literature*—as many of them were, albeit litera-ture of a particular *sort*—was through their media tie-in novels. The collection has been ongoing since I was about 10 or 11 in the dead-middle 1960s. And as an adult, with the advent of anti-quarian booksellers networked via internet, I've been especially interested in finding the books I would naturally have missed, that came before.

And so one fine day in 2017, while browsing eBay, I saw listed the 1962 novelization of a 1961 film I'd never heard of, *Too Late Blues*, by an author new to me.

The by-line was Stuart James.

It's so *no-frills* a name that I wondered if it was a pseud-onym. *Too Late Blues*, I quickly learned, had been director-screenwriter John Cassavetes' second film (screenplay co-written with Richard Carr). A drama set in the nourish milieu of nightclub jazz.

Intriguing.

---

1   No more about William Scharf here, but he was an interesting character, worth looking up.

I ordered the book.

It arrived in unread condition (lucky me). Looked new, smelled new, and it was an early Lancer from the days when their edge-paper dye was lime-green. And like a lot of their books of the period, its print was *teeny*. So despite being crammed into merely 140 pages, *Too Late Blues* was a fairly substantial novel for your forty cents.

Never having seen the written screenplay, I can't attest to how rigidly the actors adhered to it—I have only the movie for comparative reference—but as with most Cassavetes films, there are sequences that seem improvised around a struc-ture, the particular lines of dialogue less important than just coherently getting from one establishing or story point to the next.

And of course, there's no prose equivalent of letting the actors *ad lib*.

The very act of crafting a sentence to be read *defies* the ran-dom performance energy of improvisation.

There is, however, the *illusion*.

And what's clear from reading the book is this: Stuart James resonantly understood that John Cassavetes was all about atmo-sphere and environment—and so he devised his novelization accordingly.

The book started out impressionistically—actual impres-sionism—*essences* of character through snatches of dialogue, information through high context rather than adjective-noun-simile description, teasing that along as the members of the band made their way out of the club where they'd just finished a gig to a bar and pool hall where they liked to hang out; and there, *there,* really *late* in the proceedings by any objective measure, Stuart James *finally* described his characters, as if offering *fulfill-ment,* a *reward* for your accepting the invitation, hanging in with him, *engaging* with him … and did it not via "reportorial" nar-ration, but just as impressionistically, through the prism of their pool game, all hipster slang, rhythm and sound, punctuated by the *click click* of the pool balls.

"And *that* in one long, almost stream-of-consciousness paragraph. With shifting points of view. Employing what I can only describe as *word jazz*.

And there was no fakey literary bullshit about it, as so often accompanies the attempt to wrangle the abstractions of fine art to coherent language. It had the authenticity of the smoke, the booze, the night, the hunger, the dexterous keyboard improvisation over a chord progression.

There was so much renegade, *fearless* craft bending to it—yet it was so *clearly* by a guy who knew his craft inside and out—that it rocked me to my core.

As importantly, none of this was in the film, yet it was *completely* in sync with what was *equivalent* in the film, a breathtaking *extrapolation* and expansion.

Stuart James' riff on *Too Late Blues* not only retained the heart and intention of its source but he profoundly made it his own.

And that damn pool hall paragraph. I kept returning to that passage. Reading it over … and over … and over … To the point where—I don't think I've ever *felt* anything quite like this before either—I was like: *Who* IS *this guy and why the hell have I never heard* mention *of him?*

Of course I collected the rest of his novelizations. That was a no-brainer.

And they of course led me to his other novels of the period.

All of them … *all* of them … to be found in the world of sleaze.

By his own admission, Stuart James broached his writing career like many of his contemporaries: via making multiple submissions and getting a lot of rejections. Once his work was good enough to earn a steady marketplace berth, however, he would sell over 300 short stories and novelettes to the pulps—mostly men's magazines. None have been subsequently collected or anthologized, but from the evidence of numerous collectible/preserved issues, his seems to have been a familiar, cover-featured byline in that niche. Copyrights on his books indicate that James was prolific and fast, so these stories probably appeared within a relatively short period, around 1955–1959.

Then came 1960—and being a published novelist. Numerous times.

As was not generally acknowledged at the time, but in later decades became an open secret, sleaze was a deceptive genre. Most of its publishers were fly-by-night outfits and many of its offerings were the dashed-off soft porn they appeared to be ... but there were many books that punched far above the genre (whose only qualification, really, was that someway, somehow, sex had to figure into the story)... and among their writers were many making their bones on the path to greater glories. Some would become hardcover brand names (usually working sleaze pseudonymously), some would remain paperback mainstays (surprisingly often writing sleaze under their actual names)—a few would even emerge as sleaze specialists who became brand names in *that* world, their work to be revived and heralded by later generations.

Stuart James was easily among the best of them. One way or another, all of his books are as strikingly memorable as *Too Late Blues*. And he himself seems not to have been obscure.

But despite this exposure having established at *least* as much foundation to build upon as that achieved by any of his historically notable sleaze contemporaries, Stuart James, as a literary presence, vanished all-but-completely after his early-'60s sleazers and screenplay novelizations.

For about 25 years.

❧ ❧ ❧

Three of his early books were big sellers:

- *Carnival Girl* (Chariot 1960), which he wrote under his only known pseudonym, "Max Gareth" (reissued some months to a year after with a bold "2nd Printing" banner).
- The novelization of *Jack the Ripper* (screenplay by Jimmy Sangster) which had two simultaneous US editions (Frederick Fell, hardcover; Monarch paperback [likely also distributed in the UK], both 1960) and two consecutive, separate releases from Australian publisher Horwitz.

—and, most significantly as a prime artifact of its era, symbolizing both how far James had come and how far he hadn't/woudn't—

- *Bucks County Report* (Midwood 1961), which had a bold, bright-orange cover, sporting big official-looking lettering, its only graphic an official ink-stamp tool outlined in white; a novel which would be reissued in sleazier wraps as *Devil's Workshop* (Midwood 1963)—unaltered but completely re-typeset—its front cover image now a painting of a woman in a see-through negligée entering an appraising man's bedroom.

Bucks County Report also had a second and transparently *mercenary* reissue in 1967, as a *non-sleaze mass market paperback*, after Tower Books had absorbed Midwood and "inherited" their backlist. The bottom half of the cover was a painting of a couple on a bed, still clothed but clearly meaning business; and the top half of the cover was the book's title—the reinstated *original* title—in large Courier font, against a white background.

But the byline was changed to "Irwin Wallach." And why?

There are no surviving records, but the answer is obvious, because in 1960, acclaimed hardcover novelist *Irving Wallace* hit the bestseller lists with *The Chapman Report*—which was *also* a novel that featured a sex survey team and its subjects; subsequently adapted into a hit film, released in '62.

However, copies of the *Bucks County* by "Wallach" edition are so spectacularly rare as to suggest that the ploy fooled few and the book sold poorly;

—*and/or* that Wallace's people sent a cease-and-desist warning to Tower;

—*and/or* that Stuart James himself logged a legal objection;

—any or all of which would have resulted in copies being front-cover stripped (for proof of no-sale refunds) and pulped.

Tower was a fly-by-night outfit and it's easy to believe that its management never informed the author or even considered that his byline was not *itself* a pseudonym and his book a bought-and-paid-for consumable property.

Did they know it had been a Midwood bestseller *only a few years before?*

Did they care?

Did they just think the title was conveniently exploitable?

The mere *existence* of the Tower edition is a comment on the transitory and capricious nature of any popularity conferred by sleaze bestsellerdom. Whatever brand Stuart James may have established by being prolific and visible at first had been forgotten in the few years between. And strictly speaking, this was already three years into his literary and known-whereabouts disappearance.

And adding to the irony, if we go back to the first, orange Midwood edition—we don't know whether Stuart James' choice of title and subject matter were coincidental or *themselves* a deliberate (if wry) improvisation off *Chapman*'s notoriety.

What we *do* know is that in substance, James and Wallace tell two *completely* different stories: Wallace's book—in paperback a small-print, 383 page week's-worth read—is about events informing the actual study of its fictional survey team. Whereas in James' book—188 pages of moderate print you could knock off in a night or two—the observers are secondary and enter late; *Bucks County Report* is really a *Peyton Place* potboiler about a suburban town.

As to his other pre-disappearance books:

- *Chita,* another sleazer, also as Max Gareth (Midwood, 1960). Copies of this one are almost impossible to find.
- *The Enemy General* (Monarch 1960), a novelization of a WWII intrigue; it was published as by Dan Pepper and Max Gareth, but the truth of the attribution is convoluted. "Dan Pepper" was a joint pseudonym for James and Lou Morheim, who collaborated on the screenplay; the use of the pseudonym suggests that they took their names off the film. That James would claim an additional byline as Gareth on the book suggests that he did the novelizing solo while deciding to remain pseudonymous.[2]

I believe that *The Enemy General* is also the first piece of hard evidence that Stuart James put in some time as a Hollywood scriptwriter.

- *The Stranglers of Bombay* (also 1960), another novelization under his own name for Monarch, also unusual in how

---

2 There may have *also* been a tacit authors' statement being made about story integrity: The film's screenplay is attributed to Dan Pepper *and Bert Picard,* about whom nothing is known. But since the connection is made with an "and" instead of an ampersand [&], *this* suggests, according to Writers Guild protocol, that Picard was brought on for *subsequent alterations* to the James-Morheim script and didn't work with them directly. Which may be why they took their names off it. Whew! (And not incidentally, a colleague's alerting me to the copyright registration for the novelization is what provided the connection to the Gareth pseudonym.)

sensitively it was written, especially given that it was based on a sensationalistic Hammer horror screenplay by David Zelag Goodman (who would go on to nobler films).

- And there was the aforementioned 1962 novelization of *Too Late Blues.*

And, finally, perhaps the two most revealing works. Also published between sleaze covers but even *more* deceptively than the others.

Frisco Flat (copyright 1960 but published by Midwood in 1964).

And *Judge Not My Sins* (Midwood 1961).

What may be most important about the Gareth sleazers is that they're unabashedly sleazarific. A dispassionate synopsis of either *Carnival Girl* or *Chita* lays out a tale that seems *objectively* to be fairly lurid stuff. Each one follows the trajectory of a much abused 19-year old woman who starts out at a roadside eatery (one as a waitress, one as a desperate runaway)," trapped by circumstance yet yearning for a better existence, who is suddenly offered the chance to escape and takes it. This leads to an odyssey of further abuse, alternating with the more positive beats of inner-strength building, the dangling promise of true love, and getting ever closer to the light at the end of the tunnel. To say more would spoil reading them, but the stories hit all the expected titillation points. Any non-discerning male hoping for a sexploitation book would probably have considered his thirty-five or fifty cents well-spent.

But for those of us who would, as the phrase goes, "buy *Playboy* for the articles and interviews," the stories are not *quite* so titillating as all that. Stuart James won't let you objectify his heroines so easily.

With manipulative skill, he paints portraits of these poor girls that are poignantly three-dimensional and compassionate. He doesn't make believe that pain isn't painful, nor that hope isn't worth clinging to by your fingernails, even against, as Franklin says in *1776,* greater odds than a more generous God would have allowed. And in these, as in all of his '60s books, even the most minor character is portrayed boldly, memorably and with surprising dimensionality—because most of them are also reaching out ... (Well, except for the worst of them. But then James makes it clear that their souls are dead. And that *lack* of dimension becomes itself a dimension.)

And therein lies the thread that runs through all of Stuart James' paperbacks of the 60s: The quest for salvation.[3]

But alongside that also lies what Stuart James thereafter abandoned: formula.

He clearly knew that he might have spun his "tragic girl" template into several more variations—but that it would be dishonest to try. For indeed, he admits as much in the *Judge Not My Sins* dedication referenced at the top of this essay.

A dedication which, as I say, doesn't *quite* make sense unless you know about the Gareth books.

Because, as noted, the books under his own name—something he seems to have cared about deeply—are nothing to minimize.

There's honesty aplenty in *Bucks County Report,* which he himself described, in an author's note prefacing the first edition, as "(e)ssentially ... a long lecture on morality and love and the various aberrations distorting human emotion." It is, in fact, the most discursively philosophical small-town potboiler you're ever likely to read. (But in a good way.)

---

3   To some degree this is also true of his novelizations. Remember, adaptation is interpretive, and even when internalizing characters created by others, James finds and exploits, as their driving force, a need for expiation and rebalance.

And there's the seaside thriller *Frisco Flat*—my personal favorite of his original novels. This one is about a prodigal son returning to his home town, to investigate the circumstances behind the death of his father. There he encounters, among others, a good girl in trouble, a troubled girl in trouble, the corrupt town Boss and the brutal sheriff, who is also the Boss's enforcer. If the pitch-line and ingredients seem familiar—one might loosely describe *Bad Day at Black Rock* in similar terms—the tale's realization is pure Stuart James. Due in no small part to James having worked on fishing boats during his wildly peripatetic job history, *Frisco Flat* teems with so much verisimilitude that you can smell the brine and feel the muscle.

And then there's *Judge Not My Sins.*

With available information, it's impossible to know the order in which his post-Gareth books were written, but *Sins* was obviously his epiphany, and as such, it's the most haunting (and curiously the shortest) of his novels.

A few interesting facts surround it, aside from what's revealed in the dedication. In Google researching, I came upon passing reference to James having been one of several Midwood novelists who also served as an editor there; and it would seem that he himself placed *Judge Not My Sins* in its catalog (possibly after being unable to sell it elsewhere). *Judge Not My Sins* also bears the distinction of being the only sleaze imprint book I've ever seen—perhaps the only one in *existence*—upon whose back cover *there's a cameo headshot of the author.* So Stuart James not only put his *name* on it; he put his *face* on it.

And on the pages ... he put him*self,* one *has* to assume, *in* it.

The novel is about David Markham, a thirtysomething writer who has made a living selling short stories to the pulp market, men's magazines primarily, who is well on his way to better things, a movie deal pending ... when he gets caught up in a destructive, career-threatening love affair with a bipolar woman. Of course, at the time Stuart James was writing, terms like *bipolar* and *manic depressive* were not part of the common vocabulary, so Leslie is presented not as a person who can be parsed via pathology; she is instead portrayed as a broken but charismatic devourer of David's soul, bouncing unpredictably between needfulness, vulnerability, self-martyrdom and abusiveness.

The book contains long stretches of philosophy—articulated by David—about love, marriage and the futility of either if there is not also compatible sex... and the sex scenes themselves are far more about graphic psychology than graphic sensuality. In one particularly disturbing passage, with the ceaseless roller-coaster of the relationship fueling David's need for *some* kind of control, he decides, as intercourse begins, "to master her" and proceeds to methodically keep bringing her to the point of release only to back off again, until she's thoroughly enslaved by him, as much in fear as ecstasy, finally orgasming explosively. And in the aftermath, this:

> I had won. I had lost. It served my ego to know that no other man had brought her to that point before, that no matter with whom she made love in the future, it would be a failure, that there would always be the subconscious remembrance of this night. But I had also reduced her for myself, and knew that the only thing that would bind us now would be this compulsive mating. I have said before that a relationship between man and woman is welded in bed, that the physical mating must be strong and reciprocal. But I must add; when there is nothing else, when a man and a woman exist for each other only in the hot sweat of lunging bodies, it is dual masturbation.

I not only think that this is as far from sleaze or even soft porn as one can get... I propose that, *had* the novel seen hardcover publication in 1961, it might well have been banned, making its way to America at first only in contraband French editions, alongside renegade books as diverse as *Lolita* and *Candy.* This is the stuff of Henry Miller and D.H. Lawrence, fantastically displaced between covers for the high-up cigar store racks.

And as I say, after these novels, a quarter-century gap with two cameo appearances...

...in 1967 he is credited for the screen story (though not the screenplay) for *Come Spy With Me,* a flop espionage film starring Troy Donahue...

...in 1979 he shows up as author of *The Firefighter,* a novella for young readers, published by Scholastic, its text illustrated with actor-posed black-and-white photos rather than drawings—the publisher's unique experiment?—in the manner of cinema verité movie stills. Apparently crafted for a series of variously-authored books about common careers, *The Firefighter*'s language is perforce more direct and less prone to poetic imagery than in the adult books...but it's an unusually mature and nuanced story for a YA chapbook anyway, the dimensionality of the characters and story bearing the unmistakable Stuart James imprimatur. (Scholastic will reprint the book just prior to the new millennium under its *Action 2000* banner)...

...the quality and confidence of *The Firefighter* make one wonder if James has kept writing all through the gap, ghosting for others, authoring genre novels under pseudonyms and house names, but there is *zero* evidence to support this speculation...

...And then he returns Big Time.

Or anyway, that was the plan.

In 1988, Bantam Books issued James' *The Spy Who Wouldn't Die,* as a lead title in their line of paperback originals. There's no question that the author is the same Stuart James (there have been others), because the headshot on the inside back cover is the same fellow whose face was on *Judge Not My Sins;* just older and more weathered, like the outdoorsman he *also* was, against a winter backdrop. The art work on the *front* cover is extravagant and eye-catching, and the author's name is above the embossed title in big, splashed letters as if he himself had signed it with an artist's paint brush.

That novel was followed in 1989 by *The Spy is Falling* (not a sequel), which was given much the same treatment. The two books looked for all the world as if Stuart James' byline was as potently recognizable as Tom Clancy's. And perhaps, to a friendly editor, it was. But James knew better. None of his early novels is mentioned in his Bantam Books bio, nor even that he ever had prior novels published. It's a bio penned by a realist.

His third Bantam espionage title, *Death Games,* wasn't released until 1992. The art work is still pretty catchy, but it's stylistically unrelated to the first two covers; the *title* is the "star"; and James' byline, while hardly marginalized, is featured in much more subdued lettering, along the bottom edge of the cover.

All three novels are beach-read length, between approximately 350 and 400 pages of average-size paperback print. They are the only Stuart James books (that we know of) to push beyond a 190 page signature.

These three books are not impossible to find "in the wild," as collectors say, but they don't always turn up readily and never in VG or better condition. This suggests that they didn't sell well and were stripped and pulped rather than remaindered. The three year gap between the second and third books suggests that Stuart James had a three-book contract, and that the publication of *Death Games* was an obligation. The completely different art work and presentation suggests, further, that Bantam *abandoned* the strategy of marketing James as the drawing card and instead gave a shot to selling *Death Games* on the merits of the story particulars alluded to on the packaging. Despite that, though, the manuscript's publication doesn't seem to have been "burned off"; its presentation is *we-should-all-be-so-lucky* respectable and may well have been an attempt to launch Stuart James *again,* in a manner that *wouldn't* recall the first two novels. I would even bet that its original title was not *Death Games,* but a variation on his *The Spy...* template, and that it was completed around 1990 (remember how *fast* Stuart James could write).

But, as we all know, the degree of commercial success attained during active career years isn't necessarily a fair barometer of quality. So how does Stuart James' unofficial espionage "trilogy" compare to the sleazers, the novelizations and the YA chapbook?

Objectively, James' spy thrillers may be fine for many. As always, he's in full control of his craft and as you read, you know you're in good hands.

But I found them disappointing. And here are my *subjective* reasons why.

Their narratives are methodical, procedural, tracking almost beat-for-beat *verité* as the central character pursues his goal. There's very little *visceral* sense—even if cold story particulars can be argued otherwise—of jumping into things in progress, of a ticking clock. It's as if length is not Stuart James' friend; as if lacking a lower word count as maximum allowable length has blunted his sense of urgency.

And his heroes seem like a more sophisticated riff on the earlier 20th century science fiction trope of "the competent man." Not that these guys are flawless: they may have somewhat stressed emotional lives—the hero in the first book, for example, seeks to smooth things over with an estranged teenage son who gets caught up in the intrigue—but they're all capable veteran agents, possessed of versatile skill sets. But not *idiosyncratically* capable agents like John Le Carré's disarmingly self-effacing George Smiley or Brian Freemantle's deceptively dissolute

Charlie Muffin. Nor are they competent but *uncertain in volatile environments*, fish out of familiar waters, like the not-quite-so-quirky leading men (and women) in the always-absorbing and even *more* realistic procedural spy novels of *Washington Post* insider David Ignatius.

No, Stuart James' "spooks" would seem to be a reflection of what Stuart James had become, and who he was as he was crafting their exploits: A competent, pragmatic professional who had been through a lot but emerged as a veteran survivor. Not at all like his earlier, desperate characters seeking salvation, who used to make the Stuart James/Max Gareth books that *looked* far less respectable *read* far more compellingly.

The heroes of the later novels *do* need to succeed.

But they don't need to be *saved*.

They're just not fucked up enough.

However…

You don't have to worry about that.

If you're reading this essay, you've experienced, or you're about to, the *essential* Stuart James, the *early* one who—for whatever reason—could never break free of the sleaze category with his original work…but who was never constrained by it either.

He made art where he could.

He seems incapable of having done otherwise.

Judge not his genre.

STUART JAMES grew up in rural Pennsylvania and at 15 went to work as a sports reporter for the *Delaware Valley Advance*. Later. while attending Temple University, he was a copy boy for the *Philadelphia Record*, then served a stint in an intelligence unit in the Army.   Newspaper work took him all across the country before he abandoned journalism, invested in a used Royal typewriter. and wrote adventure stories "by the pound"—meanwhile holding down such jobs as hunting guide, truck driver, bartender, rough carpenter, carnival barker, cannery worker, and ice cream salesman—as the rejections flooded in. At age 28, while working on a tuna boat out of Monterey, California, he sold his first story to a pulp magazine for $100. Several hundred stories later, when the short fiction markets started drying up, he became a staff writer, then executive, for a series of magazines. including *Popular Mechanics* and *True*. Finally, he quit magazines to become a a PR copywriter as well as ghostwriter and scriptwriter. "All the stuff any writer does," he said. Many of his professions inform the milieus and character portraits in his novels. In 1992, the year of his last known published book, he was making his home between residences in Greenwich, Connecticut, and Cedar Key, Florida. At this writing (October, 2020), there is no further information known as to his whereabouts (he would be in his late 90s if still alive) or passing.

DAVID SPENCER is an award-winning musical dramatist, author, critic and musical theatre teacher, whose work has been produced in the US, Canada and England. His most well-known credits as lyricist-librettist are two musicals in collaboration with composer Alan Menken: *The Apprenticeship of Duddy Kravitz,* based on the novel by Moredecai Richler and *Weird Romance* (co-librettist: Alan Brennert). His books are *The Musical Theatre Writer's Survival Guide*, the acting edition of *Weird Romance* and *Passing Fancy*, an original novel based on the TV series *Alien Nation*. David is a faculty member of BMI-Lehman Engel Musical Theatre Workshop and has also taught at HB Studio, Workshop Studio Theater in New York; and Goldsmith's College and BML in London.